Evita's REVENGE

Evita's Revenge

RICHARD J. WALTER

iUniverse®

EVITA'S REVENGE

iUniverse books may be ordered through booksellers or by contacting:

iUniverse
1663 Liberty Drive
Bloomington, IN 47403
www.iuniverse.com
1-800-Authors (1-800-288-4677)

ISBN: 978-1-4917-9011-3 (sc)
ISBN: 978-1-4917-9012-0 (e)

Library of Congress Control Number: 2016903025

Print information available on the last page.

iUniverse rev. date: 02/26/2016

For My Loyal Readers

CHAPTER ONE

May 3, 1951 – Santiago, Chile

He didn't care for Chile's capital. Santiago's architecture was drab and unimaginative. The food was indifferent, made palatable only by decent wines. Cultural life, such as it was, paled in comparison with cosmopolitan Buenos Aires, his home. There was little nightlife and even in the daytime there wasn't much that attracted him aside from the occasional spectacular view of the snow-capped Andes to the east.

Most of all, he didn't care for Chileans. They were, he thought, uniformly dull, staid, and, like their capital city, provincial. Although they were sometimes called the "British of South America," he couldn't understand why. Maybe it was because they preferred tea to coffee and admired poets. Maybe because many Chileans he had met were reserved in dress and manner. Grudgingly, he had to admit that maybe, too, it was because, like the British, they had a first-class navy. The navy that had led the way to Chile's most glorious military triumph: The War of the Pacific against neighboring Peru and Bolivia in the late nineteenth century.

More fundamentally, Chile was a rival of his native Argentina. Over the centuries, the two nations had skirmished over their shared boundary running down the spine of the Andes to the straits of Magellan. While these disputes frequently threatened to erupt into full-scale conflict, they had, up to now, been resolved by diplomacy. The famous "Christ of the Andes," a statue that straddled the border between the two nations, had been erected in 1904 as symbolic of the peaceful resolution of one of the most serious of these confrontations.

At the moment, there were no immediate crises on the horizon. But the armed forces of both countries constantly prepared for the eventuality – some even argued, the inevitability – of conflict. When he had been a young cadet in Argentina's war college, he had studied numerous contingency plans for mobilization and action in the case of a clash with Chile. He knew that the same thing occurred on the other side.

As far as his job at the moment was concerned these historic rivalries and tensions meant little. And the people who assigned him his duties cared not a whit whether he liked where he was posted. His task was to do all he could to hinder and harass the enemies of the General, up to and including assassination.

When the General had become president of Argentina in 1946, a flow of opponents began to seek exile in nearby countries. The largest group traveled across the Río de la Plata estuary to Uruguay, where most found shelter in Montevideo. Others crossed the Andes into Chile and settled in Santiago. Smaller numbers fled to other Latin American countries and a few to the United States and Europe. From the safety of exile, they organized propaganda campaigns and engaged in activities designed to discredit the General and his regime.

At first, the General, enormously popular at home, paid little heed to these dissident voices. However, as political and economic troubles began to grow, the General decided to counter these opponents at the source. He had the head of the secret police assign clandestine agents to Argentine embassies as special attachés, instructed to use whatever tactics necessary to counter opposition efforts.

His first assignment had been the year before in Montevideo. While he considered the Uruguayan capital almost as provincial as Santiago, there was much that was familiar – the same European immigrant population as in Argentina, the same Spanish accent, the same food. But again, these things were not important. From his embassy cover, he was to do all he could to discourage and dishearten the enemy.

The job was dangerous, demanding, and complicated. He had to intimidate the opposition without revealing his identity – and, of course, without being caught. If he were caught, the whole plan of intimidation could unravel and the opposition would enjoy an enormous propaganda coup. At the same time, for the plan to work, the opposition had to fear the campaign unleashed against them. They had to get the message that their activities were unacceptable to the regime; that the consequences of continuing to oppose the General could be deadly. But the actions taken had to be carried out in a way that could not be traced directly back to the embassy or to Buenos Aires.

It was not an easy task. But he accepted the challenge and in Montevideo enjoyed a string of successes. He began by setting a mysterious fire in the offices of an exile newspaper, destroying its presses and all its files. The local police declared it a work of arson. But there were no clues for them to follow and they soon abandoned their investigation.

Next, he sabotaged the automobile of a leading dissident living in the suburbs. Heading for a meeting of fellow exiles in downtown Montevideo one evening, he found the accelerator of his vehicle jammed and the brakes inoperable. In a matter of seconds, the vehicle crashed into a tree, killing the driver and his passenger, another opponent of the General.

For his next attack, he used an automobile again. This time, he drove it himself, running down and hitting an exile walking home from a late-night meeting. The victim survived, but suffered grievous, life-threatening injuries.

All three of these actions had taken place in the space of two weeks. No one suspected him, but now the opposition knew they were under attack. In response, they took precautionary measures. They set up round-the-clock surveillance of their meeting places, avoided being out alone at night, and carefully checked their automobiles before using them.

In the face of these precautions, he shifted tactics. He phoned opposition leaders in the middle of the night, hanging up once they had answered. He sent untraceable letters, threatening harm to those who dared to defame the General. He hired young street toughs to beat up the teen-age children of opposition figures. On several occasions, he fired bullets into the houses of the General's critics. His superiors, however, determined that the risk of being caught using a weapon was too great. He was praised for his initiative but told to halt this particular activity. He did so with some reluctance. He believed that the hard-core opponents of the General could only be dissuaded by the danger of death to themselves and anyone near them. But he followed orders and abandoned the use of firearms.

Over the next few months, he set more fires and continued the harassing phone calls and threatening letters. His superiors at the embassy were very pleased with the results. Dissident groups met less often, had difficulty maintaining their publications, and were noticeably less visible and active. His superiors, however, were concerned that soon his luck at remaining anonymous would run out. The Uruguayan police, not known for their efficiency, were nonetheless beginning to accumulate clues and evidence that could lead directly to him. Dissidents or their sympathizers had been spotted trying to photograph embassy personnel as they entered or left the building. It was only a matter of time, they concluded, that his true identity and purpose would be revealed. Therefore, they determined that the safest course was to transfer him to another location, one where he could get a fresh start.

He was rewarded with a private dinner in the embassy before his departure. The champagne flowed and he received hearty congratulations for his effectiveness in countering the opposition. The following day, nursing a hangover, he had taken the ferry to Buenos Aires, where he reported to secret police headquarters for his next assignment. His chief, not known for generosity in handing out praise, nonetheless, in his own manner, showed his pleasure with his work in Uruguay. He asked him if he wanted some time off to relax, perhaps to meet with friends and family. He declined. He was single. Like most Argentines, he had a large extended family but he was not particularly close to any of them. An only child, he had been strongly attached to his mother and father, but they had perished in a tragic automobile accident the year before. He had a few friends, but most of them were on assignment elsewhere.

The next day, he was on the morning Pan American flight to Santiago. He had a new passport and a new identity and had made slight alterations to his appearance. By now, he had become accustomed to the false eyeglasses, the shoes with the special lifts that made him two inches taller than his normal six feet even, and the padded girdle he wore to provide a paunch. When he had been greeted at the Santiago airport by two men from the embassy, he was momentarily at sea when they called out his new name. But he recovered quickly and it soon became second nature to be "Emilio Ramírez."

While he didn't like Santiago, the work there had gone well. The dissident community was smaller than in Montevideo, but tougher and more resilient. Nonetheless, by using the same tactics, he had begun to wear them down. They had become less strident in their attacks on the General and more circumspect in their activities. He smiled as he considered the impact of his efforts. He had managed, as the North Americans would say, to give the exiles a serious case of the "jitters."

What he planned to do next brought another smile. He and his superiors in the embassy had been formulating this plot for weeks. It was designed, literally, to kill two birds with one stone.

For the past year, the embassy had been keeping close watch on a high-ranking official in the Chilean foreign ministry. That official had met frequently with the Argentine exiles. Subsequently, he informed the foreign minister that he sympathized with the dissidents and urged him to adopt a more aggressive posture toward the Argentine regime. Up to now, the Chilean government, which was controlled by a middle-of-the road party but also contained some leftist elements hostile to the General, had maintained normal relations with the Argentines. However, if the official they were monitoring, who was connected by marriage to the foreign minister, had his way, relations could deteriorate. There was also the prospect that a coalition of Communists and Socialists might win the national elections scheduled for next year, further complicating matters.

The plan he and his superiors had devised was risky but could pay big dividends. Using a mid-level employee of the foreign ministry they had bribed to spy for them, they had arranged for a clandestine late night meeting between the high-ranking official sympathetic to the General's opponents and an exile leader.

What would happen next was up to him. It would be a challenge, but he was confident he could accomplish his mission.

The meeting was set to take place at twelve fifteen. The location was one hundred meters from the entrance to the Parque Metropolitano, to the east of San Cristóbal hill, one of the landmarks of the city. At this time of night, the spot chosen for the rendezvous was completely deserted.

He looked at his watch. It was now ten minutes after twelve. The sky was clear and the air was crisp. Summer had ended and it was autumn in the southern hemisphere. The day had been warm and sunny, but nightfall had produced a drop in temperatures. While it was not yet uncomfortably cold, he was glad he had dressed warmly. He wore dark pants, a gray woolen sweater, a black leather jacket, and a watch cap. Most importantly, he had tight-fitting gloves on both hands.

There was a paved road that wound from the entrance to where he was hiding in a grove of eucalyptus trees. He barely registered the fragrance of the aromatic leaves. He again checked his watch: twelve-fourteen. Seconds later, he saw the headlights of a car moving slowly along the road. It came to a stop about twenty meters away from where he stood. There was only one occupant. The driver turned off the motor and stepped out of the car.

Even though "Emilio's" night-time vision was excellent, he could not tell from this distance if the man he saw was the foreign ministry official or the exile leader. For what he planned, it really didn't matter.

The man who had exited the car stood close to it, stamping his feet and rubbing his hands together. From his hiding place, "Emilio" could sense the man's tension. He was in an isolated spot and vulnerable. There was little noise, although in the distance could be heard the muffled sound of the Mapocho River which cut through the heart of Santiago along with the slight rustling of the eucalyptus leaves.

"Emilio" looked at his watch: twelve-twenty. He felt a twinge of anxiety. *Five minutes late! Maybe the other man wasn't coming.* He forced himself to relax. There was nothing to do but wait.

The man next to the car reached into his pocket and pulled out his own watch. After glancing at it briefly, he put it away. He continued to shuffle his feet and rub his hands together even more vigorously, a sign of nervousness. *How much longer would he wait? If the other man didn't show up, would they be able to arrange another meeting? Maybe one of them had gotten wind of the trap?*

"Emilio" resisted the temptation to check the time again. He took deep breaths and tried to remain calm. If this plan failed he consoled himself with the thought that they could always try something else. But just then, a new set of headlights appeared and another automobile made its way up the winding road. It stopped about five meters behind the parked vehicle. Turning off the motor and extinguishing the lights, the driver got out and approached the other man.

"Emilio" felt a surge of excitement, his pulse racing. *It was going to work!* But he had to move quickly. Once the men met and started to talk, they would quickly realize that the clandestine meeting was a set-up. They would waste little time in beating a hasty retreat.

As he emerged from his hiding place and advanced toward the two men, he saw them greet each other with handshakes and an *abrazo.* Before they could begin a conversation, he was only a few meters away. Absorbed in their meeting, they had not heard him approach. He called out their names, startling them. They broke their *abrazo* and turned in his direction. In the dark, even close by, all they saw was a shapeless form. He raised his hands and like a gunslinger in a western movie fired shots from two pistols into their chests. The two men were hurled backward by the force of the bullets, bouncing off the car behind them and crumpling to the ground, blood already seeping from their bodies onto the pavement.

It had only taken a split second. The blast of the gunshots echoed in his ears. He took a moment for the reverberations to clear. When they did, he listened carefully before advancing toward the bodies. He could detect no signs of alarm. The site chosen for the ambush was far enough away from any residences it was unlikely the sounds of gunshots would carry to them. Besides, most Santiaguenos were fast asleep at this time of night. Still, he had been trained to expect the unexpected. He knew he had to move quickly in the unlikely event that the shots had been heard and someone contacted the police.

He bent over the two bodies, checking to make sure they were no longer breathing. They weren't.

Now, it *was* important to determine who was who. Putting his pistols down next to the two corpses, he lit a match to provide illumination and identified the foreign ministry official. He did the same with the other body, making sure that it was indeed the dissident leader he had targeted. It was.

Then he checked their hands. Neither wore gloves. Good. He kept his own gloves on so as not to leave any fingerprints. He placed the pistol he had used to shoot the exile leader in the left hand of the foreign ministry official. He carefully wrapped the fingers of the dead official around the handle of the pistol, placing the forefinger on the trigger. He repeated the procedure with the corpse of the dissident, this time placing the pistol in the right hand.

The attention to detail was important. Through surveillance, he and his embassy allies had determined the foreign ministry official was left-handed, the exile leader right-handed. For the plan to work there could be no slip-ups on something so basic.

After placing the pistols he had used to kill the two men in the victims' hands, his next step was to rearrange the bodies where they would lie if they had shot each other. This didn't take long. Both corpses were already on their backs. He simply moved them apart and placed them with their feet pointing at each other. Fortunately, the bullets he had fired had not gone all the way through the victims' bodies. There were no bullet holes in the car to arouse suspicion.

Even though it was chilly he could feel sweat on his forehead. He paused for a moment to catch his breath and to listen again to his surroundings. There was still nothing beyond the chatter of some night birds and the distant rumble of the Mapocho.

He was satisfied with how things looked. When the police arrived on the scene, all the physical evidence pointed to the two men having shot one another. There was, of course, the question of how they had managed to fire at one another simultaneously to such deadly effect. He and his superiors had considered the possibility that the police would have doubts about the likelihood of this happening. Perhaps it could be arranged so that one man died and the other survived. But that scenario produced its own complications. Ultimately, they decided the success of the plan hinged on having both men dead. As they saying went, *Dead Men Tell No Tales.* They had to hope the investigators could come up with no other plausible explanation and ascribe the simultaneous shooting to fate.

The next question the police would ask involved motive. *Why had they shot each other?* This question, too, had been much discussed in the embassy. Why, indeed, would two men who were of the same mind when it came to Chilean foreign policy toward Argentina, end up shooting one another? The answer he and his colleagues came up with was a simple one: jealousy. As soon as word reached the foreign ministry that the high-ranking official had been found dead in the company of the dissident, their paid spy would circulate the rumor that the official was involved in a passionate affair with the exile leader's wife. It would be implied, as well, that the alleged affair was the reason the official had urged a change in Chile's stance toward Argentina – not, as was really the case, because of his personal convictions.

To add substance to the charge, the embassy team had composed a series of love letters from the official to the exile leader's wife. Standing over the dissidents body, "Emilio" removed these letters from the inside pocket of his jacket and transferred them to the same pocket of his victim. To add a dramatic touch, he made sure the envelopes containing the forged letters were stained with the victim's blood.

It wouldn't take long for the police to discover the letters. Hopefully, they would draw the conclusion the embassy desired; that the opposition leader had discovered the letters and had come armed to confront his wife's lover. The ministry official, in turn, fearing that the affair had been revealed, came armed as well. But, as with the simultaneous shooting, there was the chance that further investigation might throw this conclusion into question. The foreign ministry official was married, with two children, and was known for his rectitude and strong religious beliefs. *Would such a man stray?* Moreover, the dissident's widow would adamantly and legitimately deny such an affair. Working in their favor, however, was the fact that the official's wife was decidedly unattractive while the exile's wife was a stunning beauty. In the last analysis, he and his colleagues reasoned, the Chilean police detectives who interrogated the widow could easily believe that even the most faithful of men might stray if tempted by such a looker. And there was the undeniable fact that the official had met with the dissident couple on many occasions.

No plan was perfect. The success of this effort depended on a lot of different pieces falling into place. And even if the police accepted the scenario that had been concocted, the Argentine exile community, and probably most Chileans, would suspect the General's hand behind the whole thing. But, "Emilio" reasoned, so long as there was no hard evidence connecting him or the embassy to the shooting, people could speculate all they wanted. The story they had constructed might ultimately fell apart. But at least he had the satisfaction that no matter what, two threats to the General had been removed.

Standing up after having placed the love letters in the exile leader's pocket, he looked at his watch. Only a few minutes had passed since he had shot the two men. There were still no signs of alarm – no sirens wailing in the distance, no vehicles heading up the road from the park's entrance. Even so, he couldn't risk hanging around much longer. If he were caught, it would be a disaster.

Satisfied that he had arranged the scene as planned and had left no traces of his involvement, he moved at a brisk pace through the woods to the street below. Emerging from the park a few minutes later, he made his way to the Mapocho. Crossing the river, he entered the well-to-do Providencia district. After walking several blocks through the quiet, deserted streets, he located a public phone.

How the bodies were to be discovered had been another subject of embassy discussion. Some wanted to wait until a passer-by stumbled across them and called the police. Others argued this would most likely happen after dawn broke and people began to take the road up to San Cristóbal. In the meantime, the scene might be disturbed, perhaps by animals, maybe even by one of the vagrants who lived in the park. A vagrant would be tempted to take the wallets, guns, clothes, and perhaps even the love letters from the bodies. So it was determined it would be best to notify the police once "Emilio" was safely out of the park.

Making sure no one was watching, he entered the phone booth and called the police. When the call was answered, he changed the pitch of his voice and spoke with a Chilean accent. He kept it brief. He had been out walking his dog, he said, when he had heard what he thought were gunshots from the direction of the Parque Metropolitano. The voice on the other end was about to ask for more information when he hung up. The "mystery" call would undoubtedly arouse suspicions, but lots of Chileans didn't want anything to do with the police. Most likely, the abrupt call would be attributed to a citizen who didn't care to have his life complicated by police questioning. At least that was the hope.

His apartment was only a few blocks away. He walked briskly. As usual, there was no one on the streets at this time of night. He got to the entrance of his building without being observed. As he pulled out his key to open the main door, he heard the blare of sirens in the distance. Half an hour earlier, that sound would have caused his stomach to churn. Now, it was sweet music to his ears. Taking the stairs to his third-floor apartment, he broke into a satisfied smile. Confident that he had carried out his assignment flawlessly, he looked forward to a well-deserved good night's sleep. The General, he knew, would be pleased.

CHAPTER TWO

May 10, 1951 – Buenos Aires, Argentina

Horacio Campos, head of Argentina's secret police, enjoyed the view from his seventh-floor office. Hands clasped behind his back, he stared out the east window toward the estuary of the Río de la Plata. The late afternoon sun glanced off the water, turning it from muddy brown to a closer approximation of the color of silver for which it had been named.

Looking at the large ships that constantly came and went into the country's major port never failed to intrigue him. Most Argentines considered the Plaza de Mayo, a few blocks to the south, as the heart of Buenos Aires – if not of the country. On the east side of the plaza sat the presidential office, the Casa Rosada, the "Pink House," symbol of the all-powerful executive authority. On the north side was the main cathedral, representing the spiritual dominance of the Roman Catholic faith and the institutional power of the Church.

But to Campos, what lay in front of him was the real heart of the city. Through the port pumped the lifeblood of the nation. Leaving Buenos Aires was a steady stream of ships carrying the meat and grains that made the country rich – the "Breadbasket of the World." Entering the port were the manufactured goods that the profits from agricultural sales allowed the country to buy, mostly from Europe and the United States. Now, with recent industrial growth, the need for imported products had declined to a degree. But the demand remained steady.

At one time, passenger ships had disgorged hundreds of thousands of immigrants onto Argentina's shores. They came mostly from Italy and Spain. The Great Depression and the World War had significantly reduced European immigration. The past few years had seen some resumption, although not in the numbers of those who had entered at the turn of the century.

Campos had no problem with the economic exchanges taking place out his window. The steady flow of imports and exports kept the economy humming. A thriving economy helped maintain political stability, which made his job easier. He had mixed feelings, however, about the arrival of immigrants.

The immigrants had provided the skills and labor that had built modern Argentina. Of that, there was no doubt. Their contributions had been many and significant. Without them, the country would have remained mired in the nineteenth century, an isolated backwater. His own parents, like so many, had arrived from a small village in northern Spain at the turn of the century with only the shirts on their backs. They found housing in a tenement, a *conventillo*, located in one of the poorest districts of Buenos Aires. Both parents started out working at menial jobs, saving every *peso* they could. By the time he was born, his father had accumulated enough money to open a *bodega* in an area only a few blocks from where he now stood. By the time he was five years old, they had moved from their *conventillo* to a modest house in the middle-class barrio of Flores.

His parents' story was not atypical. While not all immigrants thrived in the new land, and many returned in disappointment to their homelands, the majority stayed and enjoyed various levels of success. Be that as it may, there was another element of the immigrant wave that bothered him greatly. Along with their skills and their ambition to *Hacer la América* – to make it in America – some immigrants also brought with them dangerous, European-rooted radical ideas. Although relatively small in number, adherents of anarchism, socialism, and communism invaded the country's shores. In the late nineteenth and early twentieth century, Anarchists engaged in violent acts, including political assassinations and setting off bombs in public places. Along with Socialists, they encouraged the working classes to organize and to protest against the abuses of employers and the state. Many of these protests had turned to violence. By the 1920s, the anarchist influence had dwindled. The Socialists, never as extreme, worked within the political process, participating in elections and electing representatives to local and national governments to promote their agenda. Campos considered them more an annoyance than a threat.

His real concern was with the Communists. Starting with a handful of intellectuals and workers in the 1920s, the party had steadily gained strength and numbers over the past two decades. Their influence had been significantly reduced with the rise to power of Campos's friend and patron, Juan Perón, elected president in 1946. Perón had achieved his rise by mobilizing the support of Argentina's working classes to a far greater degree and with much more success than any of his more radical and ideologically-driven predecessors. In the process, he had neutralized, marginalized, and to some extent co-opted the Communists.

With the onset of the Cold War between the Soviet Union and the United States, Perón had developed a foreign policy that aimed for a neutral position in the global confrontation, a so-called "third way." Part of that policy entailed some tolerance for the local Communists, who were allowed to continue their activities within certain limits.

Campos had gone along. He had no choice. As head of the secret police, it was his job to carry out Perón's orders. He was to keep a close eye on the Communists but not harass them. Still, he had his misgivings. He had been fighting the Communists for twenty years. He loathed and distrusted them and their Soviet masters. But orders were orders. And he was nothing if not a man who obeyed orders – and who expected those below him to do the same.

He also had misgivings about another order he had been given. Over the past year and a half, Perón had directed Campos to carry out a campaign against the Argentine exiles who had found refuge abroad. The secret police were to maintain their watch over domestic opponents, their main priority, but a special cadre was developed to operate outside of the nation's borders.

Campos had expressed his concerns about the wisdom of this strategy to Perón. These operations, he warned, were extremely delicate and dangerous. They could easily backfire. The chances of failure were high and Campos was not sure the results, even if successful, were worth the risk. But Perón was adamant. The plan had to be implemented at once and carried out with vigor. Campos strongly suspected that once again, as on many occasions, Perón was pushed to carry out this campaign against his critics abroad by his wife, Evita.

Campos had come to both admire and fear Argentina's first lady. Like many, he initially discounted Eva Duarte Perón as a round-heeled floozy who had seduced a man twice her age; a two-bit actress with little education and a dubious past. But she had proved exceptionally clever and more politically astute than anyone could have imagined. Accumulating power, she had moved far beyond the traditional role of first lady to assume positions of influence second to none. She had become the main link between Perón and his principal base of support, organized labor. She also had helped to mobilize Argentine women to rally behind the regime. By now, her popularity among the masses at least equaled if not surpassed that of her husband. It was no secret that Perón planned to propose Evita as his vice-presidential candidate in upcoming national elections. This was an unprecedented move that troubled even Perón's strongest supporters, especially among the military.

Campos had little doubt that if Evita wanted to run as vice president, run she would. On too many occasions to count, he had seen Perón's wife, now one of the world's most powerful women, impose her iron will on her husband and others. She let few obstacles stand in her path as she often ruthlessly eliminated obstacles, be they institutions like the newspaper *La Prensa*, which she had cowed into submission and ultimately taken over, or individuals like labor leader Cipriano Reyes, once a supporter and now a marginalized figure. When the upper-class women's charity organization, the *Sociedad de Beneficencia*, had failed to bestow on her the traditional honor of naming the country's first lady its honorary head, Evita had simply bypassed the snub and created her own much more powerful social welfare organization. As its head, she had been dubbed the "Lady of Hope" by her worshipful followers.

Campos feared little. But he found that dealing with Evita – and her passion and her ruthlessness – unnerved him. Whenever they met to discuss police business, the conversation was normally straightforward and professional. But he also had experienced flashes of her anger when he had seemed less than enthusiastic about some of her schemes to deal with opponents. He knew that his old friend Perón was pleased with his performance, but he had his doubts about Evita. He knew that if his wife voiced her displeasure with Campos to her husband and demanded his dismissal – or worse – his long-time relationship with Perón would count for little.

So far, he had escaped such a fate by dutifully following orders despite whatever personal reservations he might have. The plan to deal with the exiles in neighboring countries was a case in point. But he now had on his desk orders from above that raised the danger to him and to the regime to an entirely new level. While the orders had come from the president, there was little doubt that they sprang from the hand of Evita. And unlike previous occasions, where Campos had had the opportunity to discuss the possible ramifications of actions against enemies of the regime with the president and his wife, this time the orders had been communicated in writing and delivered directly to the head of the secret police without prior consultation.

Campos had received the top secret message the day before. Opening it at once, he saw three type-written pages underneath the presidential seal. As he read, his heart beat accelerated, he felt a sour feeling build in his stomach, and his hands, usually steady as a rock, began to tremble.

The orders were crystal clear. He was to arrange for the assassination of a United States citizen and his Argentine-born wife on U.S. soil. The targets were not even outspoken critics of the regime. This was a matter of personal revenge, a settling of an old score.

Campos knew the targets well. They were Peter Benton and his wife María. Benton, who had come to Buenos Aires in June of 1945 to straighten out affairs at a film-distribution agency, had been recruited by a friend at the U.S. embassy to gain the confidence of Juan Perón and

Eva Duarte and glean what he could about them. Benton had reported to U.S. officials what he had learned from his meetings with Perón and Eva. And he, along with officials from the British and American embassies, had tried to disrupt the transfer of tens of millions in gold from the defeated Third Reich to Perón and his allies. They had failed in that attempt, but in the process Benton had killed the German officer who had made the transfer along with two of Campos's men, including Ernesto Aguilar, one of his most promising lieutenants. Thanks to the intercession of the U.S. ambassador at the time, Spruille Braden, Benton had been allowed to leave the country along with the two Allied officials on the provision that none of the three ever return to Argentina. Benton was also forbidden to have contact with María Suárez, the secretary at the film distribution agency who had fallen in love with him. Suárez had had the temerity – and, Campos had to admit, the courage - to approach Eva Duarte in an attempt to save Benton's life. Now, according to the sheets that Campos held in his hand Benton had ended up working for the U.S. Department of Justice in Washington, D.C. Furthermore, Benton had succeeded in getting permission for María Suárez to travel to the United States where they had married.

For Campos, it was like reliving an old nightmare. Following orders that he was sure came from Evita he had been in charge of the operation to deal with Benton. He and Aguilar had devised a plan to kidnap Benton and get rid of the interfering North American while expediting the escape of the German officer. Benton somehow had managed to turn the tables. Campos still wasn't sure how he had pulled it off, but there was no denying the corpses of his two men and the German officer they found in a field off the highway from Buenos Aires to Tandil.

However Benton had managed his escape and the death of the three men, the responsibility for the colossal disaster fell directly on Campos's shoulders. Under ordinary circumstances, he would have at the least been demoted, all hopes of advancement crushed - or even dismissed from the service altogether despite his many successes over the years. Fortunately for him, at the time Perón had serious doubts about the loyalty of Campos's superior, the then head of the secret police. Perón wanted a man in that position whom he could trust without reservation, and Campos was that man. It also helped that the most important part of the whole scheme – the transfer of the German gold – had been accomplished under Campos's direction. Six months after his election as president, Perón had promoted Campos to be the head of the secret police. Perón, at least, had been willing to overlook the disaster involving Peter Benton. Evita, however, was another matter.

On personal grounds, Campos had no qualms about eliminating Benton and his wife. The North American had been responsible for the biggest black mark on what was by and large a spotless record. And while Campos was not one to let emotion color his judgment, he had had a fondness for Lieutenant Aguilar, who he had developed into one his most effective and loyal subordinates. But to carry out such an action in the capital of the United States posed an enormous risk. If the hand of the Argentine government was discovered to be behind the action the consequences would be catastrophic

After sleeping on his dilemma, Campos decided that he had to confront Perón directly. He had too many reservations. The whole thing was too risky. If forced to carry out the plan, he even considered resigning rather than agreeing to it.

First thing the morning following his receipt of the top-secret set of orders, he contacted the president's secretary and asked for an immediate appointment. In the past, despite his busy schedule, Perón had always found time for Campos. If Campos called to ask for a meeting, a fairly rare occurrence, Perón knew that it was important enough to clear his calendar and to meet with the head of the secret police as soon as possible.

Campos expected the same response this time. But after speaking with the president's secretary, who promised to get back to him at once, Campos found himself stewing in his office for more than two hours with no response. He could only surmise that Perón did not want to meet with him, avoiding any possible confrontation and disagreement. The orders had been delivered. Now Perón wanted them carried out. Just as Campos was about to call the Casa Rosada again, he was jarred by the shrill tone of his phone ringing.

Steeling himself, he picked it up on the third ring. "Horacio Campos," he said, keeping his voice steady. He was expecting to hear that Perón was too busy to meet with him. Instead, he was startled to hear the familiar voice of the president on the other end. His first thought was that Perón was going to tell him personally, and probably forcefully, that he could not meet with him and that he should follow the orders he had received without question. But instead, Argentina's most powerful man said, "Horacio my friend. I apologize for the delay in getting back to you. I had some urgent business to attend to."

Campos doubted Perón's sincerity, but responded as expected. "That's perfectly all right Mister President. I understand completely." *What else was he going to say?* That Perón probably had consulted with Evita about the advisability of meeting with him and had gotten her reluctant permission?

"Look Horacio, why don't you come over now? I have some free time."

"Certainly Mister President. I'll come right over."

Hanging up the phone, Campos went to his outer office and informed his secretary that he would be gone for at least an hour and to postpone any appointments until the afternoon. Grabbing a topcoat, he left his office and headed for the elevator. On the ground floor, he found the bodyguard who accompanied him whenever he left the building. He was a giant of a man called Bruno, whose size alone would discourage anyone who might threaten the head of the secret police. Up until about a year ago, Campos had traveled with at least three or four protectors every time he left headquarters. But once Bruno joined the team, the extra men proved unnecessary. In addition to his size, Bruno also had the virtue of maintaining a discreet silence whenever he was in charge of Campos's safety. His job was to protect his boss with his life if necessary, not try to ingratiate himself with idle chatter.

Campos's secretary had called down to the lobby to inform Bruno that the chief was on the way. Bruno met Campos as he stepped out of the elevator, towering over the man he was sworn to protect with his life.

"Come on Bruno," Campos said. "We are going to the Casa Rosada."

"Certainly *jefe*," the giant responded, leading the way to the door to the street. Flanking the door were two more guards, who stood at attention as Campos and Bruno approached. One of them opened the door and Bruno stepped out first, carefully scanning the sidewalk and the traffic along Avenida Leandro Alem. Satisfied that there were no visible dangers, he signaled for Campos to follow him out while the guards, their revolvers not too far from their hands, watched carefully as the two men exited the building.

To the casual observer, these precautions seemed unnecessary. While there had been attempts against police officials in the past, most notably the 1909 assassination of Buenos Aires police chief Ramón Falcon by an anarchist bomb thrower, they were rare. And, since the election of Perón, backed by overwhelming popular support, there had been no incidents of note. But Campos liked to guard against any eventuality, no matter how remote. Hence, the choreographed exit from secret police headquarters.

Campos and Bruno did not have far to walk. The Casa Rosada was only a few blocks away to the south. As usual, there were many pedestrians along the well-traveled sidewalk. Bruno attracted some stares, but most looked away quickly when they saw the grim and serious expression on his face, his head swiveling left and right on the lookout for any trouble. Campos was not well known to the public and few recognized him on the street. If any did happen to notice him, they quickly averted their eyes. No one wanted to cross the path of one of the nation's most feared men.

Bruno and Campos arrived at the northern entrance of the executive mansion less than five minutes after having left secret police headquarters. Three men from the president's security detail met them at the door and ushered them into the building. Following the usual procedure, Bruno stayed in the reception area with two of the guards while a third led Campos up the marble staircase to the second floor and the presidential office. The door to the president's outer office was ajar. Campos's escort gave a gentle knock and slowly pushed the massive oak door open, gesturing for him to enter.

Once Campos was inside, the guard closed the door leaving Campos alone with Perón's secretary. The secretary, a matronly woman known for her efficiency, not for her charm, greeted him formally and asked him to take a seat. "The president is on the phone," she explained.

That was it; no elaboration. No, "He'll be with you in a minute," no opportunity for small talk if Campos had been so inclined, which he was not. As far as he was concerned, the secretary's brusque manner suited him just fine. But he knew that others found it a bit jarring.

He took a seat on the edge of a comfortable brown leather couch, waiting to be called into the inner office. He kept his back straight and his hands clasped on his knees, a formal posture that indicated he did not expect to be kept waiting long. He allowed a small smile to flit briefly across his face, so fleeting someone observing him might have thought it was their imagination.

It was Perón's secretary that produced the momentary amused look. She was such an anomaly. In almost every governmental office, private business, or professional group that dealt with the public, it was standard practice to hire attractive young women as secretaries and receptionists. There was even something of a competition among these various male-dominated enterprises to have the most beautiful women they could find front and center. If they also possessed intelligence and advanced secretarial skills, that was an added plus. But these were secondary considerations.

In his own case, Campos's secretary also deviated from the norm. Since his office did not deal with the public, he saw no need to adhere to the standard practices. His secretary, who had been with him throughout his career, was plain, a bit overweight, and with little if any sense of fashion. But she was intelligent, efficient, discreet, and, most importantly, loyal. These were the qualities he considered most important in a secretary.

But Perón's case was different. His secretary most definitely *was* in the public eye. There was a steady stream of important visitors – high-ranking military men, industrialists, union leaders, entertainers, foreign dignitaries, and others – who came to see the president. And all received the same frosty reception from Perón's secretary.

The only answer Campos could come up with to explain this anomaly was that somewhere in the equation was Evita. A man often spent as much if not more time with his secretary than he did with his wife. Women in that position could exert considerable influence over a man, especially if they were attractive. Campos assumed that Evita had made sure that the presidential secretary would in no way prove a competitor either for Perón's attentions or, possibly, his affections. As far as Campos knew Perón and Evita were a close and loving couple. But why take the chance? From Evita's point of view, there should be only one woman in Perón's life – and she was the one.

Campos was interrupted in his musings by the secretary's no-nonsense voice announcing that "The president will see you now."

Campos rose from the couch and approached the door to the president's inner office, offering the secretary a brief nod. Knocking twice, he heard Perón say "Come in Horacio. Please, come in."

Grabbing the ornate handle in one hand and pushing firmly with the other against the door panel, Campos entered the president's imposing office. Although he had visited it many times, he never failed to be impressed. Lush carpets covered an intricate parquet floor, polished to perfection. Portraits of past Argentine presidents and military heroes, often one in the same, adorned the walls. The most dominant portrait was of Argentina's great hero of the wars of independence, General José de San Martín, whose likeness occupied pride of place right behind the presidential desk. The previous year, the regime had made much of the fact that 1950 marked the centennial of the great national hero's death and the presidential couple had done all they could to wrap themselves in his mantel.

To the west, two large sets of windows, today closed against the winter chill, offered a spectacular view of Buenos Aires's main square, the Plaza de Mayo. The square had special meaning for Perón. On October 17, 1945 a massive crowd of tens of thousands working-class Argentines had gathered in the plaza to demand that Perón be released from house arrest and allowed to compete in upcoming presidential elections. Perón had delivered an electrifying speech to the assembled throng and from that day forward followed what seemed an inevitable path to the presidency.

Perón, who had been scribbling something on a sheet of paper as Campos entered, rose from behind his desk and strode forward to greet him, his arms outstretched

The two men exchanged an *abrazo*, punctuated by quick pats on the back.

"Horacio, my old friend." Perón said, "So good to see you." Then, pointing to two large armchairs facing one another over a small coffee table, added "Please have a seat."

Campos took one of the chairs, Perón the other. Campos uttered an inward sigh of relief. He and Perón were alone. He had been worried that Evita might be present, making a difficult situation even more fraught.

Perón was in shirtsleeves with his tie loosened. Part of the Peronist "revolution" had been to do away with much of the formality that for decades had characterized Argentine life and politics. Appealing to the *descamisados* literally the "shirtless ones," the first couple had tried to project the common touch, disdaining pretensions of the middle and upper classes with such gestures as Perón removing his coat at every opportunity. For reasons that Campos could not explain, Evita had been more successful in establishing a bond with the working-classes, especially the women of the working classes, than her husband – despite the fact that she had accumulated a fabulous wardrobe and often attended social functions bedecked with expensive jewelry and redolent of exotic perfumes.

Perón had given up trying to convince Campos to shed his own suit jacket. The head of Argentina's secret police had no interest in showing the common touch. That was not his job. His job was to protect the regime from its enemies, not to curry favor with the masses.

Campos looked at his watch. It was eleven thirty. He hoped he would have enough time before the president's next appointment to make his case. But he didn't know how to start. He was tempted to get right to the point. But given the delicacy of the matter, that tactic might backfire. Better to let Perón make the first moves.

A few awkward seconds passed after both men had taken their seats, each waiting for the other to speak first. Perón broke the tension. "Horacio. Would you like some coffee?"

Campos didn't really want any coffee. But he realized that he better go along. He could see that Perón was nervous. There were beads of sweat on his brow and a slight tremor in his hands. It was best to go through the social conventions before getting down to business.

"Yes Mister President. Some coffee would be fine."

Perón returned to his desk and picked up the phone. Campos heard him order the coffee. Then the President returned to his chair. Once again seated, he looked at Campos with an expression that was not hard for the trained policeman to decipher. In addition to the obvious discomfort, Campos saw that Perón was trying desperately to hold back a deep sense of sadness. He thought he saw tears begin to form at the corner of the president's eyes.

Looking down in his lap for a few seconds, Perón took a deep breath and gathered himself.

"Listen Horacio," he began his voice firm. "I know why you are here."

Campos raised his hand as though to interrupt, but Perón waved him off.

"You have serious reservations about the orders I sent to you. The orders to arrange for the assassination of Peter Benton and his wife."

Campos simply nodded.

"Yes. Yes. It is an unusual and risky operation. It could have terrible consequences. It could endanger our relations with the United States, just at a time when some of the damage done by that insufferable Braden has been repaired and we are beginning to attract significant North American investment."

Campos understood what Perón was saying all too well. When serving as United States ambassador to Argentina in 1945, Braden had done all he could to block Perón from assuming the presidency. He also had been involved in the affair with Benton. Even back in Washington, he had tried to determine the course of the 1946 election by releasing a document that alleged Perón had been connected to the Axis powers during the war. Perón had cleverly used Braden's interference and the document, the so-called *Blue Book* to his advantage by playing the nationalist card of undue foreign influence. He had debunked the *Blue Book* as no more than propaganda, although Campos knew it contained considerable truth. Since that low point, relations with the United States, while not exactly warm, had noticeably improved. Now this scheme to exact revenge on Benton could change things in the blink of an eye.

Perón took another deep breath and let out a heartfelt sigh that seemed to come from the depths of his soul. "Yes my friend, I know, I know. Is it really worth it? The operation against our exiled opponents is already risky enough. If our operations in countries like Chile and Uruguay become public, it could make our relations with our neighbors decidedly uncomfortable. But to alienate the United States, the most powerful nation in the hemisphere would be a real disaster!"

For a brief moment, Campos had the hope that Perón, by laying out the serious consequences if the operation against Benton and his wife was exposed had convinced himself to cancel it. The hope was soon dashed.

"But Horacio," Perón continued, his voice cracking with emotion, "We have to do it. We just have to do it."

Leaning forward in his chair, Perón lowered his voice to just above a whisper, although there was little likelihood that anyone could hear them. "Evita," he said, choking back a sob, "Evita wants it. She wants it."

Campos's suspicious were confirmed. But he took little solace in that fact.

"And we have to do it, my friend. We have to do it."

Perón removed a handkerchief from his pants pocket and dabbed at the tears that had formed. Staring at Campos with a look that pleaded for understanding if not compassion, Perón chocked out the words. "Evita is dying Horacio. I don't think she has much longer to live. The cancer she has is eating away at her. She is incredibly strong, but it is too much, too much. I know," he said, sobbing, "I know. I've been through this before."

Campos could not help but feel sorry for his patron and friend. Perón had lost his first wife to cancer and now it seemed he would lose his second wife in the same manner. *What cruel irony!* While it was not common knowledge, the fact that Evita was not in good health was well-known among the inner circles of the regime. The exact nature of her illness, and the many attempts to treat it, however, were a closely-guarded secret. Campos, of course, was privy to that secret but not even he had realized how serious the threat to her life was. The way Perón was suffering indicated that it was very serious indeed.

With sympathy in his voice, Campos, using the President's first name, said, "I know Juan. I know. I'm sorry. Very sorry."

Gathering himself, Perón said in a steadier voice, "Thank you Horacio. Thank you."

"So you see. We have to do this thing with Benton and his wife, no matter the consequences. We have no choice. It is Evita's wish, her dy…"

Perón stopped himself, but Campos knew what he was going to say: "Her dying wish." He couldn't help but wonder if there were more items on the first lady's "dying wish list," perhaps even his own dismissal. He knew without a doubt that if he failed to carry out the orders he had been given, he would no longer be head of the secret police.

Campos kept his expression neutral as he pondered these possibilities. At that moment, there was a knock on the door. It was an *ordenanza* with the coffee that had been requested. Campos had almost forgotten that the request had been made. But it offered a welcome break. While the *ordenanza* poured the coffee and both men went through the ritual of adding sugar and stirring, Campos had time to think through what he would say next. It didn't take long. He would swallow his reservations and misgivings and follow orders, hoping against hope that the plan he had in mind would work. And if it did not, he determined, better to go out having tried and failed than to be dismissed for not having done his duty.

Campos waited until Perón had finished his own coffee before he spoke. "I understand Mister President," he began, resuming the formal terms of address. "I understand," although, if truth be told, he wasn't completely sure that he did. How could a man like Perón, so fundamentally pragmatic and calculating, succumb to the irrational wish of Evita when the consequences for the nation he led might be so dire? These were mysteries of the human heart that Campos found difficult to fathom.

"And I think I have a plan that just might work." Campos thought about adding "*although there are no guarantees,*" but decided to put as positive a face on his proposal as possible. "And I have just the man - and woman - in mind to carry out the mission successfully."

Perón put down his coffee cup and leaned forward.

"Now here Mister President is what I have in mind."

As Campos laid out his scheme, Perón listened intently. At times, he gave a slight grimace, followed by a shrug, as though accepting the inevitable. When Campos had finished, the president rose and they shook hands. Both men were grim-faced. Campos had devised the best plan he could think of, but both men knew that the risks remained enormous and that a lot of different things had to go right if it were to succeed. But the die had been cast. The President had issued the orders and the head of the secret police was committed to carry them out. Whether both would come to regret it, only time would tell.

CHAPTER THREE

June 4, 1951 -Washington, D.C.

I got on the Connecticut Avenue Streetcar at the Kalorama Road stop a little before seven-thirty in the morning. Ordinarily, I would try to walk to my office in the Department of Justice on Constitution Avenue. But the weekend had been hot and humid, with highs in the low nineties. There was a promise of showers and cooling, but later in the day. I didn't want to arrive at the office drenched in sweat.

The car was crowded with government employees, who made up the great majority of the city's workforce. They were a mixture of dark-suited men and professionally-attired women representing the legions who helped keep the wheels of government moving. Fortunately, not all the seats were yet filled and I was able to find a space near the back of the car.

Even with the windows down, the heat was already oppressive. I removed my suit coat and folded it carefully on my lap. I placed my briefcase between my legs, using my knees to secure it. It held important papers and I didn't want to lose contact for even a few seconds. Glancing around, I saw others adopting the same posture. I wasn't the only one who thought he was carrying something of vital importance to the nation's well-being.

I took out my copy of *The Washington Post* and began to scan the front page. When I had moved to Washington from New York a few months back, one of the things I feared I would miss the most was my daily *New York Times.* I soon learned that the *Post,* although not quite up to the *Times* in my view, was an acceptable substitute. And I preferred it to the *Evening Star,* the afternoon paper of record in Washington. Since I was now an employee, if only temporarily, of the federal government, I found the local papers had more news of direct value to me than did the *Times.*

Scanning the headlines, my eyes passed over the date – June 4. For a few seconds, the significance didn't register. Then I remembered. That was the day when in 1943 the Argentine military had removed the civilian government from power and had started a process that ultimately helped make Juan Perón president of the country. I had been in Buenos Aires on the second anniversary of the military takeover and had begun to establish contact with Perón and his mistress at the time, Eva Duarte. Eva, or "Evita" as she was more popularly known, was now Perón's wife and one of the most famous and powerful women in the world.

My acquaintance with the couple was not by coincidence. I had been placed in the same apartment building where they resided by my old OSS partner, David Friedman. David was attached to the United States Embassy, which, under the direction of Ambassador Spruille Braden, was trying to thwart Perón's plans to take power. David saw my presence on the scene as an opportunity to gather first-hand information on the couple. I enjoyed some success in gaining Juan and Eva's confidence, but things fell apart quickly when I was betrayed by an embassy secretary who was having a clandestine affair with an officer in Argentina's secret police. I was subsequently kidnapped and, thanks to the aid of one of the men assigned to watch over me, only narrowly managed to escape with my life. In the process, I shot and killed two secret police agents and stabbed to death a Nazi colonel by the name of von Strasser who had delivered crates of gold to the regime. Thanks to the intercession of Ambassador Braden, I had been allowed to leave the country, but only with the proviso that I never return. More hurtful, I also had to forego any contact with an Argentine woman with whom I had fallen in love, María Suárez.

Returning to the United States, I had time to let the wounds I had suffered in my escape to fully heal. But the emotional wounds of my separation from María remained. Almost miraculously, my father, an influential international lawyer, was able to get the Argentine government to allow María to leave the country and come to the U.S. A few months after being reunited, we were married in New York, where we had lived for the past six years before we moved to Washington.

My father helped María find a job while I went to Columbia law school. Ironically, her job was with the same company, Foreign Film Distributors, where I had been briefly employed and where my adventure in Argentina had its origins. The firm was under new management, the previous director having been replaced for malfeasance. María, who had been a secretary in the FFD office in Buenos Aires, began with the same position in New York. Quickly learning English, after one year she was promoted to a management position. By the time we left for Washington, she had become the assistant director of an office that had grown dramatically in size and scope.

For my part, I had entered law school with some misgivings. Law was the career that my father had chosen and in which he had achieved remarkable success. It was his wish that I follow in his footsteps. But when I returned from my wartime service in Spain, I wasn't sure that I wanted to follow the same path. Although I loved and admired my father, I wasn't sure I wanted to emulate him. Maybe I feared that I wouldn't live up to his expectations or, more likely, I had always had something of an independent streak that had produced minor rebellions against parental authority. My experiences in Argentina, however, helped change my mind. With all the dangers and complications, I had enjoyed being on what I considered the "right" side of a struggle between the forces of good and evil. Maybe that was a bit simplistic, but that's the way I saw it. And a legal career that focused on criminal law would keep me engaged in that struggle.

Law school proved to be more of a challenge than I had expected. My classes were filled with war veterans like me, all of whom were mature, highly-motived, and extremely competitive. After a rough first year, I got squared away and managed to make law review and graduate near the top of my class. My father had wanted me to focus, as he had, on international business law. He made the powerful argument, as only he could, that with U.S. economic interests increasingly ascendant throughout the world, that field of law was particularly relevant - and highly lucrative. But from the beginning, I had stuck to my goal of specializing in criminal law. Upon graduation I took an entry-level job with the District Attorney's Office for the County of New York.

They pay wasn't much and the work was often overwhelming. I put in long days, usually arriving at our Greenwich Village apartment at seven or eight at night. Maria, who herself put in long hours at the office, was always patiently waiting for me with dinner prepared. Fortunately, she was used to eating late and I had adjusted to the same routine. The work I did was often stressful, involving serious matters of life and death, and I did my best not to carry my burdens home. I tried not to be too upbeat when we managed to put crooks in jail, and not too downbeat when they managed to go free.

I was lucky to be working with Frank S. Hogan, the District Attorney. Although he was a Democrat, he had worked with Republican Thomas Dewey in the 1930s to crack down on racketeering. When named DA in his own right in 1941, he played no political favorites. He was quiet and a bit reserved, but had a will of steel. I had been part of his team that looked into landlords who gouged their tenants, investigated corruption in city government, and brought to justice the gamblers who tried to fix the outcomes of college basketball games.

These efforts aside, Hogan's main focus had been on organized crime, specifically the organization headed by New York's most infamous crime boss – Frank Costello. I had to earn my spurs to be involved in the special task force that was gathering evidence against Costello. A year ago I had made enough of an impression to be included on the team.

In fact, that was why I was now in Washington, headed for the Justice Department with my briefcase between my knees. In March, four of us from the task force were assigned to work with the department in aid of Senator Estes Kefauver, who was spearheading a congressional investigation of organized crime with special attention given to Frank

Costello. The assignment was temporary but also open-ended. None of us knew how long we would be in Washington.

While I missed New York, I was happy to be in Washington. The work we were doing was challenging, important, and with a bit of danger. And I had to admit to myself that I had missed the atmosphere of excitement I had experienced during my OSS service in Spain and, if truth be told, my adventures in Argentina. Working on the Costello case had brought back some of those same feelings.

By the time the streetcar had reached Dupont Circle, I had stopped my musings and returned to reading the *Post* with more care. The Kefauver hearings received ample press coverage, but today there was little mention of them. The main headline news dealt with the Korean conflict, where United Nations troops seemed to be making some headway. Of course, many Americans were now getting their view of the hearings not from newspapers but from live television. I hadn't yet decided whether this was an improvement or not. Television certainly offered a more immediate picture of the proceedings and probably reached a wider audience than newspapers did. But I also feared that it provided too many distractions from the evidence that was being presented. Participants on both sides too often seemed to be putting on a show for the television audience rather than addressing the specific issues in a serious manner. But maybe I was just being old-fashioned, slow to accept the increasingly popular new form of communication.

At Dupont Circle, we picked up more passengers. The car was now jam-packed, with the aisles crowded and passengers hanging on to straps and handles, trying to retain their balance as we swayed back and forth or came to a sudden halt.

When we stopped at Constitution Avenue and the doors opened, I got up from my seat and made my way to the back exit. When I descended to the street, about half the passengers in the car accompanied me. Constitution Avenue was lined with government buildings and most of those who had been on the streetcar were heading to work in one of them. The men on the car, like me, had shed their coats. Now, we slung them over our shoulders as we walked towards our respective offices. From the standpoint of comfort, it was hard to tell what was worse, the heat and humidity in the streetcar, only slightly alleviated by the faint breeze that came through the open windows, or the heat and humidity on the street.

I only had two blocks to walk to the Department of Justice Building. I found the shadiest path I could, joining most of the other pedestrians who had sought the same refuge. I could feel a slight sheen of perspiration on my forehead and sweat on my palms. I briefly switched the briefcase I was carrying from my right hand to my left, letting the air cool the palm on the right. After a few seconds, I switched the briefcase back, feeling more comfortable with a tighter grip.

I was probably being paranoid about my briefcase. And maybe I was exaggerating the importance of its contents. But inside were irreplaceable documents that detailed down to the last minute and the last penny the daily operations of parts of Costello's vast criminal enterprise. I had taken them home to work on over the weekend and was acutely conscious of what might happen if they fell into the wrong hands. Letting my OSS training kick in, I kept a constant lookout for anyone who looked suspicious; anyone who might try to snatch my briefcase from me. As far as I could tell, my concerns were groundless. No one seemed to be paying me the slightest attention.

As I approached the southeast corner entrance to the Department of Justice, I saw several FBI agents heading for the door. We were working closely with Justice Department lawyers and the FBI on the Costello case and I had gotten to know quite a few of them over the past months. At the door, I exchanged greetings with the agents I knew and we entered the building as a group. For some irrational reason, I felt a sense of relief that I had made it from my apartment to the Justice Department without having my briefcase and its precious documents snatched from me. Now I had the added protection of a coterie of FBI agents to thwart any would-be attackers.

Parting company with my "bodyguards," I went up the stairs to my third-floor office. As usual, I took some time to admire the WPA murals that lined the staircase of the building. The heroic depictions of American farmers, workers, and other everyday citizens reminded the people who worked in the building just whose interests they were protecting. I also couldn't resist a chuckle when I pictured the boss of the FBI, J. Edgar Hoover, viewing the same murals. Many of the WPA muralists had been leftists – even a few Communists – and that must have galled the fervently anti-communist Hoover. Maybe he took pains to avoid taking the stairs, or if he did, averting his eyes from the walls.

I walked down the corridor to my office, which was about half-way down the hall to the right on the Pennsylvania Avenue side of the building. Reaching my office, I took out my key to unlock the door.

I shared the office with another member of the task force, Tim O'Rourke. Tim had joined the task force at about the same time I did and we immediately became friends. A graduate of Fordham Law School, he had served in the Marine Corps in the Pacific. Although he never talked much about his service, I knew that he had won his share of medals. At about my height, a bit over six feet, he outweighed me by about twenty pounds, all of it muscle. He was smart, tough, and an exceptionally hard worker. After we had become friends, he confided in me that the main reason he had become a lawyer had been to fight the mob. His father had owned a small tavern. For years he had been forced to turn over a good portion of his hard-earned proceeds to a local gangster and his enforcers. Once, when he had refused to pay up, Tim's father had been beaten senseless in front of his then ten-year-old son. From that time on, Tim had sworn to avenge his father's humiliation.

For all his seriousness and devotion to his work, Tim also liked to have a good time. Having spent most of his young life in a saloon, he had made it a point to seek out the best watering holes that the District of Columbia had to offer. A bachelor, he also knew how to use his natural Irish charm and good looks to find plenty of female companionship with whom to share his knowledge of the best places to eat and drink. During the week, Tim was all business, often teasing me when I got to the office after he did or leaving while he still toiled far into the night. But on the weekends, it was a different story. On Mondays, I always arrived before Tim. He usually made it in by nine or nine thirty, always with a guilty smile on his face. And I usually took the opportunity to tease him back with some wisecrack.

So I was surprised to find the door unlocked. When I pushed it open, Tim was already at his desk. I was about to make some snide remark, when I saw the serious look on Tim's face. I immediately sensed trouble.

"Morning Pete," he said. "Don't get comfortable. I was told to tell you as soon as you got in that we have to meet with Joe Smathers and the rest of the force right away."

Joe Smathers was the Justice Department lawyer who headed up their organized crime investigative unit. He served as the overall coordinator of that unit and our task force.

"What's up Tim?" I asked.

"I don't know for sure Pete. But whatever it is, it's not good. I got a wake-up call around six-thirty and was told to get my butt down here pronto."

It appeared that I was not the only one who knew about Tim's weekend routine. I guess I was a more predictable quantity, not needing a phone call at home to assure that I would be

"Okay Tim. Let's go," I said, putting my briefcase down.

As we left the office, a queasy feeling began to build in my stomach as I tried to rein in my overactive imagination as to what had prompted the emergency meeting. No sense guessing what the bad news might be. I would find out soon enough.

CHAPTER FOUR

June 4, 1951 – Washington, D.C.

María Benton was humming a Puccini aria as she cleaned up the breakfast dishes. Yesterday, to escape the oppressive heat – and also because she loved opera– she and Pete had gone to the air conditioned Loew's Palace to see the latest sensation, Mario Lanza, in "The Great Caruso." Leaving the theater, they had been greeted by a torrential rainstorm that had made their return home an adventure. Soaking wet, they had stripped off their clothes and then went right to bed and made love.

That memory brought a smile and a low chuckle. Her time in Washington had not always been so pleasant.

María never failed to appreciate how fortunate she had been. She had fallen hopelessly in love with Pete when he arrived as if by magic in Buenos Aires to take over the office of Foreign Film Distributors where she was employed as a secretary. María tried not to dwell on the circumstances that complicated their relationship – Pete's spying on Perón and Eva Duarte, his kidnapping by the secret police, her own appeal to Eva to help find Pete and the sadistic pleasure Perón's mistress had displayed in toying with her, Pete's escape and the deal made by the U.S. ambassador to allow him to leave the country. But the memories would come back at unexpected moments, especially when she ran across news from Argentina. When the face of Eva, now "Evita Perón," appeared on the cover of *Time* magazine a few years ago, María could only marvel at the power and fame that the former radio actress who had treated her so cruelly had attained. María knew that behind the saintly image the Perón regime had created for "Evita" lay a vindictiveness that knew no bounds.

When Pete left Argentina, María had despaired of ever seeing him again. But six months later, thanks to Pete's father, she had landed in New York and they were soon married. She often thought that if their romance had been the plot of the Hollywood movies she helped distribute, it would seem too fanciful even for the "Dream Factory."

Reality set in soon enough. María was happy that Pete had enrolled in law school and seemed satisfied with the career he had chosen. However, in the first weeks of their marriage, while Pete was struggling with his classes, María often found herself alone in their apartment with nothing much to do. Her life in Buenos Aires had revolved around her friends and family. Now she was thousands of miles away from all that she had known. She was not yet comfortable with English, which made it difficult to get to know her neighbors or to hold her own in a conversation with Pete's friends. Pete's family had welcomed her with open arms, but María sensed a certain reserve from Pete's mother. She had no one to confide in besides Pete, and she was reluctant to register any complaints.

But then Pete's father again came to the rescue. At first, Cyrus Benton had intimidated her. He bore a striking resemblance to her husband, and María could tell by looking at the father what the son would look like in twenty-five years – tall, handsome, athletic, with a touch of gray in his wavy black hair, and a look of intelligence and distinction. Unlike Pete, who could be spontaneous and fun-loving, who liked poetry and music, Cyrus seemed all business, a bit cold and aloof.

Within a few weeks, María's opinion changed. Cyrus, for all his reserve, clearly loved Pete and was immensely proud of him. Father and son had had their differences some of them resolved when Pete had decided to follow the same career path and enter law school. But María also knew that Pete's father would support his son no matter what he did. And that same loyalty and support was extended to Pete's wife. While Pete gave no outward indication that he understood María's sense of being out of place in a new environment, Cyrus, without saying anything explicitly, seemed to sense her growing unhappiness and discomfort. Being an international lawyer had probably exposed him to situations similar to hers. But she also thought his native intuition, insight, and empathy allowed him to see things that others, including his son, might not.

As was typical with Cyrus Benton, he came up with a practical solution. Three months after María Suárez had become María Benton, Pete's father convinced the new manager of the New York Office of her old employer, Foreign Films Distributor, to hire her on as a secretary. María suspected that Cyrus had told Pete that his new wife would not be satisfied staying at home alone in an apartment waiting for him with dinner. If so, Pete never let on and seemed as happy as she was that she would be going back to work.

At first, it was difficult. While the office routine was familiar, her limited English made everything she did slow and cumbersome. But her boss, perhaps influenced by Cyrus, was exceptionally patient with her. She also knew that her looks helped. She still turned heads in the street and the men in the office, making up the majority of a staff of ten, seemed to spend an inordinate amount of time hanging around her desk. María was used to such attention and was able to deflect it without hurting anybody's feelings or bruising any male egos. When English failed her, she simply pointed to the wedding ring on her left hand.

With the added incentive of the new job, her English rapidly improved. Pete helped when he could as did the other two females in the office. Barbara and Elaine were long-time employees of the FFD. Barbara was a stenographer and Elaine helped with the bookkeeping. Both were in their late thirties. Barbara was a brunette, a little bit overweight, while Elaine was a redhead, thin as a rail. On María's first day at work, they had invited her to lunch at a nearby diner, an invitation she gratefully accepted. The conversation was a little awkward, given that they knew not a word of Spanish and María's English was halting and uncertain. But they managed to communicate somehow and were soon laughing over bits of office gossip that the two American women seemed to have in abundant and endless supply.

From that day on, the three women had lunch on a daily basis. Conversing with Barbara and Elaine greatly accelerated María's growing fluency in English. While goings-on at the office still dominated their lunch-time talk, they also increasingly touched on personal matters. Barbara was recently divorced and was in the process of trying to readjust to the single life after twelve years of marriage. Elaine was single, but had a long-time boyfriend who refused to tie the knot. She was beginning to think about issuing an ultimatum, but had yet to muster the courage to do so.

María said little about her relationship with Pete. In truth, now that she was working and beginning to make friends, things had never been better between them. When Barbara and Elaine asked her questions about her life in Buenos Aires and about her family, María initially found it difficult to say much without emotion getting in the way. But as her English improved and she became more comfortable with the two women, she found it reassuring to share with them memories of her past life. She refrained, however, from telling them about Pete's adventures in Argentina or her own meeting with now one of the world's best-known women. They probably wouldn't have believed her.

As her English and her comfort with her office colleagues improved, so too did her performance at work. At first, she thought that even with Cyrus Benton's backing, she might be dismissed. But after a rough start, she got the hang of things, which were not all that different from what she had done in the Buenos Aires office. Her boss seemed genuinely pleased to have her as his secretary. As the Americans put it, she proved to be "more than just a pretty face," managing her duties in the office with efficiency and skill.

Her life with Pete also improved. Not that they ever had any of the kind of arguments and disagreements that seemed to bedevil so many couples. But Pete had not been totally unaware of her initial loneliness. He was delighted that she had found something to do that helped her adjust to her new surroundings. And as her English became near fluent,

María found it easier to communicate and interact with Pete's circle of friends, which was an extensive one. Many were from his childhood while others included fellow law students and a few of his colleagues from his wartime service in the OSS. Some were married and some were single. They began to go out on "double dates" with some of the married couples, enjoying meals together in the city's many interesting and varied restaurants.

When time permitted, and when she could convince Pete to go, they took in Broadway shows and visited art galleries and museums. She even managed to drag Pete finally to a performance of "Rigoletto" at the Metropolitan Opera, something they had been scheduled to see at the Colón Theater in Buenos Aires just before Pete had been kidnapped. To her surprise – and to his – Pete seemed to enjoy the opera. While he did not become as addicted to it as she was, he was not at all reluctant to accompany her to future performances.

So, after a bumpy beginning to her life in the United States, María had never been happier. She loved Pete and was immensely proud of the way he was working so hard to succeed in law school. She also took pride in her job, where she got along well with her colleagues and enjoyed the work. The only cloud in this sunny picture, and it was a dark one, was her separation from her family – her mother, father, and brother, Rafael.

When she informed them that Cyrus Benton had made it possible for her to leave Argentina and reunite with Pete, they did nothing but encourage her to seize the opportunity and go to New York. They had realized from the first time they had met Pete that she had fallen in love with him. When they saw how devastated she had been when Pete had been expelled from the country and she was forbidden any contact with him, their hearts went out to her. When she left for New York, they, along with a raft of other members of the extended Suárez clan, accompanied her to the airport. Amid tears and hugs, she bid them farewell. As she boarded the plane, her last image of them was a waving sea of hands and shouts of her name, wishing her a safe and happy trip. Her heart sank when she glimpsed the tear-stained faces of her mother and father just before she entered the plane.

The separation had been – and still was – difficult and painful. The family was close-knit and supportive and she missed them terribly. And what made the separation doubly difficult were the circumstances that surrounded her departure. Maria had no doubt that Perón and especially Eva still viewed her with ill will. Whatever arrangements Cyrus had made, it did not mean that all had been forgiven. Pete dared not return to Argentina so long as Perón was running the country. Theoretically, she could go back, but Cyrus had advised against it, warning her that the deal he had made involved a high-level official who was now an ex-official and out of power. If she did go back, she might not be allowed to return to the United States. And that would mean separation from Pete. That her parents might be able to visit her in New York also seemed out of the question. María's father was a well-known critic of the regime and had barely escaped imprisonment for his outspoken views. The Perón government probably would not be unhappy to have Alberto Suárez out of its hair. But if he and his family left the country it was unlikely they would be allowed to return. Any visit to New York was too much of a risk for them to run.

María wrote lengthy letters to her parents and her brother two or three times a week. Her first missives revealed none of her uncertainties and discomforts. Instead, they were full of enthusiastic descriptions of her life in New York with Pete. When the time for the wedding neared, she filled her letters with all the details of the intricate planning that went into the ceremony and the reception. If her parents could not be present at what was up to that time the most important moment in her life, she wanted to paint for them as full and as detailed a picture as she could. And that took some doing. Cyrus Benton was a long-time resident of New York and a major figure in the legal and business world with many friends and acquaintances. The reception was held in one of the main ballrooms of the Waldorf-Astoria Hotel and was attended by the mayor and the governor. The wedding received prominent coverage in the society pages of New York's several newspapers, featuring flattering pictures of the bride and groom. One would have to have been a mind reader to discern the bittersweet regret that her parents were not present behind María's dazzling smile. But it was there nonetheless.

Before they left for their European honeymoon María made sure to include clippings of the press coverage in her letter home. And while the letter and the clippings were intended for her parents, she was fairly certain that her correspondence to her family and theirs to her was being monitored by the regime. She hoped fervently that somehow the coverage of her marriage to Pete would make it all the way to the president and the first lady. They might have been able to keep her family from joining her, but she had managed to marry Pete despite all the regime's efforts to prevent it from happening. In her mind's eye, she pictured the clippings being placed in front of Evita and the rage, jealousy, and frustration they would produce.

María was careful in her letters not to write anything that would cause her parents and her brother any trouble. There was no mention of politics or current events, either in the United States or in Argentina. And her parents and her brother were equally circumspect, although María could often read between the lines and get some inkling of the difficulties they were experiencing in a country where democracy was a sham and opponents of the authoritarian government lived in a state of constant fear and suspicion. María could take some solace in the hope that someday the regime would end and she and Pete and her family would be able to see each other without restriction. Until that happened, however, she had to content herself with contact through letters and the occasional visits to New York by friends, who gave her more direct news of how things were going thousands of miles to the south.

Another dark cloud for María involved Pete. Although they had few secrets, María felt that her husband, who like most men did not easily share his innermost feelings, was keeping something from her – and perhaps even from himself. There was no doubt that he was fully committed to his legal career. But his choice of a specialty, criminal law, worried her. There were other options beyond criminal law. *Why chose that particular field?* When she asked him that question, he answered straightforwardly and perhaps naively that he wanted to serve the cause of justice and, as he said, "get the bad guys off the streets and put them in jail."

María could only admire and approve of his motivation. Pete's sense of right and wrong mirrored her own sentiments and reminded her of her father, who was also an attorney who fought for justice. Pete also revealed that his service in the OSS as well as his experiences in Argentina had influenced his decision to be a criminal lawyer. And this was what worried María. There was something in Pete that seemed to crave adventure and danger. What he had done in Buenos Aires was a perfect example. It had not taken much convincing for his friend David Friedman to get Pete to spy on Perón and Eva. He accepted the challenge without much questioning and even with some eagerness. And while he might not have realized it at the time, it was an extraordinarily dangerous and even foolhardy thing to do. He had managed to escape with his life, but it was a very near thing.

María's fears were heightened when Pete immediately upon graduation took a position in the District Attorney's Office. She knew it was what he wanted, but she had difficulty in hiding her concern that in dealing with the aggressive investigation and prosecution of criminals he would somehow get involved in matters that would put his life in danger. She was hesitant to raise these concerns. When she finally did, Pete tried his best to reassure her that working at the District Attorney's office posed no significant risks. She was not convinced, but did not bring up the subject again. In the back of her mind, for all Pete's reassurances and his obvious enthusiasm for his job, María felt that her husband would have been happier being a police detective rather than a prosecutor, actually putting his own life on the line in the pursuit of criminals. Every time she heard about some shoot-out involving the city's police, she gave an involuntary shudder and thanked her lucky stars that Pete was not involved. She realized that her fears were probably irrational, but they remained nonetheless.

Several months after Pete had taken his post with the District Attorney there was a change in her own career that helped take her mind off her concerns for Pete. One day, unexpectedly, her boss called her into his office to discuss a personnel matter. The assistant manager of the agency was leaving at the end of the year, several months down the road, and her boss told her he wanted María to take his place. María was stunned by the offer and protested that she lacked the training and the skills required. Her boss waved away her doubts, saying that the office would pay for her to attend the necessary night-school classes in management and accounting that would make her fully-qualified for the post

The offer overwhelmed María. It went beyond anything that she had expected. She also recognized it as a unique opportunity. there were relatively few women in high-level administrative positions in any kind of business. María couldn't help but wonder if Cyrus Benton had something to do with her boss's offer. The possibility that her boss had other, more familiar reasons for making the offer also crossed her mind. But he was a seemingly happily married man with a large, close-knit family. While she knew that was no guarantee that he would not stray from the straight and narrow, he had never been anything but strictly professional in his treatment of her. There had been none of the flirting or innuendos that she frequently received from other males in the office. She finally decided that she should accept the offer and the opportunity for what it was rather than obsessing over the possible reasons behind it.

When she told Pete about her boss's proposal that night in dinner, he could hardly contain his excitement. He grabbed her in an enthusiastic hug and told her how proud he was of her. After some discussion of the details, they agreed that she should accept the offer. The next day, she informed her boss what they had decided and he beamed with pleasure. The night school classes began the following week and for the next several months she and Pete were both putting in ten- and twelve-hour days, often including Saturdays. They tried to keep Sundays to themselves, but even then work or study would intrude.

María successfully concluded her course work and by the end of the year was promoted to assistant manager. She found the job demanding but thanks to her night-school training one she could handle efficiently and effectively. The biggest problem, she found, was not the job itself but her new relationship with her colleagues. The men in the office were at first uncomfortable having a woman who had been the office secretary more or less at their beck and call now their superior. Some were jealous as well, having wanted the position themselves. Nonetheless, over time, with her own professional handling of the job, she won most of them over. She had few problems with Barbara and Elaine, who remained close friends even though she was now technically their boss.

Two years into her new position, María could scarcely believe her good fortune or the level of satisfaction she now felt. She thoroughly enjoyed her job and took great pride in the fact that she had overcome the obstacles of adapting to a new culture and new surroundings to attain a position she never would have dreamed of attaining in Argentina, where, as a woman, the kind of advancement she had achieved was almost unthinkable. She knew that in New York, her story of "immigrant success" was far from unique. And she had the added advantage of an understanding and supportive husband and an influential father-in-law. Nonetheless, she also recognized that what she had managed to accomplish was primarily due to her own hard work, self-discipline, and ability.

Just when she thought things couldn't get any brighter in her professional life, a few days after the New Year of 1951 had been rung in her boss called her into his office with yet another surprise. He was planning to retire in a few months and he was recommending to the main office in Los Angeles that she be his replacement. While this new opportunity did not come as a complete shock – she had been getting hints from her boss that what he now revealed to her might be in the offing – she nevertheless welcomed it with gratitude and enthusiasm.

She called Pete's office to tell him the news, but his secretary said that he was in an important meeting and could not be disturbed. That was not unusual. She would have to wait until he got home to tell him about this latest development. Arriving at their apartment at about six, Maria prepared a special dinner complete with a nice bottle of French wine. She planned to tease Pete a bit, not revealing her good news until they had eaten, piquing his curiosity as to what lay behind the "special occasion."

Pete got home around seven-thirty, apologizing for his late arrival. Taking off his coat and hat and placing them on the coatrack in the hallway, he took María in his arms and gave her a kiss that under other circumstances might have led to the bedroom rather than to the small dining area. María knew the signs. Pete was always affectionate, kissing her and telling her he loved her each time he went to work and following pretty much the same routine in the evening. But those kisses were usually momentary and light, signs of affection but not of real ardor. When the kisses became more serious, María knew instinctively that Pete was about to tell her something that he wasn't sure she would find agreeable.

Ending the embrace, Pete said, "Hello sweetheart. How are you?" Then, noticing the carefully laid table, their best place settings, fresh flowers that María had gotten on the way home, the lighted candles, and the open bottle of wine, he added, "And what's the special occasion?"

Maria thought she saw a look close to panic flit across Pete's face. Although she knew something was up, she decided to follow the plan she had devised.

"Nothing special sweetheart. I got home a little early from the office and decided to surprise you. That's all."

Pete didn't look convinced. But he removed his suit coat, loosened his tie, and sat down while María went to the kitchen and brought out the meal. It was one of Pete's favorites – roast beef, baked potatoes, peas and carrots, and salad.

As they ate and drank their wine, they talked about everything except what was foremost on their minds – the recent holidays, the play they had seen the previous week, what movie they might attend with one of the couples they knew during the coming weekend, the latest headlines.

When they had finished, María gathered up their plates and took them to the kitchen. Later, Pete would wash the dishes. Returning to the table, Pete poured them both a second glass of wine.

Taking a sip, María put down her glass and beamed at her husband. "Pete, dearest. I have wonderful news."

Pete looked at her, probably not totally surprised. He had known that there must have been something behind the elaborate mid-week meal. "What it is it sweetheart?"

"Roger," referring to her boss, "Roger is going to retire this year *–and he has recommended that I replace him!*"

A mixture of emotions crossed Pete's face. "That's wonderful news sweetheart. I am so proud of you. So very proud."

María expected Pete to come around the table to where she was sitting and give her a hug. But instead, he stayed glued to his chair and María could see him struggling to come up with what he would say next.

"But you see sweetheart, something has come up at the office."

María's heart began to sink. This was not going to be good news.

"You know that we are investigating organized crime here in New York, particularly the family run by Frank Costello." María knew this but could not share Pete's enthusiasm as he described how important it was to try to bring the family to justice. The Costello organization was known for its brutality and she feared that somehow Pete might become a target of its wrath. He did all he could to reassure her, but she still had her fears.

"Well the thing is, Senator Kefauver is conducting a similar investigation and we've been asked to help. And I've been selected by District Attorney Hogan to be part of a four-man task force to work with the Department of Justice to aid the senator. That's why I was late for dinner sweetheart. I was meeting with the DA and the rest of the team to work on the details."

Pete did little to hide the excitement in his voice. He had started at the bottom of the DA's office, handling mundane cases. It had been difficult, but through hard work, he had made his way up the ladder to the point where he was now part of a top-level group hand-picked by the District Attorney to carry out one of the office's most important assignments. Despite her fears and what she suspected he was going to say next, María couldn't help but feel pride in her husband's accomplishments and admire the dedication it had taken to reach this point in his career.

"Well that's wonderful Pete," she said. "It looks as though we both have good news to celebrate tonight," although María sensed that Pete was going to put a damper on their celebration.

Pete gave a nervous smile and he lowered his eyes for a moment. Then, gathering his courage, he looked at her and delivered the blow as best he could. "Yes. What a coincidence. But it puts us in a real pickle." It had taken a while for Maria to catch on to this particular North American idiom, but she had heard it enough times to understand its meaning. "The task force will be going to Washington to work directly in liaison with the Justice Department."

María's face fell, even though she suspected this would be, how do the North Americans put it?, "the fly in the ointment."

"For how long Pete?"

"It's impossible to say. Six months at least. Maybe longer."

María could barely hide her disappointment. But she did her best. She could tell that Pete was worried about her reaction. She tried to reassure him that his job came first. But at the back of her mind she couldn't ignore the feeling of resentment that her own career had to take second place to his. Especially when she thought of the struggle she had gone through to win the opportunity that now seemed to have been snatched away from her.

Over dessert and coffee, they discussed and then dismissed the possibility of María staying in New York while Pete went to Washington. Under that scenario, Pete would return on the weekends. But they both knew that Pete often worked on Saturdays and sometimes on Sundays, so that option was closed. They did not want to be separated. Finally, it was agreed that María would move with Pete to Washington, giving up her job with the hope that it might be waiting for her on their return.

The next day, María met with her boss and gave him the news. At first, he was taken aback. But he quickly recovered and graciously offered to grant her what he called "an extended leave of absence," keeping her job open until she returned, whenever that might be. So far as the promotion to manager was concerned, he could make no promises at the moment, but pointed out that he would not be retiring until the end of the year. If María should return before the year was out, then she was still his top candidate. María couldn't tell if the generosity came from her boss's good nature of if somehow the influence of Cyrus Benton was hovering in the background. At any rate, she was grateful for the offer, which took some of the sting out of her disappointment.

Two weeks later, Pete and María moved to Washington. At Pete's request, the Justice Department had found them a nice town house on Wyoming Avenue in an area called Kalorama Heights in Northwest Washington. The apartment was owned by a couple who worked for the Department of State and who were on overseas assignment. It was comfortable and tastefully furnished, with all the latest modern kitchen appliances. And it was well-located, only two blocks from Connecticut Avenue and close to Rock Creek Park. Among the elegant townhouses in the area there were small embassies and consulates scattered about, giving the neighborhood a cosmopolitan, international touch.

The first few weeks found María caught up in the euphoria and excitement of the move. Pete took her to see the impressive monuments that dotted the nation's capital. On the weekends, they were invited to a non-stop round of introductory dinner parties, where María met the other men on Pete's task force from New York as well as the Justice Department team with whom they were working. María had a chance to swap stories with the wives of two of the other team members about the challenges of moving and the new life that awaited them, taking some comfort in the shared experiences.

Pete threw himself into his work, as María knew he would. Once again, she had to put up with his grueling schedule. He left early in the morning and often did not come back to the apartment until late in the evening. As they had foreseen in New York, he often worked on the weekends as well, either at home, where he retreated to a small study, or at the office.

At first, María shared his excitement and took pleasure in how happy he was in the work he was doing. But soon, she began to experience some of the same feelings that had bedeviled her when she first arrived to the United States. She had developed a nice group of friends in New York; Elaine and Barbara at the FFD office and the wives and girlfriends of Pete's circle. But now she was again beginning to feel isolated and lonely, anxiously awaiting Pete's arrival to break the boredom of the day. The wives of the other task force members had chosen to live in the Northern Virginia suburbs and although they occasionally met for lunch, they were too distant for her to see them on a regular basis and to develop any close relationships.

She kept up her steady correspondence with her parents and stayed in touch with her friends in New York. Elaine and Barbara wrote letters that filled her in on what was happening in the FFD office, implying that things were just not the same without her there. While she looked forward to their letters, they also reminded her of how important her job had been and how much she missed it. Pete had suggested that she look for something similar in Washington, if only temporarily. But the only jobs she saw listed in the paper were for low-level secretarial positions. Maybe she should have taken one just to fill the time. But she found the prospect of essentially starting over at the lowest level so unappealing that she preferred to suffer being alone in her apartment, hoping that something more attractive might appear.

Trying to adjust to life in Washington proved more of a challenge than she expected. Everything, it seemed, involved politics. The latest topic of discussion was the decision in April by President Truman to relieve General Douglas Macarthur of his duties as commander of the forces in Korea. To María, the plain-spoken Truman was far from the picture she had formed of the typical President of the United States. And coming from a place where all she had known for most of her life had been governments controlled by the military, either outright or behind the scenes, she found Truman's actions hard to comprehend. She admired his courage in doing so, but wondered what trouble it might produce.

The newspapers and the radio were also filled with stories about Senator Joseph McCarthy from Wisconsin who seemed to think the government was riddled with Communists. And that was related to something else she found disconcerting. She knew, of course, about the so-called Cold War between the United States and the Soviet Union. It had not been absent from her life in New York. But here in Washington it seemed to take on new intensity. From the first days of her arrival, she had been unnerved by the constant warnings of a Soviet nuclear attack and what should be done to prepare for it. Washington, D.C., she was reminded incessantly, would be the principal target of such a strike. When she expressed her concerns to those she met, they tended to dismiss them, telling her that it was something they just had to learn to live with. Pete also tried to reassure her. But it was difficult to ignore the fact that schools were drilling children on what to do in case an atomic bomb exploded over their heads and the government had organized a program to send the public to shelters if the Russians attacked.

There was also a lot of news and discussion about the Kefauver committee hearings on organized crime. Since Pete was involved, María devoured the stories and when he came home at night would discuss with him how his work was proceeding. In New York, Pete had tried not to bring his job home, but in Washington he was more forthcoming and seemed pleased in María's interest. But for all her pride in Pete's role in this important investigation, which was receiving so much national attention, her concern that it might somehow place him in danger never left her mind.

María gradually got into the flow of the political life that surrounded her and seemed to consume so many with whom she came into contact. Her father had been deeply involved in politics in Argentina and she had grown up in an atmosphere where political discussion around the dinner table was the order of the day. She was not as fascinated by it as some, but she had a good grasp of the essentials and understood its importance in the larger scheme of things. She enjoyed reading the two main Washington papers, the *Post* in the morning and the *Star* in the evening. She also followed the news on the radio. The apartment did not have a television and they had debated whether or not to purchase one. They had resisted the temptation in New York but finally decided it was important to have one since the Kefauver Hearings were to be televised and had bought a set. María found the new medium helped distract her somewhat from her loneliness although she found some of the programming appallingly juvenile and banal.

Newspaper reading, radio listening, and television viewing helped in her attempts to adjust to life in Washington. But there was still a void. While the nation's capital had its cultural attractions, they paled when compared to New York. Her thirst for opera had to be slaked by listening to radio performances on Sunday afternoons. There was some theater, which was another of her passions, but it could not begin to compare with what she had been able to see on Broadway.

Art was another of her interests. The National Gallery was housed in an impressive building, but the collection did not measure up to what she had become accustomed to in New York. The night after her first visit to the National Gallery, when she expressed her disappointment to Pete, he told her that she might like to try the Phillips Gallery only a few blocks away. Someone had told Pete about the Phillips several weeks ago, but he had forgotten to mention it to Maria at the time. She mildly berated him for his forgetfulness, but looked forward to visiting it the next day.

The Phillips was a revelation. Located in a stately mansion near Sheridan Circle, it contained an extensive collection that featured some outstanding works of the French Impressionists. Both the building and the collection had been donated by the Phillips family and opened to the public in the 1930s. Arriving when the Phillips opened at ten, María stayed the entire day, fascinated by each painting that she saw. There were the occasional visitors, but for the most part María had the museum to herself.

That night, when Pete came home, María could not contain her excitement. She leapt into his arms when he arrived, barely giving him time to take off his hat and coat. Her eyes shone as she told him about her day. Pete, who had not been oblivious to his wife's unhappiness in her new surroundings, beamed with pleasure as she babbled on. Over dinner, María told Pete that she wanted to learn more about art so that she could fully appreciate this jewel that she had discovered. He suggested that she might enroll in art history and art appreciation classes at one of the local universities. The next day, she did just that, signing up for two courses at George Washington University. Although she was enrolling in mid-semester, the admissions office was willing to make an exception in her case. Fortunately, Pete had an old Yale classmate who was on the faculty at the University and was able to exert some influence for her to be admitted as a special student.

Initially, she found the classes overwhelming. She was weeks behind in the reading and written assignments and felt intimidated by all the younger – and to her mind – smarter students that surrounded her. But with Pete's help and encouragement, she quickly caught up and by the end of her first month was performing as well as any in the class.

She now was doing something she thoroughly enjoyed and had established a routine that helped ease her sense of isolation and loneliness. Her classes met in the morning each weekday, the first beginning at nine and the second at eleven. Each day she took the Connecticut Avenue streetcar to K Street, where she switched to the line that carried her to the George Washington campus. While Washington did little to remind her of Buenos Aires, riding the streetcar, a common mode of public transportation in her native city brought back some familiar memories.

After class, María would have lunch at the school cafeteria and then head to the library to work on her daily assignments. Then, as the evening approached, she would retrace her steps, stopping at a local Safeway to pick up the ingredients for that night's dinner. She had made it a point to have a home-cooked meal ready for Pete when he came from work, no matter the hour.

Learning to cook had been a challenge. In Argentina, she had lived at home and her meals had been prepared either by her mother or their maid. Otherwise, she ate out in one of the city's many restaurants. In the United States, she had been forced to learn from scratch the simplest things, like boiling eggs and cooking meat in the oven to the proper temperature. Pete had been infinitely patient, always expressing his appreciation for her efforts even though she could sometimes tell from his expression that her latest culinary experiment had produced less than satisfactory results. But in this, as in her dedication to her job at the FFD office, she had turned into what she admitted to herself to be a pretty good cook. Indeed, following six months of often hilarious trial and error, she had managed to pull off a dinner party for six of Pete's friends. She took the compliments she had received on the quality of the meal as genuine.

In fact, she had become such a good cook that Pete teased her by saying she was trying to fatten him up. If so, she was failing. He still remained the trim and athletic figure he had been since she had first met him six years earlier. No signs yet of a middle-age bulge. Pete made it a point to get a lot of exercise, both because he enjoyed it and because it provided a good way to relieve the tensions of his job. They often took long walks together through the city or out into the countryside. Once the weather and time allowed, they planned to explore hiking opportunities in the nearby mountains of Maryland and Virginia.

When she wasn't studying or performing her domestic chores, María headed invariably to the Phillips. There, she would sit in front of a particular painting for hours, studying every detail and trying to fit what she saw into what she was learning. She would bring her notebook with her and jot down her impressions as they came to her, thinking how they might be incorporated into the next paper she was assigned. Her focus was so intense that she often forgot she was in a public space frequented by others and was startled when she heard other voices or saw others looking at the same painting. For the most part, she was left alone. The staff had become accustomed to her presence and rarely disturbed her unless it was to provide a quiet reminder that the museum was closing. On a couple of occasions some men with obvious intentions had tried to strike up a conversation, but she quickly discouraged them.

It seemed to be something of a cliché, but art had filled a void in her life. It had opened up a whole new world for her to explore and had provided the routine and the structure to her life that had been disrupted by the move to Washington. But there were still pieces missing. She had no close friends in her new home, indeed hardly anyone she could call a friend, close or otherwise. She did still have the occasional lunch with the wives of the other New York task force members. But they were infrequent and while the two women were perfectly pleasant, their conversation focused on schools and children, both of which had little connection to María's life at the moment. When she told them about her new-found interest in art, they simply said "that's nice" and moved on to other matters.

Occasionally, she and Pete would go out on a double date with Tim O'Rourke, Pete's office mate. María liked Tim, who was a gregarious and fun-loving Irishman. But he never seemed to bring the same date with him twice in a row so there was no chance for a possible friendship forming through him. They also went out to dinner with Pete's old friend from Buenos Aires, David Friedman, who worked in Washington. David, who was a bachelor, had recently begun to date a young woman named Sarah who worked at the Israeli Embassy. She offered the possibility of friendship, but was so busy she barely had time for David much less for her.

María wanted and needed a real "girl" friend, someone like the many she had had in Argentina or like Barbara and Elaine in New York. She had gotten to know some of the girls in her art classes. They were friendly enough, but they were more than ten years younger than her and unmarried. She met with a few of them from time to time to work on joint projects, but aside from the classes, they had little in common. And then, from out of the blue, just last week she had encountered someone who held open the possibility for the kind of female companionship she was longing for.

María's classes had ended the week before. She had struggled with the written assignments and the examinations, but glowed with pleasure when she received "A's" in both courses. "Quite an accomplishment," Pete had said when she told him the news. "Especially considering the fact you started in mid-semester. But I'm not surprised sweetheart. When you set your sights on something, you make sure you do your best - and your best is always pretty darn good." She planned to take two more courses in the summer session, which started in a few weeks. She had the vague idea that somehow she might be able to turn her new avocation into some kind of career if things did not work out for her at the FFD.

Once again with time on her hands, she had been to the Phillips every day the previous week. There, late on Thursday afternoon she was sitting on a bench in front of one of her favorite paintings, Renoir's "Luncheon of the Boating Party," the most famous work in the museum's collection. María never failed to be enthralled by the depiction of late nineteenth-century Parisians enjoying themselves on an open boat, the details rendered beautifully, the ebullient mood captured to perfection. The painting seemed to beckon the viewer to join in the festivities.

Immersed as usual in her thoughts, María felt the bench shift as someone sat down next to her. Turning, she half expected to see some man trying to strike up a conversation. Instead, what she saw was almost a mirror image of herself – a young woman in her early thirties, with black hair, dark eyes, and, she judged, about the same height and weight as her. She wore a tasteful summer dress in a muted pattern of red and green and flat shoes, sensible for walking. She had on minimal makeup and the only jewelry she wore was a slender silver bracelet on her wrist and a gold wedding ban.

Her flawless skin, olive-hued like Maria's, was lightly tanned. In the United States, María had found it difficult to determine from somebody's appearance whether they were native-born Americans or foreigners. This was especially true in New York with its melting pot of people from all over the world. Aside from the diplomatic community, it was somewhat less difficult in Washington. But, if María had to guess, she guessed that the woman next to her was not North American. As soon as the woman spoke, betraying a heavy Spanish accent, María's guess was confirmed.

"It is beautiful, is it not?" she said in a soft voice. "I love watching at it."

María was tempted to correct the woman's English but refrained. "Yes it is. Very beautiful. I love it too."

The young woman extended her hand in greeting. "My name is Graciela Walker," she said with a smile that revealed perfectly straight, gleaming white teeth.

María hesitated for just a second. Then she grasped the offered hand in hers. "I'm María Benton," she said, returning Graciela's dazzling smile with one of her own.

"Do you come here often María?"

For a split second, Maria felt uneasy. They were alone in the room and closing time was near. There was a feeling of emptiness in the museum although she knew that members of the staff were still on hand. The feeling passed as quickly as it had come. She attributed it to that persistent fear she had that somehow danger was just around the corner – Pete threatened by gangsters, a military coup because Truman had dismissed Macarthur, an atomic bomb dropping on the Capitol. Her rational mind told her these were all exaggerations bordering on paranoia, but her heart often told her otherwise. At any rate, in this instance she dismissed them, sensing that a new opportunity was opening up for her. The possibility that she might be on the brink of establishing the kind of female friendship she had been missing for the past several months. Later, she would come to regret not heeding the warnings her heart had sent her.

CHAPTER FIVE

June 4, 1951 -Washington, D.C.

Tim and I walked down the corridor to the room where the organized crime unit held its daily meetings. Along the way, the two other members of the New York team joined us. Jim Franklin, a lanky six footer with thinning sandy hair, was a twenty-year veteran of the DA's office and was the most experienced member of the task force. As such, he was the official leader, although he governed with a light hand and gave us a free rein as we performed our respective duties. Carmine De Grazio, a short, stocky native New Yorker with an unruly mop of thick dark hair, was, like Tim and I, a newcomer to the office. Carmine had grown up in Little Italy and was intimately familiar with the workings of the Costello gang. Their faces were grim as they nodded silently in greeting.

The meeting room was to our left, in the interior of the building. The door was open and we entered. Joe Smathers was already there with the rest of the Justice Department team. "Please take a seat gentlemen." he said. There was no doubt from the serious look on his face and the tone of his voice that the news he had for us was not good.

We took our usual seats around the conference table. Windows that faced an interior courtyard let in some sunlight, but I always found the room dark, gloomy, and slightly claustrophobic. The windows were opened half way, allowing the occasional breeze to enter. Two fans listlessly stirred the humid air. It was still uncomfortably warm, even early in the morning. Along the walls were photographs of previous attorney generals with a place reserved for the current incumbent, J. Howard McGrath, when he retired.

Taking a notepad and a pen from my inside pocket, I placed them down on the table and looked around. The Justice Department team was composed of seven members in addition to Joe Smathers - three more department lawyers and three agents from the Federal Bureau of Investigation. The participation of the FBI was a significant concession from Director Hoover. Reflecting the anti-communist passion of Senator McCarthy, Hoover considered possible Soviet subversion more of a threat to the nation than organized crime. Most of the bureau's resources were now focused on trying to locate and arrest suspected "Reds," domestic and foreign. The director's willingness to assign three agents to the unit reportedly came only after considerable horse trading between Hoover and McGrath. While I supposed there was some justification for concern about the Soviet threat – I had no doubt that the Russians had spies in the U.S. and that some American Communists were probably helping them – the whole hullabaloo seemed exaggerated and out of proportion to the threat posed. It was also clear that McCarthy was stirring things up to enhance his own political stature and career. I feared that in the end he and Hoover would do more harm than good. In the meantime, organized crime continued to grow and flourish, extending its tentacles into all aspects of national life.

I exchanged nods of acknowledgement with the three FBI agents, who sat in a group directly across from me. Initially, they had been standoffish if not outright hostile toward the four of us from New York. They seemed to resent the presence of outsiders and probably were unhappy that they had been assigned to what the director considered a second-tier operation. But fortunately for me, and for the task force as a whole, there was a senior member of the bureau who had been in Buenos Aires during my time there and put in a good word on my behalf. Whatever Roy Johnson told them, it appeared to do the trick. After the first week, the tension dissipated. We New York "outsiders" now got along well enough with the FBI contingent, even if we did not suddenly become best buddies.

The three agents were all dressed alike in the familiar FBI uniform – dark suits, white shirts, black ties, wing-tips so shiny you could see your reflection. They were all clean-shaven, their hair trimmed to the exacting standards that Hoover demanded. Even though we had worked together for months, I still occasionally had trouble telling them apart. I knew their names – George Wilson, Elliot Baker, and Fred Flynn - but sometimes got mixed up as to who was who. It didn't help matters that they were all of about the same height and weight.

Shifting my gaze from the FBI men who sat directly across from me to the right and the far end of the table, I immediately felt a shiver run up my spine despite the heat. One of the seats where a department lawyer usually sat was empty. The other members of the task force were looking in the same direction, worry lines deepening on their faces.

From the end of the table, Joe Smathers cleared his throat. Smathers, who had a family connection to the Florida Senator of the same name, spoke with a soft southern accent. Behind the softness was plenty of iron. He was all business and worked at a killing pace. While Director Hoover might not consider organized crime a top priority, Joe Smathers certainly did. He took his assignment to deal with the mob in the spirit of a medieval crusader, determined to wage the good fight for justice whatever the cost.

We all liked and respected Joe. He came from a small town in Southern Georgia, where his father had been a local judge. In college at the University of Georgia, Joe had been an outstanding baseball player, heavily scouted by major league teams. The New York Giants had even offered him a contract. But Joe was determined to study law. Like me he had specialized in criminal law. He had come to work for the Justice Department during the Roosevelt Administration, making his mark as an outstanding investigator in the criminal division. When the war broke out, he signed up for the Army Air Corps. He had piloted a a B-25, flying over thirty missions. When the war ended he mustered out with a fistful of medals. Back at Justice, he picked up where he left off and became the leader of the criminal investigation division. Approaching his fifties, he still retained the physique of the college athlete – about my height, two inches over six feet, he was trim and muscular. The only sign that age was taking its toll were the worry lines on his face and a head of brown hair that was beginning to thin and show streaks of gray.

We New Yorkers particularly appreciated Joe. While he would tease us occasionally, calling us "Yankee Carpetbaggers," he showed none of the superior tone or standoffishness of the FBI cohort. He had welcomed us to the team and treated us with fairness and courtesy. And while there was no doubt as to who was the boss of the outfit, Joe put on no airs and listened respectfully to whatever ideas we might have. When we organized a staff softball team to play on Saturday afternoons, Joe still showed the skills that had attracted so many major league scouts. His range at shortstop was little short of amazing and he could still hit the ball a country mile. When we went out for beers after the game, Joe was just one of the guys.

This morning, however, the look on his face told us that the burdens of leadership were weighing heavy upon him. Gone was the twinkle in his eye when he called us "carpetbaggers" or after he had hit another colossal home run.

"I've got bad news gentlemen," he began, a slight waver in his usually steady voice. His hands with the long fingers that allowed him to gobble up ground balls were interlaced and clasped firmly in front of him. He was bouncing them lightly on the table in the kind of nervous gesture I had never before seen from him. "Something has happened to Ralph Turner. Right now he's in a coma at GW Hospital and the doctors are not optimistic that he's going to pull through."

There was a collective gasp from around the table. Even the usually stoic FBI agents showed shock.

"What happened Joe?" I asked, knowing I spoke for all of us.

Smathers looked at me and took a deep breath. "Last night, about nine o'clock, right after the big storm we had, Ralph went out to see if there had been any damage to their house. When he didn't return after fifteen minutes, Belinda went out to look for him." Belinda was Ralph's wife. They lived in a ranch house in Silver Spring, Maryland. The Turners had been especially welcoming to the New York team, helping them get settled in. We had been invited to their home on numerous occasions, enjoying the delicious meals that Belinda prepared and the easy banter we shared with Ralph. While Ralph took his job seriously, he did not take himself seriously. His lack of pretension made him a favorite in the group. "She found Ralph lying in the driveway," Joe said, "covered with blood and unconscious. She called an ambulance and they got him to the hospital in record time. If they hadn't, Ralph would certainly have bled to death."

Joe sat back in his chair and unclasped his hand. For about fifteen seconds, there was total silence as we absorbed the news. I could hear some people talking in the courtyard below and the distant sounds of traffic on Constitution Avenue. While no one was speaking, I knew what we all were thinking. This was no random act. Ralph had been beaten half to death to send us a message. Next to me, Tim's fists were clenched and his face was flushed as he tried to control his anger. Tim had been a champion boxer in college and had even fought a few professional fights. He didn't brag about it, but I knew that he had knocked out each of his opponents in the early rounds. I could easily imagine that he couldn't wait to get his hands on whoever had beaten Ralph and give them a similar going over.

One of the FBI agents, Elliot Baker, broke the silence. "What do we know Joe?"

"Right now, not much I'm afraid. Belinda called me from the hospital as soon as she could to let me know what had happened. We sent some men to check the scene, but it didn't tell us much. All they could find was Ralph's blood in the driveway," Joe said with a grimace. "They knocked on some doors to see if any of the neighbors had any useful information. Most of them had been watching television or listening to the radio and said they didn't see or hear anything unusual out on the street. One neighbor did say she thought she heard some screams at about the time Joe was being beaten, but couldn't be sure they were his or something she heard on television. We've got a larger crew out there right now and maybe they can come up with something more."

"Any chance that this might be something personal?" Elliot asked. "Something else besides what we all think this is?"

Joe looked into his lap for a moment, then raised his head and looked down the table. His eyes were moist. "The doctors at GW said that Ralph's injuries were consistent with having been repeatedly beaten either by a club or a baseball bat. They found slivers of wood in his wounds. It was not the kind of damage you sustain when its fists or feet." In other words, the attack had all the earmarks of a professional job, not the kind of beating you would expect if it was over some personal grievance. And knowing Ralph as we did, it was almost inconceivable that someone would have it out for him to the extent they would attack him in this deadly fashion.

"Of course, we are going to investigate every possibility. Maybe Ralph was in some kind of neighborhood dispute we don't know about it. Maybe it has something to do with his wartime service, someone who waited to settle some kind of old score." Sweeping his arm along the table as if brushing these possibilities aside, Smathers said grimly, "But let's not fool ourselves. This was a beating by the mob on one of our own, telling us to back off. They didn't leave a note, but the message is pretty clear."

Myriad thoughts raced through my mind. First and foremost was my concern for the Turners. Ralph and Belinda had two teenage daughters and I could imagine the pain and suffering they were going through right now. My face might not be as red as Tim's, but if I had Ralph's attackers in my grasp I would do everything I could to exact punishment. I also was in some shock. We knew we were dealing with some dangerous characters, but it was hard to fathom that they would resort to the kind of tactics they used to intimidate those they were extorting - or often on each other - on officials of the federal government. Now, it seemed, they were either arrogant enough – or desperate enough – to risk whatever consequences might come their way. *How would we respond?*

Joe Smathers began to answer my unspoken question. "I met earlier this morning with Attorney General McGrath and Director Hoover to advise them of the situation. We agreed that we need to make a thorough investigation of what happened to Ralph. But in the meantime, you all must take extra precautions. We can't assume the attack on Ralph was an isolated, one-time event. I hate to say it, but you – we – are all potential targets. And I hate even more to say this; so, too, are our families."

This warning was greeted with some nervous coughs and uncomfortable shifting in our chairs.

"Excuse me Joe," George Wilson interjected, "But isn't that a little extreme. I haven't seen any evidence that they mob would go that far. In fact…"

Carmine DeGrazio interrupted with an edge to his voice. "It happens, George. Believe me, it happens. I've seen it."

Wilson was about to respond when Smathers cut him off. "Carmine's right George. And even if it's an unlikely possibility, it's one we have to consider and prepare for."

Heads nodded in agreement. Joe continued. "Director Hoover has agreed to assign agents to provide around-the-clock protection for the lawyers on the team. We are also asking the D.C. police to assist, but need to think about how much we want to make the attack on Ralph public knowledge."

While I was grateful for the round-the-clock protection, I wondered how long it would last. How long would Hoover allow the diversion of manpower from his unflagging crusade to uncover Communist subversives? My guess was, not very long.

"In addition, we want you to be able to protect yourselves. How many of you lawyers have guns?" No hands were raised. Seeing the response, Smathers said, "Well from now on, we want you carry a revolver with you at all times. We can provide you the necessary guns, ammunitions, and special permits. Make sure you pick them up before you leave the office - *today*." Smathers didn't ask if we needed any training. All of us had served during the war and all of us were familiar with firearms, although like most veterans, we didn't want anything to do with guns once the fighting stopped. Now, it seemed, we were back at war and required the weapons needed for the fight.

The mood in the room grew even more somber. We all realized how much our situation had changed because of what had been done to Ralph Turner.

"Joe, how much is the attack on Ralph going to be made public?" I asked.

"We haven't decided yet Pete," he answered. "We need to consult with Senator Kefauver and his staff before we make a decision. Since we don't have any definite proof yet that this was a mob hit, we need to be careful in what we say. GW Hospital has agreed not to release any public statement until we give them the say-so. But it will be impossible to keep things under wraps for long. Ralph's neighbors saw and heard the ambulance that picked him up and knew from our team's questions that something happened to him. There's no way we can keep them quiet. So we'll just have to wait to see how things develop."

Greg Parker, one of the Justice Department attorneys, asked the question we all had on our minds. "What should we say to our own families Joe?"

Smathers took a deep breath. "Well Greg, you can't keep this from them. They all need to know the score. And they have to be alert and careful. Even with the protection, there's no way we can guarantee their safety at all times. When your kids go to school, for instance, we can only provide so much cover. The same when your wives go shopping."

I could see a variety of reactions around the table. The FBI agents seemed to be taking this news as though it was all part of their daily routine. Perhaps it was. Their families were accustomed to the risks inherent in their jobs. For the lawyers, it was a different story. We accepted a certain amount of danger as part of the job. But the idea that our wives and children might be put at risk rarely entered our minds. The attack on Ralph had changed all that. I could see the concern written on the faces of the New York team and the two Justice Department lawyers. Tim O'Rourke was the only bachelor among us, but the look on his face showed that he sympathized with us.

Joe Smathers read our concern. "Now maybe I'm sounding a bit too alarmist. Chances are that your families are off limits." Then, nodding toward Carmine De Grazio, "But as Carmine said, the mob has sometimes gone over the line on this score. And after what happened to Ralph, we just can't take any chances. We have to assume the worst."

Joe paused for a moment while we felt the weight of what he had said. "At our meeting this morning," he continued, "the Attorney General, Director Hoover, and I agreed that if any of you wanted out of your assignment we would understand completely. There would be no consequences. You guys here at Justice," he said, nodding towards Greg Parker and Phil Davis, "would be reassigned to other duties. The members of the New York task force would have the option of returning home or staying on here in some other capacity. The decision is up to you. And you don't have to decide right now. Take some time to think it over. You probably should discuss it with your families."

He made no mention of the FBI agents. They presumably would stay on no matter what the rest of us decided.

If we had been forced to choose at that moment, I was sure we would all vote to stay. None of us relished the idea of succumbing to mob threats. For my part, and I'm sure I was not alone, what had happened to Ralph made me even more committed to continuing the job. But Joe was right. The potential danger to our families made the situation more complex and any decision to stay or leave more difficult. I did not look forward to discussing all this with María.

"For now," Joe said, "why don't we all get back to work?"

"What about seeing Ralph?" Phil Davis asked. He and Ralph were close, having served together in the same infantry platoon in France and working together, often as a team, at the Justice Department.

"Good question Phil," Joe said. "I'll check with GW on the visiting hours." Then he added somberly, with a catch in his voice, "I'm sure Belinda would appreciate a visit." Left unsaid was the fact that Ralph would have no idea any of us had been to see him.

On the way back to my office, I stopped in the men's room. As I was washing my hands and splashing water on to my face, I heard someone vomiting in one of the stalls. When the door opened, George Wilson stepped out, looking somewhat shamefaced. I didn't say anything, simply giving a nod of comprehension. Strangely, I took comfort in his reaction. *Those agents were really human after all.*

CHAPTER SIX

June 4, 1951 -Washington, D.C.

At ten in the morning, María Benton took the same Connecticut Avenue Streetcar her husband had boarded earlier in the day. She was heading downtown to meet Graciela Walker at Garfinkels on F Street to shop for summer dresses. Afterwards they were to have lunch at the Willard Hotel.

The car was not crowded, and María found a seat near the back. She was still humming the Puccini aria as she took an art magazine out of her purse and began to leaf through the pages. But her excitement at meeting up with her new-found friend made it difficult to concentrate.

After she had met Graciela at the Phillips, she had invited her to have coffee at a nearby Peoples Drugstore. There they could chat and get to know each other. Graciela eagerly accepted.

When they got to the Peoples, they found a booth near the back and took a seat opposite one another. During the walk to the drugstore, Graciela told María that she was from Montevideo, Uruguay and had only recently arrived in the United States. Her husband worked for an important grain-exporting business and had been temporarily assigned to manage their North American operations. It was Graciela's first visit to the United States and she was finding the adjustment challenging. She had studied English in school, but was having great difficulty in communicating with Americans, who seemed to have no comprehension of Spanish whatsoever. María nodded in sympathy, telling Graciela she had gone through much the same experience when she had first arrived.

The waitress, a chubby middle-aged blond with what María had come to identify as a barely discernible District of Columbia accent, came to take their order.

María did the ordering. "Two coffees please." Then, cocking an inquisitive eyebrow in Graciela's direction, she asked in Spanish, "Cream and sugar?"

Graciela nodded yes and María repeated the order in English. The waitress had cocked an eyebrow of her own when she heard the Spanish, but didn't register any reaction beyond that. Since the drugstore was in an area frequented by diplomats, she probably was accustomed to hearing foreign languages spoken.

María looked at Graciela with a wry smile on her face. She already had told her that she was from Buenos Aires and had been in the United States for six years. "Not quite what we are used to is it?"

"No," Graciela responded. "Not at all," and began to giggle. The giggle was infectious and María couldn't help but join in.

Where they came from, a drugstore was a pharmacy. If you wanted a coffee or a snack you went to a café or a *confitería*, where the persons who waited on you were invariably male and who approached their tasks with the utmost seriousness. Neither of them could imagine any waiter at a café calling them "honey" when taking their order.

María was having difficulty not breaking out in a loud laugh. "And the coffee here is *terrible*," she said. "I think they purposely make it as weak as possible and keep it around for days as though it might get better with age. The only way I can stand it is with lots of cream and sugar to hide the taste."

Graciela emitted a throaty chuckle of her own. "I know. I know. When I drank my first cup here, I thought they had made a mistake and served me tea instead of coffee."

"It's better in New York," María said. "There, you can find some real cafés that serve espresso especially in the Italian district they call 'Little Italy.' And I've learned to make some decent coffee at home. But here in Washington, there is no Italian district and this is where you come to have coffee with a friend."

When the waitress returned with the coffee, she asked them if they wanted anything else. When María said no that would be all, the waitress took out her pad, scribbled the cost of the two coffees onto the bill, and placed the bill under the ashtray on the table, an ashtray that still held a few cigarette butts.

María and Graciela looked at each other. "And that's another thing," María said. "In places like this, they don't want you to linger too long. Eat or drink what you order and move on. The idea seems to be that 'there are other customers waiting,' even if, as now," she said, pointing to the cashier's desk, "there's nobody in line." In the cafés they were used to, there was never a rush. You could order one coffee and stay as long as you wanted.

Both women poured copious amounts of cream into their cups, along with several spoonfuls of sugar. As they stirred their cups and waited for the coffee to cool, María tactfully asked Graciela about her background. It turned out they had much in common. Graciela was, like María, a descendent of Spanish immigrants who had arrived in Uruguay in the late nineteenth century. Her father was a physician who had hoped that Graciela might follow in his footsteps, the same hopes that Maria's father, a lawyer, had for her. After a few months at the medical school of the national university, Graciela had determined that she was not cut out for a medical career. Then she had met Roberto Walker, an up-and-coming young businessman. After a whirlwind courtship they had married.

Roberto, Graciela explained, was an Anglo-Uruguayan, hence the English last name. The company for which he worked sold most of its products to Great Britain. Thanks to his fluency in English and having studied in England, Roberto had risen rapidly through the ranks of the company and had recently been named its principal representative in the U.S. He and Graciela had arrived in Washington two weeks ago and were just getting settled into their new surroundings.

For Roberto, it was not a difficult adjustment. He had traveled often to England and the United States and felt very comfortable in both countries. He also had his job to keep him busy. When Graciela confessed that the move was more difficult for her, María could only nod in understanding. Never having been out of Uruguay and with only limited English, Graciela was fighting loneliness and boredom. Roberto had suggested that she get to know the city by visiting its monuments and museums and that is how she had ended up at the Phillips gallery.

María's heart went out to Graciela, who seemed as delighted as she was to have found someone from the same background; someone with whom she could confide about the challenges of adapting to life in the United States and who could lend a particularly sympathetic ear, having gone through those same challenges herself.

Fortunately, there was no line waiting for their booth and they were able to talk without interruption for more than an hour. María shared stories of her first weeks in New York and some of the difficulties she had faced. She did not mention the circumstances that had caused her to leave Argentina and arrive in the United States, not wanting to open up too much to a person she had just met. She simply stated that she and Pete had met in Buenos Aires and fallen in love. Graciela did not push for more details, a fact that María appreciated.

When they had parted, they had arranged to meet again on Monday for a combined shopping expedition and lunch.

María arrived at the main entrance to Garfinkels a few minutes before eleven. She was a little early and, knowing the Latin American propensity to consider agreed-upon times to be flexible, expected to wait for Graciela to arrive. Instead, Graciela was already at the entrance, greeting her with a broad smile.

In the Latin tradition, they exchanged kisses on the cheek, drawing some curious stares from passers-by.

"Hello María," Graciela said in heavily-accented English. "How are you? How goes it with you?"

"I'm fine thank you," Maria responded in English. "And how are you?"

"I'm fine too, "Graciela responded, appearing a little uncertain if she had phrased things correctly.

At their first meeting, María had agreed to help Graciela with her English, starting with the basics like what to say when greeting someone. She gave her a wink of encouragement, planning to help her polish her greetings and responses later.

They went into Garfinkels arm-in-arm, grateful for the air conditioning. Heading for the women's clothing department, they spent the next hour shopping for summer dresses. At noon, they left Garfinkels with their purchases and turned west on F Street, walking towards Fifteenth. Pete had suggested that María and Graciela have lunch at the Willard Hotel on the corner of Fifteenth and Pennsylvania, only a few blocks from Garfinkels and not far from the White House. The Willard was a local hotel steeped in history. Various important statesmen had either resided in or stayed as guests at the Willard. Although it had lost some of its cachet in recent years, it still had a loyal clientele that included some of the most important movers and shakers in the capital. Pete also thought that its turn-of-the century Beaux Art style might remind María of the renowned Plaza Hotel in Buenos Aires.

Entering the hotel lobby, they attracted appreciative stares from the mostly male clientele. They got the same treatment when they entered the wood-paneled restaurant with its photos of famous politicians adorning the walls. Again, as in the lobby, most of the patrons were men. María thought she recognized a few well-known journalists and politicians as the maitre'd escorted them to a table for two in the back, where they could enjoy some privacy. Out of the corner of her eye, María could see some heads swivel as they passed by, briefly interrupting conversations that probably had to do with weighty matters of state.

The maitre'd held plush chairs for each of them, a slight smile on his lips. Welcoming them to the Willard, he handed over leather-backed menus and wished them a pleasant meal.

María and Graciela took a minute to glance around their elegant surroundings. Pete was right, María thought to herself. The whole atmosphere did remind her of some of the fashionable hotels in Buenos Aires.

Thirty seconds after they had been seated, a waiter wearing a white jacket, a bow tie, and dark pants came to ask them if they would like something to drink. Graciela shot María an inquisitive look that asked her to take the lead. María thought about ordering a cocktail, but demurred. She tried to avoid alcoholic drinks during the day.

"I would like an iced tea, please," she told the waiter.

Graciela followed suit and the waiter departed to fetch their orders.

With a quizzical look, Graciela asked, "What exactly is iced tea?"

"I know. It sounds awful doesn't it? It took me awhile to get used to it. But if you add a bit of sugar and lemon it can be quite refreshing."

Graciela looked dubious. But when the waiter returned with two glasses and she took her first sip, after following Maria's advice concerning the sugar and lemon, she had to agree. "Yes. You're right. It seems a bit strange at first, but it is refreshing."

Putting down their glasses, they opened their menus. After Graciela had asked for María's help in translating some of the items, they called the waiter over and placed their orders. Deviating from her reluctance to have alcohol at mid-day and trying to recreate the experience she and Graciela would have shared in South America, María ordered glasses of white wine to accompany their meals.

Once their orders had been placed, the two women picked up the thread of conversation that had begun when they first met. María was still circumspect when talking about her family, steering talk away from her years in Buenos Aires and focusing on what life had been like for her since her arrival in the United States. She could see an occasional look of surprise flit across Graciela's face when she described how she had learned English, educated herself, and risen through the ranks of her New York office. But when she mentioned the name of the company where she worked, there was no look of surprise. Instead, Graciela began to incline her head a fraction of an inch, as if to say, "Yes, I know" It was the briefest of gestures, lasting only a split second, and María kept on talking, not letting it interrupt the flow of her conversation. It had caught her a bit off guard, but she quickly pushed it to the back of her mind. She attributed Graciela's reaction to the fact that Foreign Films Distributors was well-known in the Río de la Plata region with Graciela simply responding to that familiar name.

María was beginning to shift the conversation to some of the problems Graciela might encounter in adjusting to life in the United States when the waiter delivered their orders. María had suggested that Graciela try the crab cakes, a local specialty. They were an unfamiliar dish for her Uruguayan friend and she thought she might like them.

After a first tentative bite, Graciela hummed with pleasure. "María," she said, "these are very good."

"I thought you would like them. Something different, no?"

They chatted amiably between bites of their food, sipping the cool glasses of white wine they had requested. By the time they had finished and ordered coffee, María, relaxed by the meal and the wine, decided to take a risk. They had been talking about the familiar and mundane, generally safe territory. Gradually, María began to steer the conversation onto trickier ground, hoping to determine just how open she could be with her new friend.

"One thing you will have to get used to in Washington," she said while she added sugar to her coffee, "is the incessant talk about politics. It is topic number one at every social gathering I have attended here. And the newspapers, radio, and now television just can't seem to get enough of it." Glancing around the room at a clientele immersed in guarded conversation with serious looks on their faces, she added, "I bet that ninety percent of what the men in here – and maybe most of the women – are talking about is something political. It can get a little overwhelming."

Graciela nodded in understanding. "Yes. Roberto also told me that would be the case." Then, after pausing for a moment, she went on. "Of course, politics is a big part of life in Montevideo. We have a very vibrant democracy and our press is full of news about the government. Each of our main parties, the *Colorados* and the *Blancos* have their own newspapers that are read daily by their loyal followers. My family belongs to the *Colorados* and we never tire of talking about its electoral chances whenever we get together."

María let a brief smile play across her face. She didn't know a lot about Uruguayan politics, but she did know that the *Colorados* were quite similar to the mostly middle-class, pro-democratic *Partido Radical* with which her own family was affiliated.

Graciela leaned forward with a look that suggested she was about to reveal a state secret. In lowered tones, she said, "But Roberto, coming from a landowning family and involved in business, is a *Blanco.* I didn't care. I'm not that wedded to the *Colorado* party. But it took some time for my family to accept him. Even now, after several years of marriage, we try to avoid political discussions when we are with my family."

"What about Roberto's family?" María asked, "Do they object to his having married into the opposition?"

Graciela let out a low chuckle. "No, no, not at all. In fact, Roberto has led them to believe that he can convert me to the *Blanco* cause. Raiding the enemy camp so to speak. Neither one of us take the party affiliation business as seriously as our parents do."

Looking at María over the rim of her coffee cup, Graciela asked, "And what about you María? Is your family involved in politics?"

The question was simple, flowing naturally from the conversation. María did not notice anything out of the ordinary in Graciela's tone of voice or facial expression. But they both knew that the circumstances in dictatorial Argentina were significantly different from those in democratic Uruguay and that such a question carried serious implications. As if to set María at ease, Graciela added, "Of course, I don't mean to pry. If you don't want to talk about the subject, I understand."

María gave the matter a few seconds thought before answering. "No. That's all right. My family is pretty political too. In fact, my father holds an important position in the Radical party. So I grew up in the same atmosphere you describe with lots of political discussions over the dinner table."

A serious look appeared on Graciela's face. "Things can't be easy for your father María. I have met some Argentine exiles in Montevideo, several from your father's party. They seem to have run afoul of the regime. A few have even been in physical danger despite being out of Argentina."

María nodded. "Yes. I know. And I worry about my family. It's frustrating sometimes, being so far away. I try not to dwell on it, but…"

"I can imagine," Graciela said sympathetically. "And, if you don't mind me saying so, I can't imagine living in Argentina these days. From what the exiles have told me, if you are not a *Peronista*, you have to watch carefully everything you say or do, otherwise…"

"Yes. Otherwise, things would not be very pleasant." María said grimly.

"And to top it off – *that woman!*," Graciela exclaimed a look of distaste crossing her face, as though the crab cake she had eaten had suddenly turned sour in her stomach. And no need for her to explain. "*That Woman*" was Evita Perón.

"Yes. *That woman*," María responded grimly. She was tempted to say more, but decided not to pursue the matter further. Maybe at some time in the future she could share her own personal experience with "*that woman*" with Graciela. But for now she was comforted by the fact that she seemed to have found a kindred spirit in whom she could confide. In some ways, meeting Graciela reminded her of how she had met Pete, as though they both had suddenly dropped out the sky to change her life in ways that, at the time she met them, she could barely foresee.

CHAPTER SEVEN

June 4, 1951 – Washington, D.C.

I left the Justice Department at five. The blast of heat and humidity hit me as soon as I stepped out onto Constitution Avenue. To the west I could see storm clouds building. Almost like clockwork, it seemed, rain showers descended on the nation's capital just as government workers headed home. These "government showers" brought some relief. But they usually lasted only twenty minutes or so, leaving the streets soaked and steaming while thoroughly drenching the unprepared. This time, however, the forecast predicted that these up-coming showers would bring with them cooler air that would stick around for a while.

I joined the crowd heading to the streetcar that would carry me home. Taking off my coat, I placed it over my briefcase, which I held tightly in my right hand. It was noticeably heavier than when I had brought it with me in the morning thanks to the .38 Smith and Wesson revolver I was now carrying with me per Joe Smather's instructions. I had made sure it was unloaded before packing it, not wanting any accidental discharge to take place in a crowded streetcar. The bullets were in separate packages. I would load the weapon once I got home.

Also in my briefcase was a shoulder holster. Joe had wanted me to put it on before I left the building, but I had demurred. I told him that the odds of someone attacking me in broad daylight on the downtown streets of Washington or on a streetcar jammed to the gills with passengers were pretty slim. He reluctantly accepted my argument. Nevertheless, he urged me to wear the gun under my arm, where it could be reached quickly if needed as a matter of course. I promised him that I would.

When I reached the corner of Constitution and Fifteenth, there was already a long line waiting for the next streetcar. Most of the men, like me, had again shed their coats. Many were wiping their foreheads with their pocket handkerchiefs.

I got in line, taking a careful look around me for anything or anybody who looked suspicious. Despite my assurances to Joe, there was always the chance that I had miscalculated the odds and there was somebody around who was looking to send me the same message that had been delivered to Ralph Turner.

I saw nothing out of the ordinary. I recognized some familiar faces, fellow passengers who followed the same schedule as I did and nodded my acknowledgement. A few were fidgeting, looking south for the next streetcar while glancing at the dark clouds gathering to the west.

We did not have long to wait. I had only been in line for a couple of minutes when I heard the reassuring clang of the streetcar bell as it approached our stop. When it came to a halt and opened its doors to let out passengers, there was room for everyone standing in line to board. I was able to find a seat near the back next to a window, which was already open to let in the breeze. As I sat, I could feel the faint waves of wind that smelled like rain. Taking the seat next to me was one of the department's secretaries. I knew her by appearance but not by name. She was about fifty and had the weary and resigned look of someone who had put in a hard day's work. I gave her a brief smile, which she returned without trying to strike up a conversation. I was grateful. Ordinarily, I was more sociable. But I, too, had had a long day and was in no mood for idle chit-chat. What had happened to Ralph Turner lay heavy on my mind.

I reached down and opened my briefcase. The revolver was on the bottom, covered by some papers from the office. I carefully removed this afternoon's *Evening Star*, which I had purchased from a vendor on the street, and began to page through it. I ignored the headlines and went directly to the local crime report. Halfway down page eighteen I found what I was looking for.

It was only two paragraphs: "Silver Spring Man Victim of Mysterious Attack." Ralph was mentioned by name but was not identified as a Justice Department lawyer. The article stated that Ralph was recuperating from his injuries but did not specify where he had been hospitalized. The local police were investigating the attack and asked for anyone who might have information to contact them as soon as possible.

Joe Smathers had reconvened the task force at noon. He informed us as to what Director Hoover and the attorney general had decided to tell the press concerning the attack on Ralph. As Joe had mentioned in the morning meeting, it would be impossible to keep news of the incident completely out of the papers. Ralph's neighbors already knew what had happened to him and had been questioned by the FBI and the local police. There was no doubt speculation already circulating among those questioned as to who might have been behind the attack. It was decided, therefore, to have the bureau contact the local papers and ask their cooperation in trying to keep the report of the attack to a minimum. No front-page coverage and no indication that we suspected this was something that originated with organized crime, at least not until we had more evidence. From what I had read in the *Star,* that newspaper had agreed to cooperate.

There was the hope, Joe had added, that someone who saw the story might have information and come forward to provide a lead. It was not entirely out of the question that a person or persons affiliated with one of the organized crime families might decide to squeal. While loyalties within the individual families were usually ironclad, there was often bitter rivalry among the various families. It was conceivable that a member of one family at odds with another would contact the police or the FBI, spilling the beans as to who was behind the assault on Ralph. Personally, I thought that to be a very remote possibility. But I also admitted that it was worth a try.

I folded the paper and put it back into the briefcase. I had tried to read the sports pages, but my mind was too cluttered to concentrate. As the streetcar passed Dupont Circle, thunder rumbled in the distance and the sky grew ever darker. I didn't believe in omens, but the approaching storm provided a fitting backdrop to my biggest concern at the moment: *How would María take the news I had for her?*

Over lunch, the three married members of the New York team had discussed what we should tell our wives. For us, accepting the risks that came with the job was something we all assumed. But putting our wives and children in danger was another matter altogether. When we had gone to war abroad, we had done so with the confidence that our family at home would be safe. But this was a different kind of war, one on the home front where nobody was safe.

After we hashed it over, we agreed that there was no way for us to soften the blow. Our families were going to be under FBI surveillance and protection. We could not conceal that fact. We had to describe the situation in full and offer what reassurances we could. Saying that was what we were going to do was one thing. Actually doing it was quite another. Nobody was looking forward to breaking the bad news about the attack on Ralph and what it meant for the rest of us.

As I got off the streetcar and crossed Connecticut Avenue heading for home, the skies had darkened even more. The wind was picking up and large drops of rain began to fall. I put my copy of the *Evening Star* over my head for protection and quickened my pace, breaking into a trot. Approaching our town house, I spotted a dark sedan parked across the street, two men in the front seat. The FBI was on the job, as promised. I wondered if María had noticed their presence.

I got to the door just as the storm erupted in full fury, complete with thunder and lightning. I could only hope the same thing would not happen when I broke the news to María about the events of the day.

CHAPTER EIGHT

June 8, 1951 – Washington, D.C.

It was twelve thirty when I left the Justice Department building and headed west on Pennsylvania Avenue for lunch with my old pal David Friedman. As had become my custom, I looked carefully in all directions as soon as I hit the street. I saw nothing suspicious.

In the days since the attack on Ralph Turner, there had been no new incidents. Nobody on the task force had reported anything out of the ordinary. Still, I was reassured by the presence of my .38 in a shoulder holster under my left arm.

Ever since I had arrived in Washington, David and I had made it a habit to meet every Friday at the Occidental Restaurant on Pennsylvania. In addition to being a fine eating establishment, it was only a few blocks from Justice and a short walk for David from the temporary War Department buildings that lined the Reflecting Pool in front of the Lincoln Memorial. They now housed the Central Intelligence Agency for which my friend now worked. David wryly noted that aside from the leaking ceiling whenever it rained or snowed, the lack of sufficient air conditioning, and the frequent encounter with rats of the four-legged variety that inhabited the building, he had little to complain about it.

The Occidental was a favorite of government bigwigs, politicians, journalists, lobbyists, and the occasional tourist. It was always crowded but we had a standing twelve-thirty reservation for a table for two near the back. An urgent call had caused me to be a few minutes late and David had preceded me. I threaded my way through the tables toward David, who stood and greeted me with a smile and a handshake.

"Sorry I'm late pal," I said apologetically.

"No problem buddy," he said, as we both sat. "Tough day at the office?"

"You could say that. But what else is new?" I replied.

David nodded in comprehension. He knew all about the task force and the mission that had brought me to Washington. But I had not yet had the opportunity to fill him in on the most recent developments involving the attack on Ralph Turner.

Our regular waiter arrived before we could continue. He handed over the menus and took our drink orders, a dry martini on the rocks with a twist for me and a bourbon and water for David. Ordinarily, neither one of us touched alcohol during the weekday afternoons. We had decided to make our Fridays an exception, although strictly limiting ourselves to one cocktail and no wine. We both had work to do later in the day.

While the waiter saw to our drink orders, I told David what had happened to Ralph Turner. I had no qualms about revealing all the gory details to my friend, who was entirely trustworthy. I took him through everything up to the point where I was about to enter my town house just as a monumental thunderstorm hit. At that moment, the waiter returned with our drinks and we spent the next couple of minutes placing our lunch orders.

After the waiter left, David asked, "And how did María react to the news?"

"At first, it was touch and go," I replied. "She had had a wonderful day with a new friend she had met, a young woman from Uruguay. Her eyes were shining and she gave me a warmer embrace than usual." I could feel my face turn red as I said this and David emitted a low chuckle. "So I felt pretty bad about spoiling the mood. But there was no getting around delivering the news. After I put down my briefcase, acutely aware of what was inside, took off my coat and loosened my tie, I asked her to sit down next to me on the couch. She could tell from my expression and the tone of my voice that something serious was going on."

I interrupted my narrative to take a sip of my martini, enjoying the taste as it made its way down my throat. "When I told her what had happened to Ralph, there was shock and fear on her face. For a moment I thought she was going to fall to pieces. But after a few seconds she straightened her shoulders and looked me square in the eye. 'What can we do to help Ralph and Belinda?' she asked. I couldn't have been prouder of her at that moment," I said, a catch in my voice.

I paused for a moment and David waited for me to continue. "We agreed to go to GW hospital that night after dinner. And we've been going nightly all this week."

"How's Ralph doing?" David asked.

"Still in a coma, I'm afraid. The doctors tell us that his vital signs are good and they are hopeful he'll come out of it eventually. But they can't give us any guarantees or even guess when that might be. So mostly we've been there for Belinda. She is devastated, as are her two girls. But María and some of the other wives are helping out with the household chores and trying to keep Belinda's spirits up. I think they all realize that any of them could have been in the same situation."

I took another sip of my martini and continued my narrative. "The way María has responded amazes me. I told her about the FBI agents parked outside our door and Joe Smathers's order that I carry a gun. She didn't blink an eye. Instead, she asked if I had the gun with me and would I show it to her. When I opened my briefcase and took it out, I was positive she would recoil in horror. She can't understand why so many North Americans seem obsessed by guns. But her reaction was just the opposite of what I had expected. There was a look of resolve on her face. She demanded that I show her how to load and fire the weapon. In fact, she wants me to get her one of her own to carry and take her to a firing range to learn how to use it." Even now I could only shake my head in disbelief as I recalled my wife's reaction.

"Pete, old buddy," David said. "I am not surprised. This is a woman who was willing to confront Eva Duarte Perón to try to save your life. And that was even before she became your wife."

"I guess you're right. But still…" I let it trail off. "At any rate, I've gotten Joe to agree to provide María with a .38 just like mine and use the FBI facilities to train. Some of the other wives are planning to do the same. I'm not sure just how happy Joe is with this turn of events. But he is willing to go along to keep the team together."

"Has anybody chosen to drop out?" David asked.

"Not so far. But I think one of the guys with three kids is weighing his options." I didn't name names but it was Jim Franklin, the oldest of our bunch. "The rest of us seem ready to stick it out."

"Any clues as to who was behind the attack?" David asked.

"The natural assumption is that Costello or one of the other gang bosses wants to intimidate us into dropping our investigation. It's a pretty heavy-handed way to go about things and might well backfire if we can trace the attack to whoever ordered it. The bureau is carrying out a thorough investigation, but so far no solid leads and no direct evidence of mob involvement. At any rate, the task force is more determined than ever to forge ahead – as is Senator Kefauver."

David reacted to my words with a worried expression on his face. "Just be careful Pete," he said in a somber voice. "It was one thing to run the risks we did in the OSS and Buenos Aires. But remember, you now have a wife to think about. It's more than just you and your pals."

David knew me well, probably better than anyone. He understood my penchant for taking risks and courting danger, having seen me in action enough times over the years. While he was no shrinking violet himself, he always took a more cautious and considered approach to any dangerous assignment than I did. Now he sensed that my emotions might be getting the better of me. Although I knew he wouldn't say it, he was more than likely thinking that I should take up Joe Smathers's offer and opt out of the task force. On the other hand, he also knew me well enough to realize that was the last thing I was about to do.

"Don't worry David. I'm taking all the necessary precautions," I said, patting the bulge under my left armpit.

He didn't say anything, just a slight shrug as if to say, "Just what I expected."

When the waiter arrived with our meals - rockfish, rice, and a salad for me, chicken, potatoes, and a salad for David - we went silent as he put the plates down. Once he had left, I asked David how things had been going with him since last we met. Between bites, he filled me in as best he could. Unlike with me, David had to be more constrained in what he was able say because of the demands of the particular job he had.

David and I had met during wartime service in the OSS in Spain. Fellow New Yorkers, albeit from quite different backgrounds, we had become partners and close friends. After the war, David joined the Foreign Service, dedicating himself to identifying and locating ex-Nazis seeking refuge in places like Argentina. When I arrived in Buenos Aires by chance in June 1945, we had embarked on the "little adventure" that had led to our expulsion from the country.

I had returned to New York and David to Washington. For a couple of years, David had continued to work for the State Department. But he grew increasingly frustrated there. The fallout from what we had done in Argentina had hung like a dark cloud over his head, limiting his opportunities for other overseas assignments and blocking any hopes he might have of tracing runaway Nazis.

When the new State of Israel was created in 1948, David seriously considered resettling in the Jewish homeland. He thought that with his background he would be accepted into the intelligence services, where he could resume his quest to hunt down and bring to justice fugitive Nazi war criminals. But as fate would have it, before he decided to go to Israel he got an offer to join the newly-created Central Intelligence Agency. The head of the agency, our former OSS boss, William "Wild Bill" Donovan, had a very high opinion of David and his abilities. Donovan did a successful job of convincing David to leave the State Department and join the new agency. The CIA chief had implied that David would find the work more satisfying and the atmosphere more congenial.

David had remained in his new job for more than three years. But it was clear he was not happy. While he didn't confide in me, maintaining the strict confidentiality that came with working for America's most secret agency, his unhappiness was written on his face. His soulful brown eyes rarely flashed the twinkle they had when we first met. The worry lines on his forehead and bracketing his mouth only deepened and his curly brown hair was turning gray and beginning to recede from his forehead. Even though we were both in our early thirties, David looked ten years older. As a sign of his frustration, he had begun dropping hints that he was again considering moving to Israel and volunteering to work for their intelligence agency. The fact that for the past several months he had been dating an official from the Israeli embassy who eventually would return home would be a major factor in that decision.

I could see he was calculating how much he could tell me. I tried to make it easier on him. "How's Sarah?" Sarah was his Israeli girlfriend.

At least he wouldn't be revealing any state secrets responding to that question. But from the look on his face, you couldn't tell. David had always been shy around women. As far as I knew he had never had had a serious relationship. His cheeks reddened as he replied. "She's fine Pete. Just fine."

When he fell silent, I uttered a low chuckle. "Come on buddy. 'Just fine.' That's all you've got for me. Come on. Give."

David looked down and played with the food on his plate. When he raised his head to look at me, I saw the long-lost twinkle in his eye. "We're thinking about getting married. No definite plans yet, but we're moving in that direction."

I wasn't totally surprised. I knew they were serious about one another and figured it was just a matter of time until they decided to tie the knot.

"That's great David. Wonderful news. So have you proposed? Does she have a ring? Can I tell María?"

A pained expression crossed his face. "No. No formal proposal yet. You know, down on bended knee and all that. It's just more of an understanding we have reached."

"When does Sarah get reassigned to Israel?"

"We don't know for sure, probably sometime in the fall. They want her to finish up some assignments here before she leaves."

"I see. Well I hope it becomes official soon so that we can have a proper celebration. María and I think Sarah is a wonderful young woman and a great match for you."

"Thanks Pete. I think she's wonderful too. And you'll be the first to know when I pop the question."

I could sense some hesitation in David's attitude. Maybe the "understanding" he and Sarah had reached was more on his side than hers. Maybe he wasn't yet completely confident she would say "yes" when he asked her to marry him. I hoped fervently that he would not be disappointed. David was a very tough and resilient guy, but in affairs of the heart he was as vulnerable as the rest of us, perhaps even more than most.

I decided to switch topics. "I read in the *Post* today that two British diplomats have gone missing, maybe on a plane to Russia."

David's look turned somber. "Yeah. Donald MacLean and Guy Burgess." He paused for a minute, probably thinking through what he could tell me. "It looks as though they've been spying for the Soviets for some time. Part of an espionage ring within British intelligence." Then another pause before he added, "We're pretty worried that there may be more. You know that Angleton," referring to James Jesus Angleton, head of the CIA's Office of Special Operations and in charge of counter-espionage, "has suspected for some time that the Soviets have a mole in the agency. MacLean and Burgess may just be the tip of the iceberg."

David turned his attention again to his food, a clear sign that he was not inclined to say anything more. I did not press him.

The waiter collected our plates and poured us each a cup of coffee. After he left, I told David how happy I was that María had found a new friend – a young woman named Graciela Walker from Uruguay. He knew how difficult the adjustment to life in Washington had been for my wife. A smile creased his face as I described María's excitement over having met a female with whom she could converse and confide. "In fact," I said, "I'll be meeting her and her husband Roberto tonight for dinner. Roberto is some kind of businessman who has been posted by his company to Washington. So they'll be here for a while. This is great for María. Something to take her mind off, you know..."

David nodded. "Glad to hear some good news Pete. I hope things work out on that front." He paused for moment. "These new friends. They're from Uruguay you say?"

"Yes. Not exactly María's home country. But close enough."

I could see him pondering what to say next. "When you two have dinner with this couple how much do you plan to tell them about your time in Argentina? The matter of how you and María met is bound to come up."

"We've discussed that. We'll stick to the story that I was assigned to manage the FFD office and from there one thing led to another. After all, that part of it is the truth – although certainly not the whole story. We've been down this road before when others have asked how we met. We stick to the basics, no elaboration."

"Good. Good. That's the best thing. We've done a pretty thorough job of keeping that whole episode under wraps. It wouldn't do anybody any good to revisit what happened. Our relationship with the Perón regime is improving and we don't want to open any old wounds." Even though David's main assignment was the Middle East, he also kept a keen eye on Argentina and was thoroughly conversant with the latest developments there. In the back of his mind, I knew he wanted to return and continue the pursuit of the Nazis who had escaped and settled in that country.

"I understand David. Mum's the word." Then a thought struck me, my memory jogged by a momentary return to my time in Argentina. "Say, do you hear anything from Bruno? How's he doing?"

Bruno was a secret policeman who had helped kidnap me back in 1945 but who I had convinced to help me turn the tables on my captors. In return for not revealing the role he had played in my escape to his superiors, the intelligence officers at the embassy had enrolled him as a double agent who would report to them whatever tidbits about the secret police he could turn up.

I owed Bruno my life and felt embarrassed that I hadn't asked David about him before this. Again, there was the studied pause as David pondered his response. "Funny you should ask Pete. Bruno is fine. He's been operating under cover for us for six years now and providing useful information. In fact, these days he has become the principal bodyguard for the head of the secret police, Horacio Campos." I nodded in recognition of the name. Campos had been in charge of the operation that had led to my kidnapping at the orders of Perón and Eva.

David leaned over the table and lowered his voice. "Bruno goes just about everywhere Campos does, including the Casa Rosada. Recently he has reported that something serious seems afoot in the executive mansion. Evita's health has deteriorated and Campos has been called in by Perón to discuss the ramifications."

My curiosity was piqued. "Does Bruno know anything more? Any details?" But then I realized that I might be putting David in a compromising position, asking him to reveal more than he should. Sensing my concern, he said, "Don't worry Pete. There is nothing more to say. Bruno isn't present when Campos meets Perón. And he doesn't dare ask his boss any questions, no matter how innocent. So all that we do know is that something might be up, we just don't know what."

I finished my coffee, which had gotten a little cold. I had considered writing Bruno a letter of thanks as soon as I returned to the U.S. But David had warned me that if any communication from me fell into the wrong hands, it would be curtains for Bruno. "Well, I'm glad to hear that Bruno is all right," I said. "Maybe someday I can get in touch with him and thank him in person for all his help."

David shrugged. He knew full well that at the moment neither one of us could go to Argentina. "Who knows? But right now, it looks as though whatever the current crisis, Perón is going to stay in power for the foreseeable future. Until he's gone, any contact you might have with Bruno could well put his life in danger."

I bobbed my head in agreement. With that sobering thought, we paid the bill and left the Occidental. Later, I would have occasion to replay some of things David and I had discussed regarding Bruno's reports and see them in a quite different light. There were clues in our conversation that might have led me to anticipate what was to come, but they were difficult to discern at the time.

CHAPTER NINE

June 8, 1951 – Washington, D.C.

David Friedman mulled over the luncheon conversation he had had with his old friend as he strolled toward his office. He shook his head and let out a deep sigh of resignation. Once again, his best friend was flirting with danger. There seemed to be something in Pete Benton's nature that sought it out. From their days in the OSS to their "little adventure" in Argentina, and now to the threats to the Justice Department task force, Pete often found himself at risk. Although David had himself to blame for putting Pete in danger in Argentina, it was a challenge that his friend welcomed with open arms. Pete's redeeming virtue was an ability to display remarkable resilience and, up to now, survive whatever had been thrown his way – albeit in Argentina, it had been a very close thing. He could only hope that Pete's luck would hold in facing this new crisis.

As he entered the exceptionally unexceptional building that housed his office, David put his concerns about Pete Benton to one side. He had his own problems to worry about.

Heading down the corridor, he passed half a dozen office doors before reaching his own small space. Each office had a small air conditioning unit in the windows facing Constitution Avenue, but most of them either failed to work altogether or put out such a small amount of cool air it was scarcely worth the effort to turn them on. In at least half the offices he passed, the doors and windows were open to allow whatever breeze was stirring outside to circulate. Hardly the ideal circumstances for an agency involved in what was supposed to be top-secret work. There was talk of a new building for the CIA across the river in Northern Virginia, but so far it was just talk.

David entered his office and immediately went to the air conditioner and switched it on. His was one of the few that actually worked. But the price was an infernal racket that often made it hard to think much less carry on a conversation.

On his desk were a pile of publications on economic conditions in major Middle Eastern countries. His boss had assigned him the task of reading them over and writing a summary in preparation for a staff meeting on Monday. It was mind-numbing work, but David was determined to finish by the end of the day.

David's girlfriend and intended fiancée Sarah's job at the Israeli Embassy demanded she attend an endless series of meetings, dinner parties, and diplomatic receptions. She and David had to squeeze in time together as her busy schedule allowed. Too often, to David's dismay, things they had planned to do together fell through at the last minute because Sarah was called upon to attend some cocktail party at some embassy. But he also understood that Sarah was much in demand for such duties - and not just because she was young and exceedingly attractive. While her official position was that of a junior political officer, in reality Sarah was working for Israeli intelligence. The more she could circulate among Washington's diplomatic circles and domestic power brokers, the more information she could gather. Whatever the inconvenience he suffered as a result, he recognized, was of no consequence compared to the important work Sarah was doing.

This weekend was going to be different. Sarah had prevailed upon her superior to give her a break. She had been on the job constantly for more than a year and needed some time off. Her superior had reluctantly agreed, even though there were some receptions at key embassies she would miss. Sarah suggested a substitute, a young female employee in the cultural affairs office who was also working for intelligence. Although the young woman was green, Sarah argued that she was ready to go into the field. Her boss gave in, recognizing that Sarah was going to dig in her heels if he objected. No sense alienating his most valuable asset.

With decks cleared, David and Sarah planned to spend the weekend at a friend's summer house on Chesapeake Bay. The friend, a colleague at the agency, wouldn't be using the house that particular weekend and was more than happy to let David and Sarah occupy it.

David didn't want to squander this golden opportunity and attacked the material on his desk with determination. Mindful of the clock, he rushed to finish his work in time to place it on his boss's desk before he left the office at five. He and Sarah were planning to depart by six, stopping for dinner along the way.

As he finished reading the dreary economic publications and began to type his report, David found his mind wandering. Earlier in the week, when it was confirmed that Sarah would indeed have the weekend free, David had bought an engagement ring. Although he hadn't thought through all the details, he planned to propose marriage to Sarah on the shores of the scenic bay in as romantic a setting as he could find.

David was naturally nervous. But he felt reasonably certain that Sarah would accept his proposal. They had discussed the possibility in an off-hand manner for the past several months. While Sarah had not made any promises, she hadn't discouraged the talk either. When David had told Sarah he loved her, she told him that she loved him too. But love was one thing, marriage was another. This was especially true in their case, where their respective situations and their relationship were fraught with complexities. The details of just how their marriage would work were tangled and complicated. It involved not only melding two personalities but also two careers.

When David had joined the Central Intelligence Agency, he had done so with a mixture of relief and gratitude. His career at the State Department was stalled, with little hope of advancement. What had transpired in Argentina with Pete Benton meant that he had virtually no chance to get another overseas assignment in the foreseeable future. Upon his return from Buenos Aires, he had enjoyed the opportunity to work with former ambassador Braden to compile the so-called *Blue Book* documenting Perón's links with the Axis. But the effort backfired and may have helped Perón win presidential elections in 1946. Discouraged by that failure and his chances of working abroad slim to none, he found himself caught in an endless cycle of meaningless paper shuffling. He also felt keenly the lingering anti-Semitism in a department top-heavy with members of the Ivy League Protestant elite. He had joined the Foreign Service initially so that he could track down Nazis who had fled Germany, expose them, prevent them from finding refuge, and bring them to justice. Being stuck behind a desk at Foggy Bottom was no way for him to accomplish that mission.

He appreciated the help he had gotten from his former OSS boss in making the switch to the CIA. He reconnected with many of his fellow OSS agents, who, like him, had served in the clandestine service in Europe during the war. Even though the agency was run by many of the same Ivy Leaguers who managed the State Department, he found the environment overall more welcoming and with greater possibilities.

It didn't take long for him to become disillusioned. At first, given his experience and his knowledge of Spanish he was assigned to the Latin American division. But it became immediately apparent that the agency was little concerned with the possibility that hundreds if not thousands of Nazi war criminals and fascists from other European countries were finding new homes in Latin America. Instead, the main preoccupation was with the threat of communism in the region as the Cold War intensified and areas outside of Europe were seen as possible targets for Soviet expansion.

While David was not happy with this development, he could understand and to some extent sympathize with it. He had few illusions about communism or about Soviet intentions. While some of his college classmates and even a few close friends had found Marxism attractive during the Depression years, David had not succumbed to the appeal. He found the ideology rigid and the Soviet leadership under Stalin cynical, ruthless, and without humanity. In fact, despite the momentary wartime alliance with the U.S.S.R. and his admiration for some of the Communists he met in Spain, he saw little difference between communism and fascism. Stalin and Hitler, he believed, were basically cut from the same cloth.

Once again frustrated, David asked for a shift to the Middle Eastern division. Two main considerations drove his request. First, he wanted to be involved in any policy decision that might affect the new State of Israel. Second, while not as many ex-Nazis had found refuge in places like Turkey, Syria, and Egypt as they had in Latin America, there were still some important figures hiding in those countries that he would like to track down and expose. Even before he requested the transfer, he had begun to study Arabic where his facility in learning foreign languages proved a boon.

When David asked for the transfer, he did not reveal the two main reasons that lay behind his request. Instead, he pointed out that the Latin American section was well staffed while the Middle Eastern section needed more manpower. The fact that he had already mastered a reading knowledge of Arabic proved a valuable asset. Fortunately for him, the deputy director in charge of the Middle Eastern division was Brent Sanderson, a former OSS colleague for whom David had worked in Spain and who had been instrumental in approving his move from State to the CIA. It was clear from Sanderson's reaction that he had his doubts about David's reasons for the shift. He knew all about David's obsession with tracking down former Nazis. But he agreed that the section was understaffed and could use some new blood.

Once settled in, David enjoyed the challenges posed in trying to understand a new part of the world. The Middle East seemed to him much more complex and opaque than Latin America. It took him a while to get up to speed on a history and a culture that stretched back millennia. Over time, he came to appreciate the complex dynamics of the region and to recognize fully the immense difficulties faced by Israel, a relatively small oasis in a very hostile neighborhood. When he began to draft reports analyzing current developments and suggesting policy lines, he took care not to show any bias toward the new Jewish state. While the anti-Semitism of the State Department was not so pronounced in the CIA, he was one of only a handful of Jews in the Middle East division and he knew that his superiors would keep a close eye on everything he produced.

Working within these constraints, during his first year in the new division David was fairly well-satisfied with his work. The policy papers he produced received careful attention and Brent Sanderson took pains to congratulate him on the astute insights they contained.

But David's frustrations continued. His position in the agency was that of analyst. As such, he had to rely on published information and whatever agents in the field might dig up and deliver to him. Over the course of the past year, those agents had failed to provide him much if anything about Nazi war criminals in the region. He entertained the idea of asking to serve as a field agent himself. But he realized that even if the lingering effects of his experience in Argentina had not been enough of an obstacle to overcome, the agency was not about to send Jewish agents to Muslim countries.

There were even more troubling matters. David knew from the time he had joined the agency that it had collaborated with the State Department to assure that certain German scientists who had worked on the Reich's V-2 rocket program ended up in the United States. The plan was to have them continue their work on rocket design, this time for their former enemies. Although he was not happy with this development, David understood the practical Cold War logic that lay behind it. The Soviets were grabbing their fair share of German scientists to help develop a rocket program of their own. In light of that fact it made sense for the U.S. to do the same.

Of greater concern was something David had picked up through water-cooler gossip. While the "rescue" of the German scientists was public knowledge, the agency was also engaged in helping other, even less desirable Germans find a new home in the United States. These Germans, it was rumored, were not scientists. Rather they were men who had been in important positions in the Nazi SS and Gestapo, a few of them involved in helping direct the Holocaust. According to the scuttlebutt, the agency was helping them relocate by providing them with new identities and generous living expenses.

At first, David dismissed the possibility that the agency would do something so outrageous. But the more bits and pieces he picked up the more he began to suspect that the CIA's recruitment of ex-Nazis was an undeniable fact, even if he did not have the hard evidence to prove it. The idea that he was working for an organization that actually helped men who sought to exterminate all Jews from the face of the earth began to eat away at him. He had more than the usual trouble sleeping and fell into a familiar pattern of missing meals, trying to stay awake with massive infusions of coffee, and losing an alarming amount of weight.

Finally, David determined to find out if what he was suspected was true. He made an appointment with Brent Sanderson, intending to ask him straight out if the agency was indeed recruiting and protecting ex-Nazis. He remembered their meeting as though it was yesterday.

CHAPTER TEN

February 13, 1950 – Washington, D.C.

It was a cold, raw, rainy Monday in mid-February. The sky was gray and overcast. A stiff wind blew across the Mall. The foul and gloomy weather matched David's mood.

His appointment was at nine sharp. David arrived at Sanderson's office on the dot. The deputy director was in the administration building, next door to where David worked. David had not bothered to carry an umbrella or put on a hat to navigate the fifteen feet or so that separated the two buildings. He arrived with raindrops scattered in his hair and speckling the top of his suit coat.

The administration building was not much different from the other temporary quarters the agency had on the Mall. But the offices were larger and better appointed. Sanderson's was no exception. There was a reception area with comfortable chairs and a shiny new wooden desk. David and most of his colleagues had to make due with drab Army-surplus office furniture.

Sanderson's secretary Julie, an attractive petite blonde, greeted David with a smile. "Good morning Mister Friedman," she said in a slight southern drawl. "I'll let Mister Sanderson know you are here. He is expecting you."

She tapped lightly on the door behind her. "Mister Friedman is here to see you sir."

David could hear the creaking of a chair and then footsteps as Sanderson opened the door.

"Thanks Julie," he said to his secretary. Then he waved for David to enter and extended his hand. "David," he began, "Good to see you. How are…?" He let it trail off. It had been at least a month since he had last seen David and he could not hide the shock his haggard appearance produced. *"My God man. What's going on? Are you ill?"*

David's handshake was firm, but his clothes hung loosely on his frame and there were deep circles under his eyes. "No. No. I'm fine Brent. Just a little tired, that's all."

Sanderson did not look convinced and continued to view David with concern. He gestured for David to take the seat opposite his desk while he returned to his chair.

"Would you like some coffee David?"

David, absently rubbing his stomach as though it could reduce the dull pain he was feeling, shook his head. "No Brent. Thanks. That's kind of you. But I've had enough coffee already."

Sanderson raised his hands in an "Okay" gesture and then placed them flat down on his desk. The desk was polished mahogany, likewise far from standard government-issue but in keeping with the deputy director's tastes and presumably paid for with his own funds. The chair David sank into was covered in soft brown leather, as was its twin to the right. Sanderson's own swivel chair was also brown leather and probably cost half of David's yearly salary. Behind Sanderson were three oak book cases, filled to the brim with reference works and well-known books on the Middle East, including a first edition of T.E. Lawrence's *Seven Pillars of Wisdom.* On the walls to his right and left were paintings that depicted views of Istanbul and Cairo. Sanderson kept the harsh fluorescent overhead lights off, preferring the illumination of a Tiffany lamp on his desk. The top of his desk, like the rest of the office, was neat and orderly. The only items on it at the moment, aside from the lamp, were a manila folder that David recognized as his own most recent report on Egypt and a pipe rack and ash tray. When David had first met Sanderson in Spain, he had been a chain-smoker of cigarettes.

Returning to the States, he had switched to a pipe, which he was currently packing with tobacco.

Brent Sanderson, like many in the upper echelons of the agency, came from a well-to-do New England family. He had attended all the right schools - Philips Exeter Academy, Princeton as an undergraduate majoring in government, and then a law degree from Harvard. Prior to the war, he had been a partner in a powerful Boston law firm. Tall and handsome, with bright blue eyes, wavy blond hair, a square jaw and aquiline nose, he had married into another family of substantial means. So far as David knew, he remained happily married to the same woman. And despite the often killing demands of his job, was an attentive and dutiful father to his two children, a boy and a girl, now, as David remembered, both off to college.

When the U.S. entered the war, it was presumed that Brent, like his father, would join the Navy. But Bill Donovan, scouting for talent, found that Brent had spent significant amounts of time in Europe on legal matters and was conversant in four languages – German, French, Spanish, and Italian – and recruited him into the OSS. David and Pete had gotten to know Brent in Spain, where he was one of a number of men who rotated in and out periodically as their immediate superiors. Their relationship did not always go smoothly. Brent was a stickler for the rules and Pete and David often carried out assignments with a somewhat broader interpretation of what constituted an unnecessary risk. But Brent could not argue with the results David and Pete produced. While they did not become personally close, they developed a feeling of mutual respect. David considered Brent a fair and trustworthy boss, one who put the wellbeing of the agents who worked for him first and foremost. And while Brent was ambitious, he did not advance by stepping on those below him. Instead, he ascended the ladder of the OSS and the CIA through intelligence, even-handedness, and, when required, being exceptionally tough-minded. To David, Brent was something of an exception – a straight shooter in a profession where deception was the coin of the realm.

Brent had been with the agency from the time of its creation. He had decided not to return to his lucrative law practice but rather to devote himself to public service, in David's eyes another point in his favor. Because of his war-time experience, he was assigned to the European division. That division was at the epicenter of the emerging Cold War confrontation with the Soviet Union, consequently the most important intelligence-gathering part of the agency. Brent swiftly rose to the top of the European desk. But in a bureaucratic reshuffling complicated by some inter-office infighting he was reassigned to be in charge of the Middle Eastern division. As was his custom, he threw himself wholeheartedly into his new post. Like David, he studied Arabic and immersed himself in the region's history and culture.

When David joined the agency, in large measure thanks to Brent, they had resumed the relationship they had established in Spain. From David's first day on the job, Brent had told him that his door was always open if there was anything he needed. Now, David had decided, was the time to put that offer to the test.

"What's up David?" Sanderson asked. "Julie didn't mention anything in particular." Pointing down to his desk with the stem of his pipe at David's most recent analysis of the situation in Egypt, Brent said "I presume it has something to do with your work on the tension between the Army and the Farouk Monarchy. First-class stuff by the way. So…?"

David shook his head. "Thanks Brent. But no. It's not about Egypt."

There was a moment of silence as David tried to muster his thoughts and his courage. Brent looked at him calmly, lighting his pipe and taking some initial puffs, waiting for the shoe to drop.

Breathing in the fragrant tobacco smell, David looked Brent squarely in the eyes and began: "This is difficult Brent. And I may be totally off base. But I've been hearing chatter here and there that suggests the agency is planning to," he stumbled for the right word, "the agency is 'recruiting' former Nazis as intelligence assets, providing them safe passage from Germany and relocating them here in the United States. Some of them are even war criminals, charged with participating in the extermination of the Jews."

Brent said nothing, keeping his expression neutral. When he didn't respond, David squirmed in his seat. "I know this sounds bizarre but it's been driving me crazy. Please tell me it's not true."

Brent took his time responding, puffing thoughtfully on his pipe. David felt the acid building up in his stomach. Inadvertently, in a nervous gesture, Brent put a finger under the starched collar of his white dress shirt as though to loosen the pressure he felt. His fingers drummed on the desk. He looked over David's head to a distant ceiling corner as though seeking divine inspiration. David noticed that Brent's hair was now more gray than blonde and there were worry lines etched ever more deeply, bracketing his mouth and creasing his forehead. Suddenly, without a word but with a finger to his lips, he went to his office door and put his ear to it. Apparently satisfied, he returned to his chair and gestured for David to move closer so that he could lower his voice

Moving his chair closer to Brent's desk, David leaned his head forward. "Listen David," Brent said in a voice barely above a whisper. "And listen closely. What I am about to tell you goes no further than this room. It is top secret and absolutely confidential. Both of us would be in big trouble if word got out that I had told you what I am about to tell you. *Understood?"*

David nodded. "I may come to regret this," Brent continued. "But we go back a ways. And I know how much this means to you." There was a glimmer of sympathy in Brent's eyes but his voice was calm and steady.

"The rumors are true. We *are* doing exactly what you have heard. We are contacting former members of the Third Reich and bringing them to the United States to help us spy on the Soviets."

David sat back, stunned. His worst fears were realized. He began to speak, but Brent again put his finger to his mouth and gestured for him to resume his posture over the desk. "Listen David. We have to keep this quiet. It's just too sensitive." Then, gesturing to the door. "I do trust Julie to be discreet, but no sense taking unnecessary risks."

"But Brent," David stammered, his voice a hoarse whisper. "How can we do this? How can we work with such monsters?" Then, close to tears, he added, "I just can't believe it. After all the terrible things they have done. *To reward them like this! To recruit them!* It's just, just..." David couldn't find the words and slumped back in his chair, his shoulders sagging, a look of excruciating pain on his face.

Brent looked at him with a sober expression, nodding in silent agreement. Then he again gestured for him to come closer. "I know David, I know. And believe me, I'm not happy about this either. But we need to look at the bigger picture." Internally, David shuddered at the term "bigger picture," one he had come to fear and loathe as an excuse to cover up sins too numerous to mention. "We are now engaged in a new war, a war that if it gets out of control could make what happened previously look like a walk in the park. We're talking about a catastrophe on a global scale. Perhaps the end of life as we know it. And like any war, you have to employ all the weapons available to you if you hope to prevail. I'm afraid that these "monsters," as you rightly describe them, are one of those weapons. We are going to use men who worked in German intelligence to help us locate and identify Soviet agents both at home and abroad. You may not like it and I may not like it, but the director has given the project a green light and we have no choice but to go along with it."

To David, Brent's words seemed to echo the familiar refrain of the Nazi war criminals convicted at Nuremburg: "Just following orders." And while his head could understand the logic of what the agency was planning to do, his heart and his stomach found it too much to accept. He thought about arguing with Brent, but knew it would be a futile exercise. The decision had been made at the highest levels and was being kept a secret from most of the staff at the agency. If word leaked about the scheme, he knew there would be hell to pay. In fact, he wondered why Brent had dared to confide in him. It was clear that he found the agency's actions distasteful and perhaps he wanted to share that distaste with someone else.

Still hunched over Brent's desk, David whispered to Brent. "Thanks for telling me this. I know you have gone out on a limb. You have my promise that it will stay between us." Soon, David would come to regret that promise.

Brent nodded. The two men leaned back. In a normal voice Sanderson asked, "Now do you want to talk about your Egypt report?"

David shrugged, watching the smoke from Brent's pipe trace intricate patterns around the Tiffany Lamp. "Sure. Why not?"

CHAPTER ELEVEN

February 17, 1950 – Washington, D.C.

David spent half an hour with Brent Sanderson, going over the Egypt file. He could barely concentrate his mind in a whirl after his worst fears about the agency had been confirmed. When he returned to his office, he was still in a fog. He had mumbled greetings to the others he met in the hallway, doing his best to hide his emotions but without much success. A couple of fellow analysts stopped him to ask what was wrong. He told them he was a little under the weather, something that was easy to believe given his appearance.

Once in his office, he locked the door and stumbled to his desk. There, he spent a few minutes staring into space, trying to determine what to do next. Finally, he decided that while the memory was fresh, he ought to write down all he could remember from his conversation with Brent Sanderson. He knew it was dangerous to have the notes of a top-secret and confidential conversation in his possession. But he wanted to make sure he had at least some tangible proof of what the agency was doing, even if it would only be his version. Also, by putting the words down on paper, he could give some concrete reality to what seemed a horrible nightmare.

Over the next few days, David wrestled with an intractable moral dilemma. On the one hand, how could he sit by and do nothing while the agency for which he worked carried out a program that, in his mind, meant not only condoning evil but even rewarding it? Moreover, his silence made him complicit in the agency's endeavor. On the other hand, he had promised Brent that he would keep their conversation confidential. That promise put him in a bind. He couldn't talk with any of his colleagues about the agency's program without breaking that promise and potentially forcing the dismissal of both himself and Sanderson. For a moment, he entertained the wild thought of going straight to the director, Walter Beedel Smith, and begging him to abandon the recruitment scheme. He got along well with Smith and thought he might be able to convince him that what the agency was doing was beyond the pale. But with sober reconsideration, he realized he was being naïve and that such a move would prove a fool's errand, also undoubtedly leading to his and Brent's dismissal.

David spent the next several days in emotional and physical agony. He couldn't sleep, had to force himself to eat, and became even more haggard. Finally, after another sleepless night, he came to a decision. He could no longer work for the agency and had to resign in protest of its policy of recruiting ex-Nazis.

But before he took this step, there was another option to consider. A few months earlier, he had met a member of the Israeli mission to the United States at one of those diplomatic cocktail parties in Georgetown that he usually avoided like the plague. His name was Moshe Levinson, a political officer at the embassy who was about David's age and as committed as he was to trying to track down and bring to justice Nazi war criminals.

David and Moshe began to meet for the occasional dinner and quickly established a close friendship. It didn't take long for David to reveal to the Israeli official his frustrations with what he saw as the failure of the U.S. government, the Nuremburg trials notwithstanding, to pursue more aggressively the ex-Nazis who had escaped justice. In the course of their conversations, Moshe hinted rather broadly that if David's frustrations reached an intolerable level, he would be most welcome as a citizen of the new State of Israel. There, he assured David, no obstacles would be put in his way. Instead, he would be eagerly accepted into the ranks of those dedicated to finding, exposing, and punishing the war criminals who had been involved in the Holocaust.

On the Friday after David had met with Brent Sanderson, he sat down for lunch with Moshe Levinson at an out-of-the-way restaurant near American University. When he arrived a few minutes after noon, the smells of spilled beer and grease filled his nostrils as soon as he opened the door. On the jukebox, Tony Bennett was singing "Cold, Cold Heart." David wondered if this was some kind of omen.

Moshe was waiting for him in a booth in the back corner. David shook his hand and settled in across the table. There wasn't much of a crowd and the chances of being overheard were slim. Nonetheless, right away David asked Moshe if they could speak in Hebrew in case anybody might pick up snatches of their conversation. Moshe agreed.

When David looked at Moshe it seemed almost like viewing himself in the mirror. His Israeli friend had the same curly brown hair, sad brown eyes, and slim build. Like David, he was soft-spoken and reflective. With his horn-rimmed glasses, he looked more the rumpled scholar than the polished diplomat he was. He had once told David that if the Germans had not invaded his native Poland, he had planned to study philosophy and become a university professor. But behind Moshe's benign and gentle appearance was plenty of toughness. As a teenager, Moshe had participated in the Warsaw uprising against the Nazi occupation. He had been among the fortunate few to escape, ultimately ending up in Palestine. There he had taken part in the fighting against the British and the Arabs, suffering some serious wounds in the process.

David struggled to begin. What he was about to do represented the most momentous decision of his life. He had faced many tough choices before in Spain and in Argentina. But they had all been in the service of his country, a country he had risked his life for many times. He considered himself a loyal and patriotic American and had a deep love for his homeland. But he also had a strong sense of his Jewish identity and a profound emotional commitment to the new state that had been created out of the ashes of the Holocaust. Now he was about to betray one to serve the other.

David could see that Moshe sensed his anguish. In an effort to get him to relax, the Israeli tried to lighten the mood.

"I've never been here before David," he said, taking a glance around the down-at-the-heels establishment. "What do you recommend? What's the specialty of the house? Any good wines available?"

That produced a slight smile from David. "I don't think *any* wines are available Moshe. This is strictly a beer and whiskey kind of place."

At that moment, a waiter came over and deposited some grease-stained menus in front of them. "Anything to drink gentlemen?" he asked.

"I'll have a National Bohemian," Moshe replied, requesting the most popular beer in the Washington area.

"Just water for me," David said. Then, after the waiter left, "So Moshe, I guess you are adapting to the local customs."

The Israeli smiled and shrugged. "When in Rome…"

David returned the smile, but then his face turned somber. "Listen Moshe, I have something important to…"

Moshe held up his hand. "Let's wait until we order so that we won't be interrupted."

David nodded in agreement. They chatted about this and that while the waiter brought their drinks and took their orders, vegetable soup and a salad for David, a cheeseburger for Moshe.

Once their orders arrived, David ignored his food. Taking a deep breath, he told Moshe about the rumors concerning the CIA recruiting ex-Nazis, the confirmation of those rumors by Brent Sanderson, and his decision to ask the Israelis to take him in as a citizen where he believed he could do the most good. Moshe had told him that a few months earlier the Israeli government had created an organization called the Mossad, which coordinated the new state's intelligence services much in the way of the CIA. An important part of its mission was the locating and bringing to justice of Nazi war criminals. David suggested that he very much wanted to be part of that mission. With his background he might prove a valuable addition to the new intelligence service.

Moshe listened intently as David spoke, taking small bites from his cheeseburger and small sips of his beer. He kept his expression neutral, nodding on occasion. By the time David had finished his recitation Moshe had cleaned his plate and drained his glass. After a long interval, he said, "Listen David. I know how difficult this is for you and I…"

At that moment, their waiter arrived to clear their plates. When he noticed that David had not touched his soup or his salad, he asked, "Anything wrong with the food sir?"

"No," David responded. "I'm just not very hungry." But then, as the waiter was removing his plates, he said, "Wait a minute. Bring me what my friend had. A cheeseburger and a National Bo – and add some fries."

Moshe looked at David in astonishment. After the waiter left, David said, "You know. For some reason, all of a sudden I am starving."

After bottling up his secrets for so long, unable to confide in anyone, finally letting it all out provided a catharsis that seemed to bring David new energy. Whatever the response from Moshe at least he had shared his thoughts and worries with someone else. The cards had been laid on the table and David would just have to wait and see how the game played out.

"As I was saying David," Moshe resumed. "I know how difficult this is for you. And I appreciate the fact that you have trusted me with this information." Moshe paused for a moment, considering carefully what he would say next. "We have been picking up some of the same rumors, but have not been able to confirm them. Now we can. And that is extremely valuable intelligence for us. But the question we have to ask is how best to use it? And to answer that, I have to consult my superiors."

David's face fell in disappointment. "I know that you have taken an enormous risk," Moshe continued, "and made a monumental decision. But right now I cannot make any promises. If I did, without official blessing, and somehow there was an adverse decision on your request, well that would make a difficult situation even worse for you. I hope you understand."

David nodded. "Sure Moshe. We're both professionals. I understand completely. I just hope I don't have to wait too long for you and the people at the embassy to come to a decision. I don't think I can take much more of this uncertainty."

Moshe nodded in sympathy. "I know David. I know. But I'm not sure I can make any promises on that score either. This is something really big we are talking about. The embassy will have to contact the government. The prime minister will have to be notified. The diplomatic consequences of all this are enormous. Just try to be patient. One thing I can promise is that I shall do all I can to make sure your interests are looked after. And as soon as I receive the go ahead to let you know what has been decided I'll get in touch with you at once."

"Okay Moshe," David said. "I'll try to be patient." Then he chuckled, "I guess I really don't have any choice do I?"

Moshe simply shrugged. When the waiter brought David his order, he ate everything on his plate and downed his beer in deep gulps. Whether it was the last meal of a condemned man or a congratulatory feast to celebrate a new start in life remained to be seen. Whatever it was, David's appetite was definitely back.

CHAPTER TWELVE

February 27, 1950 – Washington, D.C.

Over the next week, David Friedman began to return to normal. After his lunch with Moshe, he called his office to say he was taking the remainder of the day off. Then he went straight to his apartment where he slept like a baby for eighteen hours, awakening rested and ravenous. Back at the office, he found he could now focus more clearly on his work and even started to crack jokes at staff meetings. His colleagues noticed the change and asked what had caused the turnaround. Thanking them for their concern, David gave them a vague answer that he had been going through some personal difficulties outside of the office and that they were now resolved.

While that was part of the truth it wasn't the whole truth. Nothing had yet been resolved. But for some reason, David, usually pessimistic by nature, felt a sense of optimism bordering on euphoria. He had convinced himself that he had made the right decision in contacting Moshe and that things would turn out for the best. In his more sober moments, he thought to himself, a psychiatrist would probably describe his attitude as delusional. Nonetheless, in the course of a few days he had gained back much of the weight he had lost, found no difficulty in sleeping, and felt a gradual easing of the pain in his stomach.

A week after his lunch with Moshe, David received a phone call at home from the Israeli. David knew that his office phone was tapped, either by the agency or the Soviets or both, and suspected the same held true at his apartment. While David wanted dearly to get the news, good or bad, as soon as he heard Moshe's voice over the phone, he knew he would have to wait. Moshe set up another lunch for the following day, making it appear no more than a normal social engagement between two friends.

They agreed to meet at the same restaurant. This time, David arrived first, taking the same booth in the back. Once again, there wasn't much of a crowd. David was more relaxed than during his previous visit, but he still drummed his fingers nervously on the table. This time the jukebox played Les Paul and Mary Ford's "How High Moon." Another omen? The same waiter approached with a single menu, but David waved him off, saying he was meeting a friend.

A few minutes later, the friend came through the door. But, to David's surprise, Moshe was not alone. Accompanying him was an exceedingly attractive female. As they approached the booth, David could not take his eyes from her as he registered her features – wavy black hair to her shoulders, full lips, a pert nose and chin, and startling green eyes. He guessed that she was in her late twenties.

Moshe, who could not help but notice David gawking at his companion, made the introduction: "David Friedman, meet Sarah Feldman."

Sarah Feldman extended her hand. For a moment David froze. Then, surreptitiously wiping his palm against his trousers, he took her hand in his and squeezed gently. "Very pleased – and surprised – to meet you," David blurted out, his cheeks beginning to redden.

Sarah Feldman smiled and removed her trench coat. Underneath, she was wearing a gray wool dress that hugged her trim figure. Her only jewelry was a silver lapel pin and a small gold watch with a black leather band. Trying not to be too obvious, David was inordinately pleased to see no wedding ring on her hand.

Hanging their coats on the hooks at the corner of the booth, they slid into the bench opposite David, Moshe on the inside Sarah on the outside. David was desperate to get the conversation started and discover what decisions had been made. Reading his thoughts, Moshe held up a hand. “Let’s order first David. We have a lot to discuss and might as well do it on a full stomach.”

David was about to object but realized it would do little good. Moshe would tell him what he needed to tell him when he was ready to, not before. He simply nodded and beckoned the waiter over so they could place their orders. David and Moshe asked for the same beers, cheeseburgers, and fries they had had before, the waiter absorbing their order with a knowing smile. Sarah asked for a tuna fish sandwich and a salad along with a coca cola.

While there was no one nearby, they again spoke in Hebrew. Before their food arrived, David asked Sarah the obvious: “Are you with the embassy Sarah?”

“Yes I am. But rather new I’m afraid. I just arrived the day before yesterday.”

David was about to continue when Moshe interrupted. “Sarah’s posting is a little complicated David. Let’s hold off until later. Then I’ll explain everything.”

David tried to hide his annoyance. The waiting game was sorely trying his patience. Even the most innocuous questions seemed to be off limits. They descended into safe topics like the weather and the current political gossip in Washington, of which there seemed to be an endless supply.

When their food came, David was tempted to swallow it down as quickly as possible so that they could get to the heart of the matter they were there to discuss. But Moshe and Sarah set the pace, continuing the rambling conversation while taking tiny bites of their sandwiches. Reluctantly, he followed suit, realizing that he was in danger of reigniting his stomach pain if he did not.

Finally, they finished. When the waiter took their plates, Moshe and David asked for coffee and Sarah tea. Once the steaming cups were delivered, Moshe finally got down to business.

Keeping his voice low, he looked David squarely in the eye and delivered the news that would determine his fate one way or the other. “Well my friend, the news you gave me last week stirred up quite a commotion.” David nodded. “In the embassy we have talked about nothing else for days. In Tel Aviv the prime minister and the cabinet put the matter at the top of the agenda and have been wrestling with just how to respond. What we have collectively come up with is this." David braced himself. "*We don't think you should leave the agency.*"

"But Moshe..." David began with a note of panic in his voice, a look of deep disappointment on his face.

The Israeli held up his hand, palm out. "Hear me out my friend. Hear me out." David's shoulders slumped, but he quietly waited for what would come next. "Here's our reasoning," Moshe continued, sounding much like the professor he once wanted to be giving a lecture to a befuddled student, "On the one hand, we would gladly accept you as an Israeli citizen and there would be no problem getting you assigned to the Mossad. We could always use another hand in the effort to deal with Nazi war criminals. But on the other hand, we already have many people at work on that. And you, my friend, are in a unique position to help us. If you stay with the CIA, you would have access to the kind of information that could be most helpful to us. Whatever you could find out about this program to recruit and relocate ex-Nazis in the United States would be of invaluable assistance. In Tel Aviv, you would be one of many. Here, you would be our most precious resource."

David thought the sales pitch was getting a bit heavy and was about to interrupt. But Moshe again raised his hand. "Let me finish David. As I am sure you can appreciate, the news you delivered puts the Israeli government in a bind. We are appalled that you – that is, the agency – would consider giving asylum to these monsters. But if we were to expose the plan, what would be the consequences? The CIA would simply deny the accusation and the relationship between Israel and the United States would be put under great strain. We desperately need U.S. support if we are to survive, so the diplomatic questions involved are extremely touchy. Moreover, if the matter were to become public, you yourself might be in the crosshairs. We don't want you to be put in danger."

David felt a chill run up his spine. He began to realize that for all his agonizing, he had not considered all of the possibilities of his decision to inform Moshe of the ex-Nazi relocation plan. His Israeli friend was suggesting that if the leaking of such sensitive information was traced to him and the plan became public, being fired from the agency would be the least of his worries. He could face significant prison time at best or death for treason at worst.

Moshe seemed to read his thoughts. "So what we have is a situation where neither side wants to make this nefarious plan public: The Israeli government because it would greatly complicate the crucial relationship with the U.S. and the U.S. government, namely the CIA, because they don't want the American people – or the Soviets – to know what they are up to."

Moshe paused to let David absorb what had been laid before him. Sarah had remained silent. But her expression was one of sympathy and understanding for the new dilemmas that David now confronted.

Finally, David said with more than a touch of sarcasm, "So what you are telling me Moshe is that the Israeli government wants me to be a spy for the Mossad within the CIA."

When Moshe responded, David could detect some of the toughness behind the Israeli's gentle manner. There was a look of resolve in his eyes and some harshness in the tone of his voice. "Remember David, you came to us with this information and offered to do what you could to be helpful to the State of Israel. And we have decided that what we have suggested is the way you can be most helpful. What you ultimately choose to do, of course, is entirely up to you."

Sarah appeared ready to interrupt, perhaps to soften the tone. But Moshe gave her a warning look and she remained silent.

David, feeling a bit like a scolded schoolboy, took some time to reply. "Assuming I were to agree Moshe, just how would this work? Would I be reporting directly to you? And do you expect me to provide any and all information you request?"

Moshe looked at David like a fisherman who had seen the hook set in the big catch he wanted to reel in. "Fair questions David," Moshe began his tone now less harsh. "First, you will be reporting to Sarah here. That's why I brought her along; so you two could get acquainted."

Sarah nodded and smiled. "I am looking forward to working with you David. I think we'll make a good team."

David said nothing in response, feeling that he was being pushed into a corner with no way out. *Had the Israelis brought in this beauty to influence him?* He had no doubt that they had.

"As for me David," Moshe said. "I have been reassigned and will be leaving by the end of next week. So you and Sarah can make the necessary arrangements for the transfer of information. Second, we don't expect you to be – what should we call it? – 'an all-around spy.' We just expect information on this ex-Nazi relocation plan. That's it. Nothing more."

David had his doubts on that score, but kept them to himself. "Well Moshe," he said. "I have a lot to think about. Give me some time before I make a decision one way or the other."

"One more thing David," he said. "If you decide that you don't want to help us by staying on at the agency and still want to resign and move to Israel that possibility remains on the table. We can do that for you." The way Moshe said it clearly indicated it was not the option he wanted David to choose.

Sarah sweetened the pot. "And David," she said. "If at any time after we begin to work together you change your mind, we'll make sure you will be able to settle in Israel no questions asked."

"Okay," David said. "I'll think it over. When do you want an answer?"

"That's up to you my friend. Entirely up to you. You have my number at the embassy as well as my home number." Then, taking out a card, he passed it over to Sarah. "Why don't you give him your home number as well?"

Sarah took out a pen and wrote her number on the back of the card. Handing the card to David, she said, "Feel free to call me at any time, even if it's just to talk."

"Thanks," David said. "I just might do that."

CHAPTER THIRTEEN

February 28, 1950 – Washington, D.C.

David had taken Sarah up on her offer. After a restless night, he called her the day after their lunch and asked if they could meet. She seemed a little surprised to have heard from him so soon, but agreed to meet him that night for dinner.

It was a quiet Sunday in Washington and many restaurants were closed. But David knew of a small bistro not far from his apartment in Georgetown that was open. They arranged to meet there at six. David was already at a table in the back when Sarah arrived, her cheeks flushed from the cold. David rose and helped her with her coat and held her chair for her as she took her seat.

"Sorry I'm late," she said, struggling to catch her breath. "I'm still getting to know my way around. I got a little lost."

David nodded in understanding. "I know. It takes a while to get the lay of the land."

A waitress appeared with menus and asked if they would like something to drink. When Sarah hesitated, David said, "If you like French wines, they have some good choices here. Perhaps we could share a bottle."

"I adore French wines," Sarah said with a warm smile.

David took that as a "yes" and ordered a bottle of Bordeaux.

While the waitress fetched their wine, David asked Sarah if this was her first visit to Washington.

"I came once before as part of a trade delegation. But we spent most of our time cooped up in a hotel and really didn't get a chance to see the city. I'm looking forward to being here and taking in the sights."

David did not miss the opening. "Well, if you'd like Sarah, I'd be glad to show you around."

"That would be wonderful David. I would like that very much."

"It's settled then," David said. Opening his menu as Sarah did the same, he said, "You'll find the food here is a lot better than the place where we met for lunch. They have a French chef and he really knows his stuff."

Sarah chuckled. "That will be a pleasant change."

The waitress returned with the wine and poured them each a glass. They touched their goblets and took a sip. "This is really, really good," Sarah said, her green eyes sparkling with surprise and pleasure.

"I'm glad you like it. I'm not exactly a connoisseur, but a friend of mine recommended it and I trust his judgment."

After they had given their meal orders to the waitress there was an awkward silence. Sarah broke it: "Well David, what would you like to talk about? I presume you are still wrestling with whether to work with us or not. If so…"

David cut her off. "Yes. You're right. I am still wrestling with it. But I thought that if I am to be working with you, I should at least get to know a little bit about you before I say yes."

Sarah nodded. "That's perfectly understandable David. I would feel the same if I were in your shoes."

The story she told him was not unlike that of other Israelis he had met. Sarah had been born into a wealthy Jewish family in Paris. Her father was a successful banker, her mother an accomplished pianist who performed with the Paris symphony. They lived in a well-to-do neighborhood and had many friends, both Jewish and gentile. When the Germans invaded France and were on the verge of capturing Paris, her parents, fearing the worst, sent Sarah, who was then fifteen years old, and her two younger brothers to live with an aunt and uncle in

England. Three years later she received the horrible news that her father and mother, who had chosen to stay in Paris and participate in the Resistance, had been sent to a concentration camp, never to be heard from again. When Sarah related this part of the story her voice was calm but her eyes reflected the still painful memory.

In England, Sarah threw herself into her studies, ultimately graduating from the London School of Economics. She was tempted to stay in a country where she now felt at home and where she had bright career prospects. But when those Jews who had escaped the Holocaust began to migrate to Palestine, she determined to join their ranks. With the blessings of the aunt and uncle who had sheltered her and her brothers, she made her way to the new homeland and became a permanent resident. Her two brothers soon followed. Her fluency in English along with her academic background gave her the necessary credentials to attract the Ministry of Foreign Relations and she eagerly signed on. The posting to Washington, she told David, where she was replacing Moshe as the junior political officer in the embassy, was her first overseas assignment.

David had some questions in the back of his mind, but was reluctant to ask them. While he accepted most of her story, he suspected that Sarah was hiding things from him. It was too much of a coincidence that she appeared on the scene only days after he had approached Moshe. There had to be some connection. But he was enjoying her company too much to break the mood with probing questions. If the Mossad had cooked up a plan to have a beautiful, intelligent, charming woman entice him to serve their purposes it was working. Even if his suspicions turned out to be accurate, his heart was telling him that he needed to keep seeing Sarah regardless of whatever decision he ultimately made about working for the Israelis.

By the time Sarah had finished her life story, their meals had arrived. Over dessert, Sarah asked David about his background and career. While he spoke, she nodded at the appropriate intervals and shook her head in disbelief when he sketched in the details of his "little adventure" in Argentina with Pete Benton.

When David paid the bill, he asked the waitress to call a cab for Sarah. She was staying at an apartment the embassy had rented for her in Northwest Washington, about two miles away. She had taken the trolley to the restaurant and had missed a connection, which had caused her to be delayed. David told her that late on a Sunday night it was better and safer to take a cab, which he insisted on paying for. When the cab arrived, David gave the driver Sarah's address and handed over a ten dollar bill that more than covered the fare. As he held the rear door open for Sarah, she took off her glove and offered David her hand. "I'm glad you called me David," she said. "I really enjoyed the evening."

David still harbored the lingering suspicion that Sarah was playing some sort of role, but chose to believe that her sentiment was sincere. He held her hand in his for a few seconds. "I'm glad. I did too," he said. Then he let go of her hand and Sarah slid into the backseat of the cab. David closed the door behind her and as the cab took off, she gave him a wave and a smile. He turned and walked back to his apartment, ignoring the late February chill and the fine mist that was falling. His thoughts were a jumble of mixed emotions and he still was no closer to making a final decision. But of one thing he was certain: he wanted above all to spend more time with Sarah Feldman.

David waited a few days and then called Sarah for another meeting. They had dinner at the same bistro and then spent Saturday evening seeing a movie. On Sunday, taking advantage of some unusually mild weather for early March, they strolled along the Mall and around the Tidal Basin. Sarah admired the monumental structures of the capital, her first chance to see them close at hand. Sitting on a bench across from the Jefferson Memorial David told Sarah that he had decided to accept the Israeli offer. He would stay on at the CIA and report to her all that he learned about the agency's plan to recruit ex-Nazis, making it clear that was the *only* information that he would forward. Looking across the choppy gray waters of the Basin, he glanced at the statue of Jefferson, who seemed to be looking directly at him. In the back of his mind, he wondered if the Founding Father would approve of the course he was taking or would instead view him as a traitor to his country. He hoped that the sophisticated and complex third president would understand the motivations that drove him.

"Oh David," Sarah said, her eyes lighting up with pleasure when he told her what he had decided, "I am so glad." For a moment, David thought she was going to hug him. Not that he would have minded. But then her expression immediately turned serious. "I know how difficult this decision has been for you. And I promise you that we shall do all we can to protect you and to look after your best interests. You have my word on that." Than after a pause, she added, "And I – we – don't want you to take any unnecessary risks. As you, better than anyone, know, this is an extremely delicate and sensitive mission. I am sure you appreciate what the consequences will be if it is revealed that you are working for us."

David nodded. "Yes I do Sarah. Indeed I do. And I'll try to do everything I can to make this work, without, as you say, taking any 'unnecessary risks.'"

Even though David had made his decision, over the next few weeks he still experienced mixed emotions. He firmly believed that the agency's plan to recruit ex-Nazis was immoral, illegal, and went against everything he had devoted his life and career to since the world war began. He also felt he had a duty and an obligation to assist the new State of Israel however he could. And, of course, there was Sarah. As they continued to work together, his feelings for her deepened and he sensed that she was beginning to feel the same towards him. Whatever his rationales and justifications for his actions, however, he could not brush aside the fact that he was betraying his oath when he joined the CIA. In any court of law he could be charged with treason.

During the next few months, certain developments helped clarify things for David and assuage some of the guilt he felt. Despite his best efforts to gain information on the ex-Nazi recruitment plan, it remained a tightly-held secret. Even the water-cooler chatter on the subject died away. As the weeks passed, he grew increasingly frustrated. He thought about trying to approach Sanderson again, but was afraid that bringing up the subject would arouse his boss's suspicions. At one point, he suggested to Sarah that he might try to break into the office of one of the deputy directors who he thought might be involved in the program to see if he could find anything. Sarah scotched this idea at once, arguing that it clearly represented one of the "unnecessary risks" they had sworn to avoid. Even if carried out successfully it might turn up nothing.

By the end of the summer, it appeared that David's career as a spy for the Israelis within the CIA might come to an end. The fact that he had failed to provide anything further on the ex-Nazi recruitment plot prompted a decision at the highest levels of the Israeli government to shut the operation down. The Mossad had determined that the damage to Israeli-U.S. relations if David's spying were discovered outweighed any advantages that might accrue if he were able to gain further details.

There was also the question of just what exactly the government could do if such information became available. Sarah told David that there had been considerable debate on this subject. There were some who favored exposing the plan and condemning it either outright with a government statement or through leaks to the press. Others suggested that if David were able to get hold of names and locations of those ex-Nazis recruited, perhaps they could be "neutralized" one way or the other. But that would require Israeli action on American soil, action that most considered off-limits. Finally, it was determined that the best course was to thank David for what he had done and ask him to cease his efforts on their behalf.

But then a fortuitous twist of fate intervened. Just as Sarah was about to tell him of the government's decision, David had come into possession of new information that would keep his career as an Israeli source within the CIA alive. In the course of debriefing field agents in Syria, Turkey, and Egypt, David had been told that various Nazi war criminals had been seen living in the capitals of those three countries. He had all but given up hope that this kind of information would become available. But now he had it. David had gone to Brent Sanderson and asked for his permission to pursue the matter further. Brent agreed. David pressed the agents to get names and exact locations and report back to him.

By mid-summer, David had a list of more than twenty ex-Nazis living in Damascus, Istanbul, and Cairo. He then went back to Brent with an audacious plan. He knew, he told his boss, that the agency couldn't do anything about the war criminals he had located. There were too many diplomatic and legal complications involved. Left unspoken, too, was the agency's own plan to recruit such men for its own purposes. An aggressive campaign dealing with ex-Nazis living in the Middle East would run counter to that effort. But, David, suggested, what if he gave the *Israelis* the information he had gathered? They would then be free to do whatever they determined to deal with men they were trying to identify and hunt down.

Brent was taken aback. He was about to reject the idea out of hand, but David prevailed on him to give the idea some thought. The United States was committed to assisting the new State of Israel. What better way than to help them track down war criminals? Moreover, David added, in light of what the agency was planning to do with the ex-Nazi recruitment scheme, helping the Israelis in their own efforts to mete out justice to the members of the Third Reich who had either directed or had participated in the Holocaust might balance the scales a bit. Finally, doing a favor for the Israelis on a matter of such vital importance to the new state might make them more amenable in the future to aid the U.S. in trying to navigate the ever-dangerous shoals of the Middle East.

Brent looked dubious, but reluctantly gave in to David's pleading. He promised that he would consult with the director and get back to him. He also warned him not to get his hopes up.

A few days later, David was in the middle of drafting a report on Syria when Sanderson's secretary Julie called him. Brent wanted to meet with him, right now if convenient. With his heart thumping hard in his chest, David told her he would be right over. As he stepped out of the relative cool of his building into the ninety degree heat and humidity of an August day, David barely noticed. Even if it had been the middle of winter, he probably would have been sweating by the time he got to Brent's office.

Straightening his tie and running his fingers through his hair, David knocked on Sanderson's outer door. Julie told him to come in and after a quick "good afternoon" held open the door to Brent's office. After David had passed the threshold she gently closed it behind him.

Brent was seated behind his desk, wreathed in smoke from his pipe. Without a word, he gestured for David to take a chair, his expression inscrutable. David was about to initiate the conversation when Brent held up his hand palm out to silence him. Then, with the hint of a smile dancing across his lips, he said, "Well David, the director has agreed to your plan. We need to hash out the details, but you have the green light to proceed."

For a moment, David was speechless. "That's great Brent. Just great," he blurted out. "But how did you…?"

Again Brent held up his hand. "How did I convince the director to go along?"

David nodded. "Well my friend, I'm as surprised as you obviously are." Brent sat back in his chair, glancing up at the ceiling with a look of wonderment on his face. Then, with his gaze fixed steadily on David, resumed: "I laid out the arguments you presented. But, to be honest when the director asked me for my opinion I expressed my reservations. Sorry, but I'm afraid I wasn't your strongest advocate. I thought – and still think – that the whole idea of working closely with the Israelis on something that is of only tangential importance to our long-term national security interests could somehow backfire."

"You mean, if somehow the ex-Nazis we want to recruit found out we were working with the Israelis to locate their brethren in the Middle East, they would be reluctant to sign up?" David said with scarcely concealed disgust.

Brent looked uncomfortable and shifted in his chair. "Well, yes. That was a consideration. But there were others as well. However, we don't really need to go into these. Despite my lack of enthusiasm for your proposal, the director seemed to accept the arguments you made. However," Brent added, "we plan to keep you under a tight rein. If we think turning over information to the Israelis will compromise us in any way, we are going to shut you down immediately. Understood?"

"I understand Brent. I understand completely."

"Okay. That's settled," Brent said. "Now how do you plan to establish contact with the Israeli embassy?"

"That won't be a problem Brent. I already have a contact, one that I can trust totally."

David then told Brent about Sarah, spinning a tale that fudged the truth as to how they had met. Brent seemed to buy his story. They spent the next twenty minutes discussing the means by which the transfer of information would occur along with establishing the mechanisms to assure that no leaks or surprises would be sprung.

After wrapping up his meeting with Brent Sanderson, David returned to his office. He was as close to euphoric as he ever got. He immediately phoned Sarah and they arranged to meet for dinner. He didn't say anything about the good news, but she could probably tell from his unusually chipper tone that things had gone well. That night, they celebrated the start of their new collaboration with a bottle of champagne. By this time, the line between their professional and their personal relationship had blurred. After dinner Sarah spent the night with David in his apartment. And it was not for the first time.

CHAPTER FOURTEEN

June 8, 1951 – Washington, D.C.

Over the next nine months, David fed Sarah and the Israelis a steady stream of information about former Nazis who had found refuge in the Middle East. Some of it overlapped with material that the Israelis had gathered on their own, but often added new details and more up-to-date status reports. In other instances, David was able to supply new names and addresses that had slipped under the Israeli radar. The Israelis had not yet acted on the intelligence David had given them. But he knew that it was only a matter of time before they did. Fortunately, there had been none of the complications or embarrassments that had preoccupied Brent Sanderson and the director. So far, all had gone smoothly. In fact, just last month the director had called David into his office and congratulated him on the success of his operation.

Sitting at his desk, frantically trying to finish up his report by five o'clock, David took a moment to reflect on the past and the future. The last nine months, he thought, had been among the happiest in his life. He was doing something valuable and useful to further the cause to which he had dedicated his adult life and career. And then, of course, there was Sarah, his first real love. While she was often busy with her embassy duties, every minute they spent together was precious and fulfilling. David knew that he wanted to spend the rest of his life with her and believed that she felt the same.

When he contemplated the future soberly, however, there were some clouds on the horizon that made the picture a little less rosy. The director's approval of his plan to inform the Israelis about the ex-Nazis in the Middle East had gone a long way toward lessening the feelings of guilt he had over contacting them in the first place. With the perspective of time, he also believed that he had done the right thing in that instance. While he had betrayed his oath to the agency, he had served the greater good. But the fact that the agency was continuing with its ex-Nazi recruitment plan still frustrated him. And there was little he could do about it. He faced the same dilemma as before. Since he was not even supposed to know about the scheme, he couldn't object to higher ups without exposing Brent Sanderson. *And even if he did object, so what?* From the little he had been able to gather, the director and his staff had determined to proceed. Whatever arguments he might make to the contrary would be brushed aside. And even though he was continuing to do good work in what he considered a just cause, his affiliation with an agency employing the very men who had sought to destroy all Jews still ate away at him.

When he had talked with Sarah about these matters, she had reminded him of something he already knew but still had difficulty in accepting. In the field of intelligence, few things were black and white. Instead, most issues were in various shades of gray. Ultimately, pragmatism trumped idealism in almost every instance. In David's perfect world, the CIA would not be recruiting ex-Nazis. Instead it would be doing everything it could to bring them to account for what they had done. But in the real world, the new Cold War world, that course of action, unfortunately, was seen by the agency as a luxury it could not afford. Sarah, who was as appalled as David was by the ex-Nazi recruitment program, nonetheless was able to view it more objectively. She understood Brent Sanderson's point that in a war, even a supposedly cold one you had to employ every weapon at your disposal.

Another, smaller cloud on the horizon was Sarah. Even though every outward indication pointed to the sincerity of her feelings for him, there lingered at the back of his mind the smallest seed of doubt that perhaps she was playing a part to keep him viable as an Israeli asset.

She had more or less confirmed the fact that her sudden appearance as Moshe's replacement had not been a coincidence. But she assured him that over time she had come to love and respect David for who he was, not for what he did for Israel – although, she said with a chuckle, "that certainly didn't hurt." David joined in her laughter, but from time to time he would replay that conversation to see if he could find hidden meanings.

Another seed of doubt was planted when David had suggested a few months ago that perhaps he should quit the agency and the two of them move to Israel. Sarah seemed momentarily surprised, but recovered quickly. "But darling," she told him, "you are doing such valuable work for us now. I understand your frustrations. But the intelligence you are giving us is pure gold. It would be a shame to stop now. Besides, I can't just pick up and leave for Israel at a moment's notice. I have my own career to think about." When she saw his look of disappointment, she added, "Of course, if anything should happen to – what should I say? – *complicate* your situation, then we can certainly reconsider the option of getting you to Israel." David noticed the "getting *you* to Israel" rather than "getting *us* to Israel," but let it pass.

David's angst was deepened by the fact that he could not discuss his concerns with anyone else. He knew that he often let his imagination run away with him and probably was exaggerating his doubts about Sarah's sincerity. Talking things over with a third party would help clarify things for him. *But who?* Certainly no one at the agency. His parents had died a few years ago and he had no close relatives. He toyed with the idea of seeing a psychiatrist, but the agency frowned on that for a number of reasons. When Pete Benton showed up in Washington, David seriously thought about opening up to him. He had complete confidence in Pete's discretion and trusted him to be a sympathetic and helpful sounding board. But he also still harbored some feelings of regret for getting Pete involved in a plan that almost cost him his life. He was reluctant to impose further on a friend who these days had other things to worry about than David's love life.

David pushed these ruminations aside and went back to his report. He finished by four-thirty, well before the deadline. Walking over to

Brent Sanderson's office, he ran into a couple of other analysts clutching their own folders. He wondered if he looked as tired as they did, working feverishly at the end of the week to get their assignments done and on time, almost like students submitting papers to a professor. David had often thought the parallel was not too far off the mark. They entered Brent's office one after the other and turned their reports over to Julie, who jotted down their arrival and completion of duties in a small notebook.

David glanced at his watch as he left the administration building. A quarter to five. He had plenty of time to get to Georgetown and prepare for his long weekend with Sarah, a weekend that, whatever his reservations he hoped would bind them together for life.

CHAPTER FIFTEEN

June 8, 1951 – Washington, D.C.

I got back to the Justice Department at two. Tim O'Rourke was busy at his desk when I opened the office door.

"How was lunch?" he asked. "David okay?" Tim had met David soon after we all had arrived in Washington. Despite their diverse backgrounds they had hit it off at once. Irish Catholics and Jews in New York were not natural friends and allies. But their common working-class backgrounds and wartime experiences drew Tim and David together. The six of us, María and I, David and Sarah, and Tim and one of his innumerable girlfriends had begun to see a lot of each other over the past few months, sharing plenty of laughs and good times.

"Yeah. Or as good as David gets," I replied. Tim gave me a knowing look. "And things are getting pretty serious with Sarah. David says they have an 'understanding' that marriage is in the cards."

I didn't think David would mind me sharing this bit of information with Tim. It was hardly a surprise.

Tim nodded and smiled. "That sounds like David. An 'understanding.' Well, I hope it works out for him. Sarah is a terrific girl."

"Yeah. I hope so too." Thinking of my marriage to María, I said, "He deserves to have some happiness in his life."

Tim considered marriage akin to a prison sentence. But he recognized that even if it was not for him, the right wife *could* actually make a person happy. "Yes, he certainly does," Tim said.

We spent a few minutes chewing the fat and then turned to work. We had piles of paper on our desk, much of it reports from confidential informants on the inner workings of the Costello crime family. Our job was to determine what could be most useful to the Kefauver Committee, trying to verify which accounts were credible and which were not. Some of the informants had been paid for their services and we often wondered if they weren't leading us on so they could stay on the payroll. Others were members of rival organizations whose motives for ratting on the Costello gang were suspect. Most reliable, we thought, were testimonies from victims of the gang's various extortion rackets, although they too might be exaggerated. What we were trying to do was to establish patterns that we could summarize and document for the committee's use, connecting those patterns to clear legal violations. It was sometimes tedious work, but rarely boring. Some of the accounts we read sounded more like excerpts from a lurid crime novel than real-life experiences, making them all the more chilling. Every so often I would see Tim shake his head and hear him grunt in disbelief at what he was reading. But the more we read, the more committed we became to doing what we could to at least put a crimp in Costello's operation if not bring it down in its entirety. Our goal was not only to make the public aware of the serious threat organized crime posed to our society but also, if possible, put the bosses in jail.

At four o'clock the task force met in the conference room. Joe Smathers wanted to brief us for the weekend. This was the first such Friday afternoon meeting since the task force had been assembled. Usually, we met on Mondays to see where we were and where we'd be going in the upcoming week. Since many of us put in time on Saturdays and Sundays, it didn't make much sense to have a Friday meeting unless something unusual came up. The attack on Ralph Turner clearly counted as "something unusual."

As we took our seats around the table, Joe nodded a greeting to each of us. Glancing around the room, I saw tired and somber faces. Even my ever-buoyant office-mate looked a bit bedraggled and down-at-the-mouth.

Joe knew what was on our minds without anyone needing to ask. "Gentlemen," he said in his slow southern drawl, "I'm afraid I have nothing to tell you about Ralph. His condition remains the same and we have no firm leads on who attacked him. The bureau is still digging but it is tough going."

We slumped a bit in our chairs and there were a few nervous coughs. "How about any of you? Any suspicious phone calls? Anything out of the ordinary?" Joe asked, his eyes scanning each of us. We all shook our heads.

"That's a relief," Joe said. "Maybe the FBI teams assigned to you and your families have done the job."

"How much longer will we have their protection?" Phil Davis, one of the Justice lawyers asked.

Tim, who was sitting to my left perked up and put his elbows on the table, waiting for Joe's response. Tim, the only bachelor in the bunch, was not happy having two FBI agents assigned to look after him. He felt perfectly capable of handling himself in any situation. But he knew that men with families could not afford to take the same risks so he had not openly complained when two bureau men were posted outside his apartment. But he chafed at their presence and would not be at all unhappy to see them removed.

"That's hard to say Phil," Joe replied. "Director Hoover has promised to keep his men on watch until we can be reasonably sure that the threat to the rest of us has been removed. Of course, the bureau has limited resources so we cannot expect the surveillance to continue indefinitely," he added.

Tim sat back in his chair and uttered a muffled sigh. Joe seemed to notice. Looking at Tim but addressing all of us, he said, "Look. I know that some of you would prefer to do without having two bureau guys sitting in a car outside your home twenty-four hours a day. I don't much care for it myself. But consider the alternative. We don't want what happened to Ralph to happen to any of you – or to your families. And remember, there is a lot more at stake than whatever might happen to any of us. We are doing important work here, work that is vital to the overall well-being of our society. And we can't let ourselves be intimidated by the kind of tactics these criminals have used so often in the past against helpless victims."

Joe took a breath, and then continued. "We should think of it as a war. A war we are fighting on the home front to confront and defeat the kind of gangsters we had to deal with in Europe and Asia." For the low-key Joe Smathers, this was the most emotional and impassioned I had ever seen him. He reminded me of my college football coach giving us a pep talk at half time.

Jim Franklin spoke up. "Yes Joe. We all agree. This is important work. Otherwise we wouldn't be here. But when I went to fight abroad, I left my wife and children behind, sure that they would be safe while I was gone. But this 'war' is different. Now my whole family is on the front lines." For a second, I thought Jim was going to tell us that he was taking Joe up on his offer to drop out of the task force in light of the attack on Ralph. But he just sat in his chair, his shoulders sagging, a dour expression on his face. I wondered how many of the rest of us around the table were sharing Jim's sentiments.

"You're absolutely right Jim," Joe responded. "I guess I got a little carried away there." Then looking around the table, he added, "What I said on Monday still goes. If anyone wants to be reassigned, just come to see me and we'll do it, no questions asked."

There was some uncomfortable shifting in seats and more nervous coughs. Finally, I said, "I can't speak for the others Joe, but I'm still on board. If we can't stand up to these thugs, who can?"

There were nods of agreement around the table, but I didn't sense a great deal of enthusiasm.

Joe seemed to appreciate my sentiments and gave me a quick smile. "Okay, then," he said, clearing his throat. "Now remember, each and every one of you. You have to stay alert. Just because you have the bureau watching over you doesn't mean you can relax your guard. Be sure to carry your gun with you when you are out on the street, even when taking out the garbage. I don't need to remind you that Ralph was attacked in his own driveway."

Several seconds of silence passed. Then George Wilson asked Joe, "I know it sounds out of place given the circumstances, but what about our softball game tomorrow? Do we go ahead?"

We were scheduled to play a team from the Treasury Department the next day at four in the afternoon. Six games into the season we were tied with the Treasury team for first place in our league, each with six wins. Prior to the attack on Ralph, we had looked forward to the upcoming game, eager for the challenge. Now, most of us had almost forgotten it had been scheduled.

"Absolutely George," Joe said. "Absolutely. We should try to stick to our normal routine as much as possible." Aside from keeping up morale, I suspected that Smathers, whose mild outward manner hid his fierce competitive nature, wanted very much to show Treasury who had the better team.

"Uh, one thing Joe," Greg Parker, one of the Justice lawyers interjected. "Who is going to play right field?"

Ralph Turner had been our regular right fielder. Obviously he would not be available. A couple of the other guys on the task force were going to be out of town for the weekend, which left us one man short.

"I don't know Greg," Joe said. "If any of you can find a pick-up replacement, let me know and I'll try to fit him in. I'd sure hate to forfeit for lack of a ninth man." Generally, the teams had to be composed only of departmental employees to avoid the recruitment of "ringers." However, the rules did allow for one substitute who did not fit that criterion. At the moment, none of us could think of such a recruit. But we promised Joe we would look for one between now and game time.

"One more thing before we adjourn," Joe said. "Three wives are coming in tomorrow for firearms training." María would be joined by the wives of Jim Franklin and Phil Davis. "If anybody else has a wife who wants to take part, there's still time to get her an appointment on the range."

There were no takers. As the meeting broke up, Tim tried to add a bit of levity to the somber proceedings. "I'd have my girlfriend enroll," he said with a grin, "but I'm not sure I want her to be 'armed and dangerous.' She's enough trouble as it is."

That brought a laugh from one and all, including the FBI agents. It probably wasn't that funny, but we were all looking for an excuse to lighten the mood. The prospect of our upcoming softball game had provided a momentary diversion. But the mention of our wives needing to acquaint themselves with weapons of self-defense once again brought home the seriousness of the threat we now faced.

CHAPTER SIXTEEN

June 8, 1951 – Washington, D.C.

María and I arrived at the Old Europe on Wisconsin Avenue at a quarter after seven. We had arranged to join Graciela and Roberto Walker there for dinner so that I could meet María's new friend and her husband, who had only recently returned from a business trip.

We had discussed beforehand what we could and could not tell them. Nothing about my "little adventure" in Argentina, sticking to the story line we had used for years when the question came up of how we had met. So far as my current job was concerned, we would keep to the basic facts with no discussion of what had happened to Ralph Turner. There was, however, no hiding the fact that I was working on the organized crime task force, something that was public knowledge and that María had already revealed to Graciela. And it seemed logical that the Walkers might well realize that my assignment carried certain risks. As if to underscore those risks, the FBI surveillance unit had followed our taxi and was parked on the curb across from the restaurant.

After some debate, we had selected the Old Europe for our dinner meeting. The décor was faux Bavarian, with stuffed deer heads and painted steins along the walls. The waitresses were all blonds, dressed in embroidered white blouses and flared black skirts. They tried to speak in affected German accents even if they came from Pennsylvania or West Virginia. The attempt at authenticity didn't quite come off, but the atmosphere was warm and friendly and the food quite good. We thought that the couple from Uruguay, where meat was abundant and provided the basis for almost every meal would enjoy the prime rib that was the restaurant's specialty.

We had expected that the Walkers would adhere to the Río de la Plata custom of being fashionably – sometimes outrageously – late. So even though we had told them we would meet at seven, we purposely delayed our arrival for fifteen minutes, calculating that we would still get there before our invited guests with time to spare.

Much to our surprise, the Walkers were already seated in a booth near the front when we walked through the door. María spotted them at once as Graciela waved to her. My wife's cheeks briefly reddened with embarrassment at *our* late arrival.

As we wound our way through the tables to the booth, the Walkers rose to greet us. "I'm so sorry we are late," María said as she and Graciela embraced and exchanged cheek kisses.

María was about to offer some sort of excuse – caught in traffic, Pete late from work, a last-minute phone call – but Graciela beat her to the punch. With a twinkle in her eye, she said laughingly in Spanish, "That's okay María. You thought we would be late, like all Uruguayans and Argentines. But, you see, we are trying to adapt to yanqui customs. In fact, would you believe it? We even got here ten minutes early!"

They both giggled. Then there was a brief awkward moment as María tried to choose the right protocol for introductions and the language in which they would be made. I decided to take the lead, hoping I was doing the right thing. "Hello Graciela," I said in Spanish. "I'm María's husband Pete and am very pleased to meet you."

Graciela extended her hand and bent forward for me to kiss her on the cheek. "Hello Pete. It is my pleasure. María has told me so much about you. And finally we get to meet."

Turning to María, Graciela introduced Roberto. "María," she said with a broad smile and a proud look, "this is my husband Roberto." Roberto and María then went through the same hand-shaking cheek-kissing ritual and exchanged the usual pleasantries. Once they had disengaged, Roberto turned to me and offered his hand. "Pete. So pleased to meet you," he said with a grin. "Same here Roberto," I replied, taking his hand and returning his firm grip.

After the introductions, we sat. I was against one wall facing Roberto across the table with María to my side facing her new-found friend. Graciela was as María had described her, an attractive woman in her early thirties. She looked enough like my wife that they might be mistaken for sisters. She had the same lustrous black hair, parted in the middle and falling in waves to her shoulders, sparkling dark eyes, and an olive complexion. She was a bit more slender than María and I judged an inch or two shorter. She was wearing a red and yellow print sleeveless sundress that I knew she had bought with María during a shopping expedition at Garfinkels. María wore something similar in green and blue. Graciela's arms were tanned and more muscular than I would have expected given her frame.

Roberto looked about as I suspected he would. He had a full head of glossy black hair slicked back from his forehead, ending in curls at the back of his neck. He was clean-shaven, although I could see some five o'clock shadow on his cheeks and chin. I guessed that he was an inch or two shorter than my six-two but like his wife seemed fit and athletic. I would not call him movie-star handsome, but he had rugged good looks. His nose looked as though it had been broken and then poorly re-set, but not so askew as to be particularly noticeable. His most distinctive feature was his light-blue, almost gray eyes, betraying his British heritage. Like me, he wore a light-weight sport coat, an open-necked dress shirt, and casual slacks. He viewed me across the table in a friendly manner but I saw some calculation taking place behind his blue-gray eyes as he sized me up.

Before we had a chance to begin conversing, a waitress arrived with menus. She introduced herself as Trudi, short for Gertrude, and asked if we would like to order cocktails. There was a moment of hesitation as the four of us looked at each other to see who would go first. I broke the ice and ordered a gin martini, my second of the day. María asked for a gin and tonic and Roberto and Graciela ordered the same.

Once the waitress had left to fetch our drinks, the next order of business was to decide which language to use. Roberto was fluent in

English, which he spoke with a British accent. Graciela's English was a work in progress, but she insisted that we converse in that language so she could improve her skills. And if she ran into trouble, there were the three of us to help translate.

With that out of the way, there was another awkward pause as we waited to see who would speak first. Again, I broke the ice. "Roberto," I said. "I want you to know how happy we both are to have the chance to get together with you and Graciela. Your wife and mine seem to have become fast friends. I can't tell you how pleased I am that circumstances have brought them together. It has meant a lot to us."

In similar situations, my wife had mentioned that I had not always gotten off on the right foot. But this time I seem to have hit the perfect note. Out of the corner of my eye I could see María beaming and nodding.

"María tells me," I continued, "that you are here in Washington representing a Uruguayan export-import company and plan to stay for an indefinite period. Isn't that somewhat unusual? Washington isn't a center of business activity, unless you count politics as a business. I would have thought New York or Chicago would be the more logical choices."

Whatever good will I had built up with María quickly eroded. I could hear her gasp as I spoke, undoubtedly thinking that I had crossed some sort of line. In my defense, it was a natural question to ask. While I had only been in D.C. for a few months, I did know that not that many commercial companies operated in the capital.

Roberto did not take offense. In fact, he bailed me out. "Yes Pete. A perfectly logical observation," he said in a pleasant tone. "But it so happens that my company, which exports agricultural products and imports manufactured goods has several contracts with the United States government. Therefore, because I speak English and have had previous experience here and in Europe, I was sent to Washington to make sure that all proceeds smoothly with these contracts. At least we hope all goes smoothly," he said with a grin. "And I am not the only one. There are representatives of other Latin American companies here doing the same thing."

What he said made sense. But I noticed that he had not mentioned the name of his company. I was about to ask that question when María gave me a gentle nudge in the ribs that said "Enough with the prosecutorial interrogation." I got the message and kept my mouth shut.

The waitress arrived with our drinks and asked if we were ready to order. As we hadn't even opened our menus, we asked her to come back in a few minutes while we decided.

We sipped our drinks and engaged in small talk. Roberto told me that his company had a small office in a four-story building on K Street. He and Graciela were renting an apartment just off Dupont Circle, which made it easy for him to walk to work. His main business was with the Departments of Agriculture and Commerce, also within walking distance or easy enough to get to by streetcar. He preferred to walk when he could as he needed the exercise.

While our wives were engrossed in their own conversation, Roberto bent his head forward and gestured for me to do the same. Lowering his voice, he whispered in English, "I can't begin to tell you how happy I am that Graciela and María have struck up a friendship. It's been a great relief. When we first arrived, Graciela was like a fish out of water – so depressed that I thought we would have to return to Uruguay. But meeting María, who by the way seems to be a wonderful woman, has been a lifesaver. I can't tell you how gratified I am that they have found one another. If they hadn't ..." For a few seconds his eyes moistened and there was a catch in his voice.

I nodded. "I understand Roberto. We've been through the same thing. And I'm just as grateful that fate brought the two of them together. It's been a lifesaver for me too."

Our wives, chattering away, appeared not to have overheard us. I interrupted their conversation with a suggestion that we look at our menus so we could order our food. I recommended we all try the prime rib, the specialty of the house. When Trudi reappeared at our table, I placed the requests for the four of us – prime rib medium rare, mashed potatoes, string beans, and a salad. We discussed sharing a bottle of wine, but I recommended the beer instead. It was a German brew that came in a large stein.

After Trudi left, we resumed our conversation. Graciela apparently had already informed Roberto how María and I had met in Buenos Aires so that particular question did not arise. "So Pete," Roberto said, "Graciela tells me that you are in Washington as part of a special task force for the Department of Justice looking into - how do you call it? – 'organized crime.' That must be very interesting work."

"Yes it is. Very interesting," I said.

"I've been reading about the Senate hearings in the paper. Is your group involved in that?"

I hesitated for a moment, debating what to say. There was no sense hiding the basic facts of our role in the proceedings as they were more or less well-known. But I didn't want to elaborate, so I kept my answer simple and straightforward. "Yes. Yes we are."

"I don't know much about this Frank Costello and his gang who are being investigated. We have something similar in our country, what we call a *mafia*, or a crime family. As you are probably aware, we have a large Italian immigrant population," Roberto said with what I detected as a slight note of disdain, "and while most of them are hard-working and honest there are a few who are criminals involved in extortion, gambling, and prostitution. Perhaps not operating on the scale I understand to be the case here, but a problem for us nonetheless. They are not very savory characters, violent bullies for the most part." Then he paused for a moment before asking, "Do you have any concerns that some of these criminals you are investigating might pose a danger to you personally or other members of your task force?"

I was momentarily caught off guard by his question and immediately wondered if somehow he knew about the attack on Ralph Turner. Reflexively, I touched the revolver under my left arm, hoping that the bulge and gesture went unnoticed. María stiffened next to me, and I saw Graciela looking at me keenly for my response. I put my paranoia aside and decided that Roberto's question was what anyone who heard what I was doing might ask. In fact, some of my friends in New York and others we had met in Washington outside of the task force had posed the very same question. Up to this week, I had been able to respond with a bit of bravado that the danger was remote and the risk was part of the job. The attack on Ralph had changed the equation.

"Of course, Roberto," I said. "That is always a possibility. But it is a pretty remote one." I didn't add that what had happened to Ralph on Monday had made that possibility much less "remote." "Costello and his gang are already under a lot of pressure and the last thing they need is more bad publicity by doing anything to anybody who is investigating them."

I could see that my answer did not satisfy Roberto, who had a skeptical look on his face. Just as he was about to pursue his line of questioning, Graciela put a restraining hand on his arm. Perhaps sensing the unease María and I were feeling at her husband's questioning, she said, "*Por favor* Roberto. We are here to have a relaxing evening. Don't spoil it by bringing up unpleasant things."

A quick flash of annoyance crossed Roberto's face, soon followed with a nod of understanding and a rueful smile. "Sorry Pete. I didn't mean to make you uncomfortable."

I was about to reassure him that I was fine with his question, hiding the fact that I was grateful for Graciela's intercession. But before I could get the words out of my mouth, Trudi arrived with our dinners. With a cheerful smile, she set our plates down in front of us while another waitress brought us our beer, filled to the brim of the chilled steins with a foaming head spilling over the top.

With the arrival of the food, the flow of conversation halted as we began to eat. After a couple of bites, the Walkers pronounced the prime rib as good as advertised. We nodded in agreement, pleased that we seemed to have made the right choice of restaurant. As they ate, María and Graciela continued their conversation, ignoring their husbands, leaving us to our own devices. Roberto asked me where I was from originally. I filled him in on my family background, my undergraduate years at Yale, law school at Columbia, and signing on with the New York DA's office. I omitted my OSS service and of course the details of my time in Argentina. He paid close attention to everything I said and nodded and smiled as I related the story of my life and times.

"But enough about me," I said. "How about you Roberto?"

He chuckled. "Not too different Pete. I come from an established family of Anglo-Uruguayan landowners. My father wanted me to run one of our estates, but I determined to try something different. So I went to England to school and became interested in international business. When I returned to Uruguay, I joined the company I work for now and could not be happier. I have a chance to travel, to live abroad as is the case now here in Washington, and," he added with a twinkle in his eye, "make a fair amount of money."

He saw the look of surprise on my face. "Yes. I know Pete. My family is wealthy and I stand to inherit some valuable property. But I wanted to show my parents that I could do well on my own without depending on their resources." I could sympathize. I loved my parents and everything they had done for me. But I had wanted to chart my own independent course and had rather consistently engaged in minor rebellions against their wishes and plans for me.

"I understand Roberto. Everybody should want to be his own man and stand on his own two feet."

He nodded in agreement. By this time, we had finished our meals. The ever-attentive Trudi came by to remove our dishes and to ask if we wanted dessert and coffee. I suggested we all try the apple pie with vanilla ice cream, something not usually found in South America. When I received unanimous consent on the choice, Trudi gave us an approving smile and promised to be right back with our orders. I told her not to rush as we were in no hurry to leave.

Roberto and I continued our conversation. I carefully avoided treading on potentially dangerous ground, especially any mention of politics or what he thought of the regime across the estuary in Argentina. Instead, I asked him about his schooling in England. He told me he had attended a boarding school as a teenager and then gotten a degree in economics from Cambridge. "Very impressive," I thought to myself. He had returned to Uruguay soon after the war in Europe broke out and had then embarked on his business career.

As he related this, a serious look crossed his face. "You know Pete that was a difficult time for me. I loved England and hated to see what the German bombing was doing to the country. After all, it was the homeland of my ancestors. I even thought about joining the British army, but my family insisted that I return home." He looked down at the table for a moment and when he lifted his head I could see regret etched on his face. "They argued that I could do more to help England by providing it with the agricultural products we were exporting than risking my life in battle. I saw their point, but still…" He let it trail off.

"I understand Roberto," I said. "We all had difficult choices to make." Almost immediately, I wished I had not opened the next door with that observation.

"Tell me Pete, if you don't mind me asking, what did you do during the war?"

It was a perfectly reasonable question, but one that I would have preferred to avoid. My family and my closest friends – as well as my OSS colleagues – knew of my service in Spain. But it was not something I wanted to advertise. For a few seconds, I struggled with how to respond. Usually I deflected the question with some vague reply. But for some reason, I flashed back to the answer that I had given Juan Perón when he had posed the same question. "My story is not too different from yours Roberto. I wanted to enlist but I was instead recruited to work for the State Department in a special office set up by Nelson Rockefeller to improve our cultural relations with Latin America. Mr. Rockefeller, a family friend, convinced me that my Spanish language skills and understanding of Latin America would do more for the war effort than toting a rifle and hurling grenades somewhere."

"So we both served the Allies in our own ways," Ricardo said. "Me with meat and you with words," he added with a rueful grin.

I laughed at the observation, relieved that I had been able to spin my yarn successfully.

After swapping "war stories," we moved on to the common ground that so many men found comfortable – sports. Roberto said that one of the best things about being in England had been the opportunity to participate in a wide range of athletic activities. They ran the gamut – cricket, rowing, soccer, golf, tennis, and even polo, which he had begun to play when a youngster in Uruguay. His favorite, however, was rugby. Pointing to his nose, he added, "And this is the major trophy I earned."

"I have a few of my own from playing American football," I said with a chuckle. "One of my favorite games is squash, which is a combination of handball and tennis played indoors with rackets. My father and I have played weekly games for years. But since my transfer to Washington we've haven't been able to. I miss the exercise and the ritual," I said a bit wistfully.

"I understand. Graciela and I used to play tennis on a regular basis in Uruguay. But since the move, we haven't had the opportunity and we both miss it. Hopefully, now that I don't have any trips planned for the next few weeks, we can take it up again. Do you and María play? Perhaps we can try some doubles."

I shook my head. I had long since given up trying to interest my wife in things like golf and tennis. "I'm afraid that María never learned to play tennis Roberto. But we both like to go on long walks as time permits. There are some very pleasant places to hike and perhaps you and Graciela would like to join us sometime."

Roberto was quick to respond. "That sounds wonderful Pete. We would love to do that."

"Love to do what darling?" Graciela said, placing her hand on Roberto's arm. Apparently there had been a lull our wives' non-stop conversation and Graciela had picked up on Roberto's response.

"Pete has suggested that you and I join them on a long walk in the country. I hope I didn't speak out of turn in agreeing that we would love to accompany them."

There was a slight note of concern in Roberto's voice, as though he might have broken some sort of spousal rule that he not make any commitments before consulting his wife. But Graciela put him at ease with a smile and a reassuring pat on the arm. "Of course darling. That would be wonderful. A wonderful idea."

There were smiles all around the table. María was beaming as though I had somehow surpassed her expectations. Perhaps she had feared that I might find the Walkers not to my liking. But the opposite was true. I liked them very much and was looking forward to spending more time with them. Of course I knew how important Graciela had become in María's life. Like Roberto, I was delighted she had found a friend with whom she felt so at home and so comfortable. And Roberto had exceeded my expectations. I had feared that he would be standoffish and perhaps even a bit arrogant. But he had proved down-to-earth and with a nice sense of self-deprecating humor. I felt somehow I had found a kindred spirit, perhaps a new-found friend of my own. And while I was very close to my fellow task-force members, especially Tim O'Rourke, and fortunate that David Friedman was close by, it was something of a closed circle, almost like an exclusive fraternity. Getting to know Roberto would help me break out of the circle. Moreover, it would have the not insignificant benefit of pleasing my wife to no end.

María and Graciela resumed their conversation and began to sketch out the details of when and where we might hike together. As I listened to them, a thought hit me. "Say Roberto," I said, "Have you ever played baseball?"

As soon as the words left my mouth I realized I had probably blundered, and blundered badly. While baseball was popular, even insanely popular, in certain parts of the Caribbean, it was unheard of in most of South America. My question to Roberto from out of the blue seemed to unnerve him for a second as a look of confusion appeared on his face. But he recovered nicely. "Well Pete, I'm afraid not. I'm familiar with the sport. Something like cricket isn't it? But no, I've never played. Why do you ask?"

María had overheard my question and seemed as puzzled as Roberto. "Yes darling. Why do you ask?" There was a hint of disapproval in her voice and I feared I had threatened to undermine all the good will I had accumulated.

"Well, I realize it probably sounds a bit daffy," I said, shifting my gaze from my wife to Roberto, "but you see, our task force at the Justice Department has a softball team that plays in a government league with games on Saturday. And it so happens that we are short one player." I did not, of course, elaborate on why one of our teammates was out of action. "And if we don't come up with a substitute by tomorrow, we'll have to forfeit the game. I know it seems silly, but the competition means a lot to us, a way to relieve some of the pressure we are under. And tomorrow we play the only other undefeated team in our league.

We would hate to lose to them on a technicality. So I was just wondering Roberto, if you did play baseball and if you were free tomorrow, maybe you could be our ninth man."

I could feel my face redden as I spoke and imagined that the others at the table probably thought I had gone off my rocker. But Roberto bailed me out. "You know Pete, it so happens I don't have anything on my schedule tomorrow and would love to play with your team. Of course, I cannot guarantee I'll be much of an asset, never having played the game before. But at least you won't have to forfeit."

If Roberto had been a woman, I probably would have leaned over the table and kissed him. Instead I just smiled in appreciation. "That's just great Roberto. Just great. And if you have played cricket, at least you have some idea of how to swing a piece of wood at a ball and to catch one after it's hit."

He nodded in agreement, a grin on his face. "I look forward to the challenge Pete. I hope I don't disappoint you."

"Listen," I said. "The game is scheduled for four in the afternoon. Why don't we plan to meet at about three and I'll try to give you a few pointers. I'll bring a glove as well. Are you right-handed or left-handed?"

"Right-handed."

"Great. So am I. And I happen to have a couple of extra gloves. I'll bring them with me tomorrow."

Just then, Trudi brought our pie a-la-mode and coffee. As we ate, we shifted our conversation to other matters. The Walkers said that they enjoyed going to the movies and even had a taste for opera, so we added those to the agenda of things we might do together. I suggested that after the softball game tomorrow, we plan to go out to eat. It was customary for one of the team members with a house and yard, usually Joe Smathers, to have us all over for a cookout after the game. I felt pretty sure that Joe would not mind adding the Walkers to the list after Roberto played for us, but didn't want to make the commitment until I talked with him. If it was okay with Joe, we could always switch plans.

We finished our dessert and coffee and I asked Trudi for the bill. Roberto offered to pay, saying he could list it as a business expense. But

I insisted that I pay: they were our guests and it had been our invitation. "Okay Pete," he said with a shrug. "But the next time, it's on me."

After I had paid, I asked Trudi to call a cab. Ten minutes later, she informed us that the cab was waiting at the curb on Wisconsin. I thanked her for her attention and slipped her an extra five dollars, which she quickly put in her pocket. Outside, the night was warm and humid, but there was enough of a breeze so that it was not oppressive. María and the Walkers got in the back of the taxi while I sat in front with the driver. I instructed him to head first to Dupont Circle, where we would drop off the Walkers, and then on to our town house.

As he headed south on Wisconsin, I could see the FBI sedan make a U-turn and fall in one car behind us. I hoped the Walkers would not notice. The evening with them had been extraordinarily pleasant. But the presence of the FBI surveillance team was a stark reminder that our life was not normal, that we lived in the shadow of danger, and, unfortunately, that shadow could well fall on anyone who happened to be close to us. I tried to shove that unwelcome thought away, but it persisted, just like the headlights of the car behind us.

CHAPTER SEVENTEEN

June 9, 1951 – Washington, D.C.

María and I got to the Justice Department a little after nine. When we reached the shooting range in the basement, Ruth Franklin and Kathy Davis were already there. Husbands Jim and Phil were at their side, ready, as was I, to provide moral support. We greeted each other rather somberly as María and I took up a shooting lane to their right. Two FBI instructors were also present to supervise and assist. They introduced themselves; Bill Rogers and Sean Casey. They were standard-issue FBI – in their thirties, slim and fit, their hair neatly trimmed. The only concession they made to the circumstances was to shed their suit coats and roll up their sleeves. Their ties remained firmly in place.

We were the only ones at the range. When I mentioned this fact to Bill Rogers, he said, "The director told us to keep the range clear for you and your wives for as long as you needed it."

"That is pretty generous of Hoover," I thought to myself. "Maybe he has given the threat to the task force a higher priority than I had imagined."

Casey then took the lead. "Well ladies, here are your weapons," he said, pointing to three Smith and Wesson .38 pistols he held in his hands. "Why don't you take one and we'll get started. And don't worry. They are not loaded."

The three wives took the guns from Casey. Ruth and Kathy looked nervous as they gripped the revolvers by the handle. María, however, took her weapon with a look of calm and confidence. I had already familiarized her with my own weapon. And, despite her general abhorrence of guns, she had had experience shooting at wild game on the family estancia. She also told me she was a pretty good shot. Maybe she had said that only to reassure me. We would soon find out.

Casey, with Rogers assisting, took the three women over the basics. He showed them how to load the bullets into the cylinder, explained how the safety worked, and helped them with their grips. He demonstrated how to assume the shooting position and advised "Just aim at the target and squeeze, don't pull the trigger." He also warned them that when they fired for the first time they would experience some recoil and perhaps be startled by the sudden loud noise. "All that is perfectly normal," he assured them. "Even veteran agents sometimes have to get the first couple of shots off before they are comfortable." He might have added that it was one thing to fire at a paper target in controlled circumstances. It was quite another to have to think about all of these steps when facing someone else who was armed and quite capable of shooting back.

"Okay ladies," Casey said. "Let's give it a try." Each woman stood at their stations, facing the targets at the end of the range thirty feet away. The instructors helped them position themselves with their shoulders square, their feet apart about fifteen inches and well planted, the gun in one hand pointed at the target, the other supporting the hand with the gun to steady it.

Once they were lined up, Rogers took over. "All right. Everything looks good," he said in a reassuring voice. "Now release the safety." There were three soft clicks. "Fine. Remember to *squeeze* the trigger. Take a deep breath and keep your eyes open. Whenever you are ready, fire away."

Ruth Franklin shot first. She gave a little squeal, when, as predicted, the gun recoiled in her hand and the noise, echoing in the closed space, startled her. She missed the target altogether and her face turned red with embarrassment. "Not to worry sweetheart," Jim said to her. "You'll do better next time."

Kathy Davis was next. My guess was that she, like Ruth, had probably never fired a gun before. She was better prepared but also flinched as she squeezed the trigger. Nonetheless, she was able to hit the target, although high and wide from the body outline.

Almost simultaneously María fired her gun, her hand steady as a rock. There was no squeal, only the exhaling of her breath as her bullet pierced the heart of the target. I was standing a few feet behind her to her right. She looked over her shoulder at me with a look that said, "See. I was telling you the truth. I am a pretty darned good shot."

All of us were stunned. Then, to let us know it wasn't just luck, María emptied her revolver in rapid succession, grouping her shots around the heart of the target in a way that would be the envy of any professional.

"Darned good shooting ma'am," Casey said in awe. "I guess you have had some practice."

"Just a little," María said with a grin. "My father taught me to shoot when I was a child on our farm." To call her family's estancia, which covered thousands of acres, a "farm" was, unlike her aim, a bit off the mark. But she used the term that would make most sense to those unfamiliar with the large estates of her homeland.

I was afraid that María's proficiency would intimidate Ruth and Kathy. But she instead gave them encouragement and a few practical tips to improve their performance. They seemed to accept her advice more readily than from the male instructors, who after a while just sat back and let María take charge. Soon, the two other wives were hitting their targets with regularity.

When the women had finished, Jim, Phil, and I took our turns. It had been a while since I had fired a revolver. In fact, not since my time in Argentina when I was forced by extreme circumstances to pull the trigger of someone else's .45 Colt in order to save my life. I'd gotten off some blind shots that fortunately hit their targets. This time, under more favorable conditions, I was able to draw on my OSS training to rack up some respectable scores. My groupings were not quite as tight as María's, but I was able to hit the heart of the target with some consistency.

After about thirty minutes of practice, we had had enough. We packed our guns away with the men putting theirs back into shoulder holsters, the women theirs into large purses, all of us making sure the safeties were on before we did so. Casey and Rogers congratulated us and wished us luck. "Come back anytime," Casey said, "if you need more training or practice."

We thanked them for their help and headed up to the first floor. As we walked up the stairs, I once again marveled at how tough and determined my wife was. And full of surprises. *Who knew she could shoot like that?* I would bet a month's salary that Casey and Rogers, no matter how buttoned-up they might be, would be regaling their fellow instructors with details of how this beautiful woman they were supposed to instruct could shoot the eyes off a fly at thirty paces. More to the point, María's ability with a revolver helped ease some of the anxiety I had felt over her safety ever since the attack on Ralph Turner. She was more than capable of taking care of herself if need be.

Out on the street, we said our goodbyes to the Davises and the Franklins. We would meet again later in the day for the softball game and then a barbecue at Joe Smathers's home. I had called Joe earlier to let him know that I had lined up Roberto to be the ninth player. He admitted that he had not slept well that night, concerned that we might have to forfeit. I chuckled to myself. *What a competitor,* I thought. With all the things he had to worry about, the idea he might have to forfeit a softball game was what kept him awake. He was extremely grateful that I had found a substitute and told me to invite Roberto and Graciela to join everyone later for the barbecue.

We played our games at fields on the north side of Constitution Avenue, not far from the Lincoln Memorial. When I arrived a little after three, Roberto was already there, watching a game in progress.

"Hello Pete," he said with a grin, extending his hand. "How are you?"

"Just great Roberto. And you?"

"Very well, thank you. Very well." Then, turning to the field, he said, "I have been watching for a while. I think I understand some of the basic rules. But maybe you could explain a few things for me."

"Sure Roberto. I'll be happy to." I did my best to describe what was happening. I introduced Roberto to some of the subtleties of the game like when to lay off a bad pitch, how to position himself in the outfield, and what base to throw to if a ball was hit his way. Our plan was to have him play in right field, the position where he probably would have the fewest chances. I was going to play center field, which would allow me to coach him. He picked up on things right away and asked some good questions as the game proceeded.

I had brought a ball, a bat, and an extra glove. We found some empty space and began to toss the ball back and forth. I gradually increased the distance between us and the velocity of my throws. Roberto seemed a natural. He didn't drop a single throw. I could see that he had very quick reflexes, able to move easily in any direction to snag some of my errant tosses. I also encouraged him to increase the velocity of his own return throws. I could tell that he had a strong arm when a couple of his returns stung my palms.

Next came hitting. I took the bat and showed him the proper stance. "Not quite like cricket, is it?" he said.

"Aside from holding a piece of wood in your hand and swinging at a ball, no it isn't." I replied.

I had him take some practice swings. He was awkward at first, not sure how to accomplish the right combination of upper and lower body movement. I adjusted his stance and told him to keep his swing as level as possible, always with his head turned toward the pitcher and his eye on the ball. After some trial and error, he seemed to have mastered the essentials. The true test would come when he faced a real pitcher in live action.

By this time, the rest of the team had shown up. I introduced Roberto as our ninth man. Joe greeted him with a handshake and a big smile on his face. "Roberto. Nice to meet you," he said. "I can't tell you how happy I am you could join us. I really appreciate it."

Roberto smiled back at him. "Well Mr. Smathers, I..."

"Please. Call me Joe."

"Well… Joe. I hope you are as happy after the game is over. As Pete may have told you. This is all new to me. I've never played your game of baseball in my life."

Joe glared at me. I simply shrugged. I had left out this rather important detail when I told Joe that we had a ninth man. My look said "Beggars can't be Choosers."

"I'm sure you'll do just fine Roberto." Then, with a piercing glance in my direction, "And I'm sure that Pete will do all he can to prepare you to play with us."

The message was received, loud and clear. "We've been practicing Joe. Roberto is ready to go."

Joe looked dubious, but realized there was no alternative. Fortunately, we were able to have a little batting practice before the game began. We let Roberto get in the first licks. Tim, who was our pitcher, lobbed some easy throws his way. At first, Roberto missed wildly, taking awkward, off-balance swings. But after a little coaching, he began to get the hang of it and sent some stinging line drives to the outfield. I gave him as much encouragement as I could. I was pleased and not a little surprised that he had been able to get into a groove so quickly. His hand-eye coordination was superb and he had plenty of power when he connected. I warned him that Tim's tosses were at about half the speed of what he would face once the game began and the opposing pitcher took the mound.

We were the home team and would take the field first. Just before we headed out, María and Graciela showed up to cheer us on. They joined some of the other wives, who occupied the bleacher seats behind our bench. María introduced Graciela to the assembled women and then gave me a wave and a smile. Despite her general lack of interest in sports, María had picked up the rules of softball quickly. She had decided that part of becoming an American meant learning all she could about the national pastime. I could see her begin to explain some of the basics to Graciela.

As we took the field, I accompanied Roberto to his position in right and told him where to stand. I had seen the Treasury team play before and knew that their lineup, like ours, was made up primarily of right-handed batters who would most likely send the balls they hit to left field and center. Nonetheless, I had Roberto play back a little more than our normal right fielder did to try to assure that nothing got over his head. Treasury's clean-up hitter was a raw-boned left-handed batter who, like Joe Smathers, had once been a major league prospect. When he came to bat, I planned to motion Roberto to move even farther back.

I thought we would get through the top of the first without Roberto being tested. Tim struck out the lead-off hitter and got the next man to pop up to the infield. But the third-place hitter sent a line drive directly at me. I had to field it on the hop and my throw to second held him to a single. When their clean-up man strode to the plate, I gestured for Roberto to back up about thirty more feet. I did the same. I didn't want to guy to hit it over my head either. Tim managed to get two quick swinging strikes, but then fell behind with three straight balls. On a three and two count, the lefty stung a wicked line drive into right field that landed just inside the foul line. I had visions of it skipping past Roberto for extra bases. But quick as the proverbial cat, Roberto raced to the line, snagged the ball in his glove hand, and whirled to throw. I shouted at him, "Second base Roberto. Second base," figuring there was no way he could catch the lead runner before he reached third. A throw to second would at least prevent the hitter from advancing past first. But Roberto either didn't hear me or chose to ignore my advice. To everybody's amazement, he uncorked a rocket that landed in the glove of our third baseman, Carmine De Grazio, who tagged the runner for the third out.

As we trotted in from the outfield, I clapped Roberto on the back. "What a throw Roberto. What a throw. Boy, you sure catch on fast." In the stands, I could see María and Graciela jumping up and down and waving their arms in excitement.

"I just followed your lead Pete," he said. "I saw how you handled that ball hit to you and tried to do the same." Then, in a lowered voice and with a wry look, he confessed, "I *was* trying to throw to second base, just as you instructed. But in the excitement, I totally forgot which was which and sent it to third base instead. Please don't tell anyone."

I laughed. "Don't worry Roberto. I won't. And it was still a hell of a throw."

When we got settled on the bench, everyone came over to congratulate Roberto. He accepted the handshakes and the slaps on the back with a grin and a shrug. "Beginner's luck," he said when Joe Smathers told him that was one of the best throws from the outfield he had ever seen, and he had seen a lot of them. "Looks as though we've got a regular Carl Furillo here Pete," he said, pointing to Roberto. When Joe left, he asked me, "Who is this Carl Furillo?"

"The right fielder for the Brooklyn Dodgers," I explained. "With a cannon for an arm."

Roberto had certainly gotten off to a roaring start. But it was still early in the game. Baseball could be humbling. It didn't take much to go from hero to goat. And if you were lucky, back to hero again. How Roberto would hold up over the next six innings remained to be seen.

In our half of the inning, the first two batters went down on strike-outs. Batting third, I managed to poke a hit between the fielders in left and center and with some aggressive base running stretched it into a double. Standing on second base, I could see María and Graciela again on their feet, clapping their hands in glee. The Treasury pitcher, who had a wicked fast ball and an effective curve, bore down on our clean-up man, Joe Smathers. Joe whiffed on the first pitch, but managed to foul off three more before sending a single into right field that allowed me to score. The next batter grounded into a force-out at second.

We had broken on top early. But it didn't last long. In the top of the second, the Treasury team strung together some scratch singles to even the score. After that, both pitchers settled down and hits for both sides were hard to come by. Roberto struck out on three swings his first time up. But he wasn't the only one. I swung and missed on a third strike the next inning after fouling off a couple of sizzling fast balls. In the field, both of us handled some soft fly balls. Roberto had another chance to show off his arm, charging a slowly hit grounder between first and second and holding the runner, who showed no inclination to advance, to a single. The next time he was at the plate, Roberto showed some progress. After missing the first pitch, he sent a foul over the backstop and then popped out to the first basemen. He was late on his swing, but he was making contact.

We held the Treasury team scoreless through the top of the seventh inning. If we didn't score with the last at bats in the bottom of the inning the game would end as a tie. The rules did not permit extra innings. A tie would be better than a loss, but we wanted to win. I had managed to single over the shortstop's head in the bottom of the sixth. I thought we might go ahead when Joe Smathers hit a long fly ball to deep left. But their fielder made a beautiful over-the-shoulder catch to end the inning and the threat.

Tim O'Rourke was our fifth place hitter and led off the bottom of the seventh with a solid single to left. The next batter, George Wilson, followed with a sharp ground ball that barely eluded the second basemen to dribble into center field, allowing Tim to reach second and into scoring position. But Jim Franklin struck out and Carmine De Grazio popped up to the catcher. That left everything up to Roberto. As he strode to the plate, accompanied by words of encouragement from all of us, I remembered the old "hero to goat" cliché. I could hear María and Graciela yelling loudly behind me as I kept my eyes on the batter's box, where Roberto adjusted his stance and stared at the opposing pitcher.

Before he had left the bench, I had told Roberto not to be too anxious. The pitcher was tiring. "If you see pitches that look like strikes, try to foul them off," I advised. "Don't swing at pitches out of the strike zone. In these circumstances, a walk is as good as a hit." My worst fear was that Roberto would swing wildly, our last hope for a win going down with him. And while I knew that my team members would forgive him – we all had struck out at one time or another in similar situations – I worried that Roberto would take it hard, thinking that he had let me and the team down. If he somehow managed to coax a walk, at least he would not be our last chance.

I shouldn't have worried. Roberto gave me a wink, his bat held jauntily over his shoulder. "Right Pete. I understand. A walk is as good as a hit." Then he stepped to the plate, made sure his feet and shoulders were as I had coached him, took a few practice swings, and stared out at the pitcher. The expression on his face was one of complete calm and relaxation. A slight smile of anticipation played on his lips. The pitcher, who sensed easy prey, looked at him the way a lion spotting a helpless antelope might. He went into his windup, released the ball, and waited for the expected thump as it hit the catcher's mitt for a called strike. Instead, what he heard was the clear smack of the fat part of Roberto's bat meeting the pitch and sending it on a line over the second baseman's head and into the gap between the center and right fielders. Tim raced home with the winning run, although he could have trotted as the two fielders tried to track down the ball Roberto had hit.

We erupted from the bench to mob Tim and Roberto. Joe Smathers, who usually kept his cool under any circumstances, hurled his glove into the air in exultation. María, Graciela, and the other wives in attendance ran onto the field to join our celebration, hopping up and down and embracing us. It was all kind of silly of course. Grown men going giddy over a boy's game. But we had needed it. For a moment, at least, we were able to put the cares of our office and what had happened to Ralph Turner behind us.

Joe grabbed me in a bear hug. Even though I outweighed him by some twenty pounds, he easily lifted me off the ground and swung me around in a circle. Putting me down, a little embarrassed, he said, "Way to go Pete. Way to go. You saved our bacon."

"You mean *Roberto* saved our bacon," I said.

"He sure did Pete. He sure did. And I'm not certain just how he did it. I never saw someone who hadn't played a game in his life perform like that. But it's all thanks to you that he was here to provide the heroics in the first place."

We spent a few more minutes celebrating. Then, promising to see the others at Joe's barbecue, María and I and the Walkers gathered our belongings and headed to the streetcar stop. The plan was to freshen up and change clothes before heading to the Smathers's home.

"That was really, really exciting darling," María said, hugging my arm, her eyes dancing. Turning to Roberto, she added, "And you were wonderful Roberto. Wonderful. Playing for the first time and getting the game-winning hit. That was really something."

"Well, to tell you the truth María, despite Pete's instructions, I just closed my eyes and swung. It was pure luck, that's all. Pure luck. But," he added, "I'm glad it worked out the way it did. That was a lot of fun."

I appreciated Roberto's modesty. But I was watching him closely as he batted. His eye was on the ball the whole time. It wasn't luck. It was skill that delivered the key hit. He had amazing natural athletic skills that combined strength with coordination and grace. I imagined there were not many physical challenges he could not overcome with ease. The real piece of luck was me finding a fitting substitute for our team, a substitute who proved more than adequate.

All in all, I thought, as we clambered aboard the streetcar, it had been a day of surprises. First, I had no idea that my wife was an Argentine Annie Oakley. Her ability to handle a revolver came as quite a revelation. Second, to be frank, I had expected the worst from Roberto. My hope had been that not too many balls would be hit in his direction and that at bat he didn't hit into double plays. Needless to say, I never in my wildest dreams expected him to play flawlessly in the field and actually win the game for us with his bat. I could only wish that in the future other surprises would be so pleasant.

CHAPTER EIGHTEEN

June 15, 1951 – Washington, D.C.

I sat at my desk, trying to digest and summarize more witness testimonies. It was almost noon and I hurried to finish before heading to my Friday lunch date with David Friedman. Tim O'Rourke was slaving away over much the same material. I heard him utter a combination of muffled sighs, grunts, and gasps of disbelief as he jotted notes down on his yellow legal pad.

It had been a relatively quiet week. The best news arrived on Wednesday when Ralph Turner came out of his coma. He was still struggling with his speech and his memory. He couldn't provide much useful information on his attackers other than the fact he thought two men had been involved. But he had survived and the prognosis was hopeful.

Earlier in the week, Director Hoover and Attorney General McGrath determined to reduce the FBI watch over us and our families. Since the attack on Ralph there had been no further signs of trouble and the manpower was needed for other assignments. In addition, we were all now armed and on the alert for any danger. I also wondered if word had reached the director that at least one of the wives was more than capable of defending herself if need be.

My task force teammates were still buzzing over the game we had won on Saturday. They never seemed to tire of re-living it at every occasion. At Joe's barbecue, Roberto and Graciela had been the center of attention. Everything was done to make them feel welcome. We sat with them at a large picnic table along with others of the task force where they were introduced to the all-American delights of hot dogs, hamburgers, and potato salad. It was, I knew, not quite like the barbecues, the *asados,* that they were accustomed to in Uruguay, with the heaping plates of finer cuts of meat. But they seemed to enjoy the food and the company. Graciela struggled with her English, especially with some of the slang words, but was clearly making progress. María at her side helped with translations.

After we ate, the men gathered around one table while the wives and Tim's girlfriend cleaned up. Roberto sat next to me and remained mostly silent as we engaged in some shop talk. During the conversation, Jim Franklin seemed to forget that Roberto was present and blurted out: "I'm glad our wives are learning to shoot. After what happened to Ralph…" Before he could finish, Tim poked him in the ribs and nodded in Roberto's direction. Jim quickly realized his mistake and did his best to shift to another topic. Roberto didn't say anything at the time but I was afraid the cat was out of the bag.

I was right. Our wives, having taken care of the domestic chores, rejoined us and we lapsed back into general chatter about life in summertime Washington. By ten o'clock María and I and the Walkers, having had a long day, thanked our hosts for their hospitality and excused ourselves. The Smathers's home was in Chevy Chase, Maryland. As we were the only guests without a car Joe offered to drive us home. But I didn't want him to leave his party. Instead, I asked him to call us a taxi. With a look of gratitude on his face, he didn't put up much of a struggle and made the call. He was probably as tired as we were.

While we waited for the taxi to arrive, Roberto pulled me to one side. "Pete," he said in a low voice, "I couldn't help but notice what Jim had to say. Has your task force run into some kind of trouble? Are you and María in danger?"

He saw the look of confusion on my face as I tried to come up with an answer and hastily added, "I'm sorry if I am – how do you say it? – butting into your business. It's just that Graciela and I have become very fond of you both. If there is anything that we can do…"

I was touched by his concern. "That's very kind of you Roberto. Very kind indeed. But no," I lied, "we are not in any danger. Having our wives learn how to handle a weapon is just a precautionary measure. Nothing to be alarmed about."

He looked at me skeptically but did not push it. "However, I would appreciate it," I told him, "that you don't mention to anyone else what you overheard tonight. We are trying to keep all aspects of our investigation as confidential as we can."

"I understand completely Pete," he said as the taxi arrived. "I won't say a word to anyone."

On the ride home, Roberto and Graciela told us how much they had enjoyed meeting our friends and on the warmth with which they had been greeted. María and Graciela made plans to meet for lunch during the week and we all agreed to try to do something together the following weekend. In the back of my mind, I wondered if Roberto, after getting hints of the attack on Ralph and despite my disclaimers, might worry that somehow he and his wife were courting danger by being with us. When I shared this concern with María later, she did not brush it aside as an exaggeration on my part. Instead, she said practically, "Well darling, let's just wait and see. We can't let fear dictate our lives." I knew she was right, but the worry lingered nonetheless.

When I got to the Occidental, David had again arrived before me. He was sitting at our usual table, absorbed in thought. I made my way through the crowded room.

"Hey David," I said, as I approached. "Sorry I'm late."

His face lit up when he saw me. "Not to worry Pete. I've only been here a few minutes myself."

I took my seat and looked at him. I could tell from the gleam in his eye what the answer would be to my first question. "So, did Sarah say yes?"

A big grin split his face. "Yes she did Pete. She certainly did."

"That's wonderful David. Great news. I'm so happy for you. And María will be too when I tell her the news."

When the waiter approached, I was tempted to order some champagne. But then I thought better of it. Best to hold off until we could all be together for a proper celebration. Instead, I asked for my usual martini and David his bourbon and water.

"So tell me buddy," I said after the waiter left, "María is going to want all the details. Have you set the date? Will the wedding be here or in Israel? Will you both be staying here in D.C. or moving to Tel Aviv? What…?"

He interrupted my barrage of questions. "We haven't firmed things up Pete," he said. "We want to wait a few months before we settle everything." Then a sober look replaced the grin. "There are some complications you know. We both have our careers to consider. At the moment, the plan is for a wedding here in the fall and perhaps another celebration in Israel. As for settling in Israel, that all depends on what the Foreign Office has in mind for Sarah. And I'm not sure I'm ready to cut loose from the CIA. You know how it is."

In fact, I didn't. He saw the quizzical look on my face. "It's very complicated Pete. Very, very complicated."

I knew David well enough to recognize that it would do no good to press him to elaborate. Instead, I backed off from the questioning. "I get you pal," I said. "But is it all right to let María and Tim in on the good news? Maybe have a little celebration just among ourselves?"

He gave me a wry smile. "Sure thing Pete. That would be fine. But just something simple okay?"

"You got it. Simple it is."

The waiter came to take our lunch orders. After he had left, David asked, "So how was your dinner with María's new friend and her husband?"

I filled him in on the weekend's events. When I told him about Roberto's exploits on the softball diamond, David raised his eyebrows in surprise and shook his head in disbelief. He was an avid baseball fan and not a bad player himself. In fact, if he had not been out of town for the weekend I would have asked him to fill in as the substitute on our team.

After I had finished, he said, "This Roberto Walker sounds like quite a guy."

"Yes. Not at all what I expected."

"What were you expecting?"

I hesitated for a moment. "Well, you know. An Anglo-Uruguayan from a wealthy family. I figured he would be snobby and stand-offish."

David gave me a reproachful look. "I know. I know," I said defensively. "General stereotyping. Guilty as charged. But he was very natural and easy-going. No airs. No pretensions."

"You say he's involved in some kind of business that has him based in D.C.?"

"Yeah. It would seem so. He was a little hazy on the details. But he said he represents a Uruguayan export-import firm that has contracts with the U.S. government; hence, the need for him to be here."

"Did he mention the name of the company he works for?"

I ransacked my memory and came up empty. "No. Now that you bring it up, he didn't. Any reason for your curiosity?"

David was silent for a moment. A miasma of political gossip swirled around us. From time to time I could hear the names McCarthy, Macarthur, Kefauver, and Eisenhower float through the air. "No. Not really Pete," David said. "Just my espionage instincts kicking in. You know how it is in the spy business. Everybody is a suspect." Then he leaned over the table and lowered his voice. "And these days the agency is on heightened alert after the Burgess-Maclean debacle. Angleton is more convinced than ever there is a Soviet mole in the agency and is moving heaven and earth to try to flush him out. I guess I've caught some of the fever."

I chuckled. "Well anything is possible I suppose. But I'm pretty sure that Roberto Walker is no Soviet spy. We didn't talk politics, but if I had to guess I would bet he is pretty conservative."

David uttered a skeptical "uh-uh." Our OSS experience had taught us that spies came in all shapes, sizes, and cover stories. And there were few better covers than to pretend you were the opposite of what you really were.

"No. Really David. I'm a pretty good judge of character. Roberto Walker is no more a suspicious character than you or I."

As I uttered these words, a brief look of panic crossed David's face. If I hadn't been looking straight at him I would have missed it. For a moment, I got the sense that he was about to reveal some deep, dark secret. But he quickly composed himself. "I'm sure you're right my friend. Letting my imagination running away with me I'm afraid. Occupational hazard."

"To tell you the truth David," I said. "I had some of the same questions. But Roberto answered all of them straight up. What he told me made perfect sense. I've had a lot of practice and think I have a good feel when someone is lying and someone is telling the truth. And I had no hint that Roberto was being anything but honest with me."

Again, David graced me with the skeptical "uh-uh."

"Okay Pete," he said. "I don't want to inflict my paranoia onto you. And I'm very happy that you and especially María have found some kindred spirits here in Washington."

"Thanks buddy. I couldn't be happier that María now has a female friend with whom she feels comfortable. And the fact that I have taken a shine to her husband is just an added bonus."

Our food arrived and we focused on eating. Between bites, I told David about María's prowess on the shooting range. He shook his head in admiration. "From the time she dared to confront Eva Duarte to try to save your life," he said, "I knew that she possessed unusual courage, determination, and self-reliance. I have no doubt that if for some reason her life is in danger, she will be more than capable of defending herself. And you too."

"Well, I hope it doesn't come to that. Since the attack on Ralph, there have been no further threats to any of us. Good news on that front by the way," I added. "Ralph is out of his coma and the prognosis is hopeful. Sorry I didn't mention it sooner."

"I'm really pleased to hear that," David said.

"Yeah. We were expecting the worst. So that's a real relief. But…"

"But the danger is still out there, isn't it?"

"I'm afraid so." I looked around to see if anyone might be listening to us. There were no signs of interest from nearby tables. Nonetheless, I again lowered my voice. "And Director Hoover and the attorney general have been forced to remove the FBI surveillance. The manpower apparently is needed elsewhere," I said with a tinge of sarcasm.

"You mean to keep an eye on suspected Reds and homosexuals in the State Department and elsewhere," David said.

"More than likely," I agreed. "But at least we are all now armed and presumably prepared to defend ourselves if attacked."

David had that worried look I knew so well. "Okay Pete," he said. "But just be careful, okay? The threat is still out there. You can't assume that they'll stop with Ralph Turner. After all, you guys haven't let that attack slow your work. So these thugs, whoever they are, aren't likely to give up trying to intimidate you."

David was a compulsive worrier and sometimes exaggerated the prospect of danger. But this time he was right. His reasoning was completely in tune with what I and the rest of the task force thought as well. We hadn't given in to the threat and we knew that our enemies, whoever they were, would likely continue their efforts to get us to halt our investigation.

"You're right David," I told him. "We are all staying alert." Then, patting the gun under my coat, I added, "And we aren't backing down either."

We paused while the waiter cleared our plates. "So David," I asked, "When can we plan a party for you and Sarah and have a proper celebration?"

He held up his hand. "I appreciate the thought Pete. But we are both pretty busy right now. This Maclean-Burgess thing has us working around the clock and on weekends to try to assess and contain the damage. And Sarah has a lot going on at the embassy as well. So let me get back to you when the dust clears, okay? But I do appreciate the offer."

"Okay buddy. But don't let this slip through the cracks."

"I won't. I promise."

Our waiter returned with coffee for me and tea for David. He knew us so well that he hadn't even bothered to ask if that was what we wanted. As David stirred sugar into his tea and added lemon, he asked, "So, any plans for the weekend?"

"Well, as a matter of fact, we are going to see quite a bit of the Walkers. María lined up tickets for the four of us for the Watergate Opera on Saturday night. Then on Sunday we're taking a hike on the Chesapeake and Ohio canal towpath presuming the weather cooperates."

"Sounds like fun. A lot more fun than what I'll be doing," David said wistfully. Then that old worried expression reappeared. "I don't want to be a killjoy, but have you given any thought to the possibility that you might be putting your new friends in danger? After all, Ralph Turner was attacked in his own driveway. What's to say that whoever is trying to intimidate the task force won't try to take advantage of the opportunity to attack you and María – and whoever is with you – when you are in an isolated spot on the towpath? Maybe you should stick to crowded public places, especially when you might be involving innocent parties like the Walkers."

I could not dismiss David's concerns. They were not entirely unfounded. Taking a last gulp of coffee, I put the cup down. "Well, to tell you the truth, while we've discussed the problem in general terms, we haven't given that possibility as much thought as we should have. I'll talk it over again with María. She is very keen on the whole idea of hiking with the Walkers. She and Graciela are already looking forward to a trip to the Blue Ridge Mountains next weekend. The walk along the towpath is a kind of dress rehearsal for that. But maybe you are right. While we don't want to let fear dominate our own lives, we cannot ask others to share the risk without knowing what they might be in for. Maybe we should reconsider given the circumstances."

"Have you considered telling the Walkers about those 'circumstances'"?

"That's another complication. Our instructions are to keep pretty close-mouthed about what happened to Ralph. But I think Roberto picked up on the fact that something is amiss when he overheard one of our guys briefly mention the attack on Ralph at Joe's post-game barbecue. He asked me about it later and I put him off. But he's no dummy and I'm sure he suspects that something is up."

"Well," David said, after the waiter brought us the bill and we pulled out our wallets to pay, "it looks as though both of us are in pretty complicated situations right now."

I nodded in agreement. There was a difference, however. David had a clear idea of my "complications." I had only the vaguest notion about his.

CHAPTER NINETEEN

June 17, 1951 – Washington, D.C.

Over dinner Friday night, María and I wrestled again with the issue that had arisen after Joe's barbecue and the concerns that David had expressed at our lunch – namely, that by spending time with the Walkers we might be putting them in danger. We agreed that we could not let fear rule our lives. Besides, we reasoned, it seemed unlikely that whoever had attacked Ralph Turner, alone in his driveway at night, would take the risk of confronting four people together, especially if he – or they - had gotten wind of the fact that two of them were armed. Nevertheless, the possibility that we might be putting the lives of innocent people at risk, especially the lives of two people we had grown close to, was a dilemma that lingered over our heads like the proverbial dark cloud, with no easy resolution in sight.

On Saturday, we met the Walkers for dinner at O'Donnell's Sea Grill on E. Street. Later, we went to the Watergate to hear a fine performance of "Carmen." The opera was performed on a barge on the Potomac in the shadow of the Lincoln Memorial, providing a unique and historic setting. Fortunately, the weather cooperated. The temperature was in the seventies and a gentle breeze off the river made for a pleasant experience.

During the intermissions, we had plenty of opportunity to converse. Roberto had not been able to play in our softball game that day since we were back to a full complement. Nonetheless, he had showed up to watch and was warmly greeted by the whole team. We went over the game, which we had won handily, and he expressed his eagerness to participate again if the occasion should arise.

The questions David had raised about Roberto lingered at the back of my mind. During the second intermission, when María and Graciela went to fetch some cold drinks, I casually asked Roberto how his work was going, hoping to steer him in the direction of providing more details.

"Just fine Pete," he said. "In fact, better than fine. I've had some real success nailing down the details of our contracts. It looks as though our company is in line to make quite a bit of money. A few more weeks and we can begin shipping our products directly to the United States."

"That's great Roberto," I replied. "Does that mean that you and Graciela will be here in Washington for a while?"

He gave me a grin. "It looks that way. Probably for at least six more months. That is, if everything continues to go as smoothly as it has up until now."

"By the way," I said, "What's the name of your company? Maybe I should think about buying some stock in it."

I was looking him straight in the eye as I asked the question, looking for any telltale clues he might be dissembling. I could see none. He was relaxed and natural. "I'm sorry Pete. I thought I had mentioned the company name when we first met. At any rate, it's Oribe and Hermanos Exporting." Then he chuckled, and added, "As for buying stock, I'm afraid we are not listed on your exchange. At least not yet. If we ever are, I'll let you know."

I laughed in return. "Thanks Roberto. I'll keep that in mind."

Roberto's easy response had gone a long way towards convincing me that he was the genuine article with nothing to hide. However, I determined to go the extra mile and see what I could find out on my own about Oribe and Hermanos. I also considered getting David involved. While the CIA was prohibited by statute from operating domestically, looking into the bona fides of a foreign company operating in the U.S. would not be unduly stretching the agency's authority. Or at least I hoped it wouldn't.

We didn't linger after the opera. We planned to get going early on our hike the next day. Luckily, we found a taxi right away. We arranged to meet the next morning at eight thirty.

Before we went to bed, María and I sketched out our plan of action for the following day. Earlier, María had bought sandwiches at a local delicatessen along with some bottles of soda, planning on a picnic lunch at the mid-way point of our hike. We would share the load, totting the items in our respective knapsacks. In addition, I would carry two canteens of water. We had encouraged the Walkers to bring their own canteens and advised they have some insect repellent with them as well. Mosquitos and gnats could make walking in the woods very uncomfortable. We also suggested they invest in a good pair of hiking boots and break them in before we set out. Much of the trail was hard-packed dirt and easy walking, but there were rocky stretches along the way.

We struggled over the question of what to do with our pistols. I was under orders to have mine with me at all times and María had become accustomed to carrying hers in her pursue. But on the towpath, María would not have her purse. Moreover, we would be dressed casually and there was no way we could have them on our person and concealed from view. Nor did we want to explain to our new-found friends just what we were doing armed like western gun-slingers. We debated simply leaving them at home, doubtful that the four of us would be attacked. But just to be on the safe side, we determined that I would take my pistol in my knapsack. If we were attacked, it might not do much good as I likely would not be able to retrieve it in time to be effective. However, it gave us some sense of security to know that it would be there if needed.

We met the Walkers at Dupont Circle the next morning. Roberto and I were dressed in short-sleeved shirts and light-weight khaki pants. Graciela and María looked stylish in matching gray slacks and cream-colored short-sleeved blouses. Once again I noticed Graciela's well-toned arms. Roberto had taken my advice and had invested in a sturdy pair of hiking boots. He also had a canteen strapped to his belt. Graciela, on the other hand, had on shoes more appropriate for tennis than hiking.

I hoped that her choice would not result in blisters, or worse, a twisted ankle. María, like me, had on well broken-in boots.

After exchanging the usual *abrazos* and cheek kisses, we boarded the Cabin John trolley. Even though it was early on a Sunday morning, the car was packed. The trolley to Cabin John stopped at the Glen Echo Amusement Park, a few miles northwest of the District line on the Maryland side of the Potomac and a very popular destination in the summer time. We found two seats in the back for our wives while Roberto and I stood. María sat with her knapsack on her lap. I was tempted to give her mine to hold as well, but the quarters were too tight for me to make the necessary maneuver. As other passengers got on and the press of bodies increased, I could feel the weight of my revolver digging into my back. I had double-checked to make sure the safety was on before I put the gun into my knapsack. Nonetheless, I couldn't shake the image of my revolver going off by accident in a crowded streetcar.

We planned to get off near Chain Bridge, well before the trolley reached Glen Echo and disgorged most of its passengers. As the stop approached, María pulled the cord to signal our intention to descend. The trolley lurched to a halt and we had to fight our way through the mob to get to the exit door. Once on the ground, we breathed a collective sigh of relief. Although it was early in the day and the temperature was still in the seventies, we were all perspiring freely. "Sorry for the rough ride," I said, wiping my forehead with a handkerchief.

"Don't worry Pete," Graciela said. "Roberto and I are used to riding crowded trams. It's even worse in Montevideo. At least nobody pinched my bottom."

That brought a laugh from all of us. "Okay," I said. "Follow me."

I led the way down to the parking lot under Chain Bridge, a narrow span which connected the District with Virginia. Our plan was to follow the towpath from Chain Bridge past Glen Echo and Cabin John to Great Falls on the Potomac, where we would stop for lunch. The distance was a little more than five miles, most of it easy walking until you reached the falls. Then, depending on how we all felt, we would either continue on past the falls or return to Chain Bridge. María and I figured that a ten mile hike would be plenty for the Walkers. But, considering the obviously fine physical condition of both perhaps they would be up for more exercise. At any rate, we would cross that bridge when we got to it.

At the towpath, I suggested that we apply our insect repellent before we proceeded. The Walkers had forgotten to bring some so I supplied a bottle that had more than enough for the four of us. Graciela wrinkled her nose at the odor as she applied the lotion to her arms and the back of her neck. "Not the most pleasant smell is it?" I said with a smile. "But it's effective." We could already see swarms of gnats circling us and I heard the distinct whine of a mosquito in my ear as I applied a liberal dose to my exposed arms, neck, and ears.

Before we set out, I provided a history lesson. Sounding like a tour guide, I pointed to the canal in front of us. "This is one of the first east-west canals in the United States. It is claimed that George Washington helped survey the land for its construction. It was finished in the early nineteenth century and runs from Cumberland, Maryland to Washington. For a long time, it was used primarily to ship coal by barge from West Virginia and Pennsylvania to the east coast. Mules along the path we are about to walk pulled the barges along the water. When other means of transportation proved more efficient, the canal fell into disuse in the 1930s and the federal government assumed control and turned it into a national park. The tow path we are about to walk…"

Graciela interrupted. "Excuse me Pete. What exactly means a 'towpath.'?"

"I'm sorry Graciela. I should have explained more clearly. It's the path that, as you see, runs parallel to the canal and allowed the mules to 'tow,' or pull the barges."

"Sorry Pete. Now that you explain it, I see. But it's the first time for me to hear this word. We do not have anything like this in Uruguay."

"It's no problem Graciela. No problem at all. Please, if you have any questions, don't hesitate to ask." I paused for a moment. "Now where was I? Oh yes, the towpath we are going to follow to some waterfalls is flat, smooth, and easy to walk. As you can see," I said, waving my right arm above my head, "there are trees that provide plenty of shade. We'll be thankful for that once the sun gets higher in the sky." Then, pointing southward across the canal, I added, "And over there is the Potomac River. The canal runs generally parallel to the river, which not only provides some pleasant scenery but also produces a cool breeze from time to time." My lecture concluded, I said, "So if we are all ready, let's get started."

Roberto and I took the lead, our wives close behind us. I set a moderate pace, not wanting to overdo it. I had no doubts about Roberto's ability to keep up. He had shown himself to be quite the athlete and in excellent physical condition. I was more concerned about Graciela, who despite looking fit was wearing what I thought were the wrong kind of shoes and not fully prepared for the rigors ahead. After we walked about a mile, I suggested we stop and have some water. While it was not exceptionally warm, we were all perspiring freely and needed to replenish the lost fluids. I had brought some salt tablets with me just in case and offered them to anyone who wanted one. There were no takers, but it was early and I suspected they would come in handy later.

So far, Roberto and Graciela were doing fine and seemed to be enjoying the outing. After a five-minute break, we resumed walking. We passed a few other hikers on the trail and exchanged greetings, but for the most part had the path to ourselves. Behind us, María and Graciela kept up a steady stream of conversation in Spanish. At first, Roberto and I were less chatty, simply enjoying the walk and the chance to be out in nature and away from the city. From time to time, he would ask me questions about the vegetation and the occasional wildlife we spotted, which I did my best to answer.

After another period of silence, I asked Roberto, "So my friend. How are you finding life in the United States? Everything going all right?"

"Yes Pete," he replied. "Yes, everything is fine. And largely thanks to you and María. Your friendship has made all the difference. All the difference in the world. Especially for Graciela. Meeting María – and you of course – has been a blessing. If not, I don't know how she would have been able to make the adjustment."

I was a little embarrassed and at first didn't know how to respond. "Well," I said, "it's been important for us too Roberto. And María and I are delighted to have you as friends. But what I meant was, how are you finding things in the United States in general? Is it what you expected?"

He smiled. "Well, yes. I think so. Having spent so much time in England and having visited the States, I had a pretty good idea of how things work here. And thanks to you Pete, I have taken up an interest in something I had never paid much attention to before."

"Let me guess," I said. "It's baseball. Right?"

He laughed. "Yes, it is. Ever since our game I've been reading the sports pages and trying to understand how the games have gone; which teams won and which teams lost and why. It's still a little puzzling, but I think I'm getting the hang of it."

"It can be complicated Roberto, even for some who have grown up with the game. Say, maybe we could go to one of the Senators' games and I could help explain a few things to you."

"That would be great Pete. That's the local major league team, right?"

I laughed. "Well technically 'major league.' They really are not very good. But they do play in the major leagues. In fact, I think they are playing the New York Yankees sometime this week. I'll check the schedule and see if I can get tickets. It probably won't be much of a contest as the Yankees are the far better team. But it might be fun for you to see great players in action."

"I'd like that Pete. I really would."

We lapsed into another period of silence. After a few minutes, Roberto said, "Pardon me Pete, but maybe you could help me with something."

"Sure Roberto. What is it?"

"I got a letter from my home office the other day asking for my assessment of the current political situation here in the United States. They wonder if anything is happening that might affect our business. I've been trying to keep up with things as best I can by reading the newspapers. But I thought maybe you could provide more insight. For example, I can't quite understand what this Senator McCarthy is trying to do. I read this week that he was claiming that General Marshall was involved in some kind of Communist plot. Isn't the General one of your most famous and respected men?" Then he added, "I hope I'm not being impertinent Pete. I've heard that the three things you should never discuss with North Americans are sex, religion, and politics."

I laughed. "That's a rule that is often broken." Then, more seriously, I continued, "I'm not sure I can add much to what you have read beyond my own personal opinion..."

"That's okay Pete. I value your opinion."

"Well, for what it's worth I think that Senator McCarthy with his campaign to unearth supposed Communists is doing the country irreparable harm. I have no sympathy for Communists. And I do think there are some – if not outright party members then at least their sympathizers – in certain branches of government. A few have already been exposed. But finding them is up to the Justice Department, not a demagogue like McCarthy, who throws accusations around recklessly, smearing many innocents. To accuse General Marshall of being in cahoots with the Communists is simply absurd. He was a distinguished and widely admired commander during the war, playing a major role in our victory over the Axis. And as secretary of state he developed some of our most successful policies to try to contain Soviet advances in Europe and elsewhere. I don't think many people would buy the line that McCarthy is trying to sell so far as Marshall is concerned – at least I hope that is the case. I think the good senator may have overstepped the lines in attacking such a respected figure."

"Why does he do it, this McCarthy?"

"Well he does it because it makes him prominent and powerful. He plays on the fears of the general public that somehow we have an enemy that has infiltrated our government. He has taken advantage of a strain in our history to latch on to conspiracy theories to explain events that we do not fully understand. In fact, if I believed in such theories I might suspect that Senator McCarthy himself was a Soviet agent, intent on sowing suspicion and division and discrediting our leaders and our institutions."

Roberto seemed surprised. "Do you really think that might be possible?"

"Anything's possible. But, no I don't. I think Senator McCarthy is simply an opportunist who has latched onto an idea that has made him powerful – and feared." I hesitated a moment. "There is also the possibility that along with his ruthlessness he is a bit deranged. It's no great secret that he is an alcoholic."

"He sounds like a very unpleasant character."

"Yes he is, at least in my opinion. But you should also know that he has many admirers and fervent supporters, those who believe that he is a great patriot doing what needs to be done to counter the so-called Communist menace."

We then talked about other issues of the day. Roberto wanted to know more about President Truman's standoff with General MacArthur, the on-going stalemate in Korea, and the prospects for the presidential election next year. Once again, I gave him my opinions: that Truman had done the right thing in dismissing MacArthur, reaffirming civilian authority over the military. So far as the Korean War was concerned, I didn't see much hope for a definitive military solution. Rather, I speculated, there would be some kind of negotiated settlement that would bring a cease-fire and a still divided country. With regard to the 1952 elections, I told him that it seemed General Eisenhower was the leading candidate, although at the moment it wasn't clear whether he would run on the Democratic or Republican ticket. President Truman, whose public approval rating was at an all-time low, was being cagey about running for re-election after his upset win in 1948. Some Republicans, I said, were encouraging General MacArthur to run as well.

"It seems to me Pete, that here, as in much of Latin America, military men are very influential in your political life."

"At this moment, that seems to be the case."

Roberto had a bemused look on his face. "In my country, Uruguay, the military is not so important. Our armed forces are small and rarely interfere in our democratic politics." He paused for a moment. "Of course across the estuary in Argentina that is not the case. The military has been running things ever since they ousted a civilian president in 1930. Right now they have another General in charge."

I debated a response, not wanting to get too involved in a discussion that might touch on my own experiences with the "General" in question. I proceeded carefully. "You mean General Perón, I presume?"

"That's right. *General* Perón," he replied, his voice dripping with sarcasm.

"What do you think of him?" I asked.

"I don't think much of him Pete to tell you the truth. He is a reckless demagogue, much like your Senator McCarthy. He pretends to be a friend of the working class while he and his wife enjoy a life of luxury that would be the envy of the so-called oligarchy of wealthy landowners he loves to vilify. And he labels anyone who dares to criticize him as a traitor. He has even sent his agents to Uruguay to intimidate Argentine exiles who speak against him. He is just another one of the dictators who have cursed our region for so many years. And as bad as he is, his wife is even worse. I have nothing against women being involved in politics. In fact, Uruguay has been at the forefront of granting the vote and other rights to women. But this Evita is taking advantage of her status as first lady to exact revenge on all those she believes slighted her. Despite the saintly aura the regime has created for her, she is ruthless and with a relentless ambition. There was even talk a few months ago of having her run as Perón's vice-presidential candidate. Can you imagine that?"

I was a bit taken aback by Roberto's passionate and heartfelt attack on the Peróns. It was the first time I had seen him get so worked up about anything we had discussed. His disdain for the couple that ruled Argentina seemed genuine and was natural for a person with his background, coming from the class of *estancieros* who were the target of much of Perón's demagoguery. Perón also had blamed British "imperialism" for many of Argentina's troubles and his pro-Axis position during the war certainly would not endear him to someone like Roberto Walker with his strong ties to England. I was about to come up with some sort of response when María, who had undoubtedly overheard our conversation, interrupted. "Pete, darling. Could we stop for a rest? Somehow I've gotten a pebble in my boot that is driving me crazy."

"Sure thing sweetheart," I replied.

We found some logs on the side of the trail and sat down to rest. Next to me, María removed the boot from her right foot and made an elaborate show of shaking it. "There it is," she exclaimed, pointing to a small pebble on the ground. Whether it had actually come from her boot or had been there all along I could not tell. Nor could the Walkers, whose view of the maneuver I had blocked. I strongly suspected that the whole "pebble in the boot" exercise was María's way of telling me that the conversation with Roberto over the Peróns had gone far enough and was threatening to enter into dangerous territory.

I got the message loud and clear. When we resumed walking, I shifted the conversation back to politics in the U.S. Roberto seemed content to let me ramble on, occasionally breaking in to ask me to clarify some point or another. But there was no further discussion of the situation in Argentina.

It was turning out to be a lovely morning. The sky was full of puffy white clouds against a background of clear blue. The towpath was lined with leafy trees that provided an agreeable shade. On the other side of the canal we could hear the flow of the Potomac and as we neared the falls the sound of rapids. We were maintaining a steady pace, not too fast or too slow. As I had expected, Roberto was showing no signs of fatigue. I was sure he could go on well past the falls. Graciela, too, seemed to be holding up well. Her face was a bit flushed, but her breathing was regular and the smile on her face indicated that she was enjoying the exercise. So far as I could tell, her footwear was proving adequate to the task. No indications of incipient blisters that I could notice.

We reached Great Falls a little after noon. The Walkers expressed their pleasure with the falls, the water cascading in waves over the gray rocks. "Not exactly Niagra," I said. "But it's what we have."

"It's delightful," Graciela gushed. "I've never seen anything quite like it. The only river I know is the Río de La Plata which is broad and flat, almost like a lake. We do have the Cataratas of Iguazu where Argentina, Brazil, and Paraguay meet. But I have only seen them in pictures."

"I've seen some waterfalls in Northern England," Roberto said. "But these are still quite spectacular. Thank you so much for allowing us to see them with you."

"You are most welcome," María said. "Now let's eat. I am starving!"

We found a picnic table in a spot that provided shade but also allowed us to get a full view of the falls. There were no other picnickers on our side of the river, which was just unadorned park land. On the Virginia side, however, there was a large crowd enjoying the carousel and other amusements that were available. A few brave souls were swimming farther upstream. From what I knew, the Potomac at this level was not yet subject to the contamination that was making it unhealthy for swimming downstream.

As I took off my knapsack to unload the sandwiches, I had a moment of panic. The sweat from my back had soaked the canvas and the outline of my pistol was as clear as day. I wasn't sure, but I thought Roberto's eyebrows went up in surprise. I put the pack down carefully on its back so as to hide the telltale markings and began to unload the sandwiches and drinks. María had carried the paper plates and utensils as well as a light-weight tablecloth to add a little elegance to our lunch. We had debated bringing wine but had determined that it might not go well with our exertions on a hot day.

We sat around the table and munched on our sandwiches and sipped our sodas. I was afraid that Roberto might ask what I was carrying in my knapsack besides the food, thus putting a definite pall on the conversation. But if he had noticed the pistol outline, he didn't mention it, much to my relief. Instead, María and the Walkers continued to swap stories about adjusting to life in the United States and reminiscing about their homelands. I mostly listened, interjecting a comment now and then but letting them do most of the talking.

My concern that Roberto might have discovered I was carrying a pistol had sobered me. It also reminded me, as if I needed reminding, that we were hiding from them the fact that we might be putting them in some danger by associating with us. I still thought the likelihood that the four of us would be attacked by those who had struck at Ralph Turner slim. Nonetheless, I could not dismiss the possibility entirely.

María must have noticed my pensive musings. Turning to me, she asked, "And what do you think darling?"

I shook myself out of my reverie. "About what sweetheart? Sorry, but I lost track of the conversation. Buried in my own thoughts I guess."

"We were talking about how it seems as though everybody in the United States has an automobile, sometimes even two. Graciela and Roberto were saying that this seems to be one of the main differences with Uruguay and Argentina, where fewer people own automobiles and most people depend on public transportation. They were wondering that if they stay longer, might they need to purchase an automobile for their own use. What do you think?"

I pondered the question for a few seconds, glad to be pulled away from darker thoughts. "Well, I suppose it all depends on whether they remain in the city or not. In this country, many people who work in cities like Washington and New York are moving to the suburbs. While we do have buses and trains, they are not always reliable and can be noisy, crowded, and uncomfortable. So more and more commuters are buying their own automobiles for their trips from home to office as well as for the independence they provide. On the other hand, as you might have noticed, the growing number of cars also means increased traffic and smoke in the air. Since María and I have lived in New York and now in Washington, we really have not yet seen the need to have an automobile. If we were to move to the suburbs it might be a different story.

"Of course," I added, "Right now not having an automobile poses a bit of a problem. When we go to the Blue Ridge Mountains next weekend, we will need to have a car to get there. That's really the only practical way for us to travel."

"Can we rent one?" Roberto asked.

"I'm looking into that Roberto," I said. "But I think I can borrow one from a friend." I was thinking of David Friedman. David had bought a sedan several years ago but barely used it. I had meant to ask him at our Friday lunch if I might have the use of it for our hiking trip but it had slipped my mind. I intended to call him that night with my request.

When we finished our lunch, I asked the Walkers if they would like to continue beyond the falls for a few more miles. They were keen to keep going, both of them seeming none the worse for wear. We gathered up the debris from our lunch and I placed most of it in my knapsack. I faced the dilemma of how best to hide the fact that I was shifting my pistol to a place where it would not be so conspicuous without the Walkers seeing what I was doing. Fortunately, they were distracted by something that María was pointing out to them on the other side of the river. That distraction enabled me to readjust the position of the pistol so that its outline was no longer visible.

I hoisted my knapsack onto my back. I was satisfied that my weapon was where I could reach it with ease if needed. "Say," I said as we left the picnic table. "Instead of staying on the towpath, how about trying a side trail that will lead us closer to the falls? It will only take us about fifteen minutes to navigate and will provide a wonderful view."

"Sounds like a great idea Pete," Roberto said. "Lead the way and we'll follow."

I had not actually been on that particular path, which made a loop and rejoined the towpath above the falls. But one of the Justice Department lawyers who had done a lot of hiking suggested we give it a try. The entrance to the path was only about twenty yards from where we had had our lunch and we headed for it. When we started on it, with me at the lead, I soon learned that it posed more of a challenge than the smooth and level towpath. For one thing, it was much narrower, barely room for one person. For another, the footing was treacherous, with moss-covered rocks underfoot. We also had to navigate some steep inclines, requiring us to go slowly and brace ourselves against the large boulders that loomed on each side.

As we made our way upwards, I paused every few minutes to catch my breath and to check if the others following me were all right. They assured me they were and we soldiered on. After about fifteen minutes of steady climbing, the path began to level off at the summit. There were still large boulders to our right, but to our left, the path skirted the very edge of a steep cliff giving us an unobstructed view of the roaring rapids below. It was indeed a spectacular sight.

Just as I turned my head to ask my companions what they thought of the view, I could feel my left foot slip on a loose rock. As I struggled to regain my balance, I could feel my knapsack shift toward my left side, adding impetus to my impending fall into the rapids and rocks some fifty feet below. I heard María let out a shriek of alarm as she witnessed my predicament. I did my best to halt my descent, but my right foot was also losing its grip. Just as I was about to go headfirst over the cliff, I felt Roberto's strong right arm grab me around the waist. "Don't worry Pete," he said his voice steady and calm. "I've got you." Then he told Graciela and María to grab hold of him to keep him steady, which they did immediately. Their combined efforts got me back onto solid ground.

I was both relieved and embarrassed. *Some trail guide I had turned out to be!* Just seconds away from real disaster. If I had survived the fall, I'm not sure I would have made it through the rock-strewn rapids.

María hugged me, holding tight. "Pete. Pete," she said, tears in her eyes. "I was scared to death." Then, turning to Roberto: "I can't thank you enough Roberto. You saved Pete's life. If you hadn't reacted so quickly, I don't know…"

Roberto brushed it off. "Think nothing of it María. Just a natural reaction. I saw Pete begin to slip and did what I could to prevent him from falling. Anyone would have done the same."

"But he could have pulled you over with him," María said, her voice shaking. "And I'm not so sure that *anyone* would have reacted the same way."

Roberto just shrugged. "María's right," I said. "And I'll forever be in your debt my friend. You risked your life to save mine." Being extra-careful of my footing this time, I gave Roberto an *abrazo* and pounded him on his back. "And I'll never forget it."

After some discussion and assurances from me that I was okay, we decided to continue. As we set out back to the towpath, I tried to lighten the mood. "Well, it *was* a spectacular view wasn't it?" Everybody laughed, although I could see that María was still upset.

Back on level ground, we continued heading westward. If nothing else, we had determined that the Walkers should have no trouble facing the rigors of hiking in the mountains. And Roberto had more than proved that he was up to any challenge that might arise. Even though I had already seen his strength, speed, and coordination on the baseball field, I still marveled at how quick his reflexes had been when he grabbed me around the waist. His demeanor was also impressive. He hadn't panicked, hadn't hesitated, and acted with great self-assurance. *And to think that I had once imagined him to be just another spoiled South American aristocrat!* Instead, he reminded me more of some of the men with whom I served in the OSS. He had told me of his regret that he had not been able to fight in the world war. If he had, based on what I had seen, I am sure he would have made a great soldier.

After trudging on for a few more miles, we turned around and made for Chain Bridge. When we again reached the side trail to the falls, we all agreed that once was enough and stayed on the towpath. We got to Chain Bridge at around four, all of us toasted by the sun and dripping with perspiration. We were tired but happy. Except for my misadventure on the rocks, the day had been a success. When the streetcar arrived, we once again had to fight for space but were fortunate to find four seats in the back. I assured the Walkers that one of the benefits of our planned hike in the mountains next weekend would be no crowded streetcars to contend with. We got off with them at Dupont Circle just as dark clouds appeared on the western horizon. After exchanging the usual hugs and cheek kisses, María and I told the Walkers we would see them soon and then boarded the Connecticut Avenue streetcar for home.

As we took our seats, María held on tightly to my arm. "Pete, Pete my darling, she said in Spanish. "You gave me quite a fright. Thank goodness Roberto was able to react so quickly. Otherwise, I hate to think what might have happened."

"I'm sorry sweetheart. It was a careless moment. And yes, thank goodness for Roberto being there to keep me from falling."

"It is ironic, isn't it," María said with a worried look, "that after all you have been through in the war, almost losing your life in Argentina, and now with the threats from whoever is behind the attack on Ralph you might have been done in by a simple slip on a rock."

I knew there was more behind the observation. María's preoccupation with my tendency to take risks and court danger never lay too far beneath the surface. I always did what I could to reassure her, but I knew the worry was never far from her mind. Now she had seen first-hand that no matter how many precautions I might take, fate could intervene. Instead of some external threat, I could be undone by my own carelessness.

I tried to provide reassurance. "I know María. I should have been more careful. I let myself get preoccupied with enjoying the view and didn't pay enough attention to what was underfoot. I promise that I won't let that happen again."

She snuggled closer and held my arm ever more tightly. "Please do take care Pete. The next time something like that happens, there may not be anyone like Roberto or David around to save you."

She had reminded me that during my "little adventure" in Argentina, if David Friedman had not found me lying on the pampa with a potentially mortal wound, I would not have survived. Even in the heat of a late Washington Sunday afternoon, I could feel her shiver from the memory. I, too, felt a tingle in my spine as I recalled that harrowing night. And she was right. The next time I found my life threatened, I might not be lucky enough to have anyone around to save me. As I had many times before, I shoved that thought to the back of my mind. I had survived more than a few close calls. And while it might have been false courage, I had every confidence that I would continue to do so in the future.

CHAPTER TWENTY

June 18, 1951 – Washington, D.C.

I got to my Justice Department office a little after eight in the morning on Monday. Since we were planning to leave with the Walkers for the Blue Ridge on Friday, I wanted to make sure I had all my work for the week done by Thursday afternoon. Joe Smathers had already given me approval for the day off, the first I had taken since I had arrived.

As I sat down behind my desk, I stared blankly into space, mulling over what María and I had decided the previous evening. We had come to the conclusion that before we left for the Blue Ridge with the Walkers we had to let them know the danger they might face by accompanying us. As much as we hated the possibility that it might put an end to our budding friendship, it was the right thing to do.

I had promised María that I would talk to Joe Smathers first thing the next day to get the go ahead from him. I had an appointment with him in fifteen minutes.

After María and I had made this decision, I called David Friedman from the phone in the hallway. I had a couple of things to ask him. He picked up on the second ring. "Hello David," I said. "Hope I'm not interrupting anything."

"No Pete. Not at all. What's up?"

I filled him in on our hike with the Walkers. I could hear a sharp intake of breath when I told him about my misadventure on the rocks.

I could imagine him shaking his head as if to say, "That's Pete Benton for you. Always flirting with trouble."

"Lucky for you that Roberto was there to save you from serious injury."

"Yes. It was. Really lucky." I went on. "You know that we were preparing for a weekend hike with the Walkers on the Appalachian Trail in the Blue Ridge. We plan to leave on Friday and I was wondering if I could borrow your car for the trip."

"Sure thing Pete. I won't be using it. Feel free. Why don't you come by Thursday after work and pick it up?"

"Thanks buddy. I really appreciate it."

"No problem. Was there anything else?"

I paused for a moment and made sure that María was not listening. She was in the living room, the radio tuned to some classical music. "Yes, there is. Roberto Walker told me that he worked for a company called Oribe and Hermanos. Could you check that out for me?"

There was a brief silence on the other end. Maybe David was thinking the same thing I was: *A guy saves your life and you want the CIA to look into whether he's legitimate?* But then David himself had brought it up during our last lunch.

Finally David said "I'll do what I can Pete. I have some contacts from my time in the Latin American bureau. I'll see if they can help me out. It may take a while. We're still all wrapped up in this Burgess-McLean business. And I'm knee-deep working on the consequences of the new government in Iran. So you have some doubts about Roberto? Even after his heroics on the ball field and during your hike?"

I felt a little embarrassed. "Not really. There is just a little nagging doubt that I'd like to have resolved. You know how it is."

He chuckled. "Yes I do my friend. Indeed I do. I'll get back to you as soon as I find out anything."

"Thanks again," I said. We exchanged goodbyes and hung up.

As I put the phone down, María came into the hallway. "Who were you talking to darling?" I hoped she hadn't overheard.

"David. I just wanted to check that we could borrow his car for our trip next weekend."

"And?"

"And we can. He won't be using it. I'll be picking it up Thursday night."

"That's very kind of David," she said. Then cocking an eye at me, she asked, "Are you sure you can drive? We wouldn't want anything to happen to David's car. Or to us."

Being a big city boy, I had never actually owned a car. But I could drive, as I had proved on various occasions in rural areas where there was no public transportation. The times that María had been with me, I had to admit, my skills had left something to be desired. We had barely escaped accidents of various degrees of severity.

"Don't worry," I said with false confidence. "Even though I'm a little out of practice, I'm sure I can get us to and from our destination without any catastrophes. David's car – and those within it – will be safe and sound."

She gave me a skeptical look, but nodded in a way that sent the message: "If you say so. But I'll believe it when I see it."

I didn't say anything about my request that David look into Roberto's claim to be working for a company called Oribe and Hermanos. I hated keeping this from my wife. Given how attached she had become to the Walkers, and particularly to Graciela, I didn't know how she would react to any hint of suspicion I might harbor about them. But I was sure she would not be pleased. The chances were more than good that Roberto would check out just fine. If he didn't, then we would deal with it as best we could. Better not to rock the marital boat until I got an answer. I hoped it was the right choice and one I would not come to regret later on.

I met with Joe Smathers at the appointed time. He knew we were planning to be with the Walkers over the weekend and had given us some helpful tips about our trip. When I told about our decision to let the Walkers know what they might be in for, he reluctantly agreed that it was the best thing to do. "Just keep it as vague as you can Pete," he said soberly. "It is only fair they be informed. But try not to go into too many of the details."

"Will do Joe. And thanks." I added, "I don't really think anything is going to happen. But just in case…"

"Yeah. Just in case."

As I got up to leave, Joe added, "And don't forget to take your guns – you know, 'just in case.' And, he said with a grin, "That goes for María as well. From what I hear, she is quite the marksman – or should I say marks*woman*."

I returned the grin. "Yeah. I think anyone who underestimates her is in for a real surprise."

Back at my office, Tim O'Rourke sauntered in at nine thirty, humming a show tune. Our weekly staff meeting, which ordinarily met at nine on Monday, conflicted with some other business for Joe and had been scheduled for later in the day. This allowed Tim the luxury of arriving at what he considered a more "civilized" hour after a long weekend.

He didn't seem to have a care in the world. We caught up on our respective weekends. His included the usual "great time with a great gal," a Veronica Lake look-alike he had brought to Joe's barbecue. I kidded him that it sounded as if it might be getting serious. "Maybe matrimony is in the cards," I joked.

Tim recoiled, an exaggerated look of panic on his face. "Please Pete," he said. "You know how just the mention of the word gives me the willies." But behind the mock horror, I thought I detected a hint that maybe this time this girl was different; more than just a casual fling.

When I told him about our Sunday hike with the Walkers, he just shook his head when I recounted my near fall into the abyss. I also told him about my meeting with Joe and his agreement that I should let the Walkers know what they might be in for if they spent the weekend with us in the Blue Ridge. Tim had taken a real shine to Roberto after his exploits on the softball field and I could see the gleam in his eye when he met Graciela. Not that he would consider anything out of bounds. Tim had more than enough single women to choose from. He drew the line at trying to lure those who were already married. But that didn't stop him from admiring a beautiful woman when he met one.

"I'd hate to see anything happen to the Walkers," he said.

"So would I buddy. So would I. In fact, I'm going to call Roberto right now."

I picked up the phone and dialed the number they had given us. After a few rings, Graciela picked up. Following the usual greetings and chit-chat, I asked to speak to Roberto."

"I'm sorry Pete," she said. "He has already left for the office. But I'm sure he wouldn't mind if you called him there. Do you have the number?"

"I'm sorry to bother you Graciela. Perhaps I can call some other time. I don't want to disturb him while he is working. It's not that important."

"No. No Pete. He won't mind, I assure you." She gave me the office number and seemed rather insistent that I contact Roberto.

Before she hung up, she said how excited she and Roberto were at the prospect of the coming weekend. "We are really looking forward to it Pete." Thankfully, she didn't add what she might have been thinking, "Just don't cause us any more excitement like you did yesterday."

I dialed the number she had given me. Someone picked up immediately. A female voice with a distinct Latin accent answered: "Oribe and Hermanos. How may I help you?"

Immediately, I felt my face flush. What had I expected? Roberto had told me that he worked for Oribe and Hermanos. Now I had confirmation, or at least what seemed confirmation. It was, after all, only a voice on the other end of a telephone line. "I would like to speak with Roberto Walker please."

"Certainly sir. Just a moment. I'll put you right through. Who may I say is calling?"

"Pete Benton."

"Very good sir."

After a few clicks, I heard Roberto's voice. "Pete my friend. What a pleasure. How are you? So good to hear from you."

In truth, I was feeling more than a little guilty. Just the night before I had asked David Friedman to look into whether Roberto actually worked for a company called Oribe and Hermanos and, indeed, if such a company even existed. Now, it seemed, everything Roberto had told me was on the up and up.

Of course, I didn't tell him any of this. Instead, I replied, "I'm fine Roberto. Just fine. And you?"

"Just fine Pete, thanks. Just fine." Then he laughed. "But Graciela is a bit stiff and sore this morning. It's been a while since she has gotten any real exercise."

"Well she was a real trooper yesterday. Frankly, I was afraid she didn't have on the right kind of footwear for long walks. You might suggest that she try to break in a pair of real hiking boots before we go to the mountains. Some of the trails are pretty rocky and proper ankle support is a must."

"I'll suggest that Pete. It makes sense. Whether she'll listen to me," he said with a chuckle, "is another matter. She has a mind of her own."

"I know the type," I said with a laugh. "Listen Roberto, I didn't mean to bother you at work. When I called your home Graciela gave me your work number and said it was okay to contact you. But if you're busy, I can…"

"No worries Pete," he said. "Everything here is pretty slow today. I do have meetings in the afternoon, but right now I'm just reviewing some correspondence. What's on your mind?"

"Well, yesterday we talked about going to a baseball game. I saw in the newspaper this morning that the Washington Senators will be playing the New York Yankees tomorrow night and I wondered if you would like to go."

"That sounds great Pete. I'd like that. It sounds like fun."

I arranged to meet Roberto the next day at six at Dupont Circle. After I put down the phone, I tried to gather my thoughts. Tim had overheard my side of the conversation and gave me a look that begged for elaboration.

"I guess you heard. I invited Roberto to go with me to the Senators' game with the Yankees tomorrow night. That'll give me a chance to talk with him about what risks he and Graciela might run by being with us in the Blue Ridge."

"That's the right thing to do Pete. I agree that the chances are pretty slim that the four of you would be attacked. But better to let them know what they might be in for."

"Yeah. I just hope we are not over-reacting. I'd hate to put our friendship with them in jeopardy."

"Well, it would be a lot worse if something *did* happen and you hadn't warned them."

I nodded. "No argument there Tim. You're absolutely correct."

"I guess there were some things we could not have foreseen when we signed on to this task force," he observed. "It seemed pretty straightforward at the beginning. Expose the bad guys and put them out of business. But it's gotten pretty complicated, hasn't it? Especially with the attack on Ralph."

"Yes it has." And I was worried that it might get even more complicated. I gestured to the files on my desk, "But we've got to keep going regardless."

Tim nodded in agreement and we both turned our attention to the mound of paper we had to pile through. I didn't mention to Tim anything about trying to find out more on the company for which Roberto worked. My phone call to his office seemed to verify that he did indeed work for an outfit called Oribe and Hermanos. I was tempted to call David and ask him not to look any further into the matter. He had enough on his plate. But, in the end, I figured it wouldn't hurt to give him some time to gather more information and to eliminate that little sliver of doubt we both shared. Little did I know how fateful that decision would be.

CHAPTER TWENTY ONE

June 19, 1951 – Washington, D.C.

The next evening, I met Roberto at six as planned. María had accompanied me on the streetcar. She and Graciela had arranged to have dinner and then take in a movie downtown while the "boys" were at the ball game.

The Walkers were waiting for us as we got off at Dupont Circle. Once again, I was impressed by their punctuality. They seemed to be adapting to North American customs with a vengeance.

We exchanged the usual hugs and kisses. María and Graciela told us to have fun and walked down Connecticut Avenue arm-in-arm while Roberto and I waited for the streetcar that would take us east along P Street to Seventh, where we would change to the northbound for Griffith Stadium.

I was dressed in a casual shirt and slacks, as was Roberto. The weather was warming up again and we had dressed accordingly. I had decided not to carry my revolver with me. At our Monday status meeting, Joe Smathers had again encouraged us to stay armed and alert. Even though there had been no signs of trouble since the attack on Ralph, not even a hint that anybody was being followed or observed by suspicious characters, he didn't want us to let down our guard.

It was good advice. But in this instance, I decided to ignore it. To carry my pistol meant wearing a coat, which would make me stand out.

Moreover, I was going to be in public with plenty of people around, making it extremely unlikely that I would be targeted. I insisted to María, however, that even though the same circumstances applied to her, she should still carry her revolver in her purse. She wasn't entirely happy with my suggestion. But when I told her that it would help give me peace of mind, she reluctantly went along.

We only had to wait five minutes for the next car to navigate the circle and pick us up on the south side of P Street. The car was about three-quarters full, predominately men who were headed for the same destination as we were.

Roberto and I found a seat about halfway down the car.

"I'm really looking forward to this game," he told me. "A new experience for me. And I appreciate the invitation."

"I'm looking forward to it as well Roberto," I said. "And I hope you enjoy it."

"I'm sure I will." Then he asked, "Do you attend many games?"

"Not that many here. In fact, this is only the second one this season. My work keeps me pretty busy. But in New York, I usually take in about a dozen each summer."

As the streetcar rolled past Logan Circle, I explained the make-up of the American and National Leagues and provided thumbnail sketches of the various teams in each. "I'm afraid the game tonight will not be very competitive. The Yankees are loaded with talent and are likely to win both their league championship and the World Series. The Senators usually reside at the bottom of the league. Of course, there are always upsets. But probably not tonight."

"That's okay with me Pete," Roberto said. "I'm sure I'll enjoy the evening no matter what the score."

I refrained from warning him that the news I had to deliver might make the evening less than enjoyable.

At Seventh Street, we, along with most of the other passengers, descended from the car. There was a long line waiting to get on the northbound trolley up to the stadium, so we decided to walk the remaining six or seven blocks. Our route took us through a predominantly Negro neighborhood, past a mixture of homes, restaurants, bars, churches, and shops. We could hear jazz playing as we passed open windows and saw families sitting down for dinner.

While we walked, Roberto told me in Spanish that this was a new experience for him. He had heard about places like Harlem in New York, but had never been in close proximity to a Negro neighborhood. There were some Negro areas in Montevideo, but they were in isolated areas on the outskirts, not right in the center of the city. I pointed out that in the vicinity of the stadium sat Howard University, an all-Negro institution.

"I don't see any Negroes headed to the stadium," Roberto observed. "Do they not like baseball?"

"Actually, many of them love baseball. But up until recently, Negro players were not allowed into the major leagues. Instead, they had to content themselves with an all-Negro League of their own. A few years ago, however, the first Negro to break the color barrier started playing for the Brooklyn Dodgers. You may have heard of him – Jackie Robinson." Roberto nodded. "Since then, a few others have joined, but they are just a handful. And the two teams we are going to see, the Yankees and the Senators, have yet to sign a Negro player. So there is little incentive for the Negroes in Washington to attend a baseball game until that happens. If Jackie Robinson were playing for either team, I can guarantee you that most of this neighborhood would either try to see the game in person or listen to it on the radio."

"That's very interesting Pete," Roberto observed. "Very interesting indeed. I guess I have a lot to learn not only about baseball but also about American history."

"Well, like any country," I said somewhat pompously, "we have many things to take pride in and a few to be ashamed of. I'm afraid that our treatment of Negroes falls into the latter category."

By the time I had uttered that profundity, we had arrived at the stadium. The lines for tickets were unusually long. Even though most Washington fans knew they were in for a beating, the Yankees were a big draw. And many fans knew that this might be their last chance to see the legendary Joe DiMaggio, who was in the twilight of his career. When we finally got to the ticket booth, I asked for seats in the upper deck behind home plate. I informed Roberto that even though our seats were high up in the stands and rather far from the action, we would have a good view of the pitcher and the catcher. We also might benefit from whatever breeze might be stirring. Even though by seven o'clock the sun was beginning its descent, it was still hot and muggy. But the real reason I chose those seats was in the hope that we would not be surrounded by other fans and I could tell Roberto about the potential danger he and Graciela might face if they accompanied us to the Blue Ridge Mountains.

We entered the stadium, which was about half-full. I looked up towards our seats and was relieved to see that most of the top rows were empty. Before we climbed to the top, I bought us hot dogs with mustard and two National Bohemian beers. It wasn't the best beer in the world, but National Bo was a sponsor of the Senators' radio broadcast and held a virtual monopoly on the sale of beer at the stadium. At least it was cold. "All part of the baseball experience," I told Roberto as we made our way to our seats.

Once seated, we ate our hot dogs and sipped our beer. I was certain that María and Graciela were enjoying finer fare. But there was something about being at the ballpark that made even the hum-drum hot dogs delicious and the mediocre beer taste like a heavenly brew. Roberto took it all in – the vast field of green laid out before us, the smell of cigar smoke wafting up in our direction, the calls of vendors selling peanuts and cracker jacks. After we had finished our hot dogs, I called to one of the vendors for two boxes of cracker jacks. He was about ten rows down and I signaled for him to toss the boxes to me. His throws were right on target. I tossed him a couple of quarters, which he caught one-handed with easy grace. Perhaps the best athletes, I thought, were not necessarily on the field but in the stands, serving the public.

We stood up for the national anthem, and then the game began. The pitcher for the Senators was Bob Porterfield, their ace and a serviceable right-hander with a good fastball. For the Yankees, it was Eddie Lopat, a lefthander with a looping curve ball. He didn't throw very hard, but he was extremely deceptive. For most of the night he kept the Senators off balance and off the bases. Porterfield, on the other hand, had little luck against the loaded Yankees. We saw DiMaggio hit a triple into the gap between left and center. He might have been close to retirement, but he could still run like a deer. A new Yankee star, Mickey Mantle, hit a towering home run over the wall in right, showed off a powerful arm to cut down a runner at the plate, and stole two bases with blazing speed. By the time Yogi Berra golfed another shot out of the park in the sixth inning, the Yankees led 8 to 0 and the game was essentially over.

"Well Pete," Roberto said after the Senators went down one-two-three at the bottom of the inning. "You were right. It looks as though the home team is terribly overmatched."

"I hope you don't find the one-sided nature of the game too boring."

"Well, to be frank, it could be more exciting, but I'm enjoying it nonetheless." Throughout the game, I had kept up a steady flow of chatter, trying to provide as much information about the game and the players as I could. "And thanks to you," Roberto added, "I have learned a lot."

"I hope I haven't, as we say, 'talked your ear off.'"

He chuckled. "Well, maybe a little. But then, I have a lot to learn. And you have been a great teacher."

By the top of the seventh, the crowd began to thin. Office workers had to get home and to bed. Even die-hard Senators fans knew the chances of the home team mounting a rally were meager. Lopat was firmly in control, having given up only three measly singles, and showed no signs of tiring. Around us the few fans who had huffed and puffed to the upper rows had either left or gone down to now-abandoned seats closer to the action. Nonetheless, to err on the side of caution, I switched to Spanish.

"Listen Roberto," I said my face serious and my voice low, "there is something we need to discuss."

Roberto looked a little surprised, but nodded. "Sure, Pete. What is it? Something wrong?"

"Maybe," I said. "But it's something you – and Graciela – need to be aware of before we go to the Blue Ridge this weekend. And I hope you can keep what I am about to tell you in the strictest confidence; only for you and Graciela. Is that okay?"

Roberto gave me a reassuring look. "Whatever you have to tell me Pete goes no further than me and Graciela. You have my word." Then he added, I presume it has something to do with the work you are doing here investigating organized crime. Am I right?"

I took a deep breath. "Yes, you are." I then gave him a summary of the attack on Ralph and our response to it. I tried my best to follow Joe Smathers's advice to keep things vague and without much detail, no easy task. Roberto listened attentively to everything I said without interrupting, his face somber. "So we have decided," I concluded, "that the only honorable course is to make you and Graciela aware of the risks you might be running by being with us, especially in a remote location."

"I understand Pete, and I deeply appreciate you telling me all this. You can rest assured that I won't breathe a word to anyone other than Graciela. And you can trust her not to tell anyone either." He was looking at me straight in the eye when he said this. I could detect no sign that he wasn't telling me anything but the truth.

"Thank you Roberto," I said.'

"Of course, I'll need to discuss this with Graciela before we make any decision."

"I understand Roberto." Then I added, "While I don't want to sway your decision one way or the other, at our task force meeting yesterday we were told that since the attack on Ralph Turner no other threats have appeared. Ralph still has no memory of what happened to him, so we cannot rule out the possibility that it was something random, even something personal – and nothing whatsoever to do with organized crime."

Roberto looked skeptical, but remained silent. "And Joe and I have agreed that it is most unlikely that there would be any attempt on the four of us, or that whoever might be trying to intimidate us would go to the trouble to follow us all the way to the mountains. In addition, María and I will be armed and alert for any possible trouble. And we are both pretty good shots." Roberto's eyebrows went up in surprise when I said *both*. "I've been in some tight spots before," I added, without elaboration, "and as you can see I'm still here."

I'm not sure how much comfort my brave words provided. And I hoped he didn't want more detail on the "tight spots" claim. I was already revealing enough. No need to let him know that I had served in the OSS during the war, not to mention my "little adventure" in Argentina. I did feel confident that I could handle anything that might come up, especially if I had a weapon and was ready for trouble. But there were no guarantees that if confronted everything would turn out for the best, especially with three other lives at stake.

"As I said Pete," Roberto said. "I'll need to talk all this over with Graciela. We are very much looking forward to the weekend. But what you have told us definitely puts a new light on things. I'll let you know as soon as I can what we decide."

I was tempted to say, "We'll I hope you decide: *Damn the danger. We are not going to let a bunch of gangsters tell us what to do!* But that would be trying to tilt the balance unfairly. At least now they had the full story and most of the facts, enough for them to make their own informed decision.

After the Yankees scored two more runs in the top of the seventh and the Senators again went down one-two-three in the bottom of the inning, we decided to join the others who left early. We both had to be at our respective offices early in the morning. When we parted at Dupont Circle, Roberto said, "Thanks again for inviting me to the game. I really did enjoy it. As for the other matter, I'll be in touch as soon as I can."

As Roberto headed off to his apartment, I contemplated walking up Connecticut to our town house. But at that moment, a nearly empty streetcar arrived and I climbed aboard. I was tired and sweaty, ready for a shower. Besides, I hoped that I would get in plenty of walking over the coming weekend. I couldn't tell which way the Walkers would decide. But had a strong feeling, based more on intuition than reason, that we would be hiking the Appalachian Trail together come Saturday.

CHAPTER TWENTY TWO

June 21, 1951 – Washington, D.C.

I was on my way to pick up David's car for our trip to the Blue Ridge. He had driven it to work and I was walking along Constitution Avenue to his office. The plan was for me to drive him to his apartment in Georgetown as I kind of test of my ability to maneuver through the Washington traffic. Then, after leaving him, I would take the car on my own to our town house.

Roberto had called me the evening after we had gone to the ballgame. "Pete," he had said, "Graciela and I have decided we want to go ahead with our plans for the weekend. We discussed it thoroughly and we decided that your friendship means more to us than the slight chance something might happen. After all," he said philosophically and to lighten the mood, "anything could happen. Someone could slip and fall, for example." Then, on a more serious note, he added, "And we have confidence that the four of us can handle anybody who tries to do us any harm."

I was touched by his words. And I hoped his confidence was not misplaced. "Well Roberto," I said, a slight tremor in my voice, "We are very pleased to hear that. Your friendship means a lot to us as well."

"Thanks again Pete for letting us know what we could be in for. I know that things are complicated for you. But it tells me a lot about your character that you would make sure we were fully informed before we set off for the mountains. And don't worry. What you told me will remain strictly confidential. Graciela knows this as well."

We made the arrangements to meet early on Friday morning. Maria had been listening in to my end of the conversation and asked to speak to Graciela. After she hung up, she turned to me, "Well darling, I don't know exactly how I feel. I'm thrilled that we can go ahead with our plans. I just wish it were under different circumstances."

"I know how you feel sweetheart. It's unfortunate we have this cloud hanging over us. But we do, and we'll just have to make the best of it."

I was replaying this conversation in my head as I approached the building that housed David's office. It always struck me as incongruous that one of our most important agencies in fighting the Cold War was harbored in temporary buildings that looked like a government version of Depression-Era Hoovervilles while just across the Potomac the Defense Department enjoyed one of the world's largest and most modern structures.

There was a security guard at the front door. He knew me from previous visits, but I showed him my Department of Justice credentials just the same and signed the log book. Even though it was past six o'clock and most government workers had called it a day, the lights were still burning in most of the offices I passed. David's door was ajar and I could hear the rattle of his air conditioning unit, struggling to provide some comfort in what was another hot and muggy day.

I knocked softly and pushed the door open. "Hello buddy," I said as I entered the office, "How's it going?"

David's shirtsleeves were rolled up to his elbows and his tie was loosened. He had his usual rumpled appearance, his head bowed over some reports he was reading.

"Hello Pete," he said, raising his head, flashing a smile, and pointing to a chair directly across from his desk. "Take a seat. I'll be with you in a second. Just need to go over a few more things before I leave."

I settled in. "Sure thing my friend. Take your time."

While he continued to work, I glanced around the office. It was in the usual state of chaos, bookshelves crammed to overflowing, drawers in a corner file cabinet half open, a stack of bound reports at the side of the desk. But somehow it was a system that seemed to work for David. He could find anything that he needed within seconds. There were few personal items around, but I did notice a new addition on his desk: A framed picture of David and Sarah. They both seemed to be glowing with happiness.

A few minutes later, David closed a folder on his desk and breathed a deep sigh of relief. He moved his shoulders around to release the tightness that had built up as he had focused on his work. Then he slammed his palm onto the folder as if to punish it. "That's that," he said.

Of course, I didn't know what "that" was and didn't expect David to tell me. He was working on hush-hush stuff and I wasn't about to pry.

He picked up the folder and the notes he had been taking, a look of disgust on his face. He got up from the desk, went to the corner file cabinet, and placed the folder in what I presumed was its proper place. Then he moved the contents to make sure that nothing was protruding and closed the drawer with a certain amount of force, as if to say, "good riddance." Then he took out his key chain and locked the cabinet, testing the handles to make sure everything was secure. I was not an expert, but it seemed to me that if someone wanted to break into David's office and rifle through his files, it would not be much of a challenge to pick the lock. I had once made this observation to David and asked why he didn't have a more secure place to put confidential material in what was supposed to be America's main spy agency. Maybe even a heavy safe. David had shrugged and said he had asked the same question of his superiors. They had promised to get back to him, but never had. So far, at least, there had been no break-ins of which he was aware at the agency. Maybe because few people seem to know that it existed and was housed in such non-descript quarters.

"Okay Pete," he said, grabbing his hat and coat. "Let's get going."

We passed the security guard on the way out. He was reading the *Evening Star* and sipping a cup of coffee. He looked up momentarily, nodded, and then returned to his paper.

When we were out the door, I asked David if he felt secure with a guard who looked to be in his sixties, overweight, and less than attentive. He chuckled. "Not really. He's a retired D.C. cop and good guy who I'm sure would do his best if the occasion arose. Nevertheless, most of us keep a gun in our desk drawer just in case. Not that we're in any imminent danger of a direct attack." When he saw me flinch, he hastened to say, "Sorry Pete. I wasn't thinking."

"That's all right. Don't worry about it." I was beginning to think that the nation's capital was turning into something like the Wild West what with all the guns that seemed to be proliferating. Hopefully, the preponderance of weapons would remain in the hands of law enforcement and those protecting national security.

David's car was parked in a small lot of assigned spaces, most of which were still full. He had a black four-door Plymouth sedan. He had bought it new two years ago and it still had less than 2,000 miles on the odometer. Why he needed such a large car which he seldom drove was something of a mystery. He said it made him feel more comfortable on those few occasions when he took it out for a spin, reassured that if he were to have a serious accident the size of the car would give him a good chance of survival. Whatever the reason, it was fortunate for me that he had a car that could easily accommodate two couples on a long drive.

The parking lot offered no shade. David's sedan had been baking in the hot sun all day. As we approached it, he handed me the keys.

I unlocked the driver's side door, the handle hot to the touch. I tossed the keys to David so he could do the same on the passenger's side. Once he had unlocked his doors, he sent the keys back over the roof to me.

The first thing we both did once we opened our respective doors was roll down the windows. The car was like an oven. We spent a few minutes letting as much of the hot air out as we could before getting in. David had been carrying his coat, which he flung into the back seat. His shirtsleeves were still rolled up and he also yanked off his tie and unbuttoned the first two buttons of his shirt. I would have loved to do the same, but I had the inconvenience of my .38 under my arm and had to keep it covered. The most I could do was take off my tie and open my shirt collar.

By the time I sat down on the hot seats, I was dripping with sweat. I inserted the key and started the engine, making sure the brake was on and the clutch depressed. When I put my hands on the steering wheel, it was like touching the top of a hot stove. I got out my handkerchief and after wiping my brow, I used it to provide a buffer between my hands and the wheel.

David was looking at me with some amusement. "Just relax Pete. Once we get moving, we'll get something of a breeze through the windows."

I had my doubts on that score, but anything had to be better than just sitting and baking. The engine was purring nicely as I disengaged the hand brake, lifted the gear-shift lever to reverse, released the clutch, touched the accelerator lightly, and slowly backed out of the parking slot.

It had been almost a year since I had last driven a car. I was nervous but focused, trying to remember carefully all the steps required to get moving smoothly and safely. Once I had maneuvered through the lot successfully, with no abrupt starts and stops and no fenders dented, I made a careful left turn onto Constitution Avenue. It was now six-thirty, the rush hour was over, and there was relatively little traffic. My progression through the gears from first to third was a little rough, but at least there was no grinding.

I had once ridden with David from his office to his apartment and knew the route well: Constitution to Twenty-Third Street; right on Twenty-Third to Washington Circle; Pennsylvania Avenue west across Rock Creek Parkway until it became M Street; right off of M onto Wisconsin headed north; left on P Street for three blocks to David's apartment adjoining the campus of Georgetown University.

Heading down Constitution, we proceeded smoothly at a steady speed of thirty-five miles per hour. Sure enough, there was enough of a breeze coming through the open windows that the temperature inside the car was becoming tolerable. I used my handkerchief to dry the steering wheel to the point where I could grip it directly without suffering third-degree burns. I was still perspiring but my brow was beginning to cool and I was getting more or less comfortable.

We had to stop at the light before the right turn onto Twenty-Third Street. I braked in plenty of time, with two cars in the lane ahead of me. When the light changed, I stuck my left arm out the window my elbow bent, and gave the signal for a right turn. This time, my progression through the gears was flawless and I could see out the corner of my eye that David was smiling in approval. He also was checking the rearview mirror.

"Old habits stick around, don't they?" I said.

He laughed. "Yes they do." Then, more seriously, "I didn't see anyone on our tail."

"Any reason why you would be followed?"

"Not that I'm aware of. But who knows? How about you? You told me FBI surveillance has been lifted. But that doesn't mean the threat has vanished."

I shrugged. "I haven't noticed anybody following me. And I've been paying pretty close attention. Of course…"

"Yeah. Of course they might be pretty good at what they do. Never hurts to double- and triple-check."

I nodded in agreement and reflexively glanced at the rearview mirror. No signs of anything out of the ordinary.

We approached Washington Circle and I gripped the wheel more tightly. Judging when to merge and making sure that I was in the proper lane to get onto Pennsylvania Avenue were the next big tests and demanded all my concentration. I let out a sigh of relief and relaxed my hands after I had navigated the circle successfully. Crossing Rock Creek Park, I could see some people lying on the grass below others walking slowly along the designated path. Off to the left, the sun was beginning to set on the Potomac, its rays glancing off the water and making it sparkle. Ahead, I could see the spires of Georgetown University, set on a hill overlooking the river.

As Pennsylvania became M Street, David asked, "Any questions Pete? You seem to have things under control."

"Not really. I think I've got the hang of how your car handles. But when we get to your apartment, maybe you can show me where you store the spare and the jack, just in case."

"Sure thing."

Just as I was feeling confident, the glare of the setting sun hit my eyes. I quickly turned down the visor before I was blinded and reminded myself to bring dark glasses for the trip the next day, when we would be heading west for two or three hours.

I turned onto Wisconsin without incident. A few blocks later, I made a left onto P Street and in less than a minute was parked in front of David's apartment. The neighborhood was quiet and tree-shaded. There were few people on the street at this time of day, most having dinner or getting ready to host one of the many cocktail parties for which Georgetown was famous.

When I turned off the engine, David asked, "All set for your big weekend?"

We sat in the car while I told him about advising the Walkers what they might be in for if they accompanied us. When I told him that they had agreed to accept the risk, he shook his head and had a sour expression on his face. "*You* did the right thing in warning them Pete. But I'm not sure *they* did the right thing in agreeing to go along. It would be bad enough if anything were to happen to you and María; but to involve innocent bystanders? I just don't know if that is wise."

"It's a tough call, I admit," I said. "But at least my conscience is clear. I told them the risks and they agreed to accept them."

David looked dubious. "That reminds me Pete. You asked me to look into the company Roberto Walker works for, Oribe and Hermanos."

"Right. Have you found out anything?"

"I asked a friend in the Latin American bureau to do a little sniffing around. What he discovered you or I might have turned up with a little digging. There is indeed such a company and they do have a recently-opened office on K Street. Their phone number is not yet in the book, but you can find it through directory information. And Roberto Walker is listed as their agent here in Washington. So it looks as though our worries as to his and the company's legitimacy have been set to rest."

I took a deep breath and let it out. "That's great news my friend. Great news indeed. Thanks a lot for looking into it."

When I saw the Walkers the next day, I hoped I could hide my guilt at doubting Roberto's story. As I had told David when he was making sure nobody was following us, old habits die hard. In the OSS we had been trained to be suspicious of everyone and everything. The residue of that training remained. It had saved our lives more than once during the war. But carried over into civilian life, it could be more of a burden than an asset. In this case, it was a suspicion that I had been forced to keep from my wife in a marriage where we had pledged not to have any secrets between us. The suspicion had been put to rest, and for that I felt a sense of relief whatever the lingering regrets.

We got out of the car and David opened the trunk. He showed me where the spare tire and jack were located and gave me a few tips on what to do if we should have a flat tire. I had never actually changed a tire but felt fairly confident I could do it if required.

I got back into the car and started the engine. As I pulled from the curb, David gave me a wave and wished me a good weekend. I waved back and thanked him again for the loan of the car. The expression on his face as I drove away was one I had seen many times. He did little to hide his look of concern. Whether he was worried about what might happen to the Bentons and Walkers or to his car, I couldn't tell. Perhaps it was a mixture of both.

I maneuvered through the city streets without incident. It was getting darker and I turned on the sedan's lights. Once I got to our town house, I found a spot to park on the street. I extinguished the lights, turned off the motor, set the hand brake, and made sure the doors were carefully locked. Car thefts in our neighborhood were rare, but they did happen and I wanted to make sure they did not happen to us. After all we had gone through to get the weekend in the Blue Ridge arranged I didn't want anything to throw a last-minute monkey wrench into our plans.

CHAPTER TWENTY THREE

June 22, 1951 – Washington, D.C. to the Blue Ridge Mountains

We picked up the Walkers at eight-thirty in the morning, as planned. They were waiting for us in front of their apartment just west of Dupont Circle on P Street.

I had cautiously made my way down Connecticut Avenue, which at that time of day was chocked with traffic. María sat nervously by my side, ready to shout out a warning if I got too close to any passing vehicles. I hoped that my smooth shifting of the gears and careful braking helped put her at ease. But I didn't mind admitting that I would be relieved once we got out of the District and into more open country, with less crowded highways.

Before leaving, we had put a small suitcase, a picnic basket, a thermos, and our knapsacks, which contained our respective pistols, into the trunk. I had pointed out the spare tire and the jack to María as another measure of reassurance that I was prepared.

I pulled to a stop in front of the Walkers' apartment. I got out and opened the trunk so the Walkers could add their belongings to ours. María got out as well, greeting Graciela and Roberto with kisses and hugs. I followed suit, but added that we better hurry in loading the car as I was parked illegally and we didn't want to start our trip with a summons.

The Walkers also had two knapsacks and a small suitcase. In addition, they had brought four bottles of wine, packed carefully in a small cardboard box. I placed the wine in a secure location, nestled among the other luggage so that the bottles would not be jostled about. After a few seconds of deliberation as to seating arrangements, we decided that María would sit in back with Graciela while Roberto would ride in front with me.

Once I had closed the trunk lid and we were all settled in, I carefully merged into the westbound traffic on P Street. It was much lighter than the steady flow coming from the other direction and I was able to make reasonably good progress. While María and Graciela immediately started to converse in rapid-fire Spanish, Roberto remained silent while I concentrated on my driving. He probably knew from María by way of Graciela that I was something of a novice when it came to handling an automobile and didn't want to distract me while I was engaged in trying to get us through and out of the city without incident. He seemed relaxed, but I noticed that he was paying careful attention to the traffic ahead of us. I saw him put his right foot reflexively to the floor when we came to a sudden stop, intuitively hitting the non-existent brake pedal. I smiled to myself. I had done the same on more than one occasion.

We followed P Street to Wisconsin Avenue. Then I turned left until a few blocks later we reached M Street, where I took a right and made my way to the Key Bridge. There were no delays on our side of the bridge, but traffic was heavy coming into the city. When we crossed the bridge and got to Rosslyn Circle, I entered the traffic stream of cars, buses, and streetcars, exiting onto Lee Highway and Route 29. I had some near misses in the process and heard María utter a few gasps. Roberto again made the pumping gesture with his right leg. But we got through unscathed.

By the time we reached Falls Church, the traffic had dwindled significantly. We had the windows rolled down to catch any breezes we could on another warm and muggy morning. Everybody, including me, had begun to relax. Graciela and María continued to chatter away.

As we headed toward Fairfax, I turned to Roberto and uttered the pro-forma conversation starter: "So Roberto, how have things been at work this week?"

"Oh, you know how it is Pete: Demands from your bosses to get things done yesterday. I had some very long and productive meetings with people at your Departments of Commerce and Agriculture. It looks as though things are going pretty smoothly with our contracts. We should be making deliveries soon, which will make my bosses very happy."

"That's good to hear Roberto. You know, my father has been involved in a lot of international business of the same type. He complains that it is often easier to deal with foreign governments than with our own. Of course, he has a dim view of government in general."

"He might have a point Pete," he said with a laugh. "If I were in Latin America providing some – how shall I put it? – *monetary inducements* – they would make the bureaucratic wheels move more swiftly and easily. Here in your country, I know that such practices are frowned upon."

The lawyer in me responded. "Well, that is not to say bribery has never been used in the U.S. to get business done. But it is against the law and more than a few who have tried it have been caught and punished. It happens, but it is not the norm. Most government officials here are pretty law-abiding. Things may move more slowly as a result, but in the long run we believe it is best if everyone plays by the same rules." I began to suggest that he not try bending any rules himself. But I figured he would find that insulting, so I kept quiet.

"I agree Pete. Your system really does have the advantage of fairness and of everything being above board. It is something that I admire about your country."

We then turned to some of the issues of the day. While we talked, I focused on my driving. I was feeling more and more comfortable as we traveled through the Northern Virginia countryside. Nevertheless, I kept my hands steady at ten and two on the steering wheel, maintained a safe distance behind the car ahead of me, and only passed a slow-moving vehicle when I could see a quarter of a mile ahead. From time to time, I snuck a look into my rearview mirror to see if anyone might be following us. There seemed to be nothing suspicious. No car on our tail that I could see.

After passing through Fairfax, we stopped at Manassas for a cup of coffee. I found a diner just off the highway. While the Walkers and María went inside, I lifted the hood to check the oil and water, which were okay. The tires also seemed in good shape. Entering the diner, which at mid-morning was nearly empty, I joined our group at a table near the back. They were already sipping their coffee. As I sat down, the waitress came and poured me a cup. I suggested that after we had finished, we see the nearby battlefield.

When our waitress came with the check, I asked her for directions to the battlefield park. "Just down the road a mile west of here," she said, "and then your first right. You'll see a sign pointing to the public parking lot."

Her directions were right on target. Exactly a mile from the diner, I took the turn into the battlefield park. We got out and walked around for half an hour, visiting the various monuments scattered about. I did my best to try to explain the significance of the two battles fought at Bull Run and how they fit into the larger story of our Civil War. It had been fifteen years since I had studied American History at Yale, but a lot of what I had learned came back to me. I could almost smell the gunpowder as we toured the scene of so much carnage. María and the Walkers seemed to enjoy the lesson and continued to pepper me with questions once we returned to the car and got back on the road.

We reached Warrenton about forty-five minutes later. There, we turned from Route 29 to 211, which would take us all the way to the Skyline Drive that ran along the crest of the Blue Ridge. We began to pass through rolling green hills and in the distance we could begin to see the outline of the mountains.

"Tell me Pete," Graciela said from the back seat. "Why do they call them the *Blue Ridge* Mountains? They look green to me."

I laughed. "That's usually the way they look to me too Graciela. But at certain times of day, especially at dawn and at dusk, there is a mist that shrouds the peaks at the ridge line and seems to have a blue tint. And that's why they're called the Blue Ridge Mountains." I added, "As you'll see, they are not especially imposing; nothing to compare with the

Alps, the Andes, or even the Rockies. But they have their own charm and beauty."

"Anything higher than a steep hill seems like the Andes to us," Roberto said with a laugh.

We continued to head west. The sun was not only turning up the temperature it was also beginning to get in my eyes. I lowered the visor and adjusted my dark glasses, thankful that I had remembered to bring them with me. I had been keeping to a speed just below the limit of fifty miles per hour. We were passing through an area that was mostly farm land with a few small towns along the way. There was almost no traffic but occasionally I would find myself behind a farm vehicle. Because of the hilly terrain, I often had to crawl along at twenty miles per hour for five minutes or more before I could pass safely. In between such episodes, I continued to glance into my rearview mirror. Still nothing. Roberto noticed me making the check and raised his eyebrows with an unspoken: "Anything behind us?" I just shook my head.

By twelve thirty, we had reached Sperryville, a small town on the Thornton River at the base of the mountains. When I had told Joe Smathers about our plans, he had suggested we stop at Sperryville for lunch. He had recommended a hotel with a restaurant that provided not only good food but a nice setting. Turning left, I crossed onto the bridge that led into the town, which still boasted many of the original homes and buildings that had been constructed in the early nineteenth century. Heading west on Main Street, I located the Sperryville Inn, which Joe had recommended, a few blocks from the turnoff. I parked in the small lot, which only had one space left.

Entering the inn, we were told the dining room was full but that there was a table for four on the porch. A waitress led us to the porch, which fronted the river and provided a lovely view. The porch was covered and overhead fans hummed lazily above us. It was warm, but not oppressively so.

"This place is charming Pete," Graciela said.

"Joe Smathers recommended it," I said. "I hope the food is as good as the view."

It was. We feasted on ham, fried chicken, potatoes, and salad. No alcohol was available so we made do with soft drinks and iced tea. Dessert was home-made pie and we all ordered coffee to go with it. I particularly needed the caffeine jolt for the next part of the drive, which would be the trickiest, taking us up a winding mountain road to the Skyline Drive, itself a challenge to navigate.

We got back on Route 211 at about two o'clock. As I headed west, we entered the Shenandoah National Park and began our ascent to Thornton Gap where we would intersect with the Skyline Drive. The narrow two-lane road twisted and turned its way up the mountains. I kept a steady hand on the wheel and my eyes on the road as my passengers enjoyed the view. Traffic was still sparse and we made good time, reaching the Rangers' Station at Thornton Gap in less than thirty minutes.

The Ranger on duty welcomed us to the Park and the Drive. I handed over the two dollar entrance fee, and he gave us a map in return. "By the way," he said, "there have been reports of bear sightings the past few days. They don't usually get too near the Drive, but you might want to keep a lookout for them just in case."

I thanked him for the advice and pulled away from the station. About a hundred yards further on, I turned left onto the Skyline Drive and headed south. As I maneuvered onto the Drive, Graciela asked, "I'm not sure I understood what that man in uniform said Pete. Did he say there were *osos* in the park?"

She had used the Spanish word for "bears" and I there was a note of real concern in her voice.

I tried to reassure all my passengers. "There are black bears in these mountains. But from what I hear it is quite unlikely we'll encounter any of them on the main trails. Even so, they are not a danger unless they are provoked. Besides," I added, "we are prepared to scare them off if they do."

Nobody responded, but I could guess what the Walkers were thinking. *What have we gotten ourselves into? Not only might we find ourselves attacked by gangsters, now we have to worry about bears!* In fact,

I didn't think either scenario was very likely. But I couldn't blame them for believing otherwise.

After another half hour of twists and turns on the Skyline Drive, we arrived at our destination. Joe Smathers had suggested that we stay at the Skyland Lodge some twenty miles south of Thornton's Gap. I had called earlier in the week and reserved two cabins. We pulled into the Lodge parking lot, got out, stretched our legs, and took in the view over the Shenandoah Valley to the mountain range farther west. We could see the Shenandoah River like a silver ribbon bisecting the valley, with rich farm land on either side.

We entered the Lodge to register. After we signed in, the friendly clerk gave us the keys to our cabins, which adjoined one another and were located a hundred yards to the south. We got back into the car, drove to the cabins, and unpacked our belongings. The cabins were nothing fancy, but were neat and clean and had indoor plumbing. Their main feature was a porch that looked west, providing a wonderful vista for us to enjoy.

After we settled in, we gathered on our porch to decide what to do next. It was about three o'clock and the sun was at full strength. Even at the higher elevation, it was still uncomfortably hot. The sensible thing to do, especially after a full lunch, would have been to take a nap. But instead, I suggested that we hike down White Oak Canyon to the falls below. We would be in the shade most of the way, and the guide the Ranger had given us indicated there were pools of water at the base of the falls where we might refresh ourselves.

María and the Walkers seemed eager to give the hike a try. It was, they said, a good opportunity to get some exercise after having been cooped up in the car for most of the day.

The entrance to the Canyon Trail was just across the Drive from the Lodge. Before we started down it, I said to the group, "Well, you know what to do if we run into a bear. But there are some other dangers as well. Be sure to look out for snakes, some of which are poisonous." I was pleased to see that Graciela, like the rest of us, was now wearing ankle-high boots, the single best protection against a snake bite. They all looked alarmed and I tried again to reassure them. "Snakes are like bears," I said. "They won't bother you if you don't bother them. If we run across one, we'll just wait until it has left the trail and continue on." I didn't add that sometimes you came upon a snake by surprise and letting them alone was not an option.

"The chances of encountering a snake or a bear," I said with some confidence, "are pretty rare. Of greater concern is coming into contact with poison ivy. Unfortunately, it grows in abundance around here. And exposure to it can lead to a really uncomfortable rash." I then pointed to the shiny green-leaf plant bordering the trail. "So try to stay away from this plant if you can. Some people are immune to its effects. But you don't want to risk the chance that you are not."

"One other thing I should warn you about," I said. The looks on their faces seemed to say, *What now?* I hoped I wasn't sounding too condescending, but felt I had to say it nonetheless. "Going down the Canyon is going to be fast and easy. Coming back up will be another matter altogether. So if anybody has second thoughts, it's all right to beg off."

"Don't worry Pete," Roberto said with a grin. "We are all in this together. Nothing like a little adventure to add excitement to our lives."

Graciela and María nodded in agreement. So with this blessing, off we went.

CHAPTER TWENTY FOUR

June 22, 1951 – Shenandoah National Park

White oak and hemlock trees, sheltering smaller dogwoods and pines, bordered the trail and helped to provide a welcome shade. We could hear the chirping of birds nesting in the branches overhead. There was poison ivy as well but far enough away to be avoided. I took the lead with Roberto immediately behind me, Graciela behind him, and Maria taking up the rear. We were almost like an infantry platoon, with Maria, who also wore a knapsack with her pistol inside, and I carrying the weapons that would protect us in case of an attack.

The first quarter of a mile was fairly level. As we were about to enter a steeper grade, I looked down and saw a black snake directly between my feet. Caught off guard, I jumped about a foot into the air and shouted out "snake!" I heard María utter a squeal behind me. Fortunately, the snake was more afraid of me than I was of it and it slithered quickly away into the brush.

My face was red with embarrassment as I turned towards my companions. The Walkers seemed unfazed by my antics and even a little amused.

"Was that a poisonous snake?" Graciela asked.

"I don't think so. It disappeared pretty quickly. It was probably a harmless King Snake. But I'm no expert on the snakes in this region and I don't intend to follow it into the woods," I added, trying to add a bit of levity. "Hopefully, that is the only snake we'll run into."

As we continued on, I let Roberto catch up to me. "You and Graciela seem quite composed," I said. "I guess it takes more than a snake to startle you."

He flashed a quick enigmatic smile and simply shrugged as if to say "no big deal." "Pretty cool customers," I thought to myself.

We proceeded down the trail, the path becoming steeper. We could hear the distant rush of water and the beginning of a series of falls that cascaded down the mountain side to pools below. We met hikers coming in the other direction, breathing deeply from the exertion of the climb, a reminder of what we would face on the way back. I exchanged greetings with two fishermen who were making the return trip, their rods and reels over their shoulders and baskets at their side. When I asked the proverbial "How are they biting?" they showed us four good-sized trout they had managed to bag and we all took time to express our admiration of their catch. After that, we didn't meet anyone else. Forty-five minutes later we reached the base of the first series of falls. Along the way, I had been careful to stick to the path and avoid the slippery sides of the creeks we were following. I didn't want any more embarrassing incidents.

It was four-thirty and there was still plenty of daylight left. We could continue farther down the path and then take a loop trail back to Skyland. But I warned that might take us dangerously close to dark. We decided to relax by the pool at the base of the falls, enjoying the water as it thundered down from above, before we retraced out steps.

The setting was idyllic. We took off our boots and socks, rolled up our pant legs and sitting side-by-side on some smooth rocks dangled our feet in the pool. We playfully splashed one another, grateful for the cold water on our faces.

"Is this water safe to drink?" Roberto asked.

"Maybe so," I said. "But better not to take the risk. Animals use this water and there may be other contaminants. Best to stick to what we have in our canteens. There is nothing like an upset stomach to ruin a trip."

We sat around the pool for about half an hour. A few other hikers stopped by and we exchanged pleasantries. Some were continuing on down the canyon while others joined us, dipping their feet into the water. After a while, we let our feet and legs dry in the sun and then put on our socks and boots, preparing for the return trip.

After saying goodbye to those who had joined us, we retraced our steps up the trail. It was about five when we set out and it was still warm. As expected, the trip back up was a lot more arduous than the descent. Soon, we were perspiring freely and our breathing became labored. But we were all in good condition and made it back to Skyland after an hour and half of hiking. We stopped several times to drink from our canteens, which were nearly empty by the time we arrived at our cabins.

"That was a wonderful experience," Graciela said, a gleam in her eye.

"Yes it was," Roberto agreed. "A great start to our trip. Thanks a lot Pete for arranging this."

"My pleasure. I'm so glad you enjoyed it." So far, it seemed, so good.

We retired to our respective cabins to shower and to dress for dinner. We met at the Lodge at seven thirty, cleaned up and in fresh clothes. Roberto and I wore slacks and short-sleeved shirts while the women had on the same sun dresses as the night we had eaten at the Old Europe.

The main dining room had floor to ceiling windows facing west over the valley. It was a weekend at the peak of the tourist season and the dining room was full. Again following the advice of Joe Smathers, I had called ahead and using a little Department of Justice influence had reserved a prime table for four in a corner next to the window, giving us a modicum of privacy and a great view. We were rewarded with a splendid sunset, the sky alive with mixtures of colors.

Despite the big lunch, our hike had whetted our appetites. We ordered steaks with all the trimmings. When they arrived, it was clear they were not of the quality the Walkers were used to in Uruguay, but they were still tender and juicy and our hunger made them more than welcome. Around us we could hear a buzz of conversation as people made connections with one another, mostly talking about the day they had spent hiking or hikes they planned to take the next day. I saw Graciela's ears perk up when a woman at a table next to ours said in a loud voice, "We ran into a mother bear and two cubs this morning. They were adorable." I didn't hear the rest of her tale, but I presumed she had seen the bears at a safe distance. I was sure that in a close encounter, "adorable" would not have been the word she would have used. Most likely it would have been along the lines of something like "terrifying."

After we finished dinner, we returned to our cabins. Roberto invited us to join them on their porch and share a bottle of wine. It had been a long day and I was ready to hit the sack, even though it was only a little after nine. But I couldn't refuse. We sat on the porch around a small table and looked out at the star-filled sky, the lights of Luray, Virginia twinkling in the distance. By now, the air had cooled and it could not have been more pleasant. Roberto opened a bottle of French Burgundy and poured generous amounts into wine glasses they had brought with them.

We chatted about this and that and planned for the next day. The combination of the wine and my fatigue led me to drift off for a few minutes until María playfully nudged me in the ribs. "I better get my husband to bed," she said with a laugh. "It appears that he has reached his limit."

"We are pretty tired ourselves," Roberto said. "Let's call it a night. We have a big day tomorrow and need to get an early start." We had planned to try to walk to the next major area on the Drive, Big Meadows, which would make it a healthy hike of more than twenty miles there and back.

I apologized for drifting off and we said our goodbyes. As we headed toward our cabin, María looked at me in a way that suggested we would not be going to sleep right away. Hugging my arm, as I fumbled for the key to the cabin, she whispered, "I hope you are not too tired darling."

I got the message. I winked and said, "I think I can stay awake a little while longer."

CHAPTER TWENTY FIVE

June 23, 1951 – Washington, D.C.

David Friedman was in turmoil. Last night, in his apartment, Sarah had broken the devastating news that she was being recalled to Israel for an "indefinite" period. She claimed she wasn't entirely sure what had prompted the decision by the home office, which had given her no reasons – just orders. She suspected that it had to do with inter-agency squabbling over how best to utilize her talents. She also knew that some of her male colleagues at the embassy believed she was getting special treatment because she was an attractive female and were looking for ways to get her reassigned.

Whatever the reasons were, she and David needed to decide what to do - and soon. Her orders said she had to be in Tel Aviv by the beginning of July, giving them just a week to plan for the future.

David's first choice was for them to marry as quickly as possible. He suggested they go to Elkton, Maryland, a favored destination for couples looking for a fast marriage without hurdles. Then he would resign from the agency and accompany Sarah to Israel, where he would apply for citizenship and hope to find a job in the intelligence services.

Sarah seemed receptive to the idea but wanted a few days to think about it. She was not wild about the idea of a marriage before some bored local official in Maryland. She had family and friends in Israel and wanted a traditional ceremony there if possible. She also wanted

David to consider carefully what leaving the CIA would mean for him and his mission. He was an invaluable source where he was and had provided the new state with vital information. He could not be easily replaced. Moreover, Sarah said, "You will be leaving behind all you have ever known, a country where you were born and raised, a country where you have developed deep friendships like the one with Pete Benton. Abandoning all this is not a step you should take lightly."

What she said made him uncertain and uncomfortable. "You sound as though you are having second thoughts about getting married," he blurted out.

"Not at all sweetheart," she said. "Not at all. It's just that I don't want you to have regrets at some time in the future for having made such a drastic move and then blame me for your unhappiness. That's all."

David understood the logic of her position. But it worried him nonetheless. Once again, the fear rose in him that somehow Sarah saw him primarily as a source of valuable information and secondarily as her lover. He knew this was probably irrational, but he couldn't help having the idea intrude on his thoughts.

Sarah spent the night, but neither of them got much sleep. At some point, Sarah got up to go to the bathroom. David was awake and could hear her gently sobbing through the door, even though she had run the water to cover the sound. When she returned to bed, he had reached out to her and took her in his arms, gently smoothing her hair. He could feel her tears on his bare chest. "What's wrong sweetheart?" although he already had a pretty good idea of the answer.

"I'm sorry David," she said, her voice muffled. "It's just that I didn't expect all this to happen. And so quickly."

"It's okay honey. We'll work something out. Don't worry. Just remember that I love you, no matter what. We'll get through this. I know we will."

Even as he uttered these words of reassurance, he felt his own doubts gnawing at him. Eventually, they both fell back into a fitful sleep.

In the morning, David fixed breakfast for the both of them. Neither was very hungry and he kept it simple – toast, juice, and coffee.

After they ate, Sarah gave David a long kiss and left for her apartment. She had some shopping to do and later wanted to go to the embassy to catch up on a few things. She would be back in the late afternoon. They were slated to have dinner and then go to a movie with some friends. Neither of them was feeling very sociable given the cloud that was hanging over them, but thought it best to keep busy rather than brood over their situation.

As soon as Sarah left, David cleaned up the dishes, shaved, showered, and got dressed in casual clothes. He had planned to work at the office, even though it was Saturday and technically a day off for him. But, as usual, he had a large stack of papers to go through in preparation for a meeting on Monday. He had made good progress during the week, but there was still more to do. And now, with the prospect that he might be leaving the agency soon, he wanted to make sure he left with a clean desk. In addition, he also wanted to gather as much information as he could on ex-Nazis in the Middle East, hoping he would get agency permission to take it with him if he were to leave for Israel.

When David got to his office around nine, the first thing he did was turn on the air conditioner. The heat and humidity had returned with a vengeance. The temperature was slated to hit the nineties later in the day. It was already oppressively muggy.

On the way in, he had passed open doors and exchanged greetings with other analysts. David was far from the only one working on the weekend. Most of the Middle East staff was slaving away, trying to assess the consequences of the nationalist Mossadeq taking over in Iran. As he sat at his desk, feeling the traces of cold air from the conditioner begin to hit the shirt on his back, he mused, not for the first time, that for all the CIA's faults and missteps, the taxpayers were getting their money's worth from the people who worked at the agency. While there were some who spent more time socializing than doing their jobs, the great majority were hard-working, dedicated public servants, taking on an important task on behalf of national security. Most could be making more money in the private sector, but their sense of civic responsibility outweighed any desire for greater wealth. Some, like Brent Sanderson, didn't need to worry about money. But most who worked at the agency depended on their government salary to maintain themselves and their families. And while it gave them a comfortable life, there weren't many who would get rich on what the government paid them. Of course, the budget of the CIA was a closely-guarded secret, so closely-guarded that not even David knew what it was. Nonetheless, he still felt confident that as far as the agency's workforce and its habits were concerned, the part of the overall budget that went to staff salaries was being well-spent.

David unlocked the top right-hand drawer of his file cabinet and pulled out the folder he had been looking at when Pete Benton had come by on Thursday. He had meant to review it the next day, but some pressing matters had come up and this was the first chance he had had to get back to it.

The file held depressing news. It contained the names and biographies of various ex-Nazis who were now comfortably settled in the U.S. and protected by the agency. While David's focus had shifted to information about Nazi war criminals in the Middle East, Brent Sanderson still allowed him to keep track of matters closer to home. It had been generous, and even dangerous, of Brent to allow this. But David was frustrated beyond reason that all he could do about what he considered an outrageous policy was to read about the results.

As part of his agreement with Brent, David was not to copy or take notes on the information he held in his hands. If he did, the punishment would be severe. So he tried to memorize as much of the detail as he could. He had been engaged in this task when Pete had dropped by on Thursday to pick up David's car. He had not been able to tell his friend anything about this aspect of his work at the agency, but Pete might well have noticed the distaste that crossed his face when he put the file away. His friend was pretty good at picking up facial hints, something they had both been trained to do in the OSS.

Thinking of Pete, David hoped he and María were enjoying their trip to the mountains. Pete certainly deserved the break. And the friendship with the Walkers seemed to have been heaven-sent, especially for María. David was glad he had been able to put his friend's concerns about Roberto Walker's credentials to rest and chastised himself for expressing his original doubts to Pete, inflicting on him his naturally suspicious nature. As he pictured them making the drive to the Blue Ridge, he smiled at the memory of Pete sweating profusely when he maneuvered David's sedan through the streets of Washington. Not that he was a much better driver himself. Nonetheless, in their friendly competition as to who had the best skills, David believed he was ahead on points when it came to handling an automobile.

At that moment, he was jarred by the loud ringing of the phone on his desk. When he picked up, he heard a familiar voice on the line. It was Steve Graham, a guy he had worked with in the Latin American Division at the State Department and who, like David, had made the shift to the agency. Steve was also an OSS veteran, although their paths had not crossed during the war. Steve had stayed in the Latin American section of the CIA and it was he who had checked up on Roberto Walker.

"Hi Steve," David said, with a slight sense of foreboding. "What's up?"

"Glad I caught you in David," Steve said with a certain urgency in his voice. "I called your apartment, but there was no answer so I figured you might have come to the office. Listen, I'm calling from my own office. Okay if I come over? I've discovered some additional information about the fellow you asked me to check up on - This Roberto Walker. It's pretty important and I wanted to brief you as soon as possible."

The sense of foreboding deepened and David could feel his notoriously nervous stomach begin to produce the familiar cocktail of toxic juices. "Sure thing Steve. I'll be waiting for you."

David took out his handkerchief and wiped his brow. The air conditioner was going full blast, but his body was reacting to what he was convinced would be bad news. *First Sarah's little bombshell, now this – whatever it was.*

Less than three minutes after he had hung up the phone, there was a knock on his door. "Come on in Steve. It's open."

Graham came into the office. He clutched a manila envelope in his left hand and had a grim look on his face. David gestured for him to take a seat. Like David, Graham was dressed casually in slacks and a short-sleeved shirt, no tie, for work on the weekend. He was about David's age, medium height and weight and with short-brown hair parted on the left. His father had been in the mining business and had taken his family to live in South America for extended periods of time, where Steve had picked up near native-fluency in Spanish and Portuguese. After an Ivy League education, he had been recruited by the OSS and because of his command of Portuguese, been assigned to Lisbon, a hot bed of espionage. He had served there for the duration of the war.

Graham was one of the hardest-working analysts at the agency. It was no surprise that he was in his office on a Saturday. And he probably would be there on Sunday as well. He was married and had been for fifteen years, but David suspected that it was not a happy union. Whether Steve's work habits led to the unhappiness or he found refuge in his work to escape the unhappiness, David did not know. He did know that once Steve got his teeth into something, he didn't let go until it was thoroughly chewed.

As Graham sat, he put the envelope he had been carrying on David's desk and gave it a little nudge in his direction. At the same time, he pulled out a pack of Camels, selected one, put it in his mouth, and lighted up. David pushed an ashtray to the edge of the desk within Graham's easy reach. Graham took a deep puff and then blew a perfect smoke ring, the kind you see in magazine advertisements, into the air. "You might want to take a look inside the envelope David. I think you'll find it interesting."

His colleague, like others in the agency, often liked to make the revelation of information something of a game. Instead of coming right out with whatever it was they had to say, they teased you with bits and pieces until the whole picture was revealed.

While Graham focused on his cigarette, David opened the envelope and pulled out is contents. All he found was a five-by-seven black and white photograph. It was a head-and-shoulders shot of a well-dressed man who appeared to be in his sixties. He had a fleshy face, thinning gray hair, and a neatly trimmed moustache.

David looked up from the photo. "And who, pray tell, is this?"

"That my friend is Roberto Walker - the Roberto Walker who is the leading sales representative of Oribe and Hermanos here in good old Washington, D.C. At the moment, however, *this* Roberto Walker is back in Montevideo, where he has been for the past month."

David felt the room spin and clutched the side of his desk for support. His stomach was now a fiery cauldron. For a moment, he was speechless. "But how could that be?" he finally sputtered. "Didn't you say you checked and everything seemed on the level? I just don't understand..." He let it trail off, his face a picture of agony.

Graham could see David's distress. What he was about to tell him, he knew, would do nothing to calm his fears. He took another cigarette from his pack and lit it with the dying embers of the one he had smoked down to his fingers.

Placing the now extinguished butt in the ashtray, he blew another smoke ring to the ceiling. "I'm sorry it took so long to get to the bottom of this David. We've been up to our ears in Guatemala. Can you believe it? A Commie government in our own backyard."

David shook his head with impatience. "Come on Steve. Get to the point."

"Right you are. Well when you first asked me to look into this Walker character, I did the usual. Located Oribe and Hermanos in our current files and found them to be perfectly legitimate. And Roberto Walker *was* listed as their sales representative in D.C. Everything seemed to be on the up and up. So that's what I told you. When was it?"

"Thursday."

"Thursday. Yeah." Taking another deep drag on his cigarette, Graham stared at the glowing ash in contemplation. "But then I remembered you and your friend Benton's experience in Argentina. And now Benton has run into somebody who, while not from that country, purportedly is from the same area. So I decided to dig a little deeper. On Friday, I got in touch with a friend at the *Post* who covers international business to see what he knew about Oribe and Hermanos. He confirmed the company's bona fides and the fact that Roberto Walker was indeed assigned to their D.C. office. But then I asked him if by chance he had ever met this guy Walker. He said he had not, but he happened to have a photo and a brief bio on file and would send it over. I just got to it this morning. From what you had told me about

Walker, once I saw this picture I knew something was amiss. You told me that Pete said he was in his thirties and athletic. Clearly this guy," Graham said, pointing to the photo on David's desk, "does not fit that description."

David just shook his head, his despair mounting. "This morning I heard from my source at the *Post* that Walker had been on home leave for the past month. Some sort of health issue."

David was beginning to put two and two together. He was about to speak, when Graham continued. "I don't want to alarm you my friend, but the guys working the situation in Argentina have been reporting some disturbing news. It seems that while Perón is still riding high, he has been on a campaign for the past year or two to crack down on any opposition. The press has come more and more under his control. I'm sure you've heard about the regime's takeover of *La Prensa*." David bobbed his head. "Well, we've also seen more aggressive action against perceived enemies at home – and, I'm afraid, abroad. Over the past year, leaders of the anti-Peronist exile community in places like Uruguay and Chile have either been intimidated into silence or," he paused and his voice became somber, "eliminated altogether. And all done very cleverly and expertly, with no overt traces to the regime. But there is little doubt as to who is behind the campaign."

Graham was repeating much of what David already knew and confirming his worst fears. "So you think whoever is posing as Roberto Walker is part of some sort of scheme cooked up by Perón to cow the government's opponents?"

It was more a statement than a question. Graham nodded in agreement.

David paused to digest this morsel. "But why Pete? How does he pose any threat to the regime? He's no friend of Perón, but so far as I know he's never uttered a peep about the government there since he returned from Buenos Aires six years ago. And would Perón be crazy enough to risk attacking an American citizen on American soil? If it were found it, the diplomatic repercussions would be enormous."

Graham shrugged. "I agree. It does seem a bit bizarre. But how else do you explain the appearance of an imposter who has managed to get close to your friend and win his confidence? And, as you told me, have his *wife*, if that's who *she* is, establish a friendship with María Benton?"

After lighting yet another cigarette, Graham continued. "Maybe I've been at this game too long and see conspiracies everywhere. But given Pete and María's experience with Perón and his then mistress in Argentina, there might be lingering resentments. And Evita is notorious for holding grudges and punishing anyone she perceives as an enemy. From what we know, she is not in the best of health. Maybe she has asked her husband to grant her a wish to settle an old score before it is too late. And we know that Perón usually accedes to her wishes. For God's sake, he even tried to have her be his vice-president."

Graham's speculations paralleled David's. "As unlikely as it sounds Steve, I wouldn't dismiss that possibility."

"Whatever the case, you need to let Pete know right away what he might be up against with this guy Walker and his alleged wife."

David's heart sank. "That's the problem Steve. Pete and Maria went hiking with the Walkers in the Blue Ridge. They even took my car. They are probably out on the trail right now."

Graham stubbed out his cigarette. "I have my car David. We need to get moving."

"Thanks Steve," David said. "But let me call Joe Smathers first. I don't even know where they are staying. He should know. Maybe he can help. No sense heading for the Blue Ridge without a clear idea of where they might be. It's a big area. And we don't have time to waste."

"You're absolutely right. Go ahead. I'll pick up some things from my office that we might need." David knew this meant Graham wasn't about to head into potential danger without being well-armed. As Graham went out the door, David unlocked his desk drawer and withdrew his own gun. Placing the revolver on his desk, he dialed Joe Smathers. There was no answer at the office and his sense of panic deepened. But when he called Joe's home, much to his relief Pete's boss picked up on the second ring. David gave a hurried account of what he suspected Roberto and Graciela Walker were up to. He could hear the ordinarily unflappable Smathers let out a whoosh of breath and what he assumed was a smack of his hand on his forehead.

"Listen Joe. A colleague of mine and I are driving to the Blue Ridge as fast as we can. But we don't know where the Bentons and Walkers are staying, much less where they might be at this moment. Any ideas.?"

"Yes. Since I know the area pretty well, I helped Pete plan his trip. They were going to stay at the Skyland Lodge, about twenty miles south from the Thornton Gap entrance. Today they were going to hike south to the next big campground, Big Meadows." There was a pause, and when Joe spoke David could hear the sense of doom in his voice. "And I told them about a little-known spot off the trail where they could get a great view and enjoy their lunch without anyone intruding on them. If I were the Walkers and planning an attack on Pete and María, it would be the perfect spot to make the attempt."

Joe gave David directions to the secluded area. "I'm also going to contact the State Police and the Park Rangers," he said. "But you go on ahead David. I'll need time to get some of the task force organized to follow you. We've got to do everything we can to try to stop whatever it is that the so-called Walkers are planning." After a pause, he added, "And maybe *Roberto*, if that is his name, has a perfectly logical explanation for his deception that has nothing to do with the Bentons."

David knew that Joe was grasping at straws out of a sense of desperation. He was entertaining the same thoughts. But both of them knew that a "logical explanation" was a slim hope given the circumstances. And even if it did turn out to be true, they had to act on the assumption that his and Steve's speculation was the most likely explanation for the Walkers' deception. There really was no choice in the matter.

"You may be right Joe," David said. "But I'm afraid that our suspicions are pretty well-grounded."

"I have to agree David," Joe said. "But tell you what. Before you leave, let me call Skyland. Maybe something happened to delay their plans for a hike and I can get the word to Pete on what you have discovered. I'll call you right back, Okay?"

"Okay Joe. I'll be waiting." When David put down the phone, he picked up his revolver to make sure it was fully loaded. It was. He hoped he didn't have to use it, but was ready to do so if necessary. In fact, the prospect of plugging Roberto before he could do anything to Pete brought a slight smile to his lips. But then a sobering thought hit him. He and Joe were operating on the assumption that the Walkers would make their attempt on Pete and María during their lunch sometime around noon. Looking at his watch, David saw it was already ten-thirty. Under the best of circumstances, the soonest he and Steve would arrive would be sometime around two o'clock. Maybe the Park Rangers and the State Police could get there sooner, but David didn't know how easy it would be to mobilize them. And while he and Joe had a pretty good idea where the attack might take place, there was always the possibility they were wrong and trying to locate the party along the trail would take time. There was an even more sobering thought. Suppose the Walkers already had done their worst. After all, they had been with the Bentons all day and night. Maybe they had carried out their assignment already and were on their way back to Argentina. Maybe..."

The shrill ringing of the telephone jarred David from these dark thoughts. He picked up immediately. It was Joe. "David. I just got off the phone with the manager at Skyland. He says the Bentons and the Walkers left on their hike to Big Meadows about an hour ago. He said he spoke with Pete about their plans for the day when they picked up their sandwiches at the Lodge."

David breathed a sigh of relief. At least they were still alive! Or had been an hour ago. "So what I'm thinking," Joe said, "or maybe hoping, is that they won't have lunch until about one o'clock. I'm not sure any of us can reach them before then, but at least it gives us a fighting chance."

"Thanks for the call Joe," David said. "I'm leaving right now. See you at Big Meadows."

"See you then David. And good luck."

David hung up the phone and headed for the door. As he grabbed his coat and his gun, he had a flashback to six years ago in Buenos Aires. There, he and his good friend from MI6, Miles Cavendish, had gotten into an embassy car for a mad dash across the pampa, trying to save Pete's life before he was executed on orders from Perón. Now it seemed that history was repeating itself. Once again, Perón and Eva had set in motion a plot to eliminate Pete Benton. This time, however, it was not only Pete who was targeted and in mortal danger but so too was María. Pete had been able to turn the tables on his captors six years ago. He could only hope that Pete could pull off the same trick again.

CHAPTER TWENTY SIX

June 23, 1951 – On the Appalachian Trail, Shenandoah National Park

We had slept in. The combination of exercise, wine, and love-making had left us both dead to the world. When I opened my eyes, I checked my watch. It was nearly eight. We had planned to meet the Walkers at seven for breakfast so we could get an early start on what would be a long hike.

I nudged María. "It's time to rise and shine darling. We are already an hour behind time."

She roused herself, rubbing the sleep from her eyes. "What time is it?"

"Almost eight darling. We need to hustle. The Walkers must be waiting for us, wondering what's taking us so long."

She leaped out of bed and headed for the bathroom. While she was in there, I got dressed quickly. When she came out, I went in. After I had finished my business, I found her already dressed. I think we set some kind of record. When we left the cabin and headed for the Lodge, it was only five minutes after eight.

The dining room was crowded when we arrived. The Walkers were already seated at the same table we had occupied last night, sipping coffee. We rushed over, both looking a little shame-faced.

"So sorry we are late," I said. "We didn't think to bring an alarm clock," offering the first lame excuse I could think of.

They had risen to greet us. "Don't worry Pete," Roberto said. "We just got here ourselves."

I didn't know if this was the truth, or he was just trying to put us at ease. If that were the case, I was grateful for the gesture.

We all sat down and the waitress came to take our order. I suggested a hearty breakfast as we had a long day of hiking ahead of us. They agreed and we asked for bacon, eggs, toast, hash brown potatoes, juice, and more coffee.

While we waited, we talked about things we had experienced the previous day. Roberto asked me what we could expect on our upcoming hike. Before I could say much, our food arrived and we began to eat. The conversation turned to the impressions the Walkers had of our trip so far and some of the highlights of our walk down White Oak Canyon. For some reason that I could not quite put my finger on, the Walkers seemed tense and a little uncomfortable. I wondered if they had had an argument during the night. They seemed to be a happy and loving couple. But even the best of marriages can produce occasional strains, particularly when dealing with something out of the ordinary routine.

After breakfast, we went to the main office of the Lodge to pick up the trail lunch we had ordered the day before. The manager, an affable white-haired guy in his sixties with a decided southern accent, handed us our sandwiches, snacks, and drinks and asked about our plans for the day.

"We're going on the Appalachian Trail to Big Meadows," I told him. "That's where we plan to have lunch," I added, hoisting the large paper bag he had had given me.

"That's a nice hike," he observed. "You'll see a lot of interesting things along the way – and some great views." Then, with a twinkle in his eyes, he added, "And if you are lucky, you might spot a few bears."

"Just so it's at a safe distance," I said with a chuckle.

"That's right. You don't want to get them too riled up."

I'm not sure my companions were enjoying the by-play. Graciela and María looked slightly alarmed as they again heard about the possibility of a dangerous encounter with wild creatures. Roberto seemed less concerned, but he wasn't smiling either.

I thanked the manager for the lunch and the advice and we returned to our cabins to freshen up and prepare for the hike. When we were inside, María said, "I wish we weren't hearing so much about bears, darling. Personally, I have no desire to see one when we're alone in the wilderness." She gave a little shiver. "As far as I am concerned, the only place to see a bear is in a zoo. And I'm sure the Walkers feel the same."

I did my best to reassure her that it was unlikely we would run into any kind of wild animal that would pose a threat. And if we did, I was sure that Roberto and I could handle the situation. "I certainly hope so Pete," she said, but her face showed her doubt.

I didn't want anything to put a pall on our day. Last night, María told me how happy she was with the trip and how much the friendship with the Walkers meant to her. Sharing this experience with them, she said, meant the world to her. Moreover, before we made love, she whispered into my ear that perhaps now was the time to think about starting a family. We had put off the idea of having children for long enough, she said. We weren't getting any younger. Now that she was no longer tied down to a career and a job, she could focus on being a full-time mother. For the first time since we had been married, we did not take any precautions. Who knows? Maybe a little Benton was already in the works. At any rate, I promised her I would do all I could to make the hike a pleasant one, an experience that would do nothing to ruin her good mood.

By the time we met the Walkers outside the cabins, it was a little past nine. We hoisted our knapsacks and checked our canteens. We could get more water at Big Meadows. But the sun was already making its presence known. Even before we started onto the trail we were beginning to perspire. Having plenty of water, I warned, was essential under these conditions.

Before we left, Roberto and I had split the lunch between us. As I jammed the sandwiches into my knapsack, I double-checked to make sure my revolver was where it should be - nestled between some extra socks I always carried and in a place where I could get at it quickly if need be. I hadn't thought much about the possibility we might have been followed by any thugs since we had arrived at Skyland. Certainly nobody at the Lodge or who we had met on the trail seemed at all suspicious. Nonetheless, I took a careful look around as we left Skyland and entered the trail. As far as I could tell, unless someone was lurking behind a tree, we were completely alone as we set off toward Big Meadows.

We were following the Appalachian Trail. It was well marked with blue blazes and appeared to be in good condition. As long as we stayed on the trail, there was little chance we would get lost. Unless we strayed, it would take us straight to Big Meadows. Nevertheless, I had a map in my knapsack just in case along with a compass that I carried in my pocket. The map showed that for the first four or five miles, we would be climbing in the direction of Hawksbill Gap, at a little over 4,000 feet, the highest elevation in the Blue Ridge. Then we would begin a gradual descent towards Big Meadows at about 3,000 feet. Along the way, we would find scenic overlooks of the Shenandoah Valley to our right.

The trail started out on level ground, but after a quarter mile we began to climb and had to watch our steps on the rocky terrain. I suggested we take it slow and easy. There was nothing like a sprained ankle or worse to ruin the day.

I set the pace with Roberto at my side. Behind us, I could hear María and Graciela talking in excited tones about the scenery and reliving the events of the previous day. Roberto and I swapped stories about hiking in Europe he in Great Britain in the Lake District and me in the Alps when I had accompanied my father on business trips before the war. I didn't tell him about my experiences in the Pyrenees when part of the OSS.

We took our first break at Timber Hollow Overlook, about a mile into the hike. The trail had taken us along mountain ridges on a path that skirted large gray granite boulders. There had been occasional descents into tree-lined vales, but the overall course was upward. At Timber Hollow, we sat on some boulders, enjoying the view westward. Roberto and I took off our knapsacks, grateful for the break. We were all perspiring profusely and I took out a handkerchief and mopped my soaking brow. Roberto did the same.

We rested for ten minutes and then resumed our trek. It was hot and getting hotter as the morning progressed. We did have the advantage of some mountain breezes and the occasional cloud that momentarily blocked the sun. We could also take some comfort in the fact that it was hotter down below than at our altitude. But the heat and humidity were taking their toll.

After about an hour of slow but steady climbing, we finally reached Hawksbill Gap. We took another long break. Up to that point we had not met many other hikers. A Boy Scout troop out on a weekend expedition had passed us going towards Skyland, eliciting observations from María and Graciela about how "cute" they were in their little uniforms. We had overtaken a few other couples who were navigating the trail at a slower pace than we were. Otherwise, up to that point we had been more or less alone. But at Hawsbill, there were about twenty people who had gotten out of their cars from the Skyline Drive. They were congregating at the stone wall that bordered the parking lot and provided the view westward. Many of them had cameras out and were snapping pictures while others were peering through binoculars, trying to pick out sites in the valley below or tracking the hawks and buzzards circling overhead.

María had brought our Brownie with her and took it from her knapsack. For a second, I thought I heard it make contact with the pistol she was also carrying. In the rush of the previous day, she had forgotten to bring the camera with her during our trip down White Oak Canyon. Now she had it at the ready and began to snap pictures of the three of us as well as the surrounding scenery. While she was doing that, an elderly couple climbed over the stone wall onto the trail, trying to get a different angle for the pictures they were taking.

When María saw them, she approached the man, presumably the husband, who was taking pictures of his wife. "Excuse me sir," she said with a smile that no man could resist, "Would you be so kind as to take a picture with my camera of the four of us?" gesturing to me and Walkers.

The man seemed pleased by the request, his wife less so. She eyed María and the Walkers suspiciously, perhaps identifying them by their looks as "foreigners." Looking at me, however, she seemed a little reassured.

"Why sure ma'am," the man said. "Be happy to."

María handed the man her camera, which was exactly like his own. Then she made hand signals for the four of us to gather together to pose for the photo. We assembled in a group, our arms around shoulders and waists and responded with the obligatory smiles as the elderly man said "cheese." Just to be on the safe side, María asked him to take two additional shots in case there were any problems with the film. He happily obliged, no doubt enjoying the opportunity to be in close proximity to two beautiful women, if only for a few moments.

When he had finished, María approached him and said, "Thank you very much sir. That was very kind of you."

She held out her hand for the camera. He returned it with what I suspected was some reluctance. "Your very welcome ma'am. My pleasure," he said, his face beginning to flush. I could tell that he was about to continue the conversation, when his wife said in a steely tone, "Come on Clarence. We don't have time to dawdle if we plan to make Roanoke by noon."

"Sure thing Thelma," he said, looking abashed as she practically pulled him off the trail and back up to their car. "Nice to have met you folks," he shouted over his shoulder as Thelma gave him another shove. "Same here," I said, trying not very successfully to repress a smile. María was doing her best not to burst out laughing. But she had had some acting experience and was able to contain herself until she heard Thelma and Clarence shut their car door. Then she giggled for a few seconds, having gotten a kick out of the whole experience. We expected that the Walkers would find the episode equally amusing. But their smiles were half-hearted. For some reason they seemed discomfited by the entire experience. I saw them exchange a brief look I couldn't quite fathom. Maybe they hadn't understood all the by-play that had taken place. Or maybe it had something to do with the tension I had sensed in both of them at breakfast. Whatever the reason, I found it a bit puzzling. But, determined not to let anything spoil the good mood, I let it pass.

"Well," I said, looking at my watch, "It's now about eleven. The hike to Big Meadows should be easier going now that we are headed downhill. But it's still going to be two hours with the sun reaching its peak. If you want to cut it short and head back to Skyland, that's okay by me."

Both Roberto and Graciela shook their heads. "No Pete," Roberto said. "We're fine. Really. We are enjoying the hike – the surroundings, being with you. We can make it to Big Meadows. Let's keep going."

Graciela nodded in agreement. "Okay," I said. "But if at any time you feel we should turn back, just say so. Don't be shy. We'll understand, right María?"

"Whatever you say darling. Whatever you say."

So with that blessing, we resumed our trek.

CHAPTER TWENTY SEVEN

June 23, 1951 – Big Meadows Campgrounds, Shenandoah National Park

We reached Big Meadows a little after one. The hike from Hawksbill Gap had been mostly downhill and relatively easy. But we were a little beat and looking forward to lunch.

The campgrounds were crowded, all of the picnic tables taken. I was glad that Joe had suggested an alternative. It was a quarter of a mile farther south. He told us to keep an eye out for an unmarked side trail that was not easy to locate unless you knew exactly what you were looking for.

We left the campgrounds after using the facilities and re-filling our canteens. I took the lead, explaining what landmarks we should look for to find the side trail. Not more than fifteen minutes after we had left Big Meadows, I saw the configuration of rocks and trees that Joe had described. We turned to the right and followed an ill-defined foot path, so narrow that we had to walk single-file. After going about two hundred yards, we entered a small clearing, surrounded by pines and hardwoods that afforded ample shade. At the far end was a granite overlook with a splendid view of the valley below and on to the Shenandoah Mountain Range to the west.

Even though Joe had more or less guaranteed that we would be alone, I had harbored the fear that others might also know of the place and beaten us to it. But we were the only ones there. We were not all that far from the Skyline Drive and the Appalachian Trail. But the only sounds we heard were the occasional whistling of the wind shaking the leaves in the trees, the chirping of insects, and the cries of birds.

As the others gathered around me to take in the view, María said enthusiastically, "Oh Pete, this is just perfect! What a wonderful place, almost magical."

The Walkers nodded in agreement. "You're right María," Roberto said. "It is just about perfect." Once again, I noted something in the tone of his voice that didn't sound quite right.

Just as I was about to take off my knapsack, I heard a strange rustling noise in the woods to my left. The others didn't seem to have noticed although I thought I saw Roberto's eyes narrow in reaction. My OSS experience in the Pyrenees, spending long days and nights in the mountains, had attuned me to sounds in the wild. It was probably nothing, likely just the wind in the trees. But the thought hit me that our location was not only ideal for a quiet picnic - it was also ideal for an ambush.

When I kept my knapsack on, María asked, "What is it darling? Is something wrong?" There was a slight note of alarm in her voice. The Walkers were also looking at me in a questioning manner.

"It's probably nothing, sweetheart. I thought I heard something in the woods," gesturing in the direction of the sound. "Tell you what. Why don't you three settle in while I investigate? I shouldn't be long."

"Why don't I go with you Pete?" Roberto volunteered.

"Thanks Roberto," I replied. "But I don't want to leave the two women alone."

"Okay Pete," he said. Then with a grim look that again I couldn't quite read, he added, "But if you're not back in fifteen minutes, I'm coming after you."

I was beginning to regret being such an alarmist. *Talk about spoiling the mood!* I probably was letting my imagination get the best of me. But it was too late to backtrack now.

"I'm sure it's nothing. I'll be back soon," I promised.

As I began to head into the woods, María said, "Please be careful Pete."

I gave her a reassuring wave and soon disappeared from their view. The woods were thick and the ground underneath was rocky, some of the rocks slippery with moss. I took out my compass to get my bearings. I thought the sound had come from the southeast and did my best to maintain a steady course in that direction. It wasn't easy going, but after about seven minutes of my allotted fifteen, I estimated I had reached the general area where the sound had originated.

I was tempted to take my gun out and have it ready. But there were no signs of anyone in the vicinity. I didn't see anything that looked like a boot print, no telltale traces like cigarette butts left behind by anyone tracking us, no unusually broken branches other than the ones I had disturbed forging my trail. Of course, someone – if indeed there was someone - might have heard me coming and found shelter in a place I could not see. But to be absolutely sure, I would have to spend a lot more time looking around for what was more than likely a figment of my imagination.

After about thirty seconds of scouring the area, I headed back to the clearing. I hadn't gone that far, but I knew that the woods could be confusing, especially without a defined trail to follow. I was thankful for the compass. My fifteen-minute time limit had just expired when I emerged out of the woods into the clearing.

It took several seconds for my brain to process what I saw in front of me. The first thing that registered was the sight of Graciela with her left arm around María's neck, in her right hand a .22 caliber pistol pressed against my wife's temple. There was a look of shocked disbelief on María's face. Behind her, at her heels was her open knapsack, her revolver undoubtedly having been removed.

For a moment, I was frozen. My first instinct was to head towards her, but I was brought up abruptly by Roberto's stern warning: "Stay where you are Pete," he said in a voice that froze me in my tracks, "or Graciela will put a bullet into your wife's brain."

María and Graciela were about twenty feet away, directly in front of me. I turned my gaze to my left and Roberto came into my vision. He had maneuvered himself to a place about fifteen feet to the side where he had me in his sights without blocking my view of the two women or placing himself between them and him. He had a .45 Colt Automatic pointed directly at my heart.

My OSS training had prepared me for almost any eventuality. But what I beheld was so unexpected and unreal, that I had difficulty remaining, as I had been trained to be, calm and collected. My heart was racing, my hands were shaking, and I was feeling dizzy. Slowly, I tried to exert self-control, taking deep breaths and focusing on practical solutions to what I knew was a situation that very likely would not end well for either me or María.

"First thing Pete," Roberto said the .45 steady in his hand, "I want you to remove your knapsack and throw it over to me."

I did as he said. I had no choice. He wanted my knapsack and the gun he knew was in it. "Careful Pete," he said as I slowly shrugged off the knapsack. "Now toss it over here," he ordered, pointing to a spot at his feet. "And don't try any tricks like throwing it at my face so as to distract me. Remember that María's life is in your hands."

"How could I forget," I mumbled to myself. I followed his instructions, the knapsack landing with a loud thump at his feet. Keeping his gun leveled at me, Roberto bent down, picked up the knapsack, and with one hand unbuckled the straps that kept it closed. Reaching in, he pulled out my .38. Checking to make sure the safety was engaged he put my gun in his waistband. He then chucked the knapsack to the side. In the process, the sandwiches and snacks we had prepared for our lunch spilled out onto the ground, the wrappings ripped open.

I was beginning to recover from my initial shock and surprise. It was now crystal clear that Roberto was no businessman. He was a professional assassin of some sort and he had done this sort of thing – holding people at gunpoint – before. It would not be easy to gain the advantage over him under the best of circumstances. And with María a pull of the trigger away from certain death, my options were severely limited. But I was determined not to give up without a fight.

"I'm so sorry Pete," María said, her voice trembling. "I didn't…"

"Please be quiet María," Roberto warned. "Any more out of you and I'll have Graciela shut you up for good."

I wanted to rush Roberto there and then. But that would be suicide and get us both killed. The best thing was to try to stay calm. I just nodded at María with what I hoped was a look of reassurance. Her face still reflected disbelief but I saw anger and determination there as well.

"Why don't you sit down Pete," Roberto said. "There's a rock a few feet behind you. I have a few things I want to tell you."

I turned and walked towards the rock, where I did as he ordered and sat down. "Keep your hands in your lap, palms upward where I can see them. And no sudden moves or…" He wiggled the gun to underscore the message.

"Don't worry Roberto," I said, straining to keep my voice steady. "Now what's this all about? I thought we were friends."

He laughed and I could hear Graciela chuckle as well. "*Friends.* Yes indeed. Very good friends. But even the best of friends have, how do you say it? 'falling outs.'"

"That may be true," I said, "but they don't usually go to the extreme of pointing guns at one another."

Roberto shook his head. "No they don't," he said. "But let's get to the crux of the matter." Looking to his right, he saw a boulder and took a seat, still keeping his gun aimed steadily at my heart. "This may take a while so we might as well get comfortable." Behind, I could see that Graciela had guided María to a similar set of rocks where they now sat side-by-side, the gun still pressed against my wife's temple.

Inwardly, I saw a glimmer of hope. So long as Roberto kept talking, we still had a chance. Maybe someone would stumble upon us, maybe his arm would grow weary and he would drop his guard. Maybe María could somehow grab the .22 away from Graciela. A lot of "maybes" but it was all we had.

"The first thing I need to tell you my *friend* is that we are Argentines, not Uruguayans." I tried not to react, but he probably saw my eyes widen. I was beginning to see where his story might be headed. "And we have been assigned to exact revenge for what you – the two of you - did in our country six years ago. You know what you did Pete, don't you. Spied on General Perón and Eva Duarte, betraying the friendship they had shown you. And then you killed two police agents and a German officer."

"Well, in my defense," I said, "They were trying to kill me."

He brushed my argument aside. "You were interfering in things that were none of your business. And as for your wife," he continued, "She had the temerity to approach Eva and ask her to help 'rescue' you from whomever had taken you hostage." He shook his head as though not believing that a woman who had happened to have fallen in love with me would go to such extremes.

"So, as I said, we have been given the assignment to make sure that what you did six years does not go unpunished."

"But why go to such extremes? You must realize the risks of carrying out an attack on U.S. citizens on American soil. The diplomatic repercussions will be severe."

"That's not for us to decide Pete," he said. "We have an assignment and we will carry it out. The 'repercussions' are for others to worry about. But," he added with a sly grin, "You really have provided the perfect story to deflect attention away from us. Here's how it's going to go. Once we complete our assignment…"

"You mean once you have killed us," I said bitterly.

"Yes. Once we have done that, we return to Big Meadows panic-stricken. You see, it seems that Graciela had twisted her ankle on the way to this spot and we were lagging behind when all of a sudden we heard a series of gun shots. When we finally got here, we found both of you mortally wounded, your own revolvers in your hands. We saw two large men running through the woods. I would have given chase, but I didn't want to leave Graciela, with her twisted ankle, alone just in case the two men circled back. Instead, we made our way to the campground, with me supporting a hobbling Graciela, to get help and to report what we had seen. When the authorities begin to investigate, they will come to the conclusion that this was part of the attempt by organized crime to intimidate the work of your task force. They'll connect it to the attack on Ralph Turner and we'll be in the clear."

I put on my lawyer's hat and tried to poke holes in his scheme. "I don't think it's going to work. First of all, your name really isn't Roberto Walker is it?"

He nodded. "No. There *is* a Roberto Walker who is a sales representative for Oribe and Hermanos. But he's been on home leave in Montevideo while I have taken his place."

"What is your real name?"

He chuckled. "There's no need for you to known that Pete. Just call me Roberto."

"Okay *Roberto*," I said with some sarcasm. "You do know that killing me is going to stir up a hornet's nest. Every investigative agency imaginable is going to go over your story with a fine tooth comb. It won't take them long to figure out that you are not who you say you are and to doubt your story. It has more holes in it than Swiss Cheese," I said with more confidence than I felt.

He shrugged his shoulders. "You may be right Pete. But by the time they do 'figure it all out' Graciela and I shall be long gone. We'll leave it up to our superiors to handle the consequences. That's not our job. Our job is to exact revenge. And we are going to do our job."

I had no doubts on that score. But I wanted to keep him talking. "Something else Roberto. Why this elaborate plot? Why not attack us in Washington when the opportunity presented itself? Maybe something similar to what was done to Ralph Turner. Say you didn't…?"

He shook his head. "No. We didn't have anything to do with that."

"Well. As I was saying, why not get rid of us in some kind of ambush where you could do the deed and get away without anybody being the wiser? Why the charade of becoming our friends so you could lure us to a spot like this? I don't quite get it."

"To tell you the truth Pete, that is what I would have preferred. As you might have guessed, I have done this sort of thing before. I'm not bragging when I say that I could carry out the plan the way you describe it with a hundred percent guarantee that I would never be identified as the killer. But that's not what Evita wanted." I detected a note of disapproval in his voice. "She wanted you and María to feel a sense of real betrayal. She also wanted us to have this little conversation before

I killed you so that you would know exactly why it was being done and who was behind it. Knocking you both off from out of the blue would have been easier, but it would not have sent the same message. Now you are going to die at the hands of people you thought were your real friends. Something you can take to the grave with you."

It still all seemed unreal. I knew that Eva Duarte, as I and María had known her six years ago, could be ruthless and vengeful. And as powerful First Lady Evita she had done her best to deal cruelly with those she felt had looked down at her or anyone she considered an enemy, real or imagined. But to go to this extent and to take such a risk that might do harm to her husband, who must have agreed to the scheme, and his regime seemed to cross all reasonable boundaries. But here we were. I had to accept the fact that what Roberto was telling me was indeed reality.

There wasn't much more for me to say. But I was desperate to keep Roberto talking. "I have to admire your acting abilities. You and Graciela certainly had us completely fooled."

Glancing at María I could see her begin to say something. I put my finger to my lips. She had been warned to keep quiet and I didn't want anything to happen to her.

"We are well trained," Roberto said. "And to tell you the truth Pete, it wasn't all acting. We did come to like both of you. You were our targets, but the more we came to know you the fonder of you we became. In fact, we really enjoyed the various things we did together. Although, later on we would have a laugh over how gullible you both were. 'Easy pickings' as you North Americans say."

I had a brief flicker of hope. Maybe I could turn his sympathy to our advantage. But he quickly extinguished that hope. "But we are professionals Pete. When we are given an assignment, we carry it out. Sorry, but that's the way it is. But we do have a dilemma Pete."

Hope flickered again, only to be snuffed out immediately. "Which of you should die first? Graciela – and, as you might have guessed, that's not her real name either – Graciela thought it would be best if you watched María take a bullet before you did. Give you some time to suffer the loss before I put you out of your misery. But I argued that

Evita would be more pleased if I shot you first so that María would be the one who experienced the agony of watching the man she loved die. We argued about that for a good part of the morning."

That explained the tension I had noted over breakfast. Some other things clicked into place as well: their calm reaction to the snake we encountered; Graciela's insistence that I call Roberto at his office to allay any suspicions about his credentials; Roberto's description of the isolated clearing as the "perfect place" now had quite another meaning. These things now made sense in retrospect, but recognizing them did me no good at the moment.

"And I won the argument Pete," he said. Then, keeping his .45 squarely on my chest, he stood and gestured for me to do the same. When I hesitated, he warned, "We can still change the order Pete."

Slowly, I got to my feet. I could see Roberto's finger tighten on the trigger. I was getting ready to hurl myself to the side to avoid his bullet when everything became a blur as several things happened simultaneously. First, I heard María shout out, "I love you Pete," assuming those would be the last words I would hear and ignoring Roberto's warning to keep quiet. At the same time, there was a crashing sound from the woods to our right. Incredibly, a large black bear burst into the clearing. That must have been the source of the rustling sound I had heard earlier. The smell of our sandwiches had undoubtedly attracted the animal.

Since the food was closest to the two women, that's where the bear headed. Graciela let out a shout of pure terror, removed the gun from María's temple, rose from the rock where she had been seated and fired a shot at the approaching animal. The .22 bullet did little damage. It only enraged the bear, who swatted a huge paw in Graciela's direction, knocking her to the ground screaming in agony. He then began to maul her, tearing a jagged hole in her throat. María, only inches away, stood in horror as blood began to spurt from Graciela's neck.

Roberto turned his gun from me to the bear. He fired a shot from his .45 into the back of the beast, who with a loud roar of pain fell flat on the ground, mortally wounded, his body half covering that of

Graciela. There was no saving Graciela, who lay in an ever-expanding pool of her own blood.

I saw Roberto shift his sights to fire at María. But she had the presence of mind to dive for cover behind the nearby rock on which she had been seated seconds before.

I took advantage of the distraction to launch myself in Roberto's direction. By the time I closed the distance between us to less than ten feet, he turned to face me and fired a second shot that dug a furrow into my shoulder. Just before I tackled him and we both fell to the ground, he got off another shot that whizzed harmlessly past my left ear. The sound of the shot momentarily deafened me. My struggle to grab the weapon from Roberto's grasp took place in an eerie silence. In the back of my mind I recalled a similar battle with a Nazi officer on the pampa of Argentina.

Even though I had knocked Roberto down and was momentarily on top of him, the wound to my shoulder had started to bleed down my arm to my hand. When I grabbed for the gun, I could feel the steel barrel become slippery with my own blood. Roberto had both his hands on the gun and was trying to maneuver it to a position where he could fire it into my body. But his grip was beginning to be affected by my bleeding as well and I could feel it begin to loosen. I exerted all the strength I could muster and managed to twist Roberto's hands and arms in a way that wrenched the Colt from his grip and sent it flying a few feet away.

With the gun out of the way, I reached for Roberto's throat. But he was strong and agile, and easily blocked my effort. Then, flat on his back, he managed to buck me off, sending me reeling to the side. I landed on my wounded shoulder and let out a cry of pain that seemed to come from a far distance.

Roberto got to his feet and went to recover the Colt. I scrambled after him, but he got to the gun first. He had it in his right hand and was turning toward me when suddenly a shot rang out and a perfect circle appeared in the middle of his forehead. He immediately fell backwards, the Colt falling from his lifeless fingers, a look of total bewilderment on his face.

I looked up to see María ten feet away. She was in the standard two-handed shooting posture with her feet spread and balanced that I had first seen her adopt at the FBI Range, the smoke spiraling from the barrel of her .38. Then she dropped the gun and began to crumple to the ground, her eyes locked in a vacant stare. I rushed to her and cradled her in my arms, offering words of comfort and relief. My hearing was starting to come back and in the distance I could detect the faint echo of police sirens. Help had finally arrived, late but welcome nevertheless.

I gently assisted María to her feet. "Oh Pete," she said, tears in her eyes, "I'm so sorry. Graciela had me so …"

"It's all right sweetheart. They were accomplished professionals. They fooled me too, and I have been trained to spot imposters."

She noticed the blood dripping down my arm. "Oh Pete. You're bleeding."

I made like a movie hero. "Just a scratch sweetheart. Nothing serious. Nonetheless, we better patch it up."

There was a first-aid kit in my knapsack. María helped me clean the wound and bandage it. That helped stop the bleeding, but my shoulder was sore and I would need some pain medication once we got back to civilization.

We could hear footsteps and voices approaching along the narrow path to the clearing. I thought I heard David Friedman shouting my name, but my hearing was not yet fully back to normal and I couldn't be sure. But María had heard it loud and clear. "David," she shouted. "We are over here. And we are all right."

A few seconds later, David along with five or six others entered the clearing. We could see the looks of bewilderment on their faces as they surveyed the scene. The two dead human bodies they could probably understand. I guessed they already knew that Roberto and Graciela were not who they had claimed to be. The dead bear would take some explaining.

CHAPTER TWENTY EIGHT

June 23, 1951 – Big Meadows to Washington, D.C.

While María and I tried to recover from our recent brush with death, David took charge. He ordered the State Troopers who had accompanied him to remove the bodies of Roberto and Graciela and get them to a nearby morgue in Luray until a decision was made as to their ultimate disposal. He warned them to do so in a way that would attract as little attention as possible, although just how that would be accomplished was not entirely clear. If anybody at the campground asked what had happened, they were simply to say that the "Walkers" had been the victims of an unfortunate accident.

David and Steven Graham then helped escort María and me to the campground parking lot. María was still in a state of shock. She was able to put one foot in front of the other, but I kept my good arm around her waist to offer support until we got to Steve's car. The bleeding in my left shoulder had stopped, but it was painfully sore.

Steve drove us to Skyland, where the three of us – David, María, and I transferred to David's sedan for the trip to Washington. I sat in the back with María, her head in my lap as she curled on the seat like a baby and began a quiet sobbing. I did my best to comfort her, but as we wound our way down the mountains to Sperryville, she was inconsolable. "Oh Pete," she moaned. "How could I have put you in such danger? What a fool I was. Can you ever forgive me?"

I took out my handkerchief and dried her tears. "There's nothing to forgive sweetheart. How were you to know that the Walkers were not who they seemed to be? They had me totally fooled as well. And don't forget, you saved my life. If you hadn't reacted the way you did Roberto would have shot me and then you and we wouldn't be here now."

By the time we had reached Sperryville, she had regained some control. She had stopped sobbing and sat upright, her head resting against my right shoulder. David, who had been silent up to that point, asked me what had happened back at Big Meadows. Before I told him, I had a question of my own. How had he known we were in trouble and how to find us? He explained that Steve Graham had stumbled onto the fact that the Roberto Walker we knew was not the genuine article. The two of them began to piece together what Roberto and Graciela were up to. He had found out from Joe Smathers where we would most likely be and he and Steve had hustled to Big Meadows as fast as they could.

I then gave him a blow-by-blow account of the day's events. As I related them, I still had a hard time believing the reality of what we had experienced. It was like a nightmare. I half expected to wake up in our bed at Skyland dismissing it as no more than a bad dream. But the pain in my shoulder was a stark reminder that it had been no dream.

We stopped at a hospital in Warrenton to have a doctor look at my wound. After a fifteen-minute wait in the Emergency Room, a young physician treated me. Looking at the furrow Roberto's bullet had dug, he said, "You know, I need to report any gunshot wounds to the police."

I dug out my wallet and showed him my Department of Justice credentials. He looked at them and said, "Okay. I understand. Let me patch you up and you can be on your way." He cleaned the wound, applied some anti-biotic cream, and gave me some pills for the pain. "You have lost some blood," he said, "so take it easy for a few hours. And you should have another doctor look at this in a week or so, earlier if you have a fever and soreness. But I think you'll be all right. It's only a superficial wound. You were lucky."

"Yes I was. Very lucky."

I thanked the doctor and we resumed our trip. David and I started talking about what we should do next in light of what had just happened.

As we talked, María once again curled up on the seat with her head in my lap and began to doze. I took that as a good sign.

We crossed the Key Bridge into the District of Columbia just as the sun was beginning to set. It brought back bittersweet memories of how happy and excited María and I had been crossing the same bridge in the other direction less than forty-eight hours ago.

There was little traffic on a Saturday night. David drove through the quiet streets of the capital and let us off in front of our townhouse.

"Thanks for everything David," I said, helping María out and then closing the door.

"You're more than welcome my friend," he said. "I just wish I could have gotten to you sooner."

"You did your best buddy," I said. "That's all anyone could have expected. And thank goodness you showed up when you did. I'm not sure how we could have handled things otherwise."

"Okay you two," David said. "I've got to get going. We are going to be working on this thing all night. I'll be in touch later. In the meantime, try to get some rest."

David drove away and we entered our townhouse. María headed straight for the bathroom, aiming to take a long shower. She had bloodstains on her hands and face she desperately wanted to remove. I went to the kitchen for some water when the phone rang. It was Joe Smathers.

"Hi Pete," he said. "How are you and María? We were worried sick."

"We're okay, all things considered. It could have been a lot worse; a whole lot worse."

Joe then explained that he and a couple of the agents on the task force had arrived at Big Meadows twenty minutes after we had left. Joe had overseen the transfer of the bodies of the Walkers to Luray and had issued orders to the State Troopers to keep mum.

"What about the bear?" I asked. After all, he – or she – had saved our lives and I hated to think of it simply rotting in the sun.

"That's one for the books, isn't it," he said. "It took five of us to move its body into the woods and bury it."

The thought that the beast had been treated with some respect heartened me. I couldn't very well have thanked it whatever the circumstances.

"Listen Pete," Joe continued. "Try to get some rest. We are going to be burning the midnight oil on this whole affair. There are a lot of moving parts and we want to get ahead of things before they get out of hand. If the press gets ahold of this...well, let's hope that doesn't happen. I'll call you in the morning to let you know where things stand."

"Thanks Joe. I want to be in on whatever you guys decide. Until tomorrow then."

"Until tomorrow."

After I hung up the phone, I went to the kitchen and filled a large glass with ice-water. I was tempted by the cold bottles of beer that we also had on hand. But if I were to take the pain pills the doctor in Warrenton had given me, it was not a good idea to mix them with alcohol.

María came out of the bathroom and joined me at the kitchen table. She wore a light-weight robe and had a towel around her freshly-washed hair. There was still a dazed look in her eyes, but overall she seemed calm. I got her a glass of water, which she drained in one swallow. I asked her if she was all right, probably a foolish question under the circumstances, and she assured me she was. I left her at the table and followed her example, taking a long shower and washing my hair, careful not to get my bandage wet. By the time I got out of the bathroom, María was already in bed and asleep. I took one of the pain pills and slipped in beside her, grateful for the air-conditioning unit that hummed away in the background. Whether because of the pill or because of pure exhaustion, I fell asleep at once. Later, in the middle of the night, I was awoken by a loud shout from María and an anguished cry of "No. Please, no." I pulled her into my arms, expecting to find her wide awake. But she was still fast asleep. After about five minutes, I dropped off again into a deep slumber.

CHAPTER TWENTY NINE

June 24, 1951 – Washington, D.C.

Rays of sunshine coming through the blinds and onto my face woke me. For a moment, I thought that it was just another Sunday morning. But then the events of the previous day came rushing back, the throbbing in my shoulder a painful reminder of what we had been through. I reached over to touch María, but her side of the bed was empty. Through the bedroom door, I could smell coffee brewing and bacon frying on the stove.

I put on my robe and stumbled into the kitchen. María, still in her night clothes, was standing at the stove preparing my favorite breakfast – bacon, scrambled eggs, toast, juice, and coffee. "Good morning darling," she said with a smile that never failed to warm my heart, "Did you sleep well? Ready for breakfast? I don't know about you, but I am starved."

She seemed so normal that I feared she might have blocked out entirely what we had been through the day before. "I'm fine darling. How about you? How was your night?"

"I slept like a log," she giggled. "Isn't that a funny expression? Does a *log* actually sleep?"

"I'm glad to hear that sweetheart. Very glad. But what about…?"

She raised a hand. "Yes. Yes. What about yesterday?"

I nodded. "We do need to talk about it darling," she said, her face serious. "I understand your concern. You think I'm denying the reality of what I… we went through. I am not, I assure you. I replay that horrible scene in my mind every waking minute. But right now, I just want to feel that things are normal. That we are back safe and sound in our home, doing the things we always do. Let me have that then we can talk about…things."

"Certainly sweetheart, certainly. Whatever you want. Just let me know when you're ready."

While we were having our breakfast, the phone rang. I picked it up and Joe was on the other end. "Hello Pete. How was your night?"

"Fine Joe. We got a good night's sleep and are in the middle of tucking into a hearty breakfast. What's going on?"

"Glad to hear it Pete," he said. "I'll let you get back to your breakfast. But before I do, can you make it down to the Executive Office Building, say in about an hour? We've been here all night and there are some developments we want you to know about."

I looked at my watch. It was already past ten. María and I had slept for almost twelve hours. "Sure thing Joe. I'll be there by eleven."

"Great. See you then." Just before he was about to hang up, he added, "We're in room 323 on the Third Floor. I'll let the guard at the door know you are coming."

"Room 323," I confirmed. "Got it. See you soon."

María had picked up enough of my side of the conversation to know that I would be going soon. I was reluctant to leave her alone, concerned that despite her brave front she was still in a fragile state. But she assured me that she would be fine and that I needed to attend the meeting. We were both anxious to know what U.S. officialdom was going to do about the attack on us by agents of a foreign government. We were hardly disinterested bystanders.

I arrived at the EOB a few minutes before eleven. The building, constructed in the French Empire style after the Civil War, was directly west of the White House on Pennsylvania Avenue. Its distinctive architecture had its admirers and its critics, but whatever the opinions it had become an established landmark. It had once housed the departments of State, Navy, and War, but they had since moved to other quarters. It was now used by the president's and the vice-president's staff. The fact that Joe's meeting was held at the EOB rather than at the Department of Justice signaled that the White House was involved.

When I presented my credentials to the guard, he waved me through. Tim O'Rourke was waiting on the other side. As I stepped through the door, he grabbed me in a tight Irish hug and pounded me on the back. His eyes were moist. "Hey partner," he said, his voice hoarse, "Am I ever glad to see you."

My shoulder felt better, but Tim's exuberant embrace produced a wince. "Sorry Pete," he said, "I forgot about your wound. How's it feel."

"Still sore, but nothing I can't handle," I assured him. "And hey, I'm glad to see you too, believe me. Less than twenty-four hours ago, I didn't think the chances were very good that María and I would make it."

He looked at me soberly. "Yeah. Roberto and Graciela really put on a good act didn't they? None of us suspected they weren't who they claimed to be, not to mention that they might try – you know – to get rid of the both of you."

"Well, they were highly-trained professionals, and as much as I hate to admit it, really good at what they did."

"Not good enough though, right?"

"I guess so. But if hadn't been for that bear…"

"Yeah. Too bad we can't pin a medal on him."

I chuckled. Tim's Irish humor was coming to the fore. "Joe and the rest of the team are waiting upstairs Pete. Let me show you the way."

The building was empty on a Sunday morning and our footsteps echoed loudly in the hallway. "Just so you know," Tim said, "Joe assembled the entire task force last night. We're all here along with David Friedman and Steve Graham. There are also some guys from the State Department," he said in a way that suggested he wasn't thrilled by their presence. "They are pretty much running the show," he muttered, doing nothing to hide his displeasure.

We took the stairs up to the third floor. Room 323 was down the hall to our right. Tim opened the door for me and we went in. Joe Smathers was sitting at the far end of a long rectangular conference table. Next to him, to his left were three men I did not recognize but assumed were the State Department representatives that Tim had mentioned. Scattered around the other sides were the task force guys, along with David and Steve. All of them except the State Department people rose and came over to shake my hand, one by one, each expressing their relief that María and I had made it through our experience alive. By the time I had shaken the last hand, I could feel tears begin to form at the corner of my eyes. I brushed them away and took a deep breath. "Thanks a lot, all of you."

Joe, who had been the first to greet me, took me by the elbow and guided me to a vacant seat to his right and gestured for me to sit. "Pete, you know everybody here except for these three men," he said, gesturing to his left. "They're all with the State Department." He introduced the two men farthest away first, then the one sitting next to him. "And this is Grant Spenser, who is heading up State's response to what happened yesterday."

As Joe made his introductions, I looked around the table. Almost everyone had their coats off and their ties loosened. There was stubble on their faces and weariness in their eyes. They were showing the effects of no sleep and little nourishment. Spenser, however, still had his tie firmly in place, his coat on, and looked fresh as a daisy. I judged him to be in his mid-fifties and, although he was sitting, probably over six feet in height. He had a full head of dark hair, graying slightly at the temples, and sported a moustache that mimicked that of his boss under a hawk-like nose on which perched a pair of metal-rimmed glasses. He had cold gray eyes, but on closer inspection I saw that they also were streaked with red and showed some of the strain he was under. As I took my inventory, I thought he looked familiar. Then I remembered that I had seen him on television and in newspaper photos, a constant presence at the side of Secretary of State Acheson. I didn't know his exact title, and it was not volunteered, but I knew it was high up the hierarchy of the State Department.

"Pete," Joe said. "We've been at this all night. Everybody around the table but you knows where we stand at the moment. It's important that we bring you up to speed." Joe looked down at his hands, which were clenched tightly together on the table in a gesture I knew signaled his unstated displeasure with something. "Grant here," he continued, "is in charge. So we thought he better fill you in on what's been decided so far."

"Thanks Joe," Spenser said. "Pete, a lot has happened since Joe gave us the word about the attack on you and your wife." He spoke in a calm and self-assured manner. "I'll try to keep it simple. First, we have taken this very seriously. Both President Truman and Secretary of State Acheson have been informed. They have asked me to convey their regrets that you and your wife were subject to such an attack and their relief that you both survived along with their personal best wishes for a speedy recovery from whatever wounds you might have suffered."

I was a bit overwhelmed, but simply nodded. Spenser cleared his throat and continued, "Secretary Acheson had me call the Argentine ambassador last night to register a formal complaint. As you might guess, the ambassador denied knowing anything at all about a plan to attack you and your wife. And that might even be true. According to the CIA," he said, looking at David and Steve, "this could have been an 'off the books' operation. Whoever ordered it, might have kept the embassy in the dark. Furthermore…"

David interrupted. "We know who ordered it Grant. It came from the office of the president of the country, acting on behalf of his wife. That's what the man known as Roberto Walker told Pete, and from what I know of Evita, I have no doubt she was behind it."

Spenser shifted in his seat, looking uncomfortable as heads around the table nodded in agreement with David's words. "Yes David. As bizarre as it sounds that very well might be true. But we have no *definitive* proof that is the case. My apologies Pete," he said, turning to me, "but all we have to go on are what the two people who survived the attack have told us. And I'm afraid that's not going to be enough."

"What about the evidence we turned up that Walker was impersonating someone else?" David asked, his voice testy. "Isn't that hard evidence?"

I could see Spenser get a little testy himself. "Sure David, we can prove that. But so what? There could be a multitude of explanations put forth for why he was pretending to be someone else. Maybe he was planning to steal money from the company. Maybe he was sent here as a spy to gather sensitive information."

He could see the disgruntled looks around the table. "We have asked our embassy in Buenos Aires to look into this whole matter. But we are not optimistic they'll be able to come up with any convincing evidence. And even if they do, the likely response will be a blanket denial and an accusation that we are trying to besmirch the good name of the country's leaders prior to a national election. It will be an echo of the *Blue Book*, and we all know how that turned out."

David stared daggers at Spenser, but he kept his anger to himself. He had worked on the State Department's *Blue Book*, former Ambassador Spruille Braden's failed attempt to link Perón to the Nazis that had backfired badly.

"Look," Spenser said, "I know that we are all angry and want some kind of retribution, some kind of punishment." Again turning to me, he said, "Personally, I tend to agree with Pete and his wife that the Walkers were sent here to exact revenge. And I'm incensed that the Argentine government would order an attack on American citizens on American soil. It's virtually unprecedented. In some circumstances it might even merit a declaration of war – or at least a break in diplomatic relations."

He looked around the room. "But there are other interests at play." I could see a look of disgust crop up on all the faces around the table except for the two State Department men, who remained expressionless. Obviously, all of this had been hashed out before and was now being replayed for my benefit. "We don't want to overreact. We need to maintain good relations with Argentina. It's too important a country for us to alienate. We've had a rocky relationship with the Perón government in the past, but things have been improving in recent years. We don't want to rock the boat at this stage. There's too much at stake. We've done a good job of containing communist influence in the region. Like it or not Perón has been an unspoken ally in that regard. He has taken away the working class as a basis for any kind of Marxist influence in Argentina. Besides..."

In an uncharacteristic move, Joe reached over and grabbed Spenser's arm with a bit more force than he may have intended. "Okay Grant, we get the picture. No need for another lecture."

Spenser looked annoyed and stared at Joe's hand on his arm until Joe removed it. Joe was plainly exhausted, frustrated, and angry. He was intensely protective of the men who served with him and was furious that no action would be taken in retaliation for the attack on me and María.

"Right Joe," Spenser said. "Okay. We've been over all of this. Unfortunately, our hands are tied right now. But we *are* going to deal with this problem. We want to find an appropriate response. But it's going to take some time to work something out. In the meantime, we are trying our best to keep all of this from the press and the public. I don't need to tell you what a nightmare it would be if the story got out." Again he turned to me, "Do you understand Pete? Not a word to anyone outside of this room. And I hope we can trust your wife to keep quiet about this."

I felt my face redden and balled my fists. If Joe hadn't been between me and Spenser, I might have punched him the nose. But the flash of anger passed quickly. It was a natural thing for him to ask. Mustering calm, I replied, "Yes Mister Spenser," I replied through clenched teeth, "You can trust both my wife and me to be discreet."

Spenser's eyes bored into mine as I spoke. Seemingly satisfied, he gave a slight nod. "Well then that's settled," he said. Glancing around the table, he reiterated the point: "We all have to keep this business *absolutely* confidential. Not a word to anyone outside of this room. If someone should ask you about what happened to Benton here and his wife, simply plead ignorance, at least until we have this all sorted out. *Understood*?"

The faces that stared back at him were glum. I could sense that David and Steve Graham were particularly upset. But everybody nodded and uttered quiet "understood" responses.

"Okay Joe," Spenser said. "That about wraps it up for now. Thank you all for putting so much time and effort into this thing. We'll be in touch once we see how things shake out."

Spenser gathered some papers he had in front of him and stuffed them into a briefcase. As he rose to leave, accompanied by the two State officials, Joe said, "I'll be expecting your call Grant." His expression and tone indicated that Joe was not going to let the matter rest. If he was not kept abreast of developments, he was going to raise a ruckus.

Spenser got the message. "You bet Joe."

After the State Department trio left the room, the rest of us started to get up and follow them out. Joe held up a restraining hand. "Just a minute fellows," he said. We all resumed our seats. Joe paused for moment, then began, "Look, I'm no happier about what Grant had to say than the rest of you. But orders are orders. We've got to keep this whole thing contained. We all know what might happen if…"

Eliot Baker, one of the FBI agents on the task force, interrupted. "Joe, if you ask me, this whole business stinks. First we have the attack on Ralph Turner. Now this thing from out of the blue on Pete and his wife – *and we're just supposed to keep mum?*" Elliot's face was red and his fist pounded the table. It was the first time I had seen him so agitated. Usually he was the picture of cool, unruffled calm and professionalism. "We can't let this go by without doing something."

There were murmurs of assent around the table. "Hey Elliot," Joe said. "I feel the same way. But what are we supposed to do? This is something with an international dimension that is far beyond our authority. We have no choice but to let State handle this. And remember, just how to respond to the attack on Pete and María has the attention not only of State but also the White House. We've got no choice but to accept the situation as it is. And that means keeping the whole thing under wraps. Not a word to anyone, please. If not…well, I don't need to tell you. The consequences could be pretty serious for anyone who breaks the silence."

Baker slumped in his chair. "Yeah Joe. You're right. But I still say it stinks."

At this point, I felt compelled to say something. "Joe," I said, "I'd like to say a few words."

"Sure Pete. Go ahead."

"First of all guys, I want to thank you for working so hard on this. And for the support you've given to me and María." My voice wavered and I took a moment to collect myself. "It really means a lot to both of us. But as much as I hate to admit it, Spenser is right. There are bigger things at play than this particular incident. Believe me nobody in this room wants the people who ordered the hit on me and my wife to be punished for what they did more than I do. But we have to be practical. I'm sure that the Argentine government will adamantly deny any involvement. And the only real proof we have is a confession from someone who is now dead. So what can we do? We have to just sit tight and let Spenser and State handle things from now on. And please, don't get into any trouble on my account. This attack resulted from something I – and María – did in Argentina six years ago. It had nothing to do with the task force or the attack on Ralph Turner. It's just an unfortunate set of circumstances."

I looked around the table. "For me – and I think I speak for María – the worst possible outcome of this whole affair would be if any of you had to suffer personally because you wanted the people behind the attack exposed and punished. So let me second what Joe said. Please let's keep all of this quiet until we see what State comes up with."

"Thanks Pete," Joe said. "Well, I guess that's it. Go home and get some rest. I'll see you tomorrow."

As I rose from my chair, Joe got up and put his arm around me, grabbing my good shoulder. "Great to have you back safe and sound Pete." The others came up, again shook my hand, and expressed the same sentiment. Each and every one asked me to give María their best wishes, doing little to hide their admiration for her courage in what had been a life-and-death situation. A few, including David Friedman, had tears in their eyes. I had a hard time keeping my emotions in check as well.

Even though I had gotten twelve hours of sleep, I was drained, emotionally and physically. When David offered me a ride home, I gratefully accepted. I was anxious to see María. I wanted to tell her what had transpired at the meeting. But more importantly, I wanted to make sure that the "normalcy" she had tried so hard to maintain at breakfast remained in place. We had both survived a dramatic brush with death with our bodies intact. Whether we both survived unscarred emotionally remained to be seen.

CHAPTER THIRTY

July 6, 1951 – Washington, D.C.

I took my time strolling to the Occidental for my Friday lunch with David Friedman. The temperature and the humidity were both in the nineties with no relief in sight. Everything seemed to slow down in the unrelenting heat of mid-summer Washington.

It had been less than two weeks since the meeting at the EOB. After David had dropped me off at home, I had found María remarkably calm and composed. I told her what had been discussed, how unlikely it was that the Peróns would suffer any consequences for what they had tried to do to us, and how important it was to keep what had happened to ourselves. She seemed to understand and accept the reality of the situation, telling me that it was more or less what she expected. I suspected, however, that underneath the acceptance was the kind of boiling anger that Elliot Baker had let fly. *It really did stink!*

Joe had told me to take as long as I needed to recuperate before getting back to work. By the next day after the meeting at the EOB my shoulder was feeling much better and there was no physical reason why I could not go to the office and resume where I had left off the previous Thursday, which now seemed in the distant past. But I was worried about leaving María alone to brood.

As it turned out, she seemed fine, anxious to do some preliminary studying for art history classes she had enrolled in for the fall. She even decided to return to the Phillips to look at some new paintings that had been added to the collection. I asked her if the return might stir memories of her initial meeting with Graciela, which now, in retrospect, had been part of the plot to have the two agents establish contact with us. She assured me that it would pose no problem. She was determined, she said, not to let what had happened prevent her from doing what made her happy. I wondered if she was just putting on a brave front for my benefit, but she seemed sincere.

By mid-week, it was clear that having me around the house was doing neither of us any good. In fact, now *I* was the one who was brooding and moody, not knowing exactly what to do with myself away from my desk and feeling guilty that the rest of the task force was hard at work while I tried to interest myself in pulp crime novels, the sports pages, and crossword puzzles. After two days of this, I told María that I was returning to the office the next morning. She put up no objections, sensing that as she was trying to do, it would be best for me to get back to my regular routine.

Burying myself in work proved to be the best medicine. I had fallen behind and had a lot of catching up to do. Tim and I were supposed to have our reports ready by the end of the week. Senator Kefauver was pressing the task force to assemble as much evidence as possible so he could proceed with his investigation. We both worked non-stop for the next couple of days, taking short breaks for lunch. Tim maintained his good humor and we swapped stories and jokes to lighten the mood.

Joe Smathers had scheduled a meeting for Friday at nine to discuss where we were on our assignments. Everyone arrived on time, carrying our folders full of case files and dumping them on the table in front of us. The plan was for us each to talk about where we were at the moment. Joe wanted to make sure that by the end of the day, everything was in order and he could contact the Kefauver Committee that we had assembled what they needed.

Most of us were in shirt-sleeves, the morning heat already making its presence felt. Joe greeted us with a somber look. "Good morning guys," he began. "Before we start, I have some news for you. And especially for you Pete," he said glumly.

We all knew what was coming. "I just got off the phone with Grant Spenser. He told me that State has been working all week on how to respond to the attack on Pete and María. In his words, 'It has been discussed at the highest levels.' And the decision, I'm afraid to say, is not going to make us very happy. So far as the attack is concerned, there will be no real consequences. No retaliation of any kind, no punishment. Both governments will keep the whole episode secret. The bodies of Graciela and Roberto are already on their way back to Argentina."

Shoulders slumped in resignation around the table. I heard several voices utter quiet curses. Turning to me, Joe said, "I'm awfully sorry Pete. I was hoping for something more."

I nodded. "Thanks Joe. But after listening to Spenser Sunday, I kind of figured this would be the outcome. I'm not happy about it, but I'm not surprised."

Tim, who was sitting to my right, banged the table with his fist. "Damn it Joe, we can't let this happen. I mean, we're going to let a foreign government order an attack on an American citizen on American soil and just keep silent? It doesn't make any sense. Forget about justice for a minute. What kind of message does this send? If Spenser were here now, you'd have to hold me down."

He was practically sputtering with outrage. I put a hand on his shoulder to restrain him.

Joe raised both his hands in a calming gesture. "Take it easy Tim. As a matter of fact, I raised that very point with Spenser. He told me that the secretary had sent a communication to Argentina's minister of foreign affairs making it clear that any further such attacks would have *serious consequences* for future relations between our two countries."

"Yeah," Tim said sarcastically, "More wrist-slapping and empty threats. *What a crock!*" There were murmurs of agreement around the table, with Elliot Baker nodding so hard I was afraid he was going to strain his neck.

All Joe could do was shrug.

"Thanks guys," I said. "Again, I really appreciate all the support you have given us. But we have to be realistic. As Spenser said, this matter has been discussed at the highest levels and the decision made. We just have to live with it. And I'm sorry that it has been such a distraction. Let's not forget that we still have important work to do, work to which we have dedicated months of effort and sacrifice. The best course for us now is to put all this 'Argentine' business behind us and focus on the job at hand. At least we can find some solace in the fact that the plot against María and me failed. The whole thing could have turned out a lot worse, believe me. We were very, very lucky. So let's keep that in mind and move on."

Joe looked at me with gratitude. "Thanks Pete." He cleared his throat. "You heard what the man said. Time to get back to work."

María and I had spent a quiet weekend, going to a movie and having dinner with Elliot Baker and his wife. I hadn't been particularly close to Baker before, putting him into the category of the typical humorless FBI agent. But I felt I owed him a debt for the way he spoke up to Grant Spenser and extended the invitation to him and his wife go out to eat with us. To my surprise, the Bakers proved to be quite warm and funny, especially after a couple of glasses of wine. We had a great time with them. It helped erase some of the bitter feelings from the phony friendship behind which the Walkers had hidden their real intentions.

When I entered the Occidental, David was already sitting at our regular table. As I headed in his direction, I thought of the last time we had lunch at the Occidental, when we were both so relieved that the Walkers had been made aware of the danger *they* might face if they went with us to the Blue Ridge. *Talk about irony!* The thought that *they* would pose the real danger never entered our minds.

As I approached, David rose and extended his hand. "Hey Pete," he said. "Good to see you."

I shook his hand and pulled him close for an *abrazo.*

"So Pete," David said, "How are things? How's it been going?"

He already knew what had been decided with regard to the Walkers and their attack on us. He was no happier than the rest of us. But he recognized the realities of the "bigger picture." "Believe me," he had told me, "I've had a lot of experience with the compromises that are necessary in such situations. As much as we would like to see justice done and exact a little revenge of our own, we have to recognize we are government employees who often have to make sacrifices for the greater good. As Elliot Baker said, *it stinks*. But there is only so much we can do. At least the Walkers got their just desserts."

"How's it going?" I said, "Well you know how it is pal. It's been pretty rough." He nodded in sympathy. "I've been trying to bury myself in work, but often have a hard time focusing. I keep going back over all the little clues I missed that might have alerted me to the fact that the Walkers were not who they claimed to be. María has been doing the same. She says there were a few things that didn't seem quite right about Graciela, but she had pushed them to the back of her mind. She realizes now that she had been so desperate to make a real female friend, especially one who seemed to come from the same background, that she overlooked little nagging doubts that in retrospect might have raised suspicions. And I experienced some of the same with Roberto, who after all saved me from serious injury from a fall into the Potomac."

"You know why he did that don't you?"

"Yeah," I said, "It wasn't the right moment. Their plan was to get rid of both of us and in the process make sure we knew why." I paused for a moment. "And to their credit, and to the credit of whoever dreamed up this scheme, they were exceptionally well briefed on both of us and were able to exploit our vulnerabilities to maximum effect. Objectively you have to admire how skillfully they played us. And if it hadn't been for the lucky break of that bear coming on the scene when it did, the scheme would have worked to perfection."

At that moment the waiter returned with our drinks. I took a contented sip of my martini and grinned at my friend, "And I wouldn't be here with you now enjoying this delicious martini."

David raised his glass of bourbon and water. "I'll drink to that," he said with a wry smile.

"You know," I said, "Two weeks later, I still have a hard time recognizing the reality of what happened. It was all so bizarre. And strangely enough, I can't really blame the Walkers for what happened."

David looked surprised. "Yeah, weird huh? When they held us at gunpoint in that clearing, I sure didn't feel that way. It was us or them and if I could have, I would have shot them both before they shot us.

But after thinking it over, I've come to the conclusion they were only doing what others had ordered them to do. Not too different from what we did during the war and in some ways are still doing in our present jobs. Roberto told me it was nothing personal. They were just carrying out their assignments. In fact, they had come to like us and to really enjoy our time together."

David shook his head in disbelief. "Sorry Pete, but I just can't buy that. The refrain of 'we were just following orders,' doesn't sit well with me. Isn't that what we heard at Nuremburg? It's no excuse. Everyone knows that there are lines that can't be crossed. In fact, I think that most of those who claim they were 'just following orders' only use that as an excuse to cover up what they probably would have done anyway on their own volition."

"You've got a point there buddy. But I guess in our case, the difference is that we spent a lot of time with the Walkers. We shared common experiences, mostly pleasant. That colors my perception of them, no doubt about it. Believe me, if I could get my hands on those who gave the orders, I wouldn't hesitate to extract my measure of justice."

We were halfway through our drinks when the waiter appeared to take our orders. We hadn't even looked at our menus and simply ordered from memory. After he had left, I asked David how things were going with him. He frowned and stared down at the table for a few seconds, fiddling with his silverware. When he looked up, there was a deep sadness etched on his face. "Well, I've been better Pete," he said, his voice breaking. "Sarah's back in Israel. She left earlier this week"

I knew that Sarah had been slated to return home, but hadn't realized it would be so soon. "I'm sorry to hear that buddy. What does that do to your wedding plans?"

David looked devastated. "To be frank Pete, I don't think there will be a wedding."

I was jolted and felt like reaching across the table to offer some physical comfort. "Why not? I thought things were all set."

"So did I," David said wistfully. "But Sarah says that certain unspecified circumstances have changed and it is best to put any marriage plans on hold."

"And what are those 'unspecified circumstances'?"

David gave me a jaundiced look. "I wish I knew. All very hush-hush." He paused. "You know, I always had my suspicions that Sarah might be playing a role, pretending to feel about me the way I felt about her so as to get me to…" he hesitated "…to do certain things for her. I guess I was kind of like you with the Walkers, wanting desperately to believe that she really cared for me when in fact she was, as you say, 'following orders' with another purpose in mind altogether. In your case, the Walkers wanted to take your lives. At least in that they failed. In my case, Sarah has managed to break my heart."

My own heart went out to him. He looked so sad and crestfallen. "I'm so sorry my friend." I knew that David, who had a darker view of things and tended to be more pessimistic than I was, often exaggerated. "Are you sure David? Has she actually broken things off?"

He knew what I was getting at. "Not in so many words Pete. But I'd be a fool if I believed otherwise. All the signs are there, and I can't ignore them. It's over between us. And I just have to accept that. Besides, even if I wanted to join her in Israel, I wouldn't be able to. I can't explain why, but I can't. Again, unlike the Walkers with you and María, their plan for me has worked to perfection."

David didn't need to explain. And if I asked him to, he would refuse to answer. But I could make a pretty good guess. His reference to "their plan" meant that somehow, through Sarah, the Israeli embassy had found David useful for their purposes. They had managed to put him in a compromising position from which he could not extract himself.

Just then our food arrived. We were both silent as we began to eat. But after a few bites, David, who had been listlessly pushing his meal around his plate, put his fork down and looked at me in a resigned way. "You know Pete, maybe you're right. Maybe 'just following orders' covers a multitude of sins. The Nazi underlings were 'just following orders,' the Walkers were 'just following orders,' I guess Sarah was 'just following orders.' And look at me. Now I'm doing the same, although just whose orders I'm following I can't say. In fact…" I thought he was about to reveal more, but he let the sentence drop and I didn't push it. He was under enough pressure. I didn't want to add to his burdens.

"Listen pal," I said. "We are all just parts of a larger machine. We all 'follow orders' in one way or another. It's just the way of the world."

"Maybe you're right Pete," he said, between forkfuls. "But we don't have to like it."

"No we don't." I consoled myself with the thought that at least in my case I had some options. If I disagreed with the way things were going on the task force, I could raise objections and maybe get the others to agree to a change of course. And if things became too uncomfortable, I could simply quit and return to New York where I could either resume working for the DA's office or go into private practice. David, I suspected, did not have such freedom of choice. He was stuck, and he knew it.

After we had finished our main course, we ordered coffee. While we waited for it to arrive, David asked me, "So how is María doing? She's been through a lot."

"Believe it or not," I replied, shaking my head, "I think she's recovered from the attack better than I have. At least she *seems* to be back to normal. Would you believe it, the morning after we got back from the Blue Ridge she was up before I was fixing me a full breakfast? Right now," I said, glancing at my watch, "she's just getting out of a summer school art history class at GW."

I paused for a minute. "You know, Joe Smathers told me that if I wanted to quit the task force and return to New York in light of what happened, he would understand. And I gave it some serious thought. While I would hate to give up the work, it might be better for María if she had a chance to return to her job there and to more familiar surroundings. But when I broached the subject, she was adamant that I should reject the offer. She said she knew how much the work of the task force meant to me. If I quit, it would mean the Walkers had somehow prevailed, forcing me to give up something that was of great importance to me. She claimed she had come to like living in D.C. and pursuing her interests in art. So there was no way she wanted me to accept Joe's offer, particularly on her account."

"Well, she's quite a woman Pete. Quite a woman indeed." I knew David wasn't jealous, but I noted the tone of regret. He was undoubtedly thinking of Sarah, who he had hoped would have been for him what María was to me.

"I noticed that you said *seems* to be back to normal Pete. Do you have any doubts?"

Before I could answer, the waiter brought our coffee and tea. I took a few sips of my coffee before I responded. "To tell you the truth, I'm afraid she might be over-compensating, putting on a brave front while repressing the horror of what happened. I'm no psychologist, but I'm not sure it's emotionally healthy for her not to confront the reality of what happened – betrayed by someone she thought was a friend, witness to her supposed friend's horrible death, and then killing Roberto." I had a flash back to the moment when the bear tore out Graciela's throat, spraying blood everywhere, including on María. "Every time I ask her if she wants to talk about the attack, she brushes me off, claiming she has put it behind her. That she is fine. But," I said, lowering my voice, "I hear her moaning in the middle of the night, shouting out 'No, No, please don't!' When I ask her about it in the morning, she claims not to remember. And that may well be the truth."

David's concern was evident. "Have you suggested that she see a psychiatrist?"

"Not yet. But if these nighttime outbursts continue, I'm going to give it a try."

"I think that would be best Pete. She's been through an awful lot. You may be right that she's repressing the reality of what happened."

I just nodded. While we waited for the bill, we turned our conversation to other matters. María and I had plans to go to dinner and then take in a movie with the Bakers the next day. I invited David to come along, hoping we could provide him some company to help him deal with his depression over Sarah. He hesitated at first, claiming that he would almost literally be the "fifth wheel." I assured him that we and the Bakers would love to have him accompany us. He shrugged and agreed. Deep down he realized that it was better to be out with others at this moment in his life rather than moping alone in his apartment on a Saturday night.

We split the bill and walked out of the Occidental. On the sidewalk, we prepared to go our separate ways. Walking back to the Justice Department, I turned and saw David heading toward Constitution Avenue. He was striding purposely, his head up and his shoulders back. I imagined he was exerting every ounce of will to keep a positive attitude in the face of his bitter disappointment. The three of us – David, María, and I – bore the scars of betrayal by those we had trusted. But I was confident that together we would get through these bad moments; if nothing else, to deny those who had harmed us of any final victory. With a spring in my own step, despite the July sun beating down mercilessly, I headed back to my office, more determined than ever to bring the bad guys we were after to the justice they so richly deserved.

CHAPTER THIRTY ONE

July 9, 1951 – Buenos Aires, Argentina

The ninth of July was a major holiday in Argentina, celebrating the nation's official declaration of independence from Spain in 1816. Argentina's blue and white flag flapped from every available pole, was draped over every balcony, and was carried proudly in military parades throughout the country. The regime planned a massive rally later in the day in the middle of the Avenue in Buenos Aires that bore the name of that memorable date an avenue that local citizens claimed was the "broadest in the world." The rally would bring together hundreds of thousands of *descamisados,* the Perón regime's most fervent supporters, who, fueled by free food and drink, would be banging on drums, clapping their hands, and cheering wildly for the nation's first couple, who would address them from a specially-constructed speakers stand in the middle of the avenue.

Horacio Campos, for his part, was in no mood to celebrate. Standing alone in his office, staring at the port stretched out in front of him, his hands clasped behind his back in a familiar pose, he was lost in thought. Ordinarily, the view at the activity in the port never failed to interest him. This time, he barely noticed it. He had too much on his mind.

From somewhere in his memory, he recalled a phrase that those who fail to learn the lessons of history were doomed to repeat past mistakes – or something to that effect. He should have paid heed to that admonition. For indeed, the latest attempt on the life of Peter Benton and his wife, María, had produced a catastrophe even worse than the one that befell him six years earlier. Both of his agents had been killed, the intended targets had survived virtually unscathed, and the larger consequences had been severe.

He took some solace in the fact that those consequences could have been much worse. The Americans had determined not to make the whole affair public, preferring to issue their warnings in secret. There would be no break in relations, no penalties imposed. The "larger interests" between the two countries would be protected and maintained. But the U.S. ambassador, delivering a personal letter from Secretary State Acheson to his Argentine counterpart had made it crystal clear that any repetition of such an action against American citizens on American soil – or elsewhere – would lead to an immediate break in diplomatic relations, a public airing of the details of any such attempt, and the imposition of severe economic sanctions. After consulting with Perón, the Argentine foreign minister assured the U.S. envoy that the message was received and that he had the president's personal guarantee that there would be no further attempts on the lives of the Bentons – or on any other Americans. Tellingly, there was no official apology for the attempt. Campos strongly believed that omission had been made either at the insistence of Evita or as a sop to her. At any rate, the Americans did not seem inclined to press the issue. Probably willing at this stage, as they say, "to let sleeping dogs lie."

When Campos had received notification of what had happened to his two agents in the mountains of Virginia, he almost lost consciousness. When his aide, López, delivered the news at his office, his head began to swim, the room began to swirl around him, and he felt the bile rise in his stomach. López, who had been with Campos for years and had never seen him react in such a matter rushed to his side and asked with concern, "What is it *jefe?*" He reached out to steady his boss, something he would never have considered under other circumstances. Everyone knew that the head of Argentina's secret police was averse to any physical contact beyond a brief formal handshake.

Campos recovered quickly. He brushed away the aide's hand on his arm. "I'm all right López," he said. "Just a little dizzy." Taking a deep breath and composing himself, he tried to focus on what he had to do next. "I'll need a full report López. As soon as possible. All the details you can muster." Then he asked the next question, one he dreaded: "Does the president know?"

"Not yet *jefe*. The ambassador in Washington sent a confidential cable directly to us, not to the Casa Rosada."

That spineless bastard! Campos thought to himself. *Leaving it up to me to deliver the bad news and take the blame.* Then he shrugged. Well, he thought, it *was* my plan. I'm in charge. I would have gotten all the praise and credit if things had gone smoothly. Now that the disaster had occurred, I have to assume the responsibility. He thought briefly how he might shift the blame to someone else. *But who?* He was tempted to tell Perón that if he wanted to put the onus on any one person for the plan's failure it should be directed at the person who ordered it – Evita. But he might as well put a gun to his head and pull the trigger as to utter that bit of truth.

Later that morning, López returned with the detailed report. As Campos read through it, he could scarcely believe what his eyes told him. The whole plan failed because of a *bear!* He knew that no plan was foolproof; that anything could go wrong. But a *bear* of all things. No one could have planned for that. Nonetheless, he feared that the Casa Rosada was not going to let him off easy just because of a one-in-a-million circumstance that no one could have predicted.

He found some comfort in the fact that for the moment the Americans were keeping the whole episode under wraps. So far, there had been no diplomatic repercussions, although the report indicated discussions were still taking place at the highest levels of the American government, presumably trying to determine how best to respond to the attack.

Campos instructed his secretary to call the presidential office, letting Perón know that he needed to see him at once on an urgent matter. Ten minutes later, his secretary informed him that the president was available as soon as he could get to his office. Perón knew that the planned attack on Benton and his wife had been scheduled for the weekend. Campos's call meant that he had something to report.

With Bruno again at his side, Campos walked quickly to the Casa Rosada. In his briefcase, he carried the damning report López had assembled. He was ushered in to the presidential office without delay. Perón was alone, for which Campos was grateful. Having Evita present would have made everything that much more difficult. The minute Perón saw Campos's grim face he knew the news was bad.

"What is it Horacio? What has happened?" he asked, gesturing for Campos to take a seat. Campos sat down in a chair opposite the presidential desk and opened his briefcase. Without a word, he took out the report on the attack and placed it on the desk.

Perón looked down at the report as though it might bite him. "Please Horacio. Don't keep me in suspense. Tell me what happened. I can read this later."

Campos took a deep breath. "Well Juan," he began, "you are going to have difficulty believing this." As Campos laid out the story, he could see the president turn deadly pale. He was afraid for a moment that he might have some kind of seizure. When Campos neared the end of his recital, a look of pure terror crept onto the president's normally smiling face. He could only wonder what Perón feared most: the reaction from the United States or Evita's wrath when he told her that the plan had failed – and failed disastrously.

When Campos had finished, Perón sat silently behind his desk, his head in his hands. After more than a minute in that pose, he raised his head, rubbing his cheeks vigorously as though to restore the color that had been drained from them. He fixed Campos with a stare that he could not read. "All right Horacio," he said finally. "I'm going to read this report and then meet with my aides. I'll let you know what we decide. That's all for now," he said dismissing him.

Campos was tempted to present a defense of his actions. He thought about pointing out how well-conceived the plan to entrap the Bentons had been; how close it had come to success. He and his agents could hardly be blamed for the fact that something akin to a lightning strike had foiled their efforts. But he knew the timing was not right. Perhaps after a few days had passed, Perón might be more receptive to such a rationale. But now was not the time. Besides, his fate depended as much if not more on how Evita reacted. On that score, he had little doubt that if she had her way his head would roll.

Campos spent a few tense days after his meeting with Perón, expecting any minute to receive a call that would inform him that his time as head of the secret police had ended. But when he met again with Perón in the president's office, he was astonished to learn that he would keep his post. The president and his advisors had ultimately come to agree with his unstated argument: that the plan he had devised had *almost* worked to perfection. And that no one could have foreseen the circumstances that caused it to fail. It also helped that the Americans had decided to sweep the whole matter under the rug while making it clear that any further such action would have more severe consequences for relations between the two countries. Under other circumstances, Campos could well imagine that one of the Americans' demands would have included punishment for the person who had devised and implemented the assassination scheme.

As to what role Evita had played in these deliberations, Campos could only speculate. A few of his sources had reported that, not surprisingly, she had been furious that the plot had fallen through and was out for blood – particularly his blood. But it seemed that her influence, at least on this matter, had waned. When others in the president's inner circle had heard of the whole affair, which had been instigated by the first lady, they had been horrified. To put the nation's relationship with the most powerful country in the hemisphere if not the world in jeopardy over a personal vendetta was seen as the unacceptably risky enterprise that it was. Apparently enough pressure had been put on Perón to rein in Evita on this matter and he had finally put his foot down. His wife's pleas notwithstanding, there would be no more hare-brained schemes to exact revenge on Benton and his wife. Ironically, Campos mused, both the Bentons and he had ultimately been spared the consequences of Evita's vengefulness.

At the end of the meeting, an abashed Perón told Campos that he still trusted and needed him to head up the secret police. "I have enemies everywhere," he said, "and I need you, Horacio, to keep me safe." It was almost a plea.

Campos reassured his old friend. "Don't worry Mr. President. I'll work day and night to protect you."

Perón smiled. "I know you will Horacio. I know you will." Then he paused. "There is another matter I want your help on. Last year, an important figure in the Reich sought asylum in our country and I agreed to admit him. Right now he is in Tucumán using the name "Ricardo Klement" and working as a topographical engineer. I want you to assign a team to protect him. And you must choose your best men. If word gets out that we are harboring him, there could be serious – how shall I say it? – *repercussions*."

Campos was curious as to the true identity of this mysterious Ricardo Klement. He suspected that it was someone high up the Nazi chain of command, perhaps even one of those who had a main role in the campaign to eradicate the Jews. But Campos knew that despite Perón's reassurances, he was still on shaky ground. The best course, rather than to raise questions, was the one he chose: "Certainly Mister President. I'll get to it right away," he promised.

Returning to secret police headquarters, Campos immediately called in López and ordered him to form a five-man team to carry out Perón's instructions. He asked López, "Have you ever heard of this Ricardo Klement?"

López paused to shift through the thousands of names he kept in his head like a human filing cabinet. "No *jefe*. But I can…"

Campos interrupted. "Don't worry about it López. Just get the team together and send them to Tucumán as soon as you can. We cannot afford to let anything happen to Mister Klement, whoever he is."

"Yes *jefe*. We'll have them on their way tonight."

Before López left the office, he had a bit of news for his boss. "*Jefe*. While you were meeting with the president, the bodies of our two agents arrived at Ezeiza," the international airport located some fifteen miles to the west.

A look of unbearable pain appeared on Campos's face and he slumped as though someone had just hit him in the stomach. "You said you wanted to be informed as soon as they arrived," López said apologetically.

Campos cleared his throat. "Yes López. Thank you. Please notify my driver that I want to go to the airport immediately. And Bruno should come along as well."

"Yes *jefe.* Right away."

As soon as López left the room, Campos fought to hold back the tears that threatened to pour down his face. In reality, the last thing in the world he wanted to do was go to Ezeiza to view the bodies of 'Robrerto and Graciela Walker,' the aliases they had been assigned. But he knew that it was something he had to do.

One of the proudest achievements of the Perón regime had been the construction of a new modern highway linking the city with the international airport. A showy public works project, it was designed to impress foreign visitors with the progress made under Perón's direction. Whatever its aim, it allowed Campos's driver to reach the outskirts of the airport in less than half an hour. In truth, Campos wouldn't have minded if the trip had taken forever and they never arrived.

By the time they reached the airport, night had fallen and a steady rain pelted the top of their car. Skirting the main terminal, the driver headed for a distant hangar surrounded by a high wire fence and protected by armed guards. The entire Ezeiza complex was operated by the Argentine Air Force, which provided the security for the airport and grounds.

After showing their credentials at the security gate, the chauffeur navigated a two-lane road bordered with small boulders painted white to mark the way. Pulling up to the hangar's entrance, he parked under a lighted overhang that led into the main building and provided protection from the rain. Two armed guards in Air Force uniforms were waiting at the entrance. They came forward to escort the passengers in the dark sedan into the hangar.

One of the two guards said, "Right this way gentlemen. Lieutenant Romero is waiting for you inside."

Campos simply nodded and followed the two escorts through a large steel door, Bruno close behind. Through the door, Campos surveyed the scene. The hangar was large and cavernous with a ceiling more than thirty meters from the floor. He could hear the pounding of the rain on the tin roof echoing through the massive chamber. In a corner to his right, there was a steady stream of rain running down the wall and pooling on the concrete floor.

The hangar held three Air Force planes, their silver bodies decorated with Argentina's blue-and-white flag. Campos picked up the strong odor of diesel fuel trapped in the close atmosphere. He almost gagged at the smell. To his left, in the far corner, he saw what he had expected. Placed on a large table were two wooden coffins. Lights placed on poles, similar to those used in hospital operating rooms, stood at the four corners of the table, bathing the coffins in bright light.

The two guards led the way toward the table. For a second, Campos almost panicked. *Was this something he really wanted to confront? He knew what the coffins contained. Why not turn around and head back to his office?* But this was something he had to do. Fighting back a feeling of nausea, he strode steadily toward the illuminated table.

There were three more uniformed men standing guard at the table. One of them moved forward to greet him. He was a carbon copy of the others – tall, muscular, in his late twenties or early thirties. Unlike the others, he had officer's stripes on his sleeves.

Stopping a few feet from him, the officer stood at attention and saluted. Campos was tempted to remind him that he was not part of the military and did not require a salute. But he let it pass. "Chief Campos," the officer said. "I'm Lieutenant Romero at your orders." Campos remained silent, nodding his acknowledgement. "I understand that you wish to view the bodies," Romero said, gesturing over his shoulder to the lighted table, "Before they are – uh – disposed of."

Campos cleared his throat. "Yes lieutenant. If you would be so kind."

"Right this way sir," Romero said, turning on his heel and walking to the table.

The guards at the table snapped to attention as Campos, Romero, and Bruno approached. The bright lights bounced off their shiny leather belts and polished boots.

As he neared the table, Campos saw that the coffins were simple pine boxes. He winced. But, under the circumstances, he could not blame the Americans for failing to provide something finer. As it was, they were lucky to recover the bodies at all. It would have been easier for the Americans to bury them in some distant spot and wash their hands of the whole affair.

When Campos got to the table, Romero said in a quiet voice, "We have unscrewed the tops of the coffins but left them in place until your arrival. The male is in this one," he said, pointing to the coffin to Campos's left, "the female in the other."

"Bruno," Campos said, turning to his bodyguard, "remove the lid on that coffin," pointing to the one that contained the remains of "Roberto Walker."

"Certainly *jefe*," Bruno said, moving forward. Grasping both sides of the lid he lifted it as though it weighed no more than a pillow and placed it carefully at the side of the table.

Taking a deep breath, Campos moved closer to examine the body. The bright lights illuminated every facial detail of the man the Bentons had known as "Roberto Walker." He looked remarkably peaceful. Except for the dimple in the middle of his forehead that marked the entry wound from María Benton's exquisite aim, the handsome features were completely intact.

Campos uttered a soft sigh. "Roberto" had been one of his best agents. Before being assigned to exact revenge on the Bentons, he had proved his mettle in secret operations in Montevideo and Chile. If the Benton operation had gone smoothly, his future in the secret police was a bright one. He reminded Campos of another promising officer, Ernesto Aguilar, whose career, like "Walker's" had been cut short because of Pete Benton. Now, "Roberto" would not even have the consolation of an official internment in a family tomb, his name etched in marble for all eternity. Instead, he and "Graciela" would be "disposed of" in unmarked graves somewhere in the distant pampas, all traces of their existence – and their operation – removed.

After staring at "Roberto's" unblinking face for thirty seconds, Campos turned to Bruno and said, "You may replace the lid."

As Bruno attended to his task, Campos turned to Romero. "Lieutenant. I have a favor to ask."

"Certainly Sir. At your orders."

"Could you and your men please leave me alone for a few minutes?

Romero looked surprised. "Well, my orders are…"

Campos gave him the kind of stern look that turned strong men's knees to jelly. "It will just be for a few minutes."

Romero was about to object, but thought better of it. *What would be the harm?* "Just for a few minutes sir?" Campos nodded. "Very well then," he said, motioning for the two guards to follow him to the door of the hangar.

Once they had closed the door behind them, Campos said, "Bruno. Could you help me with the lid of the other coffin? Then I would like you to leave me as well."

Bruno seemed surprised, but kept his face expressionless. "Yes *jefe.* Whatever you say."

They moved to the right side of the table. Once again, Bruno picked up the lid of the coffin and placed it carefully to the side. When he viewed the corpse inside, Campos could not hide his shock at the sight of "Graciela." Despite the best efforts of whoever had prepared the body, there was no masking the terrible disfigurement she had suffered. Half her face seemed to be missing and her exposed neck was an extensive network of dark stiches, as though her head had been reattached to her body.

"You may leave now Bruno," Campos said, his voice barely above a whisper. "I'll call you when I'm finished."

"Yes *jefe.*"

Campos kept his eyes on Bruno's back as the bodyguard walked through the hangar door and closed it behind him. He did so not because he didn't trust Bruno. He did it so as to keep his eyes averted from the horror on the table.

Once he heard the door slam shut, Campos steeled himself and looked down at "Graciela's" battered face. He couldn't control himself. He let out a mournful groan that echoed through the hangar. Tears poured down his face and he had to grip the side of the table to keep from falling. He began to retch, but managed to contain himself.

Gradually, he regained his composure. But his mind was filled with thoughts of regret. No matter how much he rationalized what had happened to one of the few female agents under his command, he knew that he would never forgive himself for what had happened to this one.

Campos had tried to keep his personal and professional lives as separate as possible. When he met with the few friends he had among the secret police, he limited the conversation primarily to office matters, only occasionally joining in discussions of things beyond the walls of headquarters. Barely a handful knew much about his life outside of work. For most at the secret police building, it was almost as though he had no home other than the one on Leandro Alem Avenue.

In fact, Campos had been happily married for more than thirty years; or at least it had been "happily" until recently. His wife Elena was the eldest daughter of Spanish immigrants who had arrived in Buenos Aires penniless and had slowly risen to middle class status, much as had his own parents. She had borne him three children, first two boys, then a girl. When Campos had joined the secret police, they had determined to keep the details of his position as confidential as possible. When family and friends inquired, they gave only vague answers. Their children were trained to do the same. Under these difficult circumstances, they tried to live as normal a life as possible. While Campos threw himself full-time into his career, Elena took care of maintaining the household and raising the children. They lived modestly in a three-bedroom apartment in the Palermo district. But Campos earned enough to send his children to a select private *colegio*, where they received a first-class education.

Campos had hoped that one or both of his sons would follow in his footsteps with careers either in the police or the military. But they chose otherwise. One became a lawyer, the other an architect. Both were now married with children of their own.

At secret police headquarters and in his official duties Campos was cold and dispassionate. At home he was a doting husband and loving and caring father, almost an entirely different person. And he loved his three children to distraction. But like any father, he had his favorite. And in this case it was his daughter, named Beatriz after her maternal grandmother.

Beatriz inherited her mother's beauty and her father's iron will. At the exclusive *colegio* she attended, she was an outstanding student and accomplished athlete, excelling at gymnastics, swimming, horseback riding, and tennis. She thrived on competition and drove herself to do her best and be the best in any endeavor she undertook.

When she graduated with honors, Campos was prepared to support her in whatever career path she chose. She was adept at drawing and perhaps like her brother, she might choose architecture or something related to the arts. Another possibility was medicine. She had won several school awards in science. While there were relatively few women doctors in Argentina, their numbers were growing. Another possibility, one that Campos found less appealing, was some kind of acting career. Beatriz had been the star of a number of school productions and displayed a talent for immersing herself completely in any role – in one case assuming the identity of a male character.

But to the surprise – and shock – of her parents, she chose none of these options. When it came time to discuss her career plans, both Horacio and Elena were floored by her decision. Campos recalled the conversation as though it were yesterday: "Papa," she said, "I want to be like you. I want to work for the secret police."

For a few seconds, both he and Elena were speechless. They had been taken totally unaware. *Where in the world has this come from?* After he recovered from the surprise, he felt an odd mixture of fear and pride; fear for his daughter's safety if she were to join the secret police and pride that she wanted to follow in his footsteps.

It was his duty to point out the obstacles: The work was both deadly boring and often exceedingly dangerous. She would be unable to lead a "normal" life, with marriage and children unlikely. She would have to follow orders from her superiors to the letter, even if she disagreed with them. Knowing his strong-willed daughter, Campos thought this to be a particularly compelling point. There were relatively few women in the secret police, an organization overwhelmingly dominated by men. And those few were mostly employed at low-level positions with little chance of advancement. In addition, their assignments usually involved seducing older men so as to gather information. Campos heard Elena utter a sob as he introduced this piece of evidence. Finally, she would be working in an organization that *he* headed with all of the complications that involved. In no way could he grant her any special treatment. The men with whom she would be working would be suspicious and resentful of her - the boss's daughter – and ready to react negatively to any hint of favoritism. As he made each point, Elena nodded vigorously in agreement. She was clearly appalled by Beatriz's sudden announcement.

Beatriz held her ground. Many jobs were "boring." She claimed she didn't mind a bit of "danger." Indeed, she welcomed it. She wasn't sure she wanted a "normal life," whatever that was. And, after all, hadn't Campos himself been able to marry and raise children? As to the lack of women in the ranks, couldn't that be seen as an argument in her favor? Wasn't there a need for more female agents, especially to do some of the clandestine work that required women? Campos found himself involuntarily nodding in agreement. So far as following orders and getting along with her male colleagues, the only way to find out if these would be problems would be for her to give it a try. She felt confident, she told them, that she could surmount any of the challenges and difficulties that came her way. She just wanted a chance to prove herself. That was all.

Campos had to remind himself that his daughter was still only twenty years old. As intelligent as she was, she was still naïve in the ways of the world. Her life had been a relatively sheltered one, isolated from many of the harsh realities that he had to deal with on a daily basis. He never brought work home from the office, never discussed the many unpleasant things he ordered his agents to do. No hint of the tortured screams he sometimes heard coming from the basement of the headquarters building. Beatriz thought of him as some kind of heroic figure, defending the fatherland from its enemies. Perhaps there was something to that image, but he knew well the darker side of his job and how muddled and morally ambiguous it often was. "Defending the fatherland" was a noble-sounding phrase that often hid unspeakable acts carried out for the basest of motives.

But he wasn't about to reveal these hard truths to her now. Both he and Elena knew the more they objected to her decision, the harder Beatriz would dig in her heels. Finally, after an hour spent trying to dissuade her, Campos and Elena finally gave in. "All right my dear," he said with a look of resignation. "If that's what you want to do – sincerely want to do – I'll not stand in your way. But remember," he added with a stern look on his face. "No special favors. You'll be treated like everyone else. And you may not always like that treatment."

Beatriz gave her father a warm embrace. "Thank you papa," she said, her beautiful dark eyes shining, "I won't disappoint you. I promise."

And she kept her promise. She went through the rigorous training program for all recruits and emerged at the top of her class. She outran, outswam, outshot, out-climbed, out-fought, out-thought, and out-performed all but a handful of male recruits. She asked no quarter and gave no quarter. Campos kept to his promise as well. He did nothing to intercede on her behalf, not that she needed his assistance. Some of her male colleagues were naturally jealous of her, but she gradually gained their respect, even if for some it was a grudging respect. When she went on her first field assignments, she performed brilliantly. Working either by herself or with a male partner, she often put her acting skills to good use to gather valuable information. More than a few of these assignments involved gaining the trust of members of the foreign diplomatic corps based in Buenos Aires. The results were often spectacular. After she turned in report after report chock-full of vital intelligence, Campos had to admit that she had been right. The secret police badly needed qualified females who had the particular attributes she possessed to fulfill their duties. He tried not to think about some of the things her daughter had been forced to do to gather such information. "Sacrifices for the defense of the fatherland," she had said with a sardonic look when he raised the issue.

As soon as Beatriz had officially joined the secret police, she had moved out of their home and into her own apartment, which she shared with another female agent. But she made it a point to join the family for Sunday dinner whenever possible. Like her father, she made it a rule never to bring up office business at home.

When he and Perón discussed the plan to exact Evita's revenge on Pete and María Benton, Campos had in mind another female agent to play the role of Graciela Walker. But back in his office, he reconsidered. He had promised Perón that he would assign his two *best* agents to carry out the plan. Beatriz was far and away his best female agent. She had already proved herself in similar assignments. And he recalled the promise he had made to her. *No special treatment. And now, with one of the most important and dangerous assignments in the history of the secret police in the works, he was not going to choose Beatriz, the most qualified for the task, because she was his daughter?* If she found out that he had protected her in that way, he feared she would never speak to him again.

All these memories raced through his mind as he looked down at the mangled corpse of his daughter. When he had broken the news of what had happened in Virginia to Elena, she had fallen to pieces, overwhelmed with grief. She had barely slept or eaten since, slipping into a kind of numb trance. Although she never blamed him directly, he could see the resentment in her eyes. When he suggested that she might accompany him to view the body, she recoiled in horror. She wanted to remember her daughter as the beautiful young woman she had been, not view the corpse of someone horribly mauled by a wild animal. *No,* she seemed to say. *You allowed this to happen. You are the one who must come face-to-face with the consequences.*

Campos wiped the tears from his eyes and bent down to kiss his daughter gently on the forehead. *I'm sorry querida. So very, very sorry,* he mumbled. Then, gathering himself, he turned and walked with a firm stride to the hangar door. He gripped the handle and pulled the door to him. Lieutenant Romero, the two guards, and Bruno were outside, waiting for him. Romero quickly extinguished the cigarette he had been smoking, a guilty look on his face. Bruno stood impassive. Campos wondered if any of them had heard his moaning and weeping through the door or noticed his red, tear-stained eyes. At this point, he really didn't care. To Romero he said, "You may seal the coffins Lieutenant. You have your orders and know what to do next."

Romero stood at attention. "Yes *jefe*. We'll take care of everything."

"See that you do Lieutenant," Campos said in a commanding voice. "And as quickly as possible."

Romero gave a quick salute, clicking his heels. "Yes *jefe*. Right away."

Campos gestured for Bruno to follow him back to the sedan.

Standing alone in his office, Campos could now hear the distant sounds of celebration echoing down the streets. He was momentarily startled from his musings by the sound of cannon fire near the Casa Rosada.

With a deep sigh, he turned from his view of the port and sat at his desk. In front of him was a file from López on "Richard Klement." He had leafed through it briefly and now studied it with more care. López had discovered "Klement's" true identity. "Klement" was none other than Adolf Eichmann, one of the principal directors of the "Final Solution" intended to eliminate all Jews from the face of the earth. Now he was being protected by the Perón government from the fate of those who had been unable to flee the defeated Reich.

Campos was not particularly disturbed by this fact on moral grounds. While he did not share the fierce anti-Semitism of some of his colleagues, he was not unsympathetic to men who he saw as carrying out the orders of higher ups. Putting himself into their shoes, he probably would have done the same thing. After all, hadn't his agreement to go along with Evita's scheme to exact revenge on the Bentons despite his own reservations been a case of doing what his superiors told him to do?

What worried him most about Eichmann's presence in Argentina was the potential danger it posed to the regime he was sworn to protect. If news got out that Perón was harboring such a notorious figure, the diplomatic consequences would be severe. It was, like the attack on the Bentons, an unnecessarily risky move. Unless Eichmann had brought with him a fortune in gold, as had been the case six years earlier with

Colonel Dieter von Strasser, what was the point of providing him a safe haven?

Nonetheless, Campos was grateful to possess the information López had provided. If at some time in the future, Evita – or even Perón – decided that he had to go, his knowledge of Eichmann's presence could prove a useful card to play in his defense. *Fire me – or worse – and I'll let it be known that you are sheltering one of the world's most notorious, reviled, and wanted men.*

Campos closed the file. For a few moments, he stared straight ahead, his thoughts a jumble. He had promised Elena that he would be home by noon so that he could share lunch with her, their two sons, and their grandchildren. Elena was still suffering. He had called in a specialist, who had prescribed some medication that had helped her begin to return to normal. But he knew that the return would never be complete. The wound was too deep. Their boys had been told of their sister's death, although without all the grim details. They knew she had been working for him and that she had died "in the line of duty." They seemed to harbor less resentment towards him than their mother, realizing that their strong-willed sister had made her own choice to put herself in harm's way. Nonetheless, they too mourned her loss.

Campos was in no hurry to leave the sanctuary of his office and face his grieving family. Opening the right-hand drawer of his desk, he stared down at the loaded pistol he kept there as a matter of habit. There was little chance he would ever be attacked in his office. There were too many layers of protection. But old habits were hard to shake.

Ever since he had received word of the failure of his plan and the death of his daughter, he had, for first time, contemplated the idea of taking his own life. He had always considered suicide the coward's way out. But now he was beginning to understand the kind of pain that drove people to such drastic action. Momentarily succumbing to a strong emotional impulse, he started to reach into the drawer and grab the revolver. But he quickly recovered and slammed the drawer shut.

No, he thought to himself *that was not the way to honor his daughter's memory.* Instead, he unlocked the middle drawer of his desk and placed the file on "Ricardo Klement" inside. *A bit of an insurance policy* he muttered to himself.

Then, for some reason, his thoughts turned to Pete and María Benton. He wondered if they were somehow celebrating Argentina's Independence Day. Probably not, he decided. The former María Suárez was now a United States citizen and had undoubtedly celebrated that country's independence five days earlier. He imagined them happy and feeling safe after escaping the trap that he had laid for them. Previously, he had found it difficult to understand the kind of vengeance that Evita had sought against the couple. Now, with the death of his own daughter, he had a clearer comprehension of what had driven the first lady to urge such drastic measures. He knew that he could not continue to pursue a similar course at the moment. But it was a thought that he would store in the back of his mind. He didn't know when he would be able to act on it – if ever – but he wanted the couple that had caused him so much trouble and so much grief to pay some price for what they had done to him and his family.

From a rational point of view, Campos knew that the Bentons were not really at fault. They hadn't been doing anything that threatened Argentina in any way, shape, or form. And when attacked, they simply defended themselves. But reason was one thing, emotion another. And in this case, Campos, ordinarily the most rational of men was listening to his heart rather than his head. Perhaps with time the emotion would fade. But he doubted it. Somewhere down the road, if the opportunity presented itself, he would try to seek his own revenge on the two people who had been responsible, at least indirectly, for the death of the person he had loved more than any other on this earth.

Oddly comforted by this thought, Campos left his office, worried that he would be late for lunch with his family.

AFTERWORD

Evita's Revenge, like Twisted Tango, is a fictional story placed within an actual historical context. In Argentina, Juan Perón and his wife, Evita, were firmly in control of the country in 1951. The other Argentine characters are fictional, and, while Evita could be vengeful and Perón did harass opponents, the plot hatched against the Bentons is purely from my imagination. Likewise, while McCarthyism was rife in the U.S. in 1951, the Kefauver committee was investigating organized crime, and the CIA was recruiting and protecting former Nazis, the rest of the story involving the Bentons and David Friedman is also completely fictional.

Printed in the United States
By Bookmasters